SILENT VENGEANCE

a Steven O'Rourke novel

JOHN SITTERLY

Author photo by Deb Sitterly
Book design by Emma Schlieder

Printed in the United States of America

The Troy Book Makers • Troy, New York • thetroybookmakers.com

To order additional copies of this title, contact your favorite local bookstore or visit www.tbmbooks.com

ISBN: 978-1-61468-278-3

*For my wife Deb, who encouraged
me to write from the day we first met*

PROLOGUE

|||||||||||||||||||||||||||||||||||||||

Rage. Pure unbridled rage. A rage that overwhelms all other feelings and thoughts. That emotion was all the tall man felt when he swung the blunt weapon in his hand with all his might at the back of the woman's head.

Her skull shattered with a sound like an axe slicing through an old tree stump. The tall man realized that the force of the blow had killed her instantly.

Even though he knew that she was dead, he looked down at the body for several minutes, allowing his anger to gradually subside. He had to stay calm and think straight now. Carefully, he took a couple tissues out of his pocket and wiped the blood off of the object in his hand before putting it back where it belonged.

Taking his time, he carefully went through the entire house. He searched every room that he had been in to make sure he had left nothing behind. He was wearing a pair of gloves now, but he made sure that everything he had touched or handled before he put the gloves on was wiped clean.

Finally he was satisfied. Before leaving, he took one thing from the kitchen that might be useful later. Then he walked down the rear stairs which led to the back door. As he closed the back door behind him, a feeling of satisfaction replaced the rage that he had felt earlier.

It was not until he was home that he allowed himself to fully assess how he had performed in his mission. Although he had killed the woman quickly enough once his anger had taken over, he was there for over an hour before finally dispatching her. He realized that he had been taken in by her seemingly innocent manner and that had left him vulnerable. That could not happen again. The next time, he would strike quickly and coldly.

There was also something else bothering him. Something was missing. He sat in the dark for an hour and it finally came to him. The woman was dead, but no one would know what she had done. The lives that she had forever ruined. In the future, he would show the world what his targets had done and he would do it without revealing himself. He would leave a message. And he would take something from each person as well. A memento. He would start with the next target.

Before he went to bed, he retrieved a spiral notebook from the spot where he had hidden it. On the first page was a list of names written neatly, one on each line. He crossed off the first name with a red marker. First mission accomplished. Many more to follow…

ONE

IIIIIIIIIIIIIIIIIIIIIIIIIIIIIIIIIIIIIIIIII

Steven O'Rourke closed his eyes and stretched out in his neighbor's chaise lounge under the late Saturday afternoon sun, the chair groaning under the weight of his muscular six foot three frame. It was a nice summer afternoon in Albany - warm but not too humid. O'Rourke was comfortable in his khaki shorts, unbuttoned Hawaiian shirt and flip-flops. He was half listening to his host, Matt Figgins, a state worker who was droning on to a few bored guests on his patio about the problems he was having at work. Matt, who had invited several neighbors over for a backyard barbecue, had already consumed a six-pack of Heineken, and the more he drank, the more he talked.

The other guests listening to Figgins had apparently come up with some excuse to move to another part of the back yard because Figgins was now standing in front of O'Rourke, blocking his sun.

"Hey, Steve, want another beer?"

"No, I'm fine." O'Rourke was still working on his second. When his kids were around, he never drank more than that.

O'Rourke looked out into the back yard where Matt's wife, Betty, was keeping watch on several children in their above ground swimming pool. O'Rourke had two kids, Lauren and Tyler. Lauren was thirteen, and was old enough and responsible enough to watch out for Tyler, who was six. They were splashing around with Matt and Betty's three children and some other neighbor kids in the pool, and seemed to be having a good time. O'Rourke was very happy about that.

O'Rourke hadn't had his kids over to the house on a weekend for almost a month and felt like he'd been neglecting them. He had been working long hours and his ex-wife Ellen hadn't really been pushing him to take the kids, but he still felt bad about not seeing them much lately.

Tonight, Ellen had a dinner date with some guy she met at work, so he was doing her a favor by taking the kids. O'Rourke had actually left work early for the first time in who knows how long, and had picked up Lauren and Tyler at Ellen's and taken them out for miniature golf before coming back for Matt's barbecue. As annoying as Matt could be sometimes, O'Rourke was grateful for the invitation. The kids were having fun and he was getting some much-needed relaxation.

Lieutenant Steven O'Rourke was a Chief Investigator for the Albany Police Department, head of the Homicide and Special Crimes Unit - "HSC" for short. Four full-time detectives worked under him, along with an overworked unit secretary, but when needed, he could pull in assistance from other units in the Department. Lately, though, things had been quiet in his unit, so his team had been helping other units with street crime issues. The month of July so far had been a hot one, and that usually meant tempers flared, especially among the gangs located in Albany's toughest neighborhoods. There had been several shootings in Arbor Hill and the South End since early June, and O'Rourke's unit had been helping to investigate them. Just yesterday, the

Department had arrested one of the shooters, an 18-year old gangbanger who had wounded another teenager who slighted him in some way or another. It was going to be a long summer for the department.

O'Rourke took another sip of his beer. Figgins was now back to giving anyone within earshot his opinions about what was wrong with state government. O'Rourke had met Matt ten years ago, shortly after O'Rourke's parents moved into the house next door in the quiet Buckingham Lake neighborhood. He assumed that his parents would spend many happy years in that house, but it didn't work out that way. His dad, former police captain Kenneth O'Rourke, died of a heart attack two years after moving in, just a month shy of seeing Steven promoted to Investigator. Almost three years ago now, O'Rourke's mother passed away from cancer. O'Rourke had a sister who lived out of town; after O'Rourke's divorce, he decided to buy out her share of the home and move into it himself. O'Rourke liked the old house and it had a lot of room for his kids when they visited on weekends.

O'Rourke finished his beer and walked over to a plastic barrel near the house where people were tossing their empties. On the way, he could hear some loud angry voices over by the pool. There seemed to be some heated discussion going on. He tossed his beer can in the barrel and headed over there.

A man and a woman were arguing loudly, and Betty Figgins was trying to calm them down. He immediately recognized the woman. Her name was Ginny Dixon. Ginny, who lived in a house down the street, was divorced and had a daughter, Molly, about Tyler's age. She was a drama teacher at the high school, a slim blonde woman around 30. O'Rourke knew her well. He had first noticed her last summer when he had seen her jogging in the neighborhood at times as he did his own morning runs. Later, they were introduced at a neighborhood party in the fall and had hit it off. They actually had a dinner date in early December, but then O'Rourke had gotten serious with another woman at work just before Christmas, and he and Ginny had gone their separate ways.

As O'Rourke got closer to the altercation, he could see the man was red-faced and yelling at Ginny. Molly was in her bathing suit, cowering behind her mother. The little girl was trembling as the man's voice got louder and angrier.

"I've got a right to see my daughter," he was shouting. "You can't keep me from taking her!"

"You're drunk," Ginny said assertively. "And you have to get out of here. I've got an order of protection."

"That doesn't mean shit to me," the man shouted. "She's my kid and I'll see her if I want, you bitch!"

O'Rourke pushed through the small crowd that had now gathered near the pool. "All right, let's calm down now," he said to the man.

The man stopped and turned toward O'Rourke. He was a big man, about thirty pounds heavier and maybe an inch taller than O'Rourke.

"Who the hell are you?" the man asked with a slurred voice. O'Rourke could smell the alcohol on the man's breath from a few feet away.

"I'm the guy telling you that you need to calm down. The lady here says she's got an order of protection against you. Is that true?"

"You need to mind your own business, asshole," the man said angrily, taking a step toward O'Rourke.

"Look, pal, I'm giving you one more chance…"

"Screw you," the man said, and took a swing at O'Rourke.

O'Rourke easily ducked away from the man's wild swing, and making a fist, rammed it into the man's substantial gut. The man doubled over, out of breath. O'Rourke moved to try to restrain the big man, but the man recovered quicker than he expected. He tried to get his hands around O'Rourke's neck.

"You son of a bitch!" he yelled drunkenly.

O'Rourke responded by grabbing the man's wrists, while bringing his knee up sharply into the man's groin. The man let out a howl and fell to the ground, clutching himself.

"Make sure he doesn't go anywhere," O'Rourke said to the crowd, although he knew the man would not be going far. O'Rourke jogged across the lawn toward his house. A minute later, he came out with a pair of handcuffs. The man was still in the same spot. O'Rourke rolled him over onto his back and put the handcuffs on him.

O'Rourke talked with Ginny as they waited for the uniformed officers to show up. Betty had taken Molly and the other kids into the house to get them ice cream sandwiches. O'Rourke had asked the other onlookers to go back near the house, while the handcuffed man remained subdued on the ground.

"Greg is my ex-husband," Ginny explained. "He just showed up here out of the blue. I do have the order of protection over there in my purse. He's not supposed to be around us. He gets like that when he's drunk…"

Ginny wiped tears from her eyes. "Sorry. I hate feeling like this. You know, afraid of him."

"Actually," O'Rourke said, "I'm impressed with the way you stood up to him. You weren't backing down."

"My daughter needed protection. That's all I was thinking."

A few minutes later, two officers arrived. O'Rourke knew them both and explained the story.

"It seems like you handled things well, Lieutenant," one of them said as they started walking Greg toward the street.

"Yeah, this guy's pretty tame now," the other cop said with a grin. "Although he is walking a little funny."

"He'll be okay in a few hours," O'Rourke said. "Thanks guys. Ms. Dixon will stop by later to press charges."

A half hour later, the party was back to normal. Several kids including O'Rourke's kids and Molly were back in the pool, while Ginny and O'Rourke talked nearby.

"I haven't seen you in a while," Ginny said.

"Work's been keeping me busy. We don't get the whole summer off like some people."

Ginny smiled. "Hey! Teaching's hard work. We need that summer off to recharge our batteries."

O'Rourke was about to come up with a clever response when a splash of water just missed his face. Tyler had just noticed his dad was standing next to the pool and decided to try to get him wet.

"Come on in, Dad! There's still room."

"Maybe later, kiddo."

Now Ginny's daughter was splashing water. Betty Figgins, who was standing near the pool, laughed and decided to get away and head back toward the patio. A large splash of cold water caught Ginny and she let out a squeal.

"Oh, jeez," Ginny said as she looked down. She was soaked from her neck down to her waist and her blouse was clinging to her. O'Rourke let his eyes linger for a moment and then handed her one of the kids' towels.

"Thanks." She flashed that smile again. "Lucky you – you

didn't get wet at all."

"I'm a cop. We've got split-second timing."

"I'll bet."

The kids were ignoring them now and were back to splashing each other. O'Rourke noticed Ginny looking at his chest as she dried herself. His shirt was still open and a jagged circular scar a few inches below his collarbone was showing. Ginny reddened a little when he caught her looking.

"Old bullet wound," he said. "Occupational hazard. It's from years ago."

She reached out and touched it gently. "That's a little scary. What happened?"

"Back when I was on patrol, my partner and I were chasing a drug dealer down an alley. It was dark. We didn't know he had a gun until too late. It hurt like a son of a bitch. Put me in the hospital for two weeks."

"What happened to the drug dealer? Did he end up in jail?"

"Nope. He never made it out of the alley. My partner was a pretty good shot."

"Oh." She had a look on her face that O'Rourke couldn't decipher. Not everyone liked to hear about a cop killing somebody. He should have been more careful about keeping the scar covered up.

"That's quite a story," Ginny said. "You probably have a lot of them."

"Probably more than you want to hear." A couple of the other parents had come over to the pool to check on their kids. "I need a soda. How about you?"

They walked together toward the patio and O'Rourke grabbed a couple of sodas from Matt's cooler. They had been chatting for several minutes when O'Rourke's cell phone rang. He carried two phones on him: one personal and one for police calls. This call was on the police phone.

"Lieutenant O'Rourke," he said briskly, annoyed at the interruption.

"Chief, it's Tony." Tony Valente, a few years older than O'Rourke, was the most senior of the four detectives that worked under him. He was a big, genial cop who was married and had five kids and one more on the way. Valente, like most of O'Rourke's team liked to call him "Chief", because, as Valente once put it, "we know you're just Chief Investigator, but we all know you're going to be chief of the whole damn department someday."

"What's up, Tony?"

"We got a murder victim up here on Central Avenue, at a photography store. It's in a strip mall just before you get into Colonie."

"I know the place – Central Studio."

"Right. The victim's wife called it in after she found her husband shot dead inside. As soon as the patrol cops made sure the scene was secure, they called it in to us. Derek and I came right over, checked it out. No witnesses at the scene. They've got some guys canvassing the neighborhood to see if anyone saw anything. Forensics should be over soon." Derek Booker was O'Rourke's right hand man, considerably younger than Valente and O'Rourke. Booker was sharp, ambitious, a quick study, and had moved up in the Department ranks quickly. In fact, Derek was the top ranking black detective on the force.

"Sounds like you've got it covered. You guys are almost done with your shift, right? You might as well stay on it, get some overtime." The timing was fortunate; if the call had come in a little later, Booker and Valente would have been gone for the day and other detectives from Division One would've handled the initial call before it made its way to O'Rourke's unit.

"Yeah…but I think you should come over here, too," Tony said.

O'Rourke looked up from the phone and saw Ginny, who was watching him with some interest. In the background, he could see the kids still splashing in the pool.

"Why? Derek's handled these calls before." Booker had handled murder scenes in the past with no problem. He would always call O'Rourke to notify him but O'Rourke's presence wasn't usually required at the scene.

"Boss, believe me, you're gonna want to see this for yourself."

Something in Valente's voice told O'Rourke he'd better get over there quickly.

"I'm on my way."

After he hung up, O'Rourke looked at Ginny. "Look, I have to run…"

"I understand," she said. She had been listening to his end of the call. There was a look of genuine concern in her eyes, but there was something else too. "Maybe you can call me sometime…"

He nodded, and then he was off to talk to Betty, who agreed to look after the kids for a few hours until their mother could get there. As he walked back to the pool, he made a quick call on his cell to Ellen, who wasn't as angry as he expected over having to cut her evening short to get the kids later. Maybe her date wasn't going so well. For some reason, that idea pleased him.

Tyler got upset when he told the kids he had to go to work.

"It's not fair! We finally get to come over and now you're leaving!" Tyler was sitting on the pool deck. He kicked at the water angrily with his foot.

"Daddy's got an important job," Lauren told Tyler. "He's got to help get catch some bad guys." Good old Lauren.

O'Rourke walked up the deck steps and gave them both a hug.

"Lauren's right," he said. "I have to go now. Mom will be here in a little while. Love you guys."

He walked briskly across the lawn to the back door of his house. He quickly put on some fresh clothes and grabbed his gun and badge. As he walked out to his car, he glanced down the driveway into Matt's back yard. Tyler and Lauren were back in the pool, laughing with the other kids. Ginny saw him and gave him a quick wave.

Generally, O'Rourke wasn't a big spender, but after his divorce, he decided to take some money out of his savings and bought himself a new red Jaguar XJ8. Something that was fun. The Department let him use it for work and paid him mileage. He liked the idea of having a car that could outrun Albany PD's regular cars. He had to shell out some of his own money to have the Department put in a police radio, but they at least threw in the portable siren for free.

Backing out of the driveway, he pulled the siren out from under the seat and reaching out the window with his left arm, attached it to the roof of the car. He didn't have to rush; the victim was already dead and wasn't going anywhere. But with Ginny watching, he decided to gun it. The siren blared as the Jaguar sped down the street. As he drove to the crime scene, O'Rourke thought about the fact that Valente had called rather than Booker, the senior man at the scene. He wondered just what the hell was going on there.

TWO

IIIIIIIIIIIIIIIIIIIIIIIIIIIIIIIIIIIIIIIIIII

Earlier that day, Randall Tucker woke up at precisely 7 AM as he did every Saturday, walked down the stairs to the kitchen, and poured himself a bowl of cereal. If he had known this was to be the last day of his life, he might have started it differently, just to shake things up. But perhaps not; after all, Randall was a man who prided himself on his routine.

As he ate, his wife Joyce came into the kitchen, straightening her nurses' uniform.

"Morning, hon," Randall muttered without looking up, flipping through the Albany Times Union looking for the score in the Yankees game.

"Good morning," she replied. "Don't forget now – try to be home by 7 tonight. Angela's coming over for dinner with her new boyfriend."

"Yeah," he mumbled. "Wonderful..."

Randall Tucker considered himself pretty open-minded for a man that just turned fifty. But he had to admit that he was not crazy about having dinner with his daughter Angela's new Jamaican boyfriend. And not just because it upset his routine.

Randall wasn't very happy when Angela started dating a

white boy in high school, but he let it slide. It was just a phase she's going through, he thought at the time. But now, Angela, who was currently attending the summer semester at the community college in Troy, was going out with this Jamaican kid named Robert. Since Angela decided to live on campus this year, even though it was just 15 miles from home, she didn't stop over that much anymore. So Randall had actually only met Robert once, when Angela dropped by briefly with him. Robert had not made a good impression on Randall. Maybe it was his dreadlocks.

"What kind of name is Robert for a Jamaican kid anyway?" he asked Joyce as he put the newspaper down.

"Haven't you ever heard of Bob Marley? Bob is probably short for Robert."

Randall grunted. "That's great. Our daughter's boyfriend is named after a pothead."

Joyce smiled. "I have to go. I'll see you tonight."

She kissed him on the forehead and took off for work. Joyce was the head nurse at the ER at Albany Med. The hospital was about a twenty minute drive from their suburban home, located in Guilderland on Peabody Lane. They had lived on that street since Angela was a baby, almost nineteen years ago. When they moved in, they were only the second black family in the entire neighborhood. Randall, somewhat jokingly, once told Joyce that he was happy to let the other black family break in the neighbors.

With only a couple minor exceptions, they really had no problems with the other families in the area. He figured that was because he and his wife were generally friendly, outgoing types, although Joyce often told Randall he could be a real grump at times. He had to admit that he could get stubborn at times. Especially about work or Angela's boyfriends.

Randall got up from the table to get ready to go to work. Since it was mid-summer, it should be a quiet day at the store. Very routine.

Several miles away, the tall man was getting ready for his day's work. He looked through his small backpack, making sure everything was there. Inside was a small can of spray paint, a pair of leather gloves, an empty glass jar, a.38 caliber handgun and its attachment, and a sharp surgical scalpel. Satisfied that he had everything he needed, he zipped the pack up. He was ready.

Less than an hour later, Randall unlocked the front door of Central Studio and flicked on the lights. The store that he owned was a small, neat shop located on upper Central Avenue, one of Albany's main thoroughfares. His business, which was officially named Central Studio and Camera Store, Inc., specialized in taking quality photographs both in the store and at weddings and parties, as well as selling high-end cameras and video equipment. It was situated in a strip mall that contained four other small stores, just inside the Albany city line east of Colonie. The street was lined with many such small businesses.

Randall was on his own today. He usually had two employees there on Saturdays; sometimes they handled customers while he was out taking photos at a wedding or other event. The older employee, Bryan Goldstein, was a friendly white kid who was taking photography classes at Albany State and liked to consume beer in mass quantities when he wasn't working or in school. This week, Bryan was on vacation in Fort Lauderdale with some friends for two weeks. He was probably sleeping off a wild night at this very moment.

Randall's niece Regina, who was two years younger than his daughter Angela, also worked in the store on most Saturdays, but she had today off. She had a good excuse; it was her high school graduation day. Randall had just hired her last fall. Randall was close to his sister Lynette and her two children. Over the last year or so, Lynette had been working long hours at near minimum wage and had a hard time making ends meet, but she refused any financial help from Randall. So when he found out last fall that her daughter was looking for a job, he asked her if she wanted to help out on nights and weekends. Regina had jumped at the chance.

Randall had almost decided to close up the store early today to attend the afternoon graduation. But although he loved his niece dearly and was especially proud of her today, he had not closed the place early on a Saturday in over 15 years and didn't want to start now. He had a regular cleaning routine he went through every Saturday after the store closed, and that was important to him.

He would see Regina tomorrow anyway, at the graduation party he and Joyce were throwing her at his house. At first, Lynette had objected to him throwing an expensive party for her daughter. But he insisted that his spacious suburban back yard was a better option than the tiny yard behind her three-bedroom flat in Albany's Arbor Hill section. It wasn't charity, he told her; he just wanted to do something nice for Regina. In the end, Lynette had grudgingly relented.

Thinking of Lynette got him brooding about her son, Michael, and of the flare-up that Randall had with Michael earlier in the week. Hopefully, he would see the boy tomorrow at the party and maybe he could talk some sense into Michael then.

The morning went quickly. Randall had one family portrait scheduled for 10 AM, and that was done within an hour. A man came in later to buy a camera, then a pretty college student came in asking about setting up a modeling shoot, and that was it. At lunchtime, he locked up for a few minutes to grab a quick lunch to bring back. When he returned, he parked his car behind the back door of his store, in a narrow access alley that ran between the strip mall and a neighboring building. By Saturday at 1 PM, the rest of the shops in the strip mall were closed, so there were no other cars back there. As he came in through the rear entrance, he heard the phone ring.

Three miles down the road, the tall man was on a payphone outside of a convenience store. He wore a hat and a pair of dark sunglasses. As he waited for someone to pick up, he took a deep breath. *Keep your voice steady*, he reminded himself.

"Hello. Central Studio," a voice answered. The tall man recognized the voice as Tucker's.

"Uh, yeah. Is Bryan there?"

"No. He's not here this week. Can I help you?"

"Oh – no. No thanks. I'm a friend of his. I'll catch up with him later. Bye."

The tall man hung up. He had received the information he expected, that he was almost certain he would. He already knew that Bryan Goldstein had boarded a plane six days earlier for a two week stay in Florida, but he wanted to make sure Goldstein hadn't for some reason returned early. He knew for certain that the girl, Regina, wouldn't be there. He had done his research well.

The afternoon was busy, but by 4:45, the last customers of the day had left. Randall locked the front door and put the "Closed" sign in the window. He flicked off the front lights, turned off the air conditioner and opened the back door like he usually did on summer afternoons. He couldn't see wasting energy on the air conditioner when no customers were inside.

He took the trash out through the back, walking past his car, and emptied it into the dumpster that was shared by a few of the shops in the strip mall. When he was done, he went back inside, leaving the door open to let in the light breeze.

Pulling out a long dust mop from the back closet, he began to run it along the ceiling tiles in the back the store, the area where he took family portraits and modelling photos. The ceiling was clean since he dusted often, but he dusted it again anyway; it was his regular routine. He continued toward the front of the store until the ceiling was done, and then filled a pail with water and started mopping the floor.

His store was small, but always very clean. He had seen many of the other camera stores and photography studios in the area and he felt his looked better than any of them. It had been at this location for sixteen years, almost since the strip mall opened. Before that, he had owned a smaller place located in the bad neighborhood where his sister still lived. When he had earned enough money, he moved his business to a nicer area and never looked back.

It had worked out well, he thought. Life was good.

The tall man was watching. He could see the back of the store well from his vantage point in the shadows of a back yard of a home less than a block away. He was situated between a tree and the wooden fence that separated the yard from the one next door. The families in both homes were related and they spent their summer weekends in Cape Cod. He had circled the block several times earlier in the afternoon, making sure they were gone, as well as checking out the studio.

He looked down and noticed his gloved hands were trembling slightly. Not surprising. Although he had done a lot of planning, he was now actually ready to go through with this. He took a deep breath and that helped. His watch read 5:25. Almost time.

At 5:30, Randall's cell phone vibrated in his pocket. Randall knew it was Joyce – she always called at exactly 5:30. He put his mop down and wiped some sweat from his brow. Leaning against the front counter, he answered the phone.

"Hi Joyce."

"Hi. Coming home soon?"

"Yup. I should be leaving in about ten minutes." Randall was facing the front window as he spoke. He could see traffic was light on Central Avenue since many people were off on summer vacation.

"Don't forget about dinner with Angela and Robert," Joyce said. "Can you pick up a bottle of that non-alcoholic sparkling cider on the way home? It's classier than soda or juice."

"We've got wine in the cupboard already."

"Don't be silly. Angela's not old enough to drink. She's only nineteen." Joyce could be so naive about Angela sometimes.

"OK – I'll get some cider. See you later."

"Bye."

A second after he hung up the phone, Randall thought he heard something behind him. He stood up from where he was leaning against the counter and walked toward the back of the room. Late afternoon shadows were starting to creep in through the back door.

At first, he didn't see the man standing there in the shadows.

A tall silent man in dark clothes was standing perfectly still, against the back wall of the store, several feet inside the back door. In his hand was a gun. And it was pointed right at Randall.

Randall let out a gasp and dropped his cell phone. It clattered loudly as it hit the floor, making him jump. The other man didn't jump. He just stood there impassively, looking at Randall.

"Wh-what do you want?" Randall asked. His own voice sounded strange to him, high and strained.

The man stood there silently. No answer. Randall tried to calm himself down, to think clearly. How long had this man been standing there? He must have entered the back door while Randall was on the phone. But Randall was only on the phone for a few minutes. He hadn't heard a car pull up. Where had he come from? What does he want?

Money.

"There's money in the register. Take it," Randall said. If he kept his cool and gave the man what he was after, the man would have no reason to shoot him.

Still no response. The silent man was just staring at him, his eyes cold, unblinking.

Randall took a step back toward the register, not taking his eyes off the man and his gun. Something about the gun looked odd, but that was the least of his concerns. The man continued to stare at Randall, not saying a word. Something about the man's eyes gave Randall a sudden urge to turn around and bolt wildly toward the front door. But that wouldn't work. The front door was locked; he would never be able to open it in time.

No. He would just pull out the tray from the register and slide it across the floor toward the man. The man could take it and leave out the back door. He must want the money. Why else would he be here, pointing that gun at him?

Randall started to take another step back and then heard a small popping noise. He wasn't sure at first what it was. Then he heard it again and at the same time, he felt an awful, searing pain in his upper chest. It happened so fast that he didn't realize he was being shot, not until he heard the sound one more time as the third bullet pierced his heart.

The tall man kept his gun aimed at Tucker's lifeless body for several moments, as if expecting Tucker to suddenly jump up and attack him. He had spent plenty of time shooting at targets but not *live* targets. Finally, he lowered his gun. He was surprisingly calm, his hands perfectly steady now. He had stupidly missed on his first shot; there was no excuse for that. But his second shot was close to the mark and the third was perfect.

"Well done," he said to himself.

He walked toward the dead man, looking toward the storefront window behind the body. Fortunately, the window contained a few large posters advertising great new deals on cameras and photo packages, so the posters took up much of the window's space. The lights were off in the front of the store, which was a good distance from the street behind the parking area in front. Someone driving by would not be able to easily see what was going on inside the store. Taking no chances though, he went to the window and peeked out anyway. Everything was fine – no one had seen anything. So far, so good. He was almost done anyway.

He took off his backpack, put his gun in it, and pulled out the scalpel, which he had wrapped in a small hand towel. He knelt down carefully next to Tucker's head. A pool of blood was forming on the floor below the dead man, so he had to be careful not to get it on his clothes. Tucker's eyes were still open; he was a little unsettled by that, but not much. Leaning over Tucker, he began to work.

When the man was done with Tucker, he went to the register and pulled out the cash from the drawer. Then he took the spray paint out of his pack and went to the back wall. Minutes later, he was gone, leaving his handiwork behind.

It was nearly dark outside when O'Rourke arrived at the strip mall. The parking lot was cordoned off by yellow police tape. Two patrol cars were in the lot blocking the entrance, lights flashing. A third patrol car was parked right in front of Central Studio to help block the store from public view. Several uniform cops were in the lot; a couple of them working on dispersing a small crowd that had gathered outside of the police tape.

Directly across the street, O'Rourke could see a larger crowd in the parking lot of a fast food fried chicken restaurant. A news van from a local TV station was already parked there; a long pole with a camera on it extended from the top of the van and was pointed at Central Studio. As O'Rourke pulled the car up to the barricade, a larger news van from a rival station was just pulling in to the parking lot of a small travel agency located adjacent to the strip mall. O'Rourke could see Trish Perkins, an aggressive young reporter for Channel Seven Eyewitness News, sitting in the passenger seat.

Sergeant Mills, an older officer from Division Three that O'Rourke had known for years, moved the police tape to let O'Rourke's car through and he parked in the lot. He got out of the car and Mills motioned for O'Rourke to follow him around the side of the building.

"How you doing, old timer?" he said to Mills, glancing over at the news van. "I see the news travels fast."

"Yeah. These TV news guys are something. They're like vultures - they listen to the police scanners and swoop in as soon as they think they've got their grubby paws on something juicy."

"That's a mixed metaphor," O'Rourke said.

"A what now?"

"Never mind. What have you got?"

"The victim's been identified as Randall Tucker," Mills said as they walked. "He owns the photography studio. Killed with two shots to the chest."

As they headed toward the alley that ran in back of the building, O'Rourke passed Derek Booker, who was talking to an attractive well-dressed black woman that looked to be in her mid-forties, probably Tucker's wife. She was wiping tears from her eyes. Next to her was a younger girl, maybe eighteen or nineteen, who looked like she could be the woman's daughter. The girl looked pretty shaky and was sobbing into a Kleenex. A tall guy with dreadlocks who was looking a little sick had his arm around her. There was a vague smell nearby like somebody just threw up.

O'Rourke decided not to interrupt Booker. He caught his eye and Derek held up a finger, indicating he would be with him shortly. O'Rourke and Mills continued the walk toward the back door.

"The wife called it into 911," Mills explained. "The Jamaican kid, the daughter's boyfriend, was waiting out front when my guys got there and they followed him around back. He was the one that found the body. He was pretty shook up; in fact, he just puked his guts out a few minutes ago. When my guys got back here, the victim's wife and daughter were standing outside the back door. The officers had to tell the ladies to back away – the killer might have still been in there. Of course, it turned out he was gone."

They walked past two patrol cars, one parked behind the other, the front one apparently being the one that took the initial call. Parked in the alley in front of those two cars was a Honda that was probably Mrs. Tucker's, and in front of that car, a Toyota with a license plate that read "CTLSTDIO" parked close to the open back door. All the cars were parked single file since the alley was narrow.

Mills stopped at the door, where a cop was standing guard. "Um, I gotta check with the rest of my guys, they've been canvassing the neighborhood. Maybe something's turned up." Mills looked like he didn't want to go back inside.

"OK. Make sure you have them talk to the people working at the chicken place. The front counter over there faces this store. See if someone saw a car parked out in front."

Tony Valente had heard them talking and came outside as Mills walked away. After a quick exchange of greetings, O'Rourke followed Valente inside. "You're not gonna like this," Valente warned.

The first thing O'Rourke saw was the large block letters painted about six feet high on the rear wall of the store not far from the back door. The words "BLACK BASTARD" were spelled out very neatly in dark blue paint. The faint odor of spray paint still hung in the air.

"Son of a bitch..." O'Rourke and his team had seen that sort of graffiti before, often accompanying cases of breaking and entering. But he had never encountered anything like this at a murder scene.

"You haven't seen it all yet," Valente said.

They walked toward the front of the store. A forensics team was milling around, looking for fingerprints and taking pictures. Although the front lights of the store were turned off, the store was well lit by portable lights that forensics had set up. One of the forensics guys that O'Rourke knew named Schade was looking at a bullet hole in the front wall.

In the middle of the store stood a pail half full of water and a mop. A few feet away was Randall Tucker's dead body lying face up on the floor. O'Rourke walked over to the body. There seemed to be an unusually large amount of blood on the floor near Tucker's mouth.

"You said he was shot in the chest," O'Rourke said to Valente. "What's with all that blood up there?"

O'Rourke and Valente squatted down next to the body. The right side of Tucker's head was against the floor, and blood trailed out that side of his mouth, pooling onto the floor. His mouth was wide open; he resembled a patient in a dentist's chair ready to have a tooth filled.

"His tongue," said Valente. "Someone cut out his tongue."

THREE

||||||||||||||||||||||||||||||||||||||||||||

"Nice, huh?"

O'Rourke jumped a bit, startled when he heard the voice behind him. Corpses with their tongues cut out could make someone a little edgy. He turned and saw Derek Booker standing over them. There was a lot of anger in Booker's eyes. "Looks like somebody wanted to leave some kind of message," Booker said.

"I thought this kind of stuff didn't happen around here anymore," Valente said.

"You think this shit only happens down south?" Booker said angrily. "Maybe it's not as obvious up here, but racism's still alive and well in the 21st century."

O'Rourke was taken off guard. Booker's anger was out of character for the usually cool-headed detective.

Valente stood up. "Hey, I didn't mean nothing," Valente said defensively, a bit taken back by Booker's tone. "Of course there's racist idiots around here, just like anywhere. But to kill someone like this…it's like somethin' from sixty years ago."

"It may have started as a robbery," O'Rourke asked, eager to interrupt the two before something was said that couldn't be taken back. "The cash register drawer is open."

"I'm not sure about that," Booker said. "The money in the drawer is gone, but the killers didn't take the larger bills underneath. Most robbers would've checked under the drawer."

The three of them walked over to the register. Another forensics guy, Harry Wilson, was over there. "Don't touch the register. We're still looking at it. There's a smudge of blood on the key that opens the register drawer. Doesn't look like we can get a fingerprint off it though."

O'Rourke thought about that. "If there's blood on the key, that means the killer must have come over to the register after he cut out the victim's tongue," O'Rourke said. "If the main intent was robbery, the logical thing to do would be to make sure he got the money out of the register first before taking the time to do that."

"But if somebody's sick enough to do that," Valente said, pointing at the body, "you gotta figure maybe he wasn't thinking logically."

"It could have been two robbers," said Booker. "Maybe more."

"Maybe. But whoever did the cutting was apparently the same person that went to the register."

O'Rourke looked over at the body. From where he stood, it appeared to be grinning grotesquely at him.

"At this point, it's all guesswork anyway until we know more. Derek, did you get anything helpful from the family?"

"Not much," Booker said, looking at his notepad. "The victim spoke to his wife at 5:30 on his cell, said he'd be home soon. When he wasn't home by quarter to seven, she got worried and called him, but no answer. She said that wasn't like him, especially since they had a nice dinner planned. She got worried; he recently turned fifty and has high blood pressure. So she, her daughter and the daughter's boyfriend drove over here. The front door was locked, so they went around back. She said he often kept the back door open while he cleaned up, especially on warm nights. His car was there. The back door was closed but not locked, and the lights in the back of the store were off. They went in, started calling for him, and then saw that nice little message on the wall. The Jamaican guy, Robert Smith, was the first to see Tucker lying there and yelled at the others to get out so they wouldn't see him that way."

"Do they have any idea who would do something like this? Have they received any threats?"

"No to both questions. Aside from getting that information, I didn't want to press them too much. They're naturally pretty upset right now. I can question them some more later."

"Okay. Why don't you give them a ride home? She shouldn't be driving. She can leave her car here, but get her keys and have someone move it so forensics can go over the alley."

"It might be good to keep a patrol car parked outside the family's house tonight."

"Good idea. We need to make sure the family's safe. Ask Mills to take care of it."

Booker started to leave, and then turned around for a second. His eyes didn't look angry anymore, just sad. "I knew this guy, you know. We had a nice portrait done by him less than a year ago. Linda and I – we put in on the Christmas cards we sent out to our families. Tucker seemed like a nice guy. He told me he had worked his way up from his small store in the ghetto all the way up to this place."

"Something to be proud of. It's a nice place."

Derek Booker looked at the writing on the wall. "It was."

Captain John Grainey, O'Rourke's boss, wasn't happy when O'Rourke called in. He had already known there was a murder on Central Avenue, but didn't have all the details until O'Rourke filled him in.

"Shit," Grainey said. "Just what we need – a hate crime. We're already getting lousy press from all those spooks shooting each other in Arbor Hill and the South End. This is probably tied in with that."

O'Rourke detested Grainey. He was an annoying S.O.B. who got his job of overseeing the detective units primarily because his father was heavily into local politics. He was the first to accept credit in the press when his men made a big arrest and the first to assign blame on them when an investigation went on too long. Plus he was a racist jerk.

A year ago, O'Rourke had gone on a vacation for a week and left Derek in charge. Before O'Rourke left, Grainey had tried to pressure him into putting someone else in charge of the unit for the week, making insinuations about "people like Booker" and how they couldn't handle being in charge. O'Rourke then made some insinuations of his own about people that got their jobs from their political connections. Since that day, an uneasy truce had existed between Grainey and O'Rourke; Grainey tolerated him because he was good at his job, but there was a limit to how far O'Rourke could go.

"All right," Grainey went on, "what we need to do is keep the gory details out of the press. All we have to say is that it appears to be a robbery that turned into a murder. They don't need to know about the graffiti and the tongue business. Hopefully, we'll get this all taken care of quick. But if the investigation does take a while, there won't be as much heat on us if we keep that stuff off of the news."

O'Rourke agreed with keeping the details out of the press, but for another reason. If they brought in a suspect for interrogation, it would be better if there were some details only the killer would know.

He realized that he was now thinking in the singular mode – "killer" instead of "killers" – and maybe that was wrong. But O'Rourke had a feeling that there was only one man involved. He couldn't explain it, but sometimes he had these feelings about things even though there was no particular evidence to support them. Some might call them hunches but they almost always turned out right.

"We'll keep it quiet," O'Rourke said. "But we're going to need a lot of staff on this investigation quickly if we don't get any leads from the neighbors. Overtime, additional detectives, the computer guys, the works…"

"All right. Tomorrow's Sunday but I'll make some calls and pull in a bunch of detectives and some uniforms for a briefing tomorrow. I'll start arranging it now – we can always cancel if we find out who did this. You'll get priority with using the computer nerds too. Take Myers and that hot tamale Oquendo too off of whatever they're on and put them on this too."

Brad Myers and Rose Oquendo were the other two members of O'Rourke's unit. The prevailing image of a typical Albany police officer was a young, tall Irish cop and Myers fit that description perfectly. Myers, who was only 25 and single, had made detective at a young age, and specifically requested to work in O'Rourke's unit. Oquendo was a street-smart detective with a husband and three kids. She was the first Hispanic woman on the force when she was hired out of college ten years ago. Somebody might have stretched the truth a little to get her past the minimum height requirement, but what she lacked in stature she made up in professionalism, energy and intelligence. The nice thing about both Oquendo and Myers was they were both young enough that they weren't yet jaded about the job.

"Make the briefing early afternoon," O'Rourke said to Grainey. "I'd like to get the forensics report first and interview the family first to see what leads we've got."

"Fine. I'll set it up for 1:00. You just make sure you keep me posted, O'Rourke."

Valente, who had been outside, came back into the store. "We don't have much so far," he said. "Mills said the uniforms have checked with most of the neighbors in the immediate neighborhood. Nobody saw anything. The guys on the register at the chicken place across the street said they didn't see any cars pull into the lot after Tucker closed up. They have a pretty good view from there. Of course, they only look out the window when they're not busy."

"It's nice outside tonight. A lot of people were probably out walking. You would think someone saw something, a car pull in or out."

"You'd think. By the way, all the cars are out of the alley now; luckily, Mrs. Tucker had a spare key for Tucker's Toyota. Forensics is going to go over the area now to check for tracks."

O'Rourke and Valente went outside, found Mills, and gave him the instructions from Grainey to keep the murder details quiet; Mills assured him none of his guys had or would say anything. Valente and Mills both pulled out cigarettes and shot the breeze for a while. O'Rourke let them hang out and went back inside. He walked back to the front counter, to the cash register. Next to the register was a small computer and printer. Wilson, the forensics guy, was in front of it, packing up his fingerprinting equipment.

"All done here?" O'Rourke asked.

"Yup. It's all yours."

O'Rourke touched the computer mouse and a homepage came up on the screen. The words "Central Studio" were on top and there was a menu below. He clicked on "Customers" and a list appeared on the screen. He went back to the menu and clicked on "Suppliers" and another smaller list came up. He printed out the screens and looked through the files for a while longer but didn't find anything else useful. When he was done, he called Valente over.

"Tony, print out all the names that you can find on the PC. We're getting a bunch of guys together tomorrow to work on this case, but I want to have someone start checking these files tonight, cross-checking these names with arrest records."

O'Rourke stayed inside for a while, watching Forensics do their job. There wasn't much more he could do inside. Plus it was getting hot and stuffy, and the dead man on the floor didn't help much. He unlocked the front door and went outside. He decided to go across the street and talk to the workers at the chicken place himself. He had just stepped over the police tape when Trish Perkins from Channel Seven News approached him with a pen and pad in hand. She covered the crime beat regularly for the television station so they knew each other well.

"What's the word, Lieutenant? Can you tell us anything about the murder?"

"It appears to be a robbery/homicide."

"We know that already. We also know it was the owner that was murdered. What else can you tell me?"

"Seems like you already know about as much as we do. There's not much else I can tell you until tomorrow, after we start assembling our facts."

"Oh, I think there's more you can tell me," Trish said coyly.

O'Rourke studied her expression. It seemed like she knew

more about the murder details - more than she should. But she was tricky and might be trying to bluff him into divulging some details.

"Like I said - tomorrow," he said abruptly and walked across the street. She started to follow him, but apparently changed her mind and walked back to her news van.

Inside, the chicken place was doing a brisk business. Customers were ordering fried chicken by the bucket and then going over to the front window to look out at the crime scene. The window seats were all taken and many customers were standing. It was like one big party. O'Rourke elbowed his way through the line at the counter, showed his badge and asked to speak with the manager. The manager, a short stocky man named Mr. Gerard, came out from behind the counter with a small bucket of chicken still in his hands and walked with O'Rourke over to an empty dining area near the back. A TV set was mounted over the tables in that area for customers to watch but no one was watching; all the customers were up front.

Other than offering O'Rourke some of the chicken, Gerard had nothing useful. He had already spoken to the cops and basically repeated what O'Rourke already knew, that no one had seen a car pull up after Tucker closed up the store. None of the staff had seen or heard anything unusual until Mrs. Tucker drove up. O'Rourke gave him his card and thanked him, and was about to leave when something on the TV set caught his eye. Channel Seven was interrupting its regular programming with a news bulletin. The local news anchor, Bill Reynolds, came on briefly and said there was more information on the story they were following – the murder of Randall Tucker. A minute later, the face of Trish Perkins appeared on the screen. O'Rourke went over and turned up the volume on the television set.

"Bill," Trish was saying, "we've just recently been informed of a new development in the murder that took place just a couple of hours ago at Central Studio in Albany. It now appears that this was not just a simple robbery that went awry. A reliable source has told us that the victim was mutilated, apparently after the murder. In addition, it appears that a racial slur was neatly written in paint on the wall of the establishment. Details are sketchy right now, but it certainly appears to be a hate crime…"

O'Rourke watched for a few more seconds as Bill Reynolds questioned Trish Perkins, but it appeared that was all the information that Perkins had. Hell, thought O'Rourke, that's all we have. O'Rourke was not happy – someone had spilled the beans about the murder details and he intended to find out who it was. He elbowed his way past the customers lined up at the store entrance and was halfway across the street to talk to Perkins when his cell phone rang.

"O'Rourke," he said gruffly.

"It's me," said Derek. "I have some news for you that you're not going to like. I just got the family home, and I was talking to Robert. It seems that while you and I were inside the store earlier, he felt sick again. He didn't want to toss his cookies in front of everybody, so he ran into the travel agency lot and upchucked. He said this nice lady came over and asked him if he was all right, offered him some tissues. It seems he got talking to her and told her what he saw inside the store. The writing on the wall, the condition of the body. From the way he described the lady, I think she was a reporter."

"No kidding. It was Trish Perkins. I'll call you later."

When he got to where Perkins was standing, the camera had just been shut off. "Pretty sneaky," he said angrily. "We wanted to keep the details quiet for now."

"Hey, we all have to do our job," Perkins answered. "How about an interview, Lieutenant? Bill, turn the camera back on."

The camera was back on before he knew it. "Any comments, Lieutenant?"

"Yeah," he said, looking directly at the camera. "We're going to catch this sick bastard."

A half hour later, two men from the Medical Examiner's office were taking the body out the back door in a body bag.

"I got everything off the computer," Valente said to O'Rourke. "Forensics is done. The uniforms are still out questioning neighbors. Anything else we need to do here?"

O'Rourke looked down at the chalk outline where Randall Tucker's body had been a short while ago. In his mind, he could still see that bloody face.

"Not right now. Why don't you call it a day? Do me a favor though: call Myers and Oquendo. We'll all get together tomorrow morning at the station."

After that, he called Ellen. She had seen the news report. "Maybe I should take the kids for a few days," she said. "I know how you get wrapped in these big cases…"

O'Rourke protested at first, but finally he grudgingly agreed. He missed the kids when he didn't see them for a while. But when he had a big case like this, he could get intense and had a hard time focusing on anything else. It might be better if they weren't around him for a while.

He spent another hour at the scene, but nothing new developed. No one in the neighborhood had seen anything, but the cops were still checking. He asked Mills to give him a call if anything new turned up and took off for home.

When he arrived home, he went straight to the fridge and

pulled out a beer. He glanced out the kitchen window. Next door, Figgin's house was dark, the barbeque long over. O'Rourke went to the living room, found a pen and paper, and made a list of what he wanted to do tomorrow. After he finished that, he called Mills, but there were no new developments. Satisfied that there was nothing else he could do at this point, he went to bed. After about an hour of twisting and turning, he finally fell asleep, a fitful sleep filled with dreams of murder, obscene graffiti, and grotesque smiles.

Elsewhere, the tall man sat down with his notebook in hand and switched on the television. It was the first time he had turned on his television in weeks; he had little use for it. All three local stations that ran the news at 11 had Tucker as the top story and one station specifically mentioned the writing on the wall. Good. People needed to see Tucker for what he was. The stations all had it wrong of course; they called it a "hate crime". That phrase applied only in the sense that the tall man hated Tucker for what Tucker had done.

After ten minutes, the stations all switched to other stories, so he shut the TV set off. He was satisfied. His second mission went more smoothly than the first. He had been more decisive and more calm this time, had not let his emotions get in the way. He opened the notebook to the first page. He neatly drew a straight line through Randall Tucker's name, the second on his list. Tomorrow, he would start thinking about the next one.

FOUR

IIIIIIIIIIIIIIIIIIIIIIIIIIIIIIIIIIIIIII

O'Rourke arrived right at seven o'clock at his second floor office at Division One Headquarters in Albany's Pine Hills neighborhood. He was in a lousy mood. He was always in a bad mood after a murder. Albany was his city and he didn't like murders on his watch.

It didn't help that Brad Myers was running late. Valente had asked the unit's secretary, Marie, to have the group in the office before 7 AM. Not wanting to waste time, O'Rourke gathered Booker, Valente and Oquendo in his office. It was a medium size room that contained a desk, four side chairs, a few file cabinets, a map of Albany on one wall, and a large New York Giants poster on another.

He had given each of his group assignments the night before and asked for updates. "What's the latest on possible witnesses?" O'Rourke asked Booker.

"Nothing. I double checked with Mills a half hour ago. They covered the entire neighborhood last night and no one saw anything. They're at it again this morning though. Maybe something will come up."

"We're putting out a press release in a few minutes, asking for anyone with any info to call the central number," Valente said.

"Rose, are we meeting with the family this morning?"

"Uh huh. I spoke to Mrs. Tucker and made arrangements for you and Derek to go over to talk with her and her daughter at 10:30 this morning."

"Why don't you go with us? You're good with this sort of thing."

"You mean I'm better at talking to crying women?" Oquendo said jokingly. "That sounds sexist, boss."

O'Rourke grinned. It was no secret that Oquendo was the best interviewer on his team. "So, what else do you have?"

"I ran a criminal records check on Tucker like you asked. Not much there. The only thing we found was a minor conviction for marijuana possession here in Albany when he was in his senior year at college. He paid a small fine and successfully completed a year of probation. Other than a couple of traffic tickets, that's it. I also ran his wife and daughter and the daughter's boyfriend, Robert Smith, just to check. No history on them at all."

"That eliminates one thing I considered this morning. When I thought about the tongue being cut out, the first thing that came to my mind is that he squealed on someone. I thought he could have been involved in something criminal in the past and turned evidence on someone in return for a reduced sentence."

"The mob used to do stuff like that to people in New York," Valente said. Valente had lived in New York for much of his early years. "Somebody would talk to the cops, and the mob would kill them and cut their tongue out."

"I guess we all had the same idea," Booker said, "I did some research on the Internet last night. They had some gruesome photos of mob hits where the victims had their tongues cut out. One had their throat slashed too. The pictures didn't look like our victim though. They were a bloody mess. Tucker was cut carefully and evenly. The killer took his time and used the right kind of tool for the job. Another thing I find interesting is that the tongue wasn't left at the scene."

"That is interesting," O'Rourke said. "So maybe this wasn't retaliation for squealing on someone. Anyone else have anything?"

"I checked life insurance records on Tucker," Valente said. "He was insured with his wife as beneficiary, but the insurance amount wasn't unusually high."

"What about the information on his computer?"

"I took the names of all of Tucker's customers and suppliers from his computer, and started checking some of the names against arrest records," Valente said. "Nothing yet."

"You can give the rest of that to the Nerd Squad to do. I called Grainey on the way over here and he said this case will be a priority for them," O'Rourke said. The Nerd Squad was what they called the Department's computer unit. They helped other units with computer research when they weren't spending time doing things like using the Internet to try to catch pedophiles by posing as teenagers using a chat room. "Grainey also said to pull you guys off of whatever you're working on now. Other units can pick it up."

Actually, O'Rourke had spoken by phone to Grainey on the ride to work and Grainey initially told O'Rourke that he was reconsidering all the overtime because the budget was stretched this summer due to the unrest in Arbor Hill. But O'Rourke had been listening to a morning radio talk show on the way over. Callers were saying that the police didn't care about what happened to minorities in the city and would probably never catch the killers. The recent surge in gang violence in the poor neighborhoods had put the Department's reputation in a bad light already and this wasn't helping. He asked Grainey to tune in for a bit and call him back. Grainey called back a few minutes later and said the case was top priority for the department, including the Nerd Squad.

Rose Oquendo had her arms folded in front of her and didn't look happy.

"I've been working on the West Hill arsons for two weeks. Now I gotta hand that case over to some flunky?" Rose's opinion of most of the other units wasn't very high.

"I'm still hoping this thing will get resolved quick and you can all get back to other stuff. But for now, this is the assignment. Homicide's always been our unit's main job, and right now, we need to be focused on this case." O'Rourke looked at this watch. "We're running late. Let's head down to the lab."

O'Rourke's office was on the second floor and the forensics crime lab was one floor below. As they exited the stairwell, they saw Brad Myers walking quickly toward them from the front of the building, fumbling with his tie as he walked.

"Sorry I'm late," he said to O'Rourke. "I had my cell phone off and didn't know Marie called. I just checked it a half hour ago and saw the messages from last night."

"Don't you ever watch the news?" Valente asked. "The murder's all over the air."

"I guess I missed it."

"Marie left messages at your home phone, too."

"I, uh, didn't catch those either."

Oquendo let out a laugh. "I think lover boy went out and found some hottie last night and never made it home."

Myers' cheeks reddened a bit and then Valente chimed in.

"Must've been a real hot date," he joked. "Cell phone off all night, no TV…"

O'Rourke stepped in and rescued Myers. "C'mon, guys, we're on a tight schedule. Let's go."

Schade and Wilson were hunched over a table in the lab, both with Styrofoam cups of coffee in their hand. It looked like they had on the same clothes as they wore the evening before, and they both needed a shave. Wilson in particular looked like he was half-asleep.

"Have you been here all night?" O'Rourke asked.

"Grainey's orders," Schade replied. "Can't complain. We get time and a half."

"All five of you are here today," Wilson noticed. "Grainey must be in a hurry to get this one solved."

"Yeah," Valente said. "He's a real humanitarian."

O'Rourke pointed to his watch. "Look, we've got a full day today, so I don't want to spend a lot of time here. You guys will be sending us up the report later, but before we head over to visit the victim's family, I want to get a quick rundown on what you've got so far."

Schade took a gulp of coffee, and then pointed to two bullets that were sitting in a tray on the table in front of him. "We found these two bullets lodged in the front wall of the store. One appeared to have gone through the victim, but the other's clean. It missed him completely. There were two entry wounds in the victim that I saw, so that makes at least three shots fired. I'm guessing the third bullet's still in him. The Medical Examiner's office should be doing the autopsy today, so you'll know more about that later."

Booker pointed to one of the bullets with a pencil. "These markings on the bullets look odd."

"You're right," Schade said, impressed that he noticed. "I

haven't seen a striation pattern like that before. I couldn't tell you offhand what it means. I'm going to send the State Police lab a photo and see what they make of it."

"OK," O'Rourke said. "What else?"

Schade opened up a small notepad. "Let's see. No signs of forced entry and no signs of a struggle. Only one set of fingerprints were found. We ran it through Criminal Justice records and they belonged to the victim."

"They would have had his fingerprints on record from the marijuana arrest," Oquendo added.

"Wouldn't there have been other prints in the store? Co-workers, customers?" O'Rourke asked.

"Normally, you would think so," Schade answered. "But Tucker kept the place immaculate. We were lucky to get the one set."

Schade flipped over to the next page on his notepad. "We looked at the blood smudge on the register key. The blood matches the victim's blood type. Not even a partial print from the smudge, so I'm guessing the killer wore gloves. He must have gotten the victim's blood on them after he mutilated the victim. There was no sign of the victim's tongue anywhere in the room or outside, by the way."

"What about footprints?"

"Nothing inside. Wilson found something outside though."

Wilson, who appeared exhausted from working through the night, didn't respond for a second, until he realized everyone was looking at him.

"Oh, sorry. Yes, I did get a partial print from a bit of soft dirt just outside the back door. It appears to be part of the sole of a typical sneaker or a running or athletic shoe. Not enough to get very specific. Since it rained earlier in the day, the print would have to have been left sometime yesterday afternoon or early evening. It doesn't match the victim's shoes so it may belong to the killer."

"It could have been from someone who came in after the murder," Valente said. "Cops, maybe one of the family…"

"I don't think so," Booker said. "The mother, daughter, and the daughter's boyfriend were all dressed nicely since they had a special dinner planned last night. None of them were wearing sneakers or running shoes. Neither were you, the Lieutenant, or myself, and definitely not any of the officers who answered the call."

"OK, so the killer probably was wearing sneakers or running shoes," O'Rourke said. "I guess that's something. What else?"

"We checked out tire tracks," Wilson said. "The only tracks we found in the alley were from the cars that were parked back there when the police arrived. If another car had been back there yesterday, there would have been some evidence of it."

O'Rourke thought about that. "So the killer might have parked on the side street or in the parking lot out in front. The guy working at the chicken place across the street told me no one saw any cars pull up out front but they weren't watching the whole time. Or the killer could have parked a distance away. That would make sense; Tucker wouldn't have heard the killer pull up then. There was no forced entry, but Tucker often left the back door open in the summer after he closed the store, according to his wife. So the killer could have snuck right in without Tucker hearing him."

"Or," Booker added, "the victim knew the killer and he let him in."

"That's always a possibility too."

It looked like Wilson was done, so O'Rourke turned to Schade. "Anything else?"

"We looked at the spray paint," Schade said. "We'll have it tested more later, but the initial analysis is that it's nothing special, the type you can purchase in hardware store or a Wal-Mart or even on-line. That's basically all we have for now. We'll fax you up the initial report once I type it up."

"Appreciate your help. Keep us posted." O'Rourke looked over at Wilson, who was sitting down with his eyes closed. "And make sure that guy gets some sleep…"

An hour later, O'Rourke was sitting on a sofa on Peabody Lane between Booker and Oquendo, who were handling the questioning of Tucker's wife and daughter. Joyce Tucker appeared very calm and collected, which seemed unusual given the circumstances. Angela, on the other hand, appeared to be distraught, a much more understandable reaction.

O'Rourke believed that people were more likely to talk to police officers they were most comfortable with, and figured that gender and race did sometimes play a part in that. Aside from briefly introducing himself to the Tuckers and Robert Smith, O'Rourke had not said much, taking notes while Booker and Oquendo handled the interview. Booker was asking the general questions, while Oquendo handled the delicate personal stuff. The plan seemed to be working; he could see Oquendo and Booker establishing a rapport with Mrs. Tucker and her daughter.

When Joyce Tucker said that she was the head nurse at the ER at Albany Med and described her job, it clicked with O'Rourke why she appeared to be so calm. Being cool in stressful situations was a necessity for her to be able to do what she did for a living. After their meeting was over, she might very well lose it. But for now, she would get through this.

Angela, on the other hand, was a wreck. Her eyes were

bloodshot, either from crying or not getting any sleep last night, and she was trembling as she spoke. Not surprising, considering what had happened so suddenly yesterday. She sat in a big stuffed chair across from the sofa, as Robert stood quietly behind her, his hand on her shoulder. O'Rourke felt a little guilty questioning them so soon after the murder, but leads in an investigation grow cold quickly.

So far, they had learned that Randall Tucker was working alone yesterday, which was unusual since he normally had one or two employees there on Saturdays. His niece, Regina, had been at her high school graduation, which Joyce Tucker had attended earlier in the day. The other employee, Bryan Goldstein, was on vacation in Florida. According to Mrs. Tucker, Randall hadn't seemed to be under any undue stress lately; nothing that might indicate he had been involved in anything unusual or been threatened. When asked if her husband had spoken to the police about anything or witnessed anything unusual lately, she said no. O'Rourke guessed that she had picked up that the reason they were asking about that was because of the business with the tongue.

Mrs. Tucker said that her husband was generally well liked around the neighborhood and had no real enemies personally or work-related. He worked long hours, rarely drank and didn't do a lot of socializing, other than belonging to a Thursday night bowling league and attending church almost every Sunday.

Oquendo was currently questioning Mrs. Tucker. "So you don't know of anyone who would want to harm your husband?"

"No, not at all," Mrs. Tucker answered.

"Have you or anyone in your family had any threats against you lately?"

"No."

"Has he been involved in any recent altercations with anyone?"

Mrs. Tucker paused before responding. "I can't think of any offhand."

"Mrs. Tucker, given the circumstances, I have to get into some sensitive issues. The writing on the wall. Has anyone made any type of racist comments around you or your husband lately, anything at all?"

"Nothing lately. When we first moved here, almost 20 years ago, there was a neighbor that had a hard time with us moving into the neighborhood. He had made some comments. But that was a long time ago. Besides, he was elderly; he moved out years ago. I believe he's in a nursing home now."

"No other racial incidents? Nothing more recent?"

She smiled slightly. "Ms. Oquendo, I find that here in the suburbs, racism is subtle. People don't make comments, at least not to your face. But it's still there. When you go to the bank, they look a little longer at your ID. When Angela was in school, she was invited to less sleepovers than the other kids. Little things like that. I could go on, but I don't imagine it would have any bearing on what you're investigating."

Oquendo nodded, and then turned to Angela. "Angela, anything that you can think of? Have you experienced any threats?"

Angela dabbed at her eyes with a tissue. Robert was still standing behind her, his hand on her shoulder. "No. I'm living on campus now. Everyone pretty much gets along there; there's a good amount of minority kids and for the most part, we're accepted OK. I'm sure there are some haters around, but I haven't had any kind of incidents. No threats or anything."

Booker picked up the questioning. "Mrs. Tucker, we have to ask about the family and get a list of your husband's' relatives."

"His parents are deceased, natural causes. He had two sisters.

Lynette lives in Albany with her two children, Michael, who's 16, and, Regina, 17. Their father took off right after Michael was born; no one knows where he is. Randall's other sister, Julie, lives in North Carolina with her husband John and three young children; they'll be coming up here tonight."

"Did your husband get along well with them all?"

Mrs. Tucker paused again before answering. "Yes," she said. "Yes, he did." O'Rourke was looking at Angela when the question was asked and he thought he saw something. A flinch.

"Next, I'd like to get a list of Mr. Tucker's friends and acquaintances," Booker began, but O'Rourke interrupted.

"Mrs. Tucker, why don't we take a break for a few minutes if you don't mind? I know all of this isn't easy."

Mrs. Tucker agreed. Oquendo went outside to grab a quick smoke and Robert went to the kitchen to make coffee while the others made small talk. O'Rourke excused himself and walked to the bathroom, which was down the hall past the kitchen. He spent a minute in the bathroom just to kill time and then stopped in the kitchen on the way back, where Robert was getting the coffee ready.

"Feeling better today?" O'Rourke asked him.

Robert smiled sheepishly. "Yes. That was embarrassing yesterday, getting sick like that in front of everyone."

O'Rourke was somewhat surprised that Robert had almost no trace of an accent. With the long dreadlocks, he half expected him to sound like a reggae singer.

"Don't worry about it. It even happens to cops sometimes, after something like that."

"Lieutenant O'Rourke, I'm sorry I gave that information to the newswoman. That was stupid. I'm sure it made your investigation more difficult. I guess I was a little out of it last night."

"Not a problem," he lied. "There is something you can help me with though."

Robert had pulled a tray out of the cabinet and began putting some coffee cups on it. "What would that be?"

"I think Angela was about to say something when we asked about Mr. Tucker's extended family. Do you know anything about that?"

Robert paused, a coffee cup in his hand. "How would I? I've never met her family's relatives."

Robert looked down and began moving some cups around unnecessarily on the tray.

"Angela has an aunt and two cousins in Albany. Has she ever talked about them?"

Robert didn't respond. He glanced into the living room. Angela was busy talking with her mother and Booker.

O'Rourke pushed on. "You know, any information you can give us might help us find out who killed Mr. Tucker."

Robert looked at O'Rourke carefully, pondering the situation. After a few seconds, lowering his voice, he responded. "If I say something, would you promise not to let Angela know I told you?"

"Of course."

"A few days ago, Angela told me she stopped over here and her father was really upset. He had gone to his sister's house in Albany earlier to talk about a graduation party he was planning for Angela's cousin Regina. It was supposed to be today, in fact. Regina has a brother, Michael. He's 16 and he's been doing poorly in school lately; his mother told Mr. Tucker that she's worried that he's starting to hang with a street gang. So Mr. Tucker went upstairs to talk to him. When Mr. Tucker went into Michael's room, he smelled smoke – marijuana."

"What happened then?"

"I guess Mr. Tucker started to lecture Michael about it and about the gang thing. Michael got angry, called him some names. 'Uncle Tom', stuff like that. He said it was easy for Mr. Tucker; he didn't have to live in the ghetto. There was some shouting, and nearly got physical. Then the kid ran out of the house. Mr. Tucker was very upset when he got home. Angela said he usually doesn't talk about family stuff like that in front of her, but he did that time. He was really upset."

O'Rourke looked into the living room; they should be getting back there.

"Thanks. That might be important. You did the right thing by telling me."

They finished up the interview with the Tuckers, getting the names of family friends, neighbors, work associates and other leads. Mrs. Tucker was still holding it together when they left, but that probably wouldn't last much longer, O'Rourke thought. In the car, O'Rourke filled in Oquendo and Booker on what Robert Smith told him.

"Sounds like maybe someone should pay Michael Tucker a visit," Booker said.

"We've got a meeting this afternoon with the additional staff that Grainey's giving us. I figured you and I could stop by the house after that."

"You know," Booker said, "I can't help thinking about the words on the wall – "Black Bastard". You would think if the murder was racially motivated, it would say something even worse, like "Nigger". "Black Bastard" just doesn't seem right. I don't know… maybe if the killer himself was also black…no, it still doesn't feel right. If the killer was his nephew, I could even see him writing "Uncle Tom" or some other crap like that, but not 'Black Bastard' ".

"Who knows what somebody's thinking when they kill someone like this," Oquendo said from the back seat. "In the heat of the moment, maybe they weren't thinking clearly, just quickly wrote out whatever came to mind."

"But they didn't write it out quickly," O'Rourke replied. "Those letters on the wall were very neat. Someone took their time doing that. With a dead body lying there, they took their goddamn sweet time."

"That takes balls," Oquendo said.

Her comment seemed so out of character that both Booker and O'Rourke burst out laughing, followed by an annoyed slap on the shoulder from Oquendo. Maybe it was having a good laugh or maybe it was getting the difficult interview with the deceased's family over with, but by the time they got back to the station, O'Rourke's mood had brightened.

FIVE

IIIIIIIIIIIIIIIIIIIIIIIIIIIIIIIIIIIIIIIII

There were about twenty plainclothes detectives and uniformed cops seated in the meeting room when O'Rourke and Captain Grainey walked in at 1 PM. The detectives and cops were scattered around the room in folding chairs which faced the front of the room, talking and joking around with each other until Grainey stepped up to the small podium in front of the room, with O'Rourke beside him. O'Rourke's staff sat at a table near the podium, also facing the small audience. Grainey, a thin man with a high voice, turned on the microphone. He told the audience how important this case was, how the Albany PD is one of the finest in New York State, and how much confidence he had that they could solve this case in a timely manner. Most of the cops were yawning or trying hard not to by the time he turned the podium over to O'Rourke.

O'Rourke turned off the mike. His voice projected enough that he didn't need to use it.

"Good afternoon," O'Rourke began. "I appreciate you all coming on short notice. Most of you had the day off, and even though it's overtime for you, I know you've all been getting more than your share of that lately with all the violence on the streets the past few weeks." More than a few of the cops nodded in agreement. A big beefy blond haired detective named Sam Wendell that was sitting up front said "Damn straight."

"You all have an outline that Detective Booker made up of the details of the case. The neighborhood was canvassed pretty well last night and there are some officers out there right now continuing that, but I want some of you to expand the search further out. We want to see if anyone saw anything or anyone unusual in the area around the time of the murder. A couple of you will be manning phones; a hot-line number has been established and the local news outlets are giving it out for anyone to call if they know anything. Some of you will be doing some research on past hate crimes in this area; Computer Crimes can pull up the most recent cases, but older stuff won't be on the database. I also want some of you to talk to Mr. Tucker's friends, neighbors, customers, and business contacts. If the victim was in trouble or had any racial remarks directed to him lately, he may have said something to someone."

Detective Wendell, apparently the joker in the crowd, turned around to face the guys in the back, and said: "Or maybe he just held his tongue." A few of the other detectives snickered.

"OK, that's enough," O'Rourke said. "We have a bizarre element in this case, that's for sure. But be careful what you say in public. The press will be keeping a close eye on this case and I don't want them to think we're taking it lightly. My hope is we can get this case wrapped up quickly, before it becomes a media event."

Wendell smiled and nudged the arm of the detective sitting next to him, whispering.

"I say we should take our time. Those jigs down in Arbor Hill will think twice before starting any more trouble if they think there's some nut job going around gunning for them."

O'Rourke took the palm of his large hand and slammed it down on the podium, loud enough that it could be heard in the corridor outside the room even with the door shut. His face was red and his voice was loud. "I SAID THAT'S ENOUGH," he shouted, looking down at Wendell, who shrank back in his seat.

O'Rourke addressed the entire group. "This is no joke. There's a man out there that's dead. He had a wife and a daughter, and they are never going to see him alive again. He didn't deserve to go out like that. He should have lived to a ripe old age, retired to play with his grandkids someday. But somebody decided to change that. And we're going to find out who that somebody is. And," he said as he stared back at Wendell, "if any of you aren't going to take this seriously, you better damn well tell me right now because I don't want you here. You got that?"

Wendell swallowed hard and nodded. The room was unnaturally silent as the rest of the cops studied their fingertips or looked down at the floor. Grainey started to say something, and then thought better of it. O'Rourke paused for a few seconds, for effect but also to give himself a chance to cool down a bit.

"I've drawn up a list of assignments for all of you," he said after a few moments, his voice lower. "We'll use this meeting room as our base of operations. You'll be working in teams and coordinating everything you do with HSC. My team is now going to give you some background on what we've got so far."

O'Rourke sat down and let Booker and the others pick it up from there. After the presentation ended without further incident, O'Rourke had the cops move their chairs around and divide into four teams, each led by one of O'Rourke's staff.

Valente's team was going to interview people that lived in Tucker's neighborhood and also continue questioning in the neighborhood. Booker's group was going to check out Tucker's friends, relatives and acquaintances, which now included getting a full history on Tucker's nephew before Booker and O'Rourke visited him later. Oquendo's people were going to focus on Tucker's business to see if there was any motive there, talking to business suppliers, competitors and customers. Myers and his team would take on what was left over, including looking at any arrests in Albany or the surrounding areas that may have been hate crimes. Although New York State had an actual hate crime database, it had only been in existence for a few years so it didn't contain older crimes. O'Rourke vaguely remembered a case being in the local news several years ago somewhere around Albany where someone assaulted a black man at night on the street and wrote something offensive on a nearby wall. He knew who could come up with information on that.

Satisfied that his staff had the teams moving in the right directions, O'Rourke exited the station. He walked down the street to an old three story building a few doors down that used to be a factory years before. Everyone called the building the Annex. The first and second floors were being temporarily used to house small units of support staff for Division One until the building where O'Rourke worked was expanded in a few months.

An older cop named Tommy McNulty that used to work with O'Rourke's father stood guard at the front desk at the Annex.

"What's up, old-timer," O'Rourke said to him.

"Not much at my age," McNulty answered with his standard response.

O'Rourke went down the hall and through a door that said "Tech Research and Computer Crimes Unit". Most of the department referred to the unit simply as the Nerd Squad.

The room was small with three desks and two smaller offices in back. The nickname Nerd Squad seemed appropriate, O'Rourke thought. One of the desks was occupied by a small guy with a beakish nose and big glasses. Another desk was occupied by a pale gangly guy with bushy bright orange hair, while a thin man with a log scraggly beard sat at a third. O'Rourke walked toward a small enclosed office with a plate glass window in the back of the room. He could see that the office was occupied by two people. Sandy Bernstein, a sharply dressed man of about fifty with a neatly clipped grey mustache, was sitting behind a desk talking to an attractive redhead in a tight skirt, Megan Ross, who O'Rourke knew very well. O'Rourke knocked on the window.

Bernstein opened the door. "Lieutenant O'Rourke, come on in," he said. "I heard you have some business for me."

"Yes, I do. A Nerd Squad special," O'Rourke said.

"Now Steven, why do you persist in calling us nerds?"

O'Rourke gestured toward the three staff members sitting at their desks in the outer room. From a distance, they resembled an owl, Napoleon Dynamite, and the lead guitarist from ZZ Top. "Not exactly a macho bunch out there," O'Rourke said.

"I'll have you know, Steven, that the man with the beard out there, Tomkins, went mountain climbing last weekend. And the one with the wild red hair, Lyons, recently won a bicycle race in Saratoga. So although they may not fit your definition of 'macho', we do have trained athletes on our staff," Sandy said, pretending to be offended.

"OK, so they're athletic nerds."

Sandy laughed but Megan had a sour expression.

"I guess we can't all be like the dashing Steven O'Rourke," Megan said with a bitter tone.

O'Rourke was always a bit uncomfortable lately when

Megan was around. He had some history with her. It started at the Christmas party last year. Everyone was standing around, having a few laughs and a few cocktails. Alcohol was officially not allowed at APD holiday parties - not allowed meaning you can't tell any outsiders about it. Before long, a group of about ten cops, including O'Rourke and Megan Ross, went down the street, to the local cop bar, Sanford's. O'Rourke and Megan got talking. Mostly just about work at first, but then about their private lives. It turned out that Megan was recently divorced, like O'Rourke. Other than that, it seemed they had nothing in common. That is until later that evening in O'Rourke's bedroom, where they found there were several things that they both enjoyed.

The affair was over by the end of spring; few others even knew about it. Nothing really clicked between them. O'Rourke considered himself kind of middle of the road politically, but to him, Megan was a bleeding heart liberal, always sticking up for the criminals. Unusual for a cop, even one that rarely did street duty. He told her once that some of her remarks rubbed him the wrong way and she changed the subject by asking what the right way to be rubbed would be. Eventually and reluctantly, knowing he would miss the sex, he decided to call it quits. He tried to end the affair in a civilized way, no hard feelings. Megan didn't take it that way. This was one of the few times he had run into her since the break-up and it was obvious to O'Rourke that she still held a grudge.

O'Rourke decided to let Megan's' comment slide. "Sandy, I need your area to take all the names from the PC at Central Studio, both business associates and customers, and check them for criminal records. I had some of the data from the PC printed out while we were there last night, but I'm sure there's more. You'll probably need Mrs. Tucker's permission to officially access the computer."

Sandy pointed his finger at the area outside his office. "You mean the one that Martin's going through over there?"

O'Rourke looked back out at the owl-like guy who was clicking away on a keyboard. "I'm impressed."

Megan smiled thinly. "We may be nerds but we're way ahead of you. We figured you'd want to run those names. I called Mrs. Tucker this morning and she gave us permission. We already went up to Tucker's store, got the PC and brought it down here," she said smugly.

O'Rourke tried not to look annoyed. "I also need a list of everyone in the state that's committed any type of hate crime and who's not in jail, details of their offenses, and their current known addresses. Plus info on any similar crimes that may not be on the database."

"That might take a while," Sandy said. "That information's spread out on three different systems. Our guys don't get paid overtime like you guys, so I'm guessing a couple of days for all that info." Sandy and Megan were part of the police department but the rest of the unit was contract staff, computer techs that were hired through an outside agency.

"How about if you limit the list for now to anyone that resides within 50 miles of Albany? That'll give us some names to start with. We can always expand the list later."

"That's more workable. It leaves out all of New York City and the rest of downstate, which would be the bulk of the data. We can probably come up with the list of names today, along with the list Martin's working on. By sometime tomorrow, we can get you the information."

O'Rourke started for the door. It was almost time to get together with Booker. "OK. Thanks for your help. Catch you later."

Megan smiled a fake smile and waved at O'Rourke as he went to leave. "Bye now," she said in a sultry voice. O'Rourke looked back at Megan, still sitting at the side chair next to Sandy's desk with her long legs crossed, looking sexy as hell and knowing it. Her tailored suit didn't quite hide her shapely assets. He knew in his mind that there were several good reasons why he had broken up with Megan. But at the moment, he could think of a few good reasons why that may have been a big mistake and none of those reasons involved his mind.

SIX

||||||||||||||||||||||||||||||||||||||||||

O'Rourke took the Jaguar to Arbor Hill with Booker riding shotgun. The house that Michael Tucker and his family lived in wasn't as run down as many of the houses on the block, but it had definitely seen better days. They pulled over a few doors down from the house. It was late afternoon and hot, and you could tell which houses didn't have air conditioning by the number of people sitting on the front steps. According to Booker, the Tucker's lived on the third floor of the three-story building. They climbed a set of stairs and rang the top doorbell. Just about everyone nearby was watching them: two guys with suits ringing a doorbell in this neighborhood usually meant cops.

No answer. They rang the bell a second time and still no response. O'Rourke rang the bell underneath, the one to the second floor. A woman's voice shouted "Who is it?"

"Police," answered Booker.

A few seconds later, a very small, very old black woman in a housedress came to the front door. O'Rourke figured she was about ninety, give or take a decade.

"You looking for the Tuckers?"

"Yes, ma'am," Booker said. "Are they home?"

"They went to Lynette's brother's house. Paying their respects. That poor man…"

"Do you know if the whole family went there?"

"Just Lynette and Regina. The boy, he didn't go. He ain't got no respect for nobody."

"Do you know if he's upstairs?" O'Rourke asked.

"No, he ain't upstairs. He's where he always is – hanging down on the corner with his *friends*." The way she said the word "friends", O'Rourke got the impression she wasn't too fond of them.

O'Rourke pointed to his right. "This corner right here?"

"No, two blocks down. The corner where all the drugs is at."

It was hardly a secret that the corner in question was an open-air drug market. Even on a hot day like this, guys hanging out there wore loosely hanging sweatshirts. Sweatshirts that could easily be filled with a variety of illegal substances.

O'Rourke wiped some sweat from his brow. "Thanks for your time. Sorry to bother you."

The old woman looked at Booker. "The news says Lynette's brother, he was a good man. Everyone they talk to on TV, they all say he was a decent man, never bothered nobody."

"Yes, ma'am."

The woman reached up to put her hand on Booker's arm, barely reaching his elbow. "You find whoever killed him. Find whoever did that awful thing to him. You hear? Both of you. You find them."

Booker nodded. "You can count on it."

O'Rourke parked the Jag a good twenty yards from the intersection where the drug dealers hung out. Small crowds were hanging out at three of the four corners of the intersection, many of the guys wearing loose hooded sweatshirts. Booker pointed to a group of four black teens standing on one corner, across the street from where the Jaguar was parked.

"The smallest kid is Michael. I recognize him from a picture of the family we saw at Joyce Tucker's home."

Michael appeared to be younger and was shorter than the other kids he was with. All four were standing there, leaning against a building smoking cigarettes; a couple of empty beer bottles were on the ground nearby.

"Why don't you let me talk to him for now? You can back me up," Booker said.

O'Rourke thought it over for a second. "OK, but at the first sign of trouble, give me a signal."

Booker got out of the car, O'Rourke staying put. As Booker crossed the street, O'Rourke saw two stocky teenage boys that were sitting on the stoop down the block look up and take notice.

Booker approached the group of four. O'Rourke rolled down his window to listen. The tallest one, a muscular kid probably about nineteen, moved forward away from the building and said something to Booker that O'Rourke couldn't quite make out. The rest of the group started laughing. Booker said something back that they apparently didn't find so funny, because the big kid tossed his cigarette aside and took a step toward him. O'Rourke started the Jag and moved it up, directly across the street from the group, then put it back in park.

Now he could hear them talking. "This is none of your business, Jukey," Booker was saying to the big teen, who was a good four inches taller than Booker. "I just want to talk to Michael."

"He's with us, man," the kid named Jukey said. "And he don't want to speak with you. He's got his rights. He don't have to say nothin'.'"

"Are you his attorney, Jukey? You sure don't look like one."

"You got that right. I don't go wearing a suit like you, pretending to be something you ain't. I think those white boys just sent you here 'cause they don't want to dirty themselves, didn't they?"

That got another laugh from the gang. This time, Booker advanced a step toward them. At the same time, O'Rourke saw in his rear view mirror that the two stocky teens that had been sitting on the steps were starting to cross the street to join the other four. O'Rourke stepped out of the car and held his hand out to the pair. "Hold it," he said sternly.

The two stopped for a moment and sized up O'Rourke, pondering their next move. O'Rourke smiled and opened his jacket, just enough so they could see his gun holster. "Let's let them work this situation out for themselves," he said.

The one in front paused for a moment, and then nodded. "No problem, man," the kid said, and the two went back to their steps and sat down.

Across the street, Jukey was angry and in Booker's face, as the other three watched. One of the three was standing behind Jukey as if ready to back him up. Michael just stood there, looking small and out of his league. "Why don't you just go back and tell your friend that Mike don't have nothing to say," Jukey said loudly to Booker.

O'Rourke took it all in but made no move.

Booker turned to Michael. "You can talk to us here or we can take you in and question you at the station. With all your family's going through, I don't think you…"

Jukey interrupted. "Maybe you didn't hear me, man. I said Mikey ain't got nothing to say," he said menacingly, jabbing a finger at Booker for emphasis. "Especially to no nigger cop."

Booker's right arm shot up quickly and grabbed Jukey's

wrist. He pulled it downward, spinning him halfway around, and taking a couple of steps forward, pushed him face first against the building. "You think you're a tough guy, huh," Booker shouted. "You think these three punks got your back? Think again, asshole. I don't see any of them making a move." Booker still had hold of Jukey's wrist and had his arm pulled way up behind his back. "And I'll bet you got a load of crack or weed in your pocket, so I might just take it and bust you all right now. Or," he said in a quieter voice, "you could all just walk away and leave Michael here to have a nice little chat with me."

He let Jukey's wrist go and stepped back. Booker's actions were so sudden that the others hadn't made a move. Jukey glared at Booker, then at the three punks who apparently didn't have Jukey's back. Then he started walking away, up the street. Two of the kids slowly started following him, leaving Michael standing there alone with Booker.

Booker put his hand firmly on Michael's shoulder and started leading him to the Jaguar. "C'mon. Let's talk."

O'Rourke drove down the street slowly while Booker and Michael Tucker sat in the back. Michael looked smaller back there, more like fourteen than sixteen. He sat with his arms folded as Booker explained that he just wanted to question the boy about his whereabouts the afternoon before and to see if he had any important information.

"We'd like your help, Michael," he was saying. "OK?"

Silence. Either scared or acting tough.

"This is important. You may not like us very much, but we want to catch the person that did this. Understand?"

More silence.

"Don't you care about your uncle?"

O'Rourke watched in the rear view mirror. He thought he caught a little crack in Michael's facade.

"Apparently, you don't care," Booker continued. "Your uncle, lying there dead with his tongue cut out, and you didn't even give a shit."

That did it. One tear trickled down Michael's face, then another. "Damn it," he said, wiping the tears away.

Booker put his hand on Michael's arm. "It's alright," he said.

Michael looked at Booker. "Why did that happen to him, man? Uncle Randy, he was a good…" The tears turned into a torrent. Michael buried his face in his hands. For several minutes, as O'Rourke slowly drove around the block back toward Michael's house, the only sound in the car was Michael's sobs.

O'Rourke thought about the situation. Michael lived with just his mother and sister. In this neighborhood. With no father. Randall Tucker might have been one of the few decent men that Michael knew. And Michael had just had a fight with him, calling him a name and running off the last time he saw his uncle alive. No wonder Michael was so distraught.

Assuming, of course, that Michael and his friends hadn't themselves shot and killed Tucker yesterday afternoon.

Booker handed the kid a couple of tissues and Michael wiped off his face. After a moment, he spoke to Booker. "I don't know anything about it. I was with those guys all day yesterday. Me and Jukey Jones and Ernest and Sam. Just hanging around on that corner. We went to the McDonald's down the street for a while, but that's the only time we left the corner."

O'Rourke decided to be the bad cop. "Selling drugs all day, I suppose?"

"We didn't even have any drugs. Jukey, he sometimes scores some pot and sells it, but he hasn't had any for a week. He just likes to pretend he does. Makes him feel cool." He looked down at his feet. "Makes us all feel cool I guess."

"Can you prove you were on the corner all day? Maybe you four decided to make a few bucks and rob Uncle Randall. Maybe it got a little out of hand."

Booker shot O'Rourke a glance. He probably thought O'Rourke was pressing too hard.

Michael sounded a little scared now, his words coming out quickly. "We were on the corner all afternoon yesterday. Ask anybody in the neighborhood. And the McDonald's where we ate was crowded; people saw us there too. I can give you some of their names. Also, the cops kept driving around all day, every half hour or so. With all the trouble going on around here, they've been driving up and down the street all weekend. They don't bother the drug dealers as long as the dealers don't get into any fights. The cops can tell you we were there."

It sounded plausible to O'Rourke. All of that could be verified.

"Besides," Michael said, "none of us got a car. We hang around here all day; if we got to go somewhere, we just walk."

O'Rourke figured Tucker's store was a good six miles from here, maybe more. A pretty long walk. They could have hopped a bus, though, or caught a ride with someone.

"Have you ever told anybody else around here that you have an uncle with a nice business out near Colonie? Do you remember ever mentioning that to any of your other friends?"

Michael looked down at the floor. "I ain't got no other friends." It seemed sad to O'Rourke that those three jerks were Michael's only friends.

They had arrived at Michael's house. Booker asked a few more questions and got a list of names from Michael of people that could verify that they were hanging around the corner yesterday. Then, Booker walked Michael up the steps. It was getting dark and O'Rourke could see from the car that the lights in the top floor apartment weren't on; apparently Michael's mom and sister weren't home yet. Booker and Michael stood there and talked for quite a while. Michael appeared to be in no hurry to go inside. Finally, Michael did go into the house and Booker returned to the car.

O'Rourke and Booker sat in silence until they were a few blocks from the station. Booker was the first to break the silence. "The kid didn't do it."

"I know."

O'Rourke could tell the kid had nothing to do with the murder but he wouldn't put it past Michael's friends though, especially the big kid Jukey. However, it sounded though they all might have an alibi if their whereabouts could be verified for the entire day. That could be checked out easy enough. If Michaels' story held up, that ruled the four of them out as suspects.

Back at the station, O'Rourke stopped in the meeting room, now used as the base of operations for the Tucker investigation, to see how things were going. Some of the detectives were still around making calls or checking computer printouts, but most were out in the field knocking on doors or had gone home for the day. O'Rourke and Valente were reviewing some information when a detective named Phillips came over.

"Lieutenant, we checked out a lead earlier. One of the guys that Randall Tucker bowled with in his league spent some time in prison twenty years ago for armed robbery."

"And?"

"Well, we went to his house to talk with him. I don't think he's involved."

"Why not?"

"I can't picture him being one of the killers. This guy's in bad shape. He's an old guy and he had a stroke a few years ago. The guy has to keep an oxygen tank with him."

"I thought you said he bowled."

"I didn't say he bowled well."

It had been a long day, so O'Rourke took off. He was a block from home when his cell rang. Albany was one of the first communities to ban talking on a cell phone while driving, but O'Rourke, like ninety percent of the city, ignored the ban.

The call was from Brad Myers.

"Boss, we got the forensics report."

"Anything new, or just what Schade and Wilson covered this morning?"

"Definitely something new," Myers said. He sounded excited. "Remember the marks on the bullets?"

"Yeah, the striation marks. Booker said they looked odd. Forensics was going to run it by the State lab."

"They did. According to the report, it's something we don't see every day around here."

"What's that?"

"You're not going to believe it."

Myers enjoying building up suspense. "Why don't you just tell me what they found," O'Rourke growled.

"A silencer. The marks were made by a silencer attached to the barrel of the gun."

O'Rourke sat in the car for over ten minutes after he pulled into his driveway. A silencer. If there was still any thought that Michael Tucker and his Arbor Hill friends had killed Randall, this just about killed that theory. Small time would-be marijuana dealers don't use silencers. O'Rourke didn't even know where someone around here would get something like that. They were illegal in New York State and it wasn't something that was even sold on the streets, at least not in Albany. Even if you could get your hands on one, they would be expensive. Probably not something you would use in a routine robbery of a small store.

According to the lab report, the silencer was the real thing, not some kind of homemade contraption. The report said there would be no way to trace it. It made O'Rourke think of spy movies, or movies about the Mafia. Valente had mentioned mobsters earlier; that they sometimes used to cut out the tongues of their victims. But the mob hadn't had a real presence in Albany since the 1930's. What the hell could Randall Tucker have been involved with that would get him killed by someone using a silencer?

O'Rourke, lost in thought, nearly jumped out of his skin when someone rapped on the driver side window. It was Ginny Dixon, dressed in jogging clothes and running in place.

He hit the button to roll down the windows. "Holy crap, you almost gave me a heart attack."

"Heart attack? The way you were staring into space, I thought you were in a coma or something."

"Very funny. I guess I've got a lot on my mind." He got out of the car. Although it was after nine, the street was well lit and it was still warm out. There were a few other people on the street, out walking, enjoying a nice Sunday evening. A far cry from the Arbor Hill neighborhood he had been in earlier.

"So, how are you holding up?" he asked Ginny.

"Pretty well, I guess. I'm more worried about Molly. She has this fear that her dad's going to come to our house and try to take her away. I spoke with my mother and she's going to watch Molly for a few days. That works out well, because I'm going to be busy dealing with the police and my attorney about this whole mess with Greg. I've been stressed out about it all day. I finally decided to get out of the house. I missed my run earlier so I figured why not get it in now."

"I missed my run today, too, but I'm too beat to do it now. It's been a long day."

"I can imagine," Ginny said. "I saw you on TV. You used some strong language there."

"I was hoping they would edit that out."

O'Rourke looked at Ginny and said: "Hey, if you're up for a run tomorrow evening, I'll make sure I get out of work on time and we can meet around eight."

Ginny wiped a bead of perspiration off of her forehead. Her blond hair was pulled back with a headband and the look was good on her. "Hmmm. It sounds inviting. But I don't usually run with strangers."

"Don't worry. If I give you any trouble, you can always call a cop."

After Ginny left, O'Rourke went into the house and had a cold beer. He called Ellen and spoke to the kids, apologizing for the abrupt end to their day on Saturday and promising to take them out sometime next week. Then he turned in early since tomorrow promised to be another long day.

Like the night before, he had unpleasant dreams, but more vivid. He dreamed he was following a man on the sidewalk, a man walking just a few yards in front of him. It was nighttime and it was foggy so he couldn't make out the man's shape very well. Since he was directly behind the man, he couldn't see a face either. No matter how fast O'Rourke walked, the man was always a few steps in front of him. O'Rourke felt he knew something about the man, some obvious detail, but he couldn't figure out what it was. The man started jogging and disappeared into the fog before O'Rourke could speed up to catch him. Just before he vanished, the man dropped a piece of paper with some writing on it. O'Rourke reached down and picked it up. The note was covered in blood but he could still read it. Just four words written in dark blue spray paint: "I'm not done yet."

SEVEN

IIIIIIIIIIIIIIIIIIIIIIIIIIIIIIIIIIIIIIII

O'Rourke started Monday morning off thinking about Ginny Dixon. But he decided that he needed to focus on the Tucker investigation, so he grabbed a much-needed cold shower before heading to work. When he arrived, the office was half empty because detectives were out looking for leads on the case.

O'Rourke took advantage of the quiet to read the reports. The lab report had nothing he didn't already know from yesterday's meeting with the lab techs. The autopsy report was more interesting; it said that Randall Tucker died from a shot through the heart. The report said the second bullet that struck him killed him, the first shot striking higher in the chest. Both shots came from about fifteen feet away, the report estimated. That means they were both good shots. This killer apparently had a lot of practice; possibly a professional killer. Of course, there was the third bullet that missed the victim completely and ended up lodged in the wall. O'Rourke assumed that would have been the first shot fired. Had the killer been nervous when he missed on the first shot? That might contradict the theory of the killer being a pro.

The other interesting thing in the autopsy report was that the tool used to remove the victim's tongue was not a knife, at least not a common type. The report stated: "The implement used was a very small and extremely sharp edged cutting tool, possibly a scalpel". The report went on to say the removal of the tongue was not necessarily done on a level requiring surgical skill, but was done very carefully, which would take a significant amount of time.

The ballistics summary was also interesting. It stated that a silencer makes the shooting of a gun less accurate. So the killer had to have been a very good shot. O'Rourke thought about the facts in the reports. It all seemed so - what was the word - sophisticated? He had never encountered a homicide like this in his time in the Albany Police Department. This was obviously no random hold-up gone bad. Nor was it a typical hate crime. The killer (O'Rourke still felt it was just one person) had prepared by bringing along a gun with a silencer, a sharp cutting tool, and a can of spray paint. Whoever did this had obviously been specifically targeting Tucker and was interested in more than just robbery. But why?

Just before noon, Sandy Bernstein called and asked O'Rourke to stop by his office, saying that he had come up with some information that O'Rourke could use. As O'Rourke was walking down the hallway of the Annex, Megan Ross emerged from the Nerd Squad room. She had on a bright red blouse that showed more than a hint of cleavage and a tight black skirt that O'Rourke could remember removing from her not so long ago.

"Well hello there, Lieutenant," she said to O'Rourke. "I take it you're here to see Sandy."

"He said he's got something I need to see," O'Rourke replied, immediately regretting his choice of words.

"So do I," Megan replied. "But I guess that ship has sailed."

Walking past O'Rourke, she whispered: "Your loss..."

Inside the Nerd Squad, the owl, Napoleon Dynamite and ZZ Top were each tapping away at their computers. O'Rourke knocked on the window to Sandy's office and went inside.

"Megan just went out to lunch," Sandy said. "It's probably just as well. I was concerned yesterday that my office was going to spontaneously combust with all that pent up sexual tension."

"That's funny, old man. At least I still think about sex once in a while."

"Hey, just because I'm fifty-three and divorced doesn't mean I don't think about it anymore. Thinking about it is about all I can do."

Sandy handed O'Rourke the paperwork on past hate crimes in the area. O'Rourke had already gotten it via e-mail and given it to Myers to follow up on. "There aren't a lot of names on this list," Sandy said.

"That's not surprising," O'Rourke responded. "A lot of prosecutors don't want to try to convict on that statute. It's a hot issue."

Sandy pointed to the fourth name down on the list. "Look at this one though. Earl Coombs. Age 33. Address: Route 30, Amsterdam, New York. Convicted of Felony Assault under the hate crime statute, served five years in prison. Several prior misdemeanor convictions, including writing graffiti."

"I remember that one. That's the case that rang a bell with me yesterday."

"I just started pulling down more details on that one and a few things jumped out at me. Coombs was in prison for beating the crap out of a black college student outside of a redneck bar over there in Amsterdam. Then he stabbed him just for good measure.

The kid was paralyzed from the waist down for several months."

"Unfortunately, that kind of crime isn't unique," O'Rourke said. "Most of these guys on this list probably have similar stories."

"Right. But here's the kicker - Earl Coombs spray painted a message on a nearby wall. It said "Niggers stay out of Amsterdam". The other thing that caught my eye was that Earl just got paroled from prison a month ago. Here, we made a file."

O'Rourke browsed through the folder. Coombs still lived in Amsterdam; a current address was listed. A recent photo of Coombs was taped to the front of the folder; he had short blond hair, cut prison style. He looked closer to forty than thirty-three. Included with the paperwork inside was a photo of the graffiti on the outside wall of an abandoned house next to the bar. The writing was sloppy, as if done in a hurry. "Hmmm. This doesn't match our suspect's M.O. From the report, it looks like Coombs ran into the kid in the bar and started arguing with him there, so the assault doesn't look premeditated like in the Tucker case. There's the graffiti angle, but the sloppy writing in these photos doesn't look anything like the words on the inside wall of the camera shop. Plus, of course, Coombs didn't shoot the kid, he stabbed him."

"But," Sandy replied, "both cases are hate crimes against black men, both with racial epithets spray painted on a wall, both ended up with the victim being cut. And Coombs has just recently been back on the street. As far as the change in M.O., people sometimes get smarter after they get caught. You don't know how many assailants were involved in Tucker's death. Maybe Coombs has a partner who writes neater than he does."

"Have you checked to see if there's any connection between him and Tucker?"

"Yes. No connection that we could find. But I still think this is a good lead."

"It's the only real lead we've got so far." O'Rourke looked at his watch. Amsterdam wasn't that far away; he could call their police department. If they were good with it, he could get there by early afternoon. "Sandy, I owe you one."

O'Rourke had been to Amsterdam before. Although it was less than 40 miles west of Albany, for some reason it had a kind of working-class redneck feel to it. Skynyrd and NASCAR. Actually not a bad combination, O'Rourke thought. Back at his office, he gave the Amsterdam chief of police a call.

Over the phone, the chief even seemed to have a redneck drawl. "Yup," Chief Sanders said after O'Rourke asked him about the suspect, "I know Earl Coombs. Bad news. He did quite a number on that college boy. Of course, the boy didn't belong in a bar like that in the first place. Anyhow, we were keepin' an eye on Earl for a while after he got out of prison, but we just didn't have enough men to do that forever. As far as I know, he hasn't gotten into any trouble since he got out."

"I'm sure you heard about our murder in Albany."

"Saw it in the papers. I figured it was connected to that racial trouble you've got over there in Arbor Hill. We don't have that problem over here." He sounded smug. No racial trouble in Amsterdam. Of course not, O'Rourke thought. He had the feeling that the chief just might have his men look the other way if one of those uppity black college kids had the audacity to visit a bar in Amsterdam and ended up getting beat to shit for it.

"We're looking at all the possibilities. It could be that Earl graduated from felony assault to murder. I'd like to come up to Amsterdam this afternoon with one of my guys and talk to him, if you don't mind."

"Well, I tell you what. Last time I heard, Earl was unemployed, so he's probably either home or at some bar. Why don't you stop by at the station here and I'll get two of my men to coordinate with you and you can all pay him a visit? I, uh, recommend that the guy you bring along with you is white."

"Thanks," O'Rourke said, hanging up before he said something that he shouldn't.

Brad Myers was at his desk. He had just finished up a phone conversation with Bryan Goldstein, the vacationing college student who worked in Tucker's store. "Goldstein's not much help, boss. He just found out yesterday about the murder, and he said he's been thinking about it all day. He has no idea who would want to kill Mr. Tucker. He said it was probably just a robbery that got way out of hand. Maybe he's right."

"But maybe not," O'Rourke said. He dropped the Coombs folder on Myers' desk. "You can read this on the way to Amsterdam."

"Amsterdam as in Holland?"

"Brad, our budget on this case is big but not that big. We're going to Amsterdam, *New York*."

"Oh," Myers said, disappointed it wasn't Holland.

After O'Rourke explained to Myers why they were going to Amsterdam, he got Booker, Valente and Oquendo together and updated them on the case.

"Brad and I will check Coombs out. You guys keep at it. Coombs is a possibility, but by no means a sure thing."

Amsterdam was about a 35-minute drive from Albany and the Jag made it in about 25. On the way, O'Rourke told Myers about his conversation with Chief Sanders.

"He sounds like a real jerk," Myers said.

"An asshole is what he is," O'Rourke replied. "But we're the outsiders here, so we've got to deal with him."

When they arrived at the Amsterdam police station, Chief Sanders wasn't at all what O'Rourke expected. O'Rourke had expected Rod Steiger but the chief, who was short and thin as a rail, looked more like Don Knotts. Sanders was standing outside of his office, speaking to two burly plainclothes cops that were both easily six feet three, making the chief look even shorter. O'Rourke and Myers shook hands with Sanders. "Chief," O'Rourke said, "I'd like to talk to Coombs as soon as possible if that's OK with you."

"I got no problem with that." He motioned to the two burly plainclothes cops. "Fitch and Harding can drive you over to Coombs' place."

O'Rourke didn't feel the need for two more cops but didn't want to cause any problems that would limit access to Coombs. "All right. But we'll do the questioning."

"Fine with me. These two ain't much on questioning anyway. But, if you want somebody to knock some heads together, they're your men."

O'Rourke didn't think that was really needed in this case, but he almost changed his mind as they rode in the back seat of Fitch's unmarked car through Coombs' neighborhood. Although the faces looked different, the area had the same depressing look as the Albany area where Michael Tucker and his friends had hung out the day before. There seemed to be a lot of guys in their twenties or so hanging out on the streets, some just sitting on the front stoop with a beer or cigarette, even though it wasn't yet two in the afternoon on a Monday.

"Amsterdam's mostly a nice city," Harding said, "but there's a lot of unemployment right now. This area's been hit the worst – the factory near here closed up a year ago."

O'Rourke nodded. "A lot of upstate New York is suffering

from businesses closing. Albany's lucky in that respect. Unemployment's not that bad there since we have the government employees, plus a lot of colleges and hospitals."

Fitch pulled the car up in front of a three-story brick building and said Coombs lived on the second floor. Before they got out of the car, a thin fortyish guy with long blond hair and a Yankees cap came over and stuck his head in the rolled down front window. "Hey, Billy, what's happening," Fitch said to him.

The guy named Billy started telling Fitch and Harding about some young guys that moved in down the block and had visitors all day and night long, most staying only 15 minutes to a half hour or so. Billy, who apparently was expecting a few bucks for this information, said he thought they were pimping some women but Fitch and Harding thought it sounded more like they were selling dope. Billy said if it was dope, they wouldn't stay so long. Fitch said sometimes dope deals took longer than the women. While Fitch and Harding continued arguing with Billy about the length of time involved in your average dope deal versus your average quickie, O'Rourke decided he didn't want to wait and got out of the back seat on the driver's side. Myers got out on the passenger side.

"We'll just take care of it ourselves," O'Rourke said to Fitch as he looked into the car over Billy's shoulder.

Fitch just shrugged. "Suit yourself. He lives on the second floor. We'll be here if you need us."

Inside the front door of the building, there were three doorbells, one for each floor. Two of the doorbells had no names written underneath, including the bell for the second floor. Myers tried ringing it and they heard nothing. Assuming it was broken, they both climbed the stairs. O'Rourke knocked on the door; from inside they could hear the voices of some children, and a radio playing.

A female voice responded loudly. "Back already? What did you do, forget your damn key again, stupid?"

"Ma'am, it's the police," O'Rourke answered, in his most official voice.

A second later, a slender blonde woman opened the door, holding a young child around eight months old in her arms. The woman had a large ugly bruise right near one eye that suggested she had been hit hard and recently. She didn't look very surprised to see a couple of cops at her door.

"If this is about all the yelling, it's over now. The lady upstairs, she calls the cops every time we raise our voices a little. Pain in the ass."

O'Rourke could see two kids, a boy and a girl about eight and nine, standing behind the woman, looking curious. They looked like they could be Coombs' kids.

"That's not why we're here. We're just looking for Earl Coombs. We'd like to speak to him."

"He ain't here. He left about an hour ago."

"Do you have any idea where he went?"

The woman hesitated. She looked like she wasn't sure whether to cooperate.

O'Rourke pointed to her eye. "Did he give you that shiner? Just out on parole and hitting you already. You better put some ice on that or it'll look worse tomorrow."

She touched the bruise near her eye and winced. "You don't have to tell me – it's not the first time." She handed the baby off to the young girl and pulled a cigarette out of a pack in her jeans pocket and lit it. "Okay, I'll tell you where that rat bastard went. Where he goes almost every day around this time. Pappy's Grill down the street. Him and Sammy Waters spend the day down there. Once in a while, they make a few bucks shooting pool for money. But usually, they just get hammered."

"Thanks, ma'am. Like I said, we just want to talk to him."

"You can throw him back in jail for all I care. I was better off without him."

Fitch and Harding had finished their debate with Billy by the time O'Rourke and Myers returned to the car, apparently deciding that Billy was right in that it probably was hookers, not dope.

"Coombs is at Pappy's Grill," O'Rourke said. "Let's head over there."

"How are you planning to do this?" asked Harding on the way. "You might want us as back up. But if all four of us go in together, it will be suspicious. He might just take off out the back door. Even if he didn't do this murder, I'll bet he's done something illegal since he's been out of prison."

"Doesn't matter who goes in," Fitch said. "He'll make these two guys as cops right away."

"How would he know we're cops?" Myers asked.

"Because you're both too clean cut and well dressed for that hole in the wall. Especially you."

O'Rourke took off his sport jacket, removed his tie, loosened his collar, and rolled up his sleeves. He took off his gun holster too; he would have to leave that behind. "Myers and I can pass for a couple of office workers out for a beer. We'll go in together; one of you can come in about ten minutes behind us so it won't be so obvious, and the other can stay outside and watch the back door."

Myers took off his tie, jacket and holster too, and then rumpled up his hair. "Can I pass for a civilian now?" he asked Harding.

"Maybe if it's real dark inside."

As it turned out, it was real dark inside. Although only mid-afternoon, there were few windows and fewer lights, giving the impression that it was late at night. About fifteen people were in the small place, which seemed like a large number to O'Rourke for a Monday morning until he factored in the high unemployment rate.

"There are a lot of people in here," Myers said.

The majority of the customers were men, long-haired types in their late twenties or thirties.

"Good, we'll stand out less." O'Rourke, older and with rugged looks, seemed to fit in much better than the younger, fresh-faced Myers.

O'Rourke needed a few minutes to adjust to the dark interior after being out in the sun, so he decided to buy some time before looking around. He went over to the bar with Myers trailing behind and ordered a couple of beers. A Molly Hatchet tune was playing on the jukebox.

"This place reminds me of the bars I used to hang out in when I went to college at Hudson Valley," O'Rourke whispered to Myers as the bartender poured the beers. "Didn't you go to college there too? You must remember those places."

"I did, but I didn't hang out at those kinds of places much." Myers looked at the glasses of beer. "We're on duty, Lieutenant."

O'Rourke took a sip. "I won't tell if you won't."

He looked around. Two men were standing by a pool table in the back of the bar. It looked like they had just finished a game and one of the two men, who had long brown hair and wore a leather vest over an AC/DC T-shirt, was putting quarters in the table for a new game. The other man, a shorter man with blond hair, had on an open flannel shirt with a Guns N' Roses T-shirt on underneath. O'Rourke recognized him from his photo; his hair was longer but it was definitely Earl Coombs.

After about five minutes, O'Rourke and Myers walked over to the pool table, beers in hand. After Coombs' buddy completed a shot, O'Rourke stacked five quarters up on the side of the table. "Do you guys mind playing partners after your game is done?"

Coombs sized them up. "We'll play you ten bucks a man each."

O'Rourke pretended to discuss the matter with Myers and after a minute told Coombs that was fine. As Coombs' pal took another shot, O'Rourke and Myers put their beers down on a table and grabbed a couple of cue sticks from the rack on the wall. They were the old-fashioned heavy wooden kind, the kind they no longer allowed in Albany bars because too many drunken college kids had used them to hit other drunken college kids over the head with.

Coombs took off his flannel shirt and hung it on the back of a chair near the pool table. Coombs arms were filled with several tattoos and plenty of muscles.

O'Rourke chalked up his cue stick and then walked over to Coombs. He held out his hand. "My name's Steve."

Coombs looked at him for a second and then shook O'Rourke's hand. Hand shaking probably wasn't a common occurrence here.

"I'm Earl. That's Sammy," he said flatly. Coomb's girl had mentioned a Sammy Waters.

"This is my friend Brad." Myers nodded at them. "We're up from Albany on business today. Figured we'd grab a couple of beers at lunch. You guys live around here?"

The mention of Albany didn't get any reaction from Coombs, as O'Rourke had hoped. Coombs who was just leaning on his cue stick, watching Waters shoot. "Yup," he said. A real talker.

Waters made a nice bank shot and was almost down to the eight ball. O'Rourke took a sip of beer and tried again. "You ever get down to Albany, Earl?"

Still no reaction, unless you count boredom. "Nope. Don't like the big city."

"I know what you mean," O'Rourke said, pretending to agree. "There are too many spooks in Albany."

Coombs looked at O'Rourke, a little more closely this time. "You got that right."

O'Rourke pressed on, playing the bigot role and feeling slimy for doing it. "Don't you sometimes wish we could just get rid of them all?"

Coombs just nodded, back to watching the pool table.

"I took a few of them out in my younger days," said O'Rourke. He didn't go into detail what he meant by that; better to let Coombs draw his own conclusion.

Another nod.

"How about you, Earl? Ever feel like doing that?"

Coombs looked at O'Rourke like he was about to say something, but thought better of it. He reached for his beer which was on the table near where O'Rourke was standing. After he drained about half the bottle, Coombs said: "I'm just a drinker, not a fighter."

"You look like you could take a few of them down if you wanted."

Waters interrupted, having just sunk the eight ball. "You rack," he said to O'Rourke.

O'Rourke plugged the quarters into the slot in the pool table and started racking the balls. Looking over at Coombs, O'Rourke kept at it. "You're right, Earl. They're good for nothing. Did you hear somebody shot one of them over in Albany?"

Before Coombs could respond, Waters stepped in between them. "I think you ask too many questions, mister," he said, glaring at O'Rourke.

O'Rourke finished racking and stood up straight. If it came to a fight, Waters was shorter than O'Rourke, but younger and muscular. "I'm just making conversation," O'Rourke said with a smile.

"Well, talk about something else." Waters' manner wasn't threatening yet, but it could get that way quickly. O'Rourke wanted to keep things calm so he could get more out of Coombs.

"No problem, buddy." He would wait until Waters was out of earshot before questioning Coombs again.

Waters looked like he was satisfied with O'Rourke's answer. O'Rourke walked back to the table where his beer was and took a sip, keeping an eye on Waters. Suddenly, something behind O'Rourke apparently caught Waters' eye and Waters' expression turned angry. O'Rourke turned around and saw Fitch was standing a few feet behind him. He had probably been watching from over at the bar and saw Waters confront O'Rourke, and had come over in case there was a problem.

Waters pointed at Fitch. "I've seen you around. You're a goddamn cop."

Coombs caught on and was furious. "You were trying to play me, man," he said to O'Rourke. Moving quickly, he picked up his cue stick by the thinner front end and swung the heavy end at O'Rourke. O'Rourke quickly grabbed his own cue stick that he had leaned against the table and holding it with one hand on each end, brought it up just in time to block Coombs' stick from cracking O'Rourke's head open.

To O'Rourke's left, Waters charged at Fitch, but Myers tackled Waters to the floor before he could get there. In the meantime, Coombs swung his cue stick at O'Rourke again, this time trying to hit him in his side. O'Rourke managed to grab the heavy end of Coombs' cue stick and pulled it to his right. Coombs went sprawling. He fell to the floor, but got up quickly on one knee. He now had a switchblade in his hand. O'Rourke brought his leg up quickly, kicking Coombs in the wrist. The switchblade went flying. Coombs was about to make another move but Fitch yelled out something and had his gun out and everybody stopped.

A few seconds later, Harding burst in through the back door and pushed aside the crowd of onlookers that had formed. Harding pulled Waters off Myers and handcuffed him, while O'Rourke cuffed Coombs with a set of handcuffs that Fitch gave him. A few minutes later, Fitch had the flannel shirt in his hands that Coombs had earlier draped over a chair. He spotted something in the front pocket of the shirt and pulled out a small vial with powder in it.

"Well look what we've got here," Fitch said. "This appears to be a significant amount of cocaine. I think these boys are in a shitload of trouble."

Twenty minutes later, O'Rourke and Myers were outside, watching a pair of uniformed cops walking Coombs and Waters toward a squad car. As he was being put into the squad car by one of the cops, Coombs turned toward O'Rourke.

"I got it figured out now. You're all trying to pin that murder you got over there in Albany on me."

O'Rourke asked the cop to hold up a minute.

"Do you have anything else to say?" he asked Coombs.

"Yeah. I didn't do it. I took care of that nigger six years ago, I admit that. But I've done my time for that. I'm not stupid enough to go back to prison again for something like that."

"Why should I believe you? You're stupid enough to have a vial full of cocaine in your pocket while you're on parole."

"I know you ain't gonna believe me, but that's not mine. I

smoke some weed once in a while, but I don't do coke."

O'Rourke motioned to the cop that he was done talking, and the cop shoved Coombs into the car.

O'Rourke, Myers, Fitch and Harding followed the squad car back to the station. Most of the talk was about the melee back at the bar. Fitch and Harding were generally impressed with the way two city cops like O'Rourke and Myers held their own.

At the station, Coombs and Waters were put in separate interrogation rooms. O'Rourke and Myers had the chance to interview Coombs and then Waters, with Chief Sanders outside watching through a one-way mirror. Each of the two men had the same stories for where they were on Saturday. They said they did some work fixing a guy's car until about five, and Coombs still had the name and number of the guy on a piece of paper in his pocket. Then they went to Coombs' apartment and drank beer until about nine. Coombs' girlfriend and her kids were there too. Later, they both went to Pappy's to shoot pool and a bar full of people saw them there. Both denied any involvement in the Albany shooting, and in fact, each of them said that they hadn't been to Albany in years. The interview with Waters ended when he asked for a lawyer. After thanking the chief for his help, Myers and O'Rourke headed back to Albany.

As they cruised east on I-90, O'Rourke switched on the local talk radio station. A black community leader named Annie Brown was talking about setting up a protest march tomorrow in Albany because the Albany police weren't doing enough to find Randall Tucker's killer.

"Well," Myers said, "maybe they'll cancel the march if they find out there are two suspects in custody."

"I don't think those two had anything to do with the murder."

"Do you mean because of their alibis? They could have easily cooked up that story about drinking in Coombs' apartment. Coombs' girlfriend is their only real witness, and she would probably cover for them, and have her kids cover for them too. The two of them could have killed Tucker after they worked on the car, and easily got back to the bar in Amsterdam by nine."

"Maybe. But I can't picture either one or both of these idiots driving down to Albany, shooting a man with a silencer, carefully cutting out his tongue with a surgical tool, leaving the money in the cash register behind, driving all the way back to Amsterdam, and then casually going to a bar and shooting pool the rest of the night."

"It makes sense when you put it that way. But stranger things have happened."

"I guess. Maybe we can go back again to question them on their alibis, see if we can poke a hole in them."

O'Rourke took the Albany exit and headed toward the Exit 24 tollbooths. "Another thing is both of those guys were wearing boots, like just about everyone else in the bar. Forensics found a partial athletic shoe or sneaker print at Tucker's back door that we figure belongs to at least one of the assailants, if there were more than one. I doubt either one of these rednecks even owns a pair of sneakers. The bottom line is they may have had nothing to do with the murder, and all we did was get them arrested by goading them into attacking us. With that cocaine in his possession, Coombs will probably end up going back to prison for quite a while. I'm not saying he doesn't deserve to go back to prison, mind you."

Myers said nothing for a few moments. O'Rourke glanced over at him and noticed a strange expression on his face.

"What is it?" O'Rourke asked.

"About that...I wasn't sure exactly what I was seeing Fitch doing back at Pappy's Grill, but now I know. While you were talking to Waters, I'm pretty sure that Fitch slipped that vial of cocaine into Coomb's shirt while it was hanging on the chair."

EIGHT

IIIIIIIIIIIIIIIIIIIIIIIIIIIIIIIIIIIIII

O'Rourke called Chief Sanders after he got back to his office and explained what Myers saw. Sanders took it in stride.

"Look," Sanders said, "maybe my guys do get a little too carried away sometimes. But look at it this way – we can use the cocaine to put some heat on these two guys. Both of them are on parole, as it turns out. Waters cut his wife with a broken bottle a few years ago; carved her face up bad. Neither one can afford a conviction on assaulting an officer and cocaine possession. One of them's bound to implicate the other in the murder."

"You're assuming they did it. I have serious doubts about that."

"I'm not necessarily sayin' that they're guilty of the murder. I'm just sayin' that you've got a lot of pressure on you over there to come up with the killers. Your minorities over in Albany are raising a big fuss. And it looks like except for Coombs and his friend, you don't have any other suspects yet. Now we've got two bad seeds over here that rightly belong in prison. If we can put enough pressure on these boys, I'll bet one of them will say that the other was the killer just to save his own skin. We end up with at least one of these guys off the streets of Amsterdam for a long time. And you end up being able to say that the killer's been caught; no more fuss from the minorities." He said "minorities" as if it pained him to use such a politically correct term. He was probably making quote marks with his fingers.

"I see. It would work out for everyone then. Except that the real killer's still out there and one of these yokels goes to prison for a murder he didn't commit."

O'Rourke spent several more minutes on the phone with Sanders and convinced him to hold off on the cocaine charges. They left it that Sanders would book the guys only on the assault charges and Albany would send over some detectives to do some more questioning about the alibis.

O'Rourke filled Captain Graney in on the whole Amsterdam story. Not surprisingly, Grainey didn't think Sanders' idea about trying to get one of the men to implicate the other on something he didn't do was all that bad. After that, O'Rourke called his team together in his office to discuss other progress on the investigation. There wasn't much.

Booker had spent much of the day talking to Randall Tucker's friends and relatives. "I spoke to Mrs. Tucker and her daughter some more," he said. "Later, I stopped over at Tucker's house again and spoke to Joyce, Regina and Michael. I was happy to see that Michael was home and not out with his deadbeat friends. I also contacted a few of Randall Tucker's friends. The bottom line is no one knows of any relationship that Mr. Tucker may have had with the mob or anything like that. From all indications we have so far, Randall Tucker was a good family man, spent most of his time either with his family or working in his store, and wasn't involved with anything shady."

Valente had been coordinating with the Arbor Hill unit. "I spoke with Lieutenant Morgan this morning. He said that with all the gang problems over in Arbor Hill lately, they did have squad cars as well as undercover cars going up and down Clinton Avenue at least every half hour on the day of the murder. They confirmed that Michael and his three friends were on that corner almost the whole day. And when they weren't at the corner, they were at the McDonalds like Michael said; there were plenty of witnesses that confirm that. The bottom line is their whereabouts are mostly accounted for at the time of the murder."

"OK," said O'Rourke. "We're probably barking up the wrong tree there. Ask Arbor Hill if they can keep an eye on Jukey and the other two though, just in case. Also, have your team continue to interview people that lived around the studio that might have seen something. Brad and Derek, work some more on checking with Tucker's friends and neighbors. Somebody has to know something."

"I made some calls to other units regarding silencers," said Myers. "No one in Albany PD, not even the old timers, recall ever hearing about a silencer used in a crime in Albany. I called the Arbor Hill and South End units. They say you can buy a lot of items on the streets in Albany, but a silencer's not one of them. I heard that you may be able to get one on the streets in New York City though. I called NYPD and they'll ask around, but it's a big city. Also, I'll bet you can probably get a silencer illegally off the Internet if you can figure out where to look."

"Good work," said O'Rourke. He turned to Oquendo. "Anything on your end?"

"We've checked out almost all of the names of business associates in Tucker's computer, and called many of them. We looked over a list of his customers too, to see if any of them had a major criminal history. We haven't found anything so far. My team is currently calling customers to see if anyone had a problem with him or heard or saw anything unusual. But so far, Mr. Tucker seems to be pretty straight. He paid his bills on time, didn't owe any major debts to anyone, nothing like that. Seems like an upstanding businessman."

"That matches what his family said," Booker added. "I doubt he had any connection with street gangs or the mob in New York City. His daughter said you might describe him as an average, down to earth guy, maybe a little bit of a neat freak and somewhat on the boring side."

"And yet," O'Rourke said, "his death was anything but boring."

As he drove home, O'Rourke remembered that he had made a date to jog with Ginny, and was running a little late. He quickly threw on a pair of running shorts and a T-shirt after he got home and then went outside. Even though Ginny lived just down the street, she had parked her car in front of his house and was just coming to his door.

"Ready, neighbor?" she asked.

"Whenever you are."

Ginny took off running. "Try to keep up," she yelled back at him.

Keeping up wasn't easy. Ginny was a few years younger than him and many pounds lighter. O'Rourke considered himself to be in good shape, but knew he could stand to lose around five pounds around the waist. He found himself out of breath trying to keep up with her and was exhausted by the time they finished their run.

O'Rourke invited her inside. He turned on the air conditioner and grabbed a couple of cold bottles of water from the fridge. They each sat on the couch, cooling down.

"So, Steven, how was your day?" Ginny asked.

"Busy," he said. "Still working on the Randall Tucker case."

"That sounds more interesting than dealing with my lawyer about my ex-husband." She sat a little closer to him. "Tell me about it."

"I doubt you want to hear the mundane details. A lot of boring procedural stuff."

"I'm sure it's not all boring." She seemed genuinely interested.

"Well," O'Rourke said, "there was a little excitement over in Amsterdam..."

He described the incident at the bar in Amsterdam, leaving the names out, but going into detail about the fight. Ginny got a kick out of him blocking Coombs' pool cue swing with his own cue.

"Where did you learn how to handle a pool cue like that? It reminds me of a sword fight. You guys were like King Arthur and his knights."

O'Rourke laughed. "I never thought of it that way."

Ginny leaned closer to him and put her hand on his shoulder. "What is it they say about men and swords? I believe I heard the sword is symbolic of something..."

O'Rourke put his arms around her and they kissed. He could feel the perspiration still glistening on her back as he held her closely. She moaned as he kissed her neck and there was a light taste of salt...

Hours later, he woke up in his bed. Ginny was naked, sleeping beside him. He couldn't recall exactly when they moved from the couch to the bedroom. He fell back asleep and when he woke again, Ginny had her jogging outfit back on and was quietly coming back into the bedroom with an overnight bag. That's why she parked her car close to the house, he thought; to keep the clothes in it without being too obvious.

"Aren't you a wily woman," he said, as she climbed back into the bed.

"Shhh," she said, as she leaned over him, and they kissed once more…

He woke up early in the morning and made breakfast in his bathrobe. He decided on bacon and eggs. Normally, he would have gone with French toast. But that was Megan Ross' favorite; he felt that would have been a bad omen.

"Here you go, my lady," he said, as he put the plate down on the kitchen table.

Ginny smiled and sat down at the table. "Ooh, my lady, you say. I guess you really are a knight," she teased.

"What?"

"Don't you remember? Last night, I mentioned King Arthur and his knights. I have this mental picture of you and the other detective – Myers – battling these two large, menacing evildoers with your cue sticks."

O'Rourke laughed. "Oh, yeah. That's us. The Albany Knights of the Round Table."

Ginny was giggling now too.

"I may have exaggerated a bit," O'Rourke said. "That menacing evildoer that I was fighting wasn't all that large. He looked pretty strong but wasn't very tall. In fact, he was wearing boots and he was still only…"

O'Rourke stopped in mid-sentence.

"Are you OK?" Ginny asked.

O'Rourke got up from the table and walked over to the far wall. He reached out to the wall with one arm as if he had something in his hand.

Ginny stood up. "Steven, are you alright?"

He looked at her. "Yeah, I'm fine… It's just… I just remembered this dream I had about the killer. There was something about him that I knew but I couldn't pin it down, if that makes sense. But I get it now. Those words painted on the wall inside Randall Tucker's store – they were about six feet high up on the wall. There's no way that Coombs could have sprayed those letters on the wall unless he reached high over his head with the spray can. And why would somebody do that? His buddy in the bar was a bit taller than him, but it would have been quite a reach for him too."

O'Rourke again reached out to the wall with one arm as if he had a can of spray paint in his hand. "I would imagine that someone spraying graffiti on a wall is usually going to hold the can at eye level or lower. You would have to if you wanted to do it neatly. And those letters on the wall in the store were done perfectly. That's what I couldn't pin down about the killer – whoever sprayed those letters on the wall must be tall. At least my height or taller."

O'Rourke dressed quickly, anxious to investigate his theory. Ginny could see he was onto something, so she got her things together. "Call me," she said, and they kissed goodbye.

Before O'Rourke left, he stopped in his garage and grabbed a can of spray paint and a measuring tape. He drove the Jaguar to Tucker's studio before going to the station. A lone officer in a squad car was parked in front of the studio to keep onlookers away. The officer had a key to the back door in case forensics wanted to return for anything and he let O'Rourke in. O'Rourke measured the height of the letters on the wall and then headed back down to the station. On the way, he caught the morning news on the car radio; the top story was the march planned for the afternoon in downtown Albany to demand that the Albany police do something about Randall Tucker's murder.

In his office, O'Rourke checked the file on Coombs again. The graffiti in an old photo from the file appeared no more than four and a half feet from the floor. Out of curiosity, he went on the Internet and looked up graffiti to see how the graffiti artists usually held out their arms while spraying paint.

O'Rourke shut off his computer and walked down the hall to Captain Grainey's office to fill him in on his theory.

"I don't know," Grainey said indecisively. "We've got two suspects over there in Amsterdam that aren't tall; this theory shoots that to shit."

"I don't buy that those two idiots in Amsterdam murdered Tucker. That doesn't fit at all."

Grainey sat back in his chair. "I hate when these things drag on. And there's that damn march downtown later." He let out a sigh. "OK, O'Rourke, it's in your hands. Pursue that theory of yours."

O'Rourke found a tablet of large paper used for brainstorming sessions and taped several sheets on a wall in a small conference room near his office. He then brought his team in.

"What's up? Are we drawing pictures?" Valente asked.

"Sort of. Rosie, I want you to take this spray can and spray your name on one of these big sheets of paper."

Rose Oquendo shrugged, then took the spray paint can and wrote her name on a sheet of paper. Since Oquendo was short, the letters were about four feet from the floor. O'Rourke had Valente, who was about five ten, repeat the process; then Booker, who was six one or so. Myers, who stood a couple of inches taller than O'Rourke at about six five, followed and sprayed his name, and O'Rourke himself did it last.

O'Rourke pointed at the names on the sheets of paper. "Notice that all five of us held the spray can at or lower than eye level. I think most people use spray cans like that; at least those that do a good job. I measured the letters at Randall Tucker's studio and those letters are exactly six foot, two inches off the floor."

"So, you think whoever painted the letters was a tall person," Myers said.

Oquendo played devil's advocate. "But what if he reached up and did the letters? Maybe to throw us off?"

O'Rourke went to a sheet of paper that he had taped high on the wall, took the spray can, reached above his head with it, and sprayed his name on the paper.

"The lettering doesn't look as neat as when you held it lower," Booker said.

"Right. The lettering on Tucker's wall was very neat, if you recall," O'Rourke said.

Valente looked at the writing. "He could have stood on a chair, and then put the chair back. Or maybe, with practice, he could learn to reach up and spray the lettering and still make it look neat."

"Anything's possible. But usually the simplest answer is most likely. The most likely assumption is that the person who painted the letters on the wall was tall, over six feet."

"Jukey Jones fits that description," said Booker. "But Michael Tucker doesn't and neither do his other friends. And neither Coombs nor Waters are very tall either from what you said."

"Let's not eliminate anyone as a suspect just yet," said O'Rourke, "but for now, let's assume that our killer is a fairly tall person. Or if there was more than one person involved, at least one of them is tall. At least this will at least give us something to consider while we look at possible suspects."

O'Rourke called Sandy Bernstein and asked him to add a height match to his search for past hate crimes throughout the state, concentrating on suspects that were over six feet tall and currently out of prison. In the meantime, Myers had compiled a stack of records from local counties of arrests that pre-dated the New York State Hate Crime Database and had racial overtones. O'Rourke had some time on his hands, so he looked through some of the records himself. Heights and weights were listed on some of them; he put records of the criminals that were tall in a separate pile. He was halfway through when Valente poked his head in O'Rourke's office.

"Boss," Valente said, "My wife just called me from home. There's something on the news about cancelling the march. She said we should check it out."

He and Valente headed to the break room, and O'Rourke waved the rest of the team in as well. There was a small TV there. Valente switched it on. Trish Perkins from Channel Seven was reporting live from downtown, only about two miles from Division One.

"As we reported," she was saying, "the march to protest the Albany Police Department's inaction on the Randall Tucker case has been cancelled based on the surprise announcement by the Albany Police Department that prime suspects have been arrested."

"What the..." O'Rourke said, and then stopped when he saw Captain Grainey on television, standing next to Perkins. He had a bad feeling about this.

Perkins turned to Grainey. "Captain Grainey, what can you tell us about the suspects."

"Well, Trish," Grainey said to the camera in his deepest voice, "we have detained two suspects in Amsterdam. As I said, we can't give out their names but I can tell you they are both Caucasian, paroled convicts, and one has a history of racial violence. Their whereabouts at the time of the murder are very much in question and they fit the profile that our department has done up."

"What profile is that?" Myers asked O'Rourke. "The only profile we have so far is that it's a tall man that used a silencer and maybe wore sneakers. Coombs doesn't fit any of that at all. "

"It's a profile that Grainey made up to fit Coombs after he was arrested," O'Rourke said with disdain.

Grainey, who looked even pastier on TV, went on. "Trish, we're confident that we're on the right track on this case. Of course, we'll keep the local media posted so that the community at large will be ensured that our department is doing everything possible to solve this heinous crime."

"Thank you, Captain," Trish replied. She turned to the camera. "We'll keep you informed as the story develops. Now, we'll return to The Price is Right, already in progress..."

O'Rourke switched off the television.

"Why would Captain Grainey indicate that Coombs is a prime suspect?" Oquendo asked.

"Grainey knows Coombs isn't the killer. He's trying to use Coombs' arrest to stop the march; he thinks the march makes the Department look bad," O'Rourke replied. "But it's going to make us look worse once everyone realizes that Coombs isn't our man."

O'Rourke spent the rest of the day looking over arrest records and any other files he could find about hate crimes. The unit as a whole went back and double checked with a lot of the people they had already interviewed and especially concentrated on those that were tall, but no one came up with any new leads. With nothing new to go on, O'Rourke left the office a little after

5 PM. As he drove home, he started wondering if the tall man theory that he was so excited about in the morning was correct. Who knows, he thought? Maybe it was possible that those two rednecks in jail in Amsterdam did kill Tucker. Then again, maybe the murder was just some single random act of violence from some lunatic, tall or otherwise, who had no criminal record at all. If that was the case and the guy never commits another crime, they might never find the killer.

Less than two miles east of Division One, the tall man was walking down State Street. He was wearing a floppy hat to conceal his hair and wore sunglasses, the same pair he had worn on the night he killed Randall Tucker. State Street ran along the northern end of Albany's Washington Park which was on the man's right; there were a few people in the park walking dogs or playing with children, but no one would be likely to pay much attention to him. He was just a guy wearing a backpack, taking an afternoon stroll.

The buildings on his left were mostly large old brownstones built a hundred years ago, made for the large families that people tended to have back then. Most of them were two or three stories high and had long ago been divided into several small expensive apartments.

There was one building in particular the tall man was interested in, one of the larger buildings. He had gone past it several times around this time of day in the last two weeks, and at this time of day, there had never been anyone around. When he got to the building, he quickly climbed the five front steps. Having checked out the building before, he was aware that the front door of the building was kept unlocked during the day to make it easier for the residents. He opened the door and walked up the inside stairs to the second floor. At the top of the stairs, he looked around the hallway to make sure no one was around. He then pulled a key out of his pocket, unlocked the door to the first apartment on the left, and let himself in. Inside, he waited for his next victim to arrive. *He has to pay,* thought the tall man. *Pay for what he did.*

NINE

||||||||||||||||||||||||||||||||||||||||

Bernard Fleming enjoyed his daily walk from the Legislative Office Building to his Albany apartment. Although he owned a car, he didn't use it to get back and forth from work since he lived only a mile away from the LOB, and it was hard to find a parking spot in the crowded neighborhood where his apartment was located. It was easier to leave his car in the LOB garage where he enjoyed free parking as one of the perks of the job.

Today, like many of his work days, had been a stressful day. In addition to having served as a state assemblyman from a densely populated district in Manhattan for the last sixteen years and being on two state legislative committees, he had the lead role in the Assembly in the push for gay rights. He had spent most of his day in meetings, conferences, or on the phone with politicians or constituents. So even on a warm day like today, he was glad for the chance to take his fifteen minute walk and unwind.

Usually, Fleming would be back in Manhattan by this time of year. But the state budget situation was still in a three-way stalemate between the governor and the Assembly and Senate majority leaders, which meant that state assemblymen were still in Albany when they normally would be off for the summer. But at least today he was able to leave his office by five. He still had several papers in his briefcase that he wanted to look over after he got to his apartment, but he would be able to relax a bit and give Jonathan a call before getting to that. Jonathan Grace was a highly paid Manhattan defense attorney and an accomplished classical pianist as well. He also had been Bernard's domestic partner for the last eight years.

As he walked across Lark Street, Fleming waved to a few passersby that he recognized from the old days. Before he settled down with Jonathan, he had frequented all of Albany's local gay nightspots in his sixteen years in Albany. Bernard Fleming had never hidden the fact that he was gay, at least not since he was an adolescent. The fact that he lived in a very liberal district in Manhattan had allowed him to be elected as one of New York State's first openly gay legislators. So naturally, after he took office, he found an apartment in a neighborhood in Albany where there was a significant gay population. Between being on television whenever there was a gay rights issue in the news and his past exploits at the local clubs, Bernie had become fairly well known in the neighborhood.

Even though he was just a few blocks from his apartment, Fleming stopped for a moment and removed his suit jacket. The afternoon heat was getting to him; at fifty-five, he wasn't as young as he used to be. He felt he could easily pass for forty-five; he had youthful features, with only a hint of grey in his hair, although he could afford to lose a few pounds. But on humid days like this, he felt his age. And his health issues didn't help.

Five minutes later, he walked up the steps to the apartment building where he resided, an old brownstone across from Washington Park. Inside the front door, Fleming retrieved his mail and then headed upstairs. Although the stairway was well lit, he had a strange feeling for a moment as he got to the top of the second floor. Was there someone else there? He looked up and down the stairs and then down the hallway, but there was no one around. It was probably just the stress of the day getting to him. Too much coffee, he thought. Feeling silly, he shrugged and unlocked his apartment door.

Inside, Fleming hung his suit jacket up in the front closet and walked through the living room into the kitchen. After his busy day, he needed a nice glass of wine. He opened the large cupboard door above the sink and chose one of the larger wine glasses. As he closed the cupboard door, something caught his eye. He turned to his right and promptly dropped the glass, which shattered on the floor. Standing there silently about ten feet away was a man pointing a pistol at him.

The man was tall, wearing a hat and a small pack on his back. Fleming had met many men in his life and had a good memory, but he did not recognize this man at all. The man's face was expressionless, yet Fleming saw something in the man's eyes. They were cold and angry.

Fleming was more outraged at the intrusion than scared. "Who are you," he said loudly. "What do you think you're doing in my apartment?"

The man took two steps toward him but said nothing.

"Listen to me carefully," Fleming said in an officious voice, as if he were addressing the assembly inside the Capitol. "I don't know what the hell you think you're doing but I have several friends arriving for a visit in just a couple of minutes. One is a police officer. I would suggest you leave right now."

The tall man spoke. "I don't believe you," he said without inflection.

Fleming was getting nervous now. He tried another tactic. "If you want money, I have some in my wallet. Take it and leave. You do not want to shoot me, son. I'm a New York State assemblyman. If anything happens to me, they'll find you. Your life will be ruined. Take my word on that."

"My life is already ruined," the man said, his voice filled with venom. "Because of what you did. You and the others."

"I don't know what you're talking about." Fleming took a deep breath to calm down. He knew how to deal with people that were upset. He lowered his voice, almost to a whisper, hoping to de-escalate the situation.

"Look," he said, "let's discuss this rationally. You look like an intelligent man. Whatever your situation is, we can sit down and talk it over."

The tall man said nothing for several seconds. Fleming desperately hoped the man was considering his offer. Finally the man answered.

"No. It's too late."

The tall man fired the gun twice. As the bullets hit Fleming in the chest, his last thought was that the sound wasn't right, that the gunshots should be louder.

The tall man put down his backpack and pulled out his scalpel. After getting a souvenir from Fleming, he took out the spray paint can and used it on the kitchen wall, just as he did in Tucker's studio. When he was done, he rinsed the blood off of the scalpel in the kitchen sink and put everything back in his pack.

He briefly thought of rifling through Fleming's desk and dressers, to make it look like a robbery, as he did with Tucker. Then he thought better of that idea. *The police aren't stupid. They've already figured out that the Tucker mission wasn't a robbery gone bad.*

After making sure he left nothing behind, he left the apartment, closing the door gently behind him. No one was in the building as he quietly walked down the inside steps. He opened the front door an inch and looked out. A few people were in the park across the street but no one was on this side of the street. He went out the door, quickly took off the leather gloves he was wearing and put them in his pocket, and put his sunglasses back on. Then he calmly walked down the five steps and walked up the street. He felt satisfied, like he did after taking care of Tucker. Not happy, but satisfied. His life might be ruined, but he still had missions to carry out, and now one more had been accomplished.

The next morning was a quiet one for O'Rourke. That wasn't good because it meant the Tucker case was getting cold. Although most of the detectives were still on the streets or on the phones checking leads, nothing was panning out so far. Coombs and Waters were still in custody and hadn't told the police anything of interest; O'Rourke was now almost certain that they didn't have anything to tell. The Arbor Hill unit was still keeping an eye on Jukey and his friends who were still hanging out on the corner; Michael was no longer hanging with them and appeared to be staying inside his house.

O'Rourke caught Captain Grainey coming out of the men's room about a half hour after he arrived. Grainey looked back as though he wanted to retreat to get away from O'Rourke, but going back in the bathroom didn't make any sense, so he stood his ground.

"I've got a major bone to pick with you," said O'Rourke. "What the hell was that 'prime suspect' stuff? You know those idiots in Amsterdam probably had nothing to do with Tucker's murder."

Captain Grainey pointed a bony finger at O'Rourke.

"I don't know anything of the kind, O'Rourke. And you haven't given me anything else to go on. I needed to give the press something. I stopped that damn march, didn't it?"

"Well, the investigation on this case is still open. The Department's going to look stupid when we come up with the real killers. And I don't want our resources cut on this case just because you think we've solved the case."

Grainey was getting red in the face. "I'm still your boss. Don't tell me what I can or can't do!"

O'Rourke glared at him but said nothing. Realizing that O'Rourke wasn't backing down, Grainey lowered his voice. "I'm not cutting back on your resources. *Yet.* If you can do your job and come up with some leads soon that will show me that someone else did this, we can tell the media there's been new developments. Then, we can justify to the public our continued use of our resources on this case."

O'Rourke took a deep breath himself. That was probably as good a deal as he was going to get. "Fine," he said. "We can discuss it more later when we both calm down."

O'Rourke needed a breather, so he took a walk over to the Nerd Squad. There was nothing much new there either. Megan was still hot and the nerds were still nerdy. Sandy's group had gotten a second list of perpetrators of hate crimes over the last several years, but most of those lived quite a distance away. He took the names back with him and made a few calls to the state parole department. Some of the perps were back in jail; he would assign the other names to Valente's group to follow up on.

At around 10 AM, Oquendo popped her head in O'Rourke's office. "Hey, boss, we got a call from Division Two." Division Two was the division that handled Albany's South End and adjoining neighborhoods. "They've got a 'questionable'. I know we're supposed to be working full time on the Tucker case, but I can make time for this."

A questionable is what APD called a death that appeared accidental but foul play hadn't yet been ruled out. O'Rourke's unit followed up on those, working with the Medical Examiner's office. The theory was if there was any suspicion at all of foul play, the quicker they started on it, the better.

"What's the story?" O'Rourke asked.

Oquendo looked at her notes. "Elderly Caucasian woman found at the bottom of the stairs inside her apartment on 690 Second Avenue. Appears to be a fall; the mailman found her. It appears she's been deceased for a few days."

O'Rourke put down the file he had been reviewing. "Did you say 690 Second Ave?"

"Yes. Why?"

"I grew up in that neighborhood, right down the street from that house. I might have even been in that house; back then, most of the families on the block had kids that we would hang with."

"I need someone to go with me anyway, Lieutenant. Interested?"

O'Rourke stood up and grabbed his jacket. "Why not?"

690 Second Avenue was the tallest house on the block, located two blocks from the top of the steep Second Avenue hill. The bottom of the hill, a few miles east, ended a few hundred yards from the Port of Albany on the Hudson River.

They took the Jaguar to the house. "This was a nice area to grow up in when I was a kid," O'Rourke said as he and Rose Oquendo got out of the car.

"Aww, cute little Stevie running around the neighborhood, playing with his little friends," Oquendo said.

"Oh, shut up," O'Rourke responded, suppressing a smile.

A single police car was parked in front of the house, which appeared to be well kept up in contrast to many of the other houses on the block. A few neighbors were gathered around. O'Rourke and Oquendo climbed the three steps to the front porch, where two patrolmen and the mailman were standing. The mailman, a short chubby man with a red beard, looked a little green, like a sick leprechaun.

One patrolman spoke up. "I'm Officer Springer," he said. "This is Officer Bremm."

O'Rourke looked at the mailman. "Are you all right?"

"I'm OK, I guess. I knew Mrs. Johnson pretty well. Nice old lady; very frail. She often came down the stairs to say hello when I delivered the mail. But I hadn't seen her for a few days. And her mail hasn't been picked up."

O'Rourke entered the front door, which opened into a small alcove. There was one door directly ahead and another on the right. A few store ads were sticking out of the top of a small black mailbox affixed to the wall on his left. The mailbox was labeled "Johnson" in pretty cursive letters. The door ahead appeared to lead to a darkened downstairs apartment, while the door on the right led to the stairs. He could tell that because the glass in the right hand door had been smashed in by the cops. A shade and a curtain that covered the inside of the door had been pushed back; he could see the steps leading up. He could also see the dead woman lying at the bottom of the stairs.

The mailman looked away from the body. "Since the mail was piling up, I rang the doorbell and knocked a few times. When I didn't get an answer, I tried to look through the door. The shade covered most of the door, but I knelt down and could see a little bit underneath. That's when I saw the body and called the police."

"Gertrude Johnson," Officer Springer said, reading from a notepad. "The neighbors say she's lived here for years, longer than any of them. No one's lived in the downstairs apartment for a long time. Officer Bremm and I broke through the door when we got here, figuring she might still be alive. Not a chance. It looks like she's been dead for a while."

There was an odor coming from the body that led O'Rourke to agree with that.

"We already checked out the house," said Officer Bremm. "No one was inside. The downstairs apartment is definitely vacant, and it looks like she lived alone upstairs."

O'Rourke carefully climbed through the doorway, avoiding the remaining glass around the edges. Seeing no sense in continuing to have everyone climb through the broken door, he took out a tissue and holding the inside doorknob with it, opened the door from the inside. He could only open it about three feet because Mrs. Johnson was sprawled out at the foot of the stairs.

Oquendo was able to easily squeeze through the narrow space, although O'Rourke had to climb up two steps to give her room to stand.

They looked down at Mrs. Johnson. She was a tiny woman, small and frail. There was a pool of blood next to her head and her face was badly bruised from the fall. One shoe was halfway up the stairs. Oquendo knelt down to take a closer look at the body, while O'Rourke went up the stairs. At the top step, he found what he was looking for. There was a small rip in the carpeting of the step, where it looked like Mrs. Johnson had caught her shoe. Most likely, she had tripped on the carpet and had tumbled all the way down the steep stairway, hitting her head in the process. Hopefully, she had died quickly.

O'Rourke noticed it was cold in the house. He could hear the hum of an air conditioner. Apparently, it had been on when she fell and it had been running ever since. Otherwise, the stench from the dead body would have been overwhelming in the heat of the day and someone would have noticed it sooner.

At the top of the stairs was a trophy case, filled with old high school sports trophies and plaques behind an opaque glass door. Peeking through the darkened glass, he could make out the name Todd Johnson on one plaque and Terry Johnson on the other. Apparently, prizes that her sons had won. Even though O'Rourke had lived nearby as a kid, he didn't recognize the names, but the sons may have been much older than him.

O'Rourke took a look around the house. The house was neat and tidy; Mrs. Johnson appeared to be a good housekeeper. There was an unwashed tea cup and saucer in the kitchen sink that apparently the old woman never had a chance to clean, but otherwise everything was clean. The bathroom and one of the two bedrooms had built-in rails on the walls of the type that O'Rourke had seen before in his grandmother's house years ago. They were to assist frail elderly folks get out of bed or the shower.

O'Rourke took a quick look in the other rooms; nothing was amiss. Experience told him that they would find no foul play in this case; just a sad but routine accidental death.

Out of personal curiosity, O'Rourke walked through the kitchen and out the back door past a set of stairs to a back porch that overlooked a sizeable back yard. The second floor porch was actually about thirty feet off the ground since the back of the house overlooked a hill. He looked off the back porch; the grass was neatly mowed and there were two patio chairs near the house. A long old-fashioned clothesline led off the porch to a metal pole that was located at the far end of the back yard.

From where he stood, you could see the tops of the higher buildings in downtown Albany. There was a tremendous view of the Empire State Plaza from here; the windows on the Corning Tower sparkled in the sunlight. This is a nice city, he thought. It made him want even more to catch the killer that was causing such fear and anger here.

Leaning over the porch, O'Rourke looked to his right and could see the back of the house he grew up in down the street. There was a swing set in the back yard, but other than that, it didn't really look that different than it had years ago. He had spent some nice times in this neighborhood. Times were simpler then, he thought. Less complicated; less violent…

He snapped out of his reverie when his cell phone rang. The work phone.

"O'Rourke."

"Chief, it's Derek. Valente and I are on State Street. We've got another homicide. You'll probably want to get over here. This looks a lot like the Tucker murder. And you're going to recognize the victim."

TEN

IIIIIIIIIIIIIIIIIIIIIIIIIIIIIIIIIIIIIII

O'Rourke got some quick details and then went downstairs, where Oquendo was talking to the two patrolmen and two guys from the Medical Examiner's Office that had just arrived. "Boss," Oquendo said, "I don't see anything unusual; it looks like she died from head trauma from the fall. We should notify the next of kin."

"Let these two officers handle that. There's been another murder. C'mon, I'll fill you in on the way."

It didn't take long to get to State Street, which wasn't more than two miles away. Parking was horrendous on the narrow one-way street on a workday since state workers routinely parked there and walked to work. Police officers had already closed off the street to traffic because their vehicles prevented cars from getting through. O'Rourke slid the Jag in behind a double parked patrol car, and he and Oquendo got out.

Sergeant Mills saw them pull in and came over as they got out of the car.

"Jeez, Lieutenant. I haven't seen you in weeks and now this is twice in five days," Mills said.

"Yeah, we've got to stop meeting like this." O'Rourke looked around. "No media this time?"

Mills pointed to the far side of Washington Park. "There's Trish Perkins and her van over there. We're not letting her any closer. No one else from the local stations are here yet. I don't know how the hell she found out about this already. We kept it off the police scanners."

O'Rourke thought about Trish interviewing Captain Grainey on the air the day before. It didn't take a genius to figure where the leak was probably coming from.

"It doesn't matter," he told Mills. "The news will be out soon enough."

Booker had told O'Rourke on the phone that the victim was Manhattan assemblyman Bernard Fleming. O'Rourke had actually met Fleming a few years back. Following a well-publicized arrest of a local attorney caught literally with his pants down with a male prostitute in Washington Park, Grainey had initiated some ill-advised raids of Albany gay bars which were intended to put pressure on the establishments. It didn't matter to Grainey that neither participant in the park rendezvous had been in a bar prior to the incident. The raids, which O'Rourke's squad was asked to assist with, caused quite a furor and the Chief of Police arranged a meeting between Fleming and police staff. O'Rourke found Fleming to be very forthright and pleasant to deal with; Fleming had the ability to look at both sides of the story and was not "anti-cop", as he half-expected the liberal politician to be. He was impressed with Fleming, who was able to convince the police to stop the raids. Since then, if O'Rourke saw an article in the paper about Fleming, he would usually read it. Although he didn't always agree with Fleming's positions, he found that the man generally presented reasonable arguments on the issues.

O'Rourke and Oquendo climbed the five front steps of the large brownstone building to the first floor entrance. The outer doors were wide open to allow the police easy access. Inside the doors, a patrolman escorted them up the stairs to the second floor apartment. O'Rourke noticed that there was no sign of damage to the apartment door that would indicate a break-in.

A short bald man wearing an expensive suit was giving a statement to Booker in the living room. O'Rourke assumed the man was the person who found the body. In the kitchen, Bernard Fleming lay face up on the floor, next to a broken wineglass. Two distinct pools of dried blood surrounded his body. The larger pool of blood had come from underneath his upper body. O'Rourke could see two bullet holes in Fleming's white shirt, right in the center of his chest. He also saw the source of the smaller pool of blood, near his outstretched left hand. The blood was coming from where his middle finger had been cut off.

O'Rourke had been so focused on the body that he didn't notice the writing on the kitchen wall immediately. On the far end of the wall was one word, neatly printed in familiar dark blue spray paint. The word was "ASSHOLE".

"We took a look around the apartment and nothing seems out of place," Valente told O'Rourke. He pointed to Fleming's pants. "His wallet's still in his rear pocket, so I'm guessing no money was stolen from it."

"Who's that talking to Booker in the living room?"

"Arnold Polanski, Fleming's chief of staff. He got worried when Fleming didn't arrive at work," Valente told O'Rourke.

O'Rourke went into the living room and introduced Oquendo and himself to Polanski.

Polanski shook hands with Oquendo and O'Rourke. Polanski's hand was trembling slightly. "I remember you, Lieutenant. You and some other policemen met with Assemblyman Fleming and me a few years back. Regarding the raids."

"I'm surprised you remembered me."

"I've got quite a memory for faces, I guess. It serves me well in my position," he said. "*Served* me well," he added, frowning.

"Mr. Polanski, I'm sure you told Detective Booker already, but can you tell me how you came to be here?"

"When Bernie left the office yesterday, around five, he didn't say that he expected to be in late today. After we couldn't reach him by phone by 10:30 this morning, I got worried and drove over here. I had to park almost three blocks away; the parking is terrible around here."

"You've been here often?"

"Dozens of times. I've worked for Bernie for nine years. He would occasionally have late night work meetings here. He also had a few parties here around the holidays. Good times," he said ruefully.

"Did you need a key to get in the front door of the building?"

"No, they keep it unlocked during the day."

"So, you came in and walked up the stairs. Was the apartment door open?"

"No. I knocked on the door a couple of times and then called for Bernie. By then, I was really worried. The door was unlocked. I came in and saw…" Polanski looked toward the kitchen for the first time since O'Rourke had arrived. His face appeared unnaturally pale. "Lieutenant, do you mind if I sit down for a moment?"

"Of course not." O'Rourke asked Oquendo if she could get Polanski a glass of water.

After sitting for a few minutes, Polanski loosened his tie and went on. "When I came in, I saw Bernie on the floor like that.

I'm surprised to say that I didn't panic. I've taken some first aid courses, so I knew to check for a pulse right away. None at all. Not surprising. There's an awful lot of blood on the floor..."

"So I called 911 on my cell," he said to O'Rourke. "Then, I went down the stairs and stood outside. I didn't think the killer was still in the apartment, but I wasn't about to take any chances. A couple of officers showed up a while later. I guess they responded rather quickly, but it seemed like an eternity at the time."

"The officers then called us after they made sure no one was in the apartment," Booker said.

Polanski wiped his brow. The apartment was very warm and the air conditioner in the apartment was off.

O'Rourke looked around at Schade and Wilson checking for fingerprints. "Did you touch or move anything while you were in here," he asked Polanski.

"Other than checking for a pulse," Polanski replied, "I don't believe I touched anything other than the doorknob. I hope I didn't ruin any fingerprints."

"I'm sure the killer wore gloves," O'Rourke said before he could catch himself.

Although upset, Polanski was still sharp as a tack and picked up on the remark. "This is related to that other murder a few days ago, isn't it?"

"We can't be certain yet. If you saw the news though, you can see the similarities. I'm sure I don't have to tell you not to mention anything to the press."

Polanski smiled weakly. "Normally, my job is to make sure the Assemblyman makes the news. But, in this case, I'll refrain from any comments."

"I'll let Detective Booker finish getting the other details. But first, I need to ask you if you would have any idea who would have done this."

Polanski took a drink of water before responding. "Lieutenant, Assemblyman Fleming is a man with strong opinions. He has made a lot of political enemies. But I can't think of anyone I've encountered in any part of the political arena who would do anything like this."

"It appears that Mr. Fleming has been dead for a while, probably since last night. It looks like that whoever did this didn't break into the apartment. I'm assuming for the moment that the killer either had a key or was let in by the assemblyman. Do you know if he had a regular…companion," O'Rourke asked, hoping that was an appropriate term.

"He's been living with the same man in Manhattan for several years. His name is Jonathan Grace. But Jon rarely comes up to Albany. In fact, he's been involved in a court case in New York City all week. Bernie spoke to him on the phone just before he left work yesterday."

"Mr. Polanski, you know the victim very well. I'm going to be blunt so I hope you're not offended. Was he the type who might have been having a sexual relationship with someone other than Mr. Grace and brought him back to his apartment? Maybe someone he picked up last night?"

Polanski paused for a long while, considering whether to answer.

"This is off the record," he finally said. "Years ago, I would have said yes. Bernie used to be quite the partier. But, not now. Bernie does go out to dinner once a week or so at a classy restaurant that caters to gay clientele, but as far as the pick-up places, he hasn't frequented those bars in many years, well before he settled down with Jon. I don't know why; maybe he just got tired of the scene, or maybe he was afraid that as he became more powerful and well-known in state politics, that it could be used against him. He hasn't frequented those places for years."

"You sound pretty sure of that."

"I'm gay myself, Lieutenant. And I haven't given up going out to the local clubs. Word gets around. If he had been frequenting the clubs again in Albany, I would have heard."

"Maybe he goes somewhere outside Albany. Does he keep a car up here?"

"Yes. But, he doesn't drive at night. He just uses it to get to meetings within Albany during the day. At night, he always leaves the car in the lot of the Legislative Building and walks home."

"So, you don't think it's likely the killer was someone he was intimate with?"

"I would very much doubt it. If you ask me, I think the killer is probably some gay-hating extremist." He pointed to the kitchen wall. "I think that writing definitely carries that message."

O'Rourke let Polanski leave and assembled his team in the living room, as Forensics continued their work in the kitchen. Brad Myers, who had been in the field on the Tucker case, had arrived while O'Rourke was questioning Polanski, so O'Rourke now had the full team together.

"Rose, why don't you see if there's anyone in any of the other apartments that saw or heard anything last night or this morning? Brad, ask Mills to give you a few officers to check out the nearby buildings as well."

That left Booker, Valente and O'Rourke in the room. O'Rourke had a pensive look on his face. "What are you thinking," Booker asked him.

"It must be the same killer, of course. The letters on the

wall look like they're the same size as the letters on the wall in Tucker's studio, and just as neatly written. And they're high up on the wall, just like they were there."

"I'll play devil's advocate for a moment," Booker replied. Booker liked doing that; O'Rourke felt that was one of his most valuable traits. "The local media has printed a lot of details regarding the writing on the wall. Although there's been no photos released, Robert Smith gave Trish Perkins a pretty good description of the first murder site. It's possible a copycat could have done this."

"Not likely," O'Rourke said. "The press has been reporting all along that the letters were written in black spray paint, because that's what Robert told Trish Perkins. When Robert arrived at the studio, it was late in the day. The letters on the wall probably appeared to be black to him without the lights on in the studio. *We* know the letters were actually dark blue, of course; but no one else except the killer would know that."

"Good point. I'm curious about the message though," Booker said. "The message on the wall is hateful like the other one. The first message references that the victim is black. This one says "Asshole". Is the killer making a point this time regarding the victims' sexuality?"

"But if he hates gays, you would expect him to write the word "fag" or something like that instead," Valente said with his usual bluntness. "And what's the deal with the killer cutting Fleming's finger off?"

"I don't know," said O'Rourke. "But it must have some significance to the killer. And since it hasn't been found, he apparently took the finger with him, like he did with Tucker's tongue."

Valente shrugged. "Maybe he's building himself a person..."

When Rose Oquendo returned, she said there was only one other resident currently in the building. "I spoke to a young woman who lives in the rear apartment upstairs, Francine Dumont. She's an artist, paints pictures in her apartment. She said she was home all day yesterday and today, and didn't hear anything unusual until she heard police sirens this morning."

"What about the other apartments? There's another one on this floor. Could anyone else have heard something?"

"Probably not. Ms. Dumont said that although every apartment in the building is rented out, the residents all work during the day. Most of them get home later than Fleming, she said. If we need their names, there is a manager, Mr. Harley, who comes in around nine PM, and is on call during the day for emergencies. She gave me his number. "

"Good. Give him a call. Get him over here now."

The manager was asleep when Oquendo called and was shocked at the news. He lived close by and said he would be over within a half hour.

While they waited, O'Rourke talked with Schade and Wilson from the Forensics team.

"There are two bullets lodged in the wall over there," Schade said, pointing to the kitchen wall, near the entrance to the living room. "So, it appears that the killer was shooting from the right side of the kitchen; the side that leads to the hallway and the bathroom and bedroom."

"What about the glass on the floor?"

"It's a wineglass. There's one glass missing from the set in the cupboard up there," Wilson said, pointing to above the sink.

"Interesting. So he had a wineglass in his hand when he was shot. That sounds pretty casual. If someone in your apartment is angry enough to shoot you, it doesn't seem likely you're going to be getting ready to have a drink."

"Could be the killer was carrying on a casual conversation with him, pretending there was no problem, then pulls out a gun and shoots him."

"Hmmm..." O'Rourke took out a pencil and put it inside of the cupboard door handle. Using the pencil to avoid disturbing any prints, he opened the door all the way. He then looked toward his right. With the cupboard door open, he couldn't see the hallway at all.

He closed the cupboard door. "Or it's possible that the killer wasn't in the kitchen with Fleming when he opened the cupboard. The killer could have been in the bedroom or bathroom. Fleming opens the cupboard door, takes a few seconds to get the wineglass, closes the cupboard door, and when he closes it, he now sees the killer standing there in the kitchen, to his right."

"Hmmm," Wilson said. "I heard you ask Mr. Polanski if Fleming could have picked a guy up last night. That goes along with that theory. Maybe the killer was in the bedroom, sleeping it off all day after an encounter with Fleming the night before."

"Or maybe the person was someone that Fleming didn't know, who could have been hiding in the bedroom or bathroom."

"But how would the killer get in the apartment?" Wilson asked. "There was no sign of a break-in."

"Good question. I see the building manager's arrived. Let's see what he can tell us."

Fred Harley was a short, pot-bellied red-faced man around sixty who smelled of cheap liquor and cigarettes. He appeared distraught as stood in the living room, looking at the dead man lying in the kitchen.

"The owners ain't going to be pleased about this at all," he said. "They always tell me they only need me to do three things: keep all the apartments rented, keep the tenants happy, and make sure there's no trouble."

"I guess this probably messes up all three," O'Rourke replied.

"Why does everything always happen to me?" Harley moaned.

"It could be worse." Valente said, pointed to Fleming. "You could be him."

Harley stopped moaning but kept a sour look on his face.

"So who are these owners?" O'Rourke asked.

"A couple of Jews from New York City. You know, the kind with the beards and the black beanies on their head. Daniel and Mark Greenberg. They own another building up the street, too."

"Do they come up to Albany often?"

"Not unless there's a major problem with the building."

"Who else has a key to this apartment?"

"Nobody. Mr. Fleming's always lived by himself."

"You would have a spare key, though, right?"

"Yup. There's three keys to every apartment. He had one and there's two spare keys in my office downstairs."

"What about the outer door?"

"It's open during the day. I lock that door at night, around nine. There's a different key for that. Every tenant has a key for that door too."

"OK. What can you tell us about Mr. Fleming?"

Harley lowered his voice to a whisper. "I don't like to talk bad about people," he said, "but Mr. Fleming was …you know…a little light in the loafers." Harley, apparently not an avid reader of newspapers, said it as though it was confidential information.

"Actually," O'Rourke said, "we've already learned that he was gay. Did he ever bring other people into his apartment?"

"Well, he used to. I clean up the building after I lock the outer door, and I usually stay here until midnight. Sometimes, Mr. Fleming would come in with someone while I was cleaning up. Not always the same person, but always a guy."

"You said he used to?"

"Yeah. I haven't seen him do that in years. He's usually home in his apartment by the time I get here, and doesn't usually go out. Except on Friday – he told me he goes out to dinner on Fridays to that fancy restaurant over there on Washington Avenue. I think it's called the Electric Company. Caters to his type, I hear. Other than that though, the lights in his room are usually out by eleven."

That was the second time the restaurant had been mentioned. O'Rourke made a note of it and would check it out.

"What about the other tenants? Is there anyone that ever gave you any kind of trouble?"

"No. These apartments are pretty expensive. All college-educated types in here." He said that as if that disgusted him. "The only trouble I ever have is the homeless guys that live in the park. Sometimes they come over this way at night, after it gets dark. They don't come over here in broad daylight though; the cops keep them away from this area."

"What kind of trouble do they cause?"

"Just last week I found some bum passed out on the steps when I left the building at night, with a bottle of cheap booze next to him. And a couple weeks ago, there was a break in."

"Someone broke into the building?"

"Yeah. I called the cops, too. You didn't do anything about it though." Harley looked at O'Rourke, Booker and Valente as if they were personally responsible.

"What apartment did they break into?"

"They didn't break into any apartment. They got in through the back door of the building that leads into the basement. It was during the day, before I got here. They got into my office and stole some rent money. I reported it to the insurance company."

"How much?"

"Um, around four grand or such," he said, looking down at the ground.

"You had four grand in rent money on hand? I would think most tenants would pay by check or credit."

"Well, yeah, you would think so...But, I, uh, had a couple of tenants that happened to have cash on hand. And I, uh, I hadn't had a chance to deposit it yet..."

Harley was obviously being elusive. "I'll have to speak to those tenants to verify that," O'Rourke said, pulling out a note pad. "Can you give me their names?"

Harley was getting agitated now. "Now, wait a minute. You don't have to do that." He mopped his brow, sweating in the hot apartment. He looked at O'Rourke and the others pleadingly.

"Look, fellas, maybe I exaggerated the amount that got stolen a little after the break-in. You know, maybe it wasn't really that much... But, that didn't hurt nobody. Just some insurance company. Those companies have plenty of money."

"Maybe you made up the whole story of the break-in," said Valente sharply. "Maybe you did it yourself."

Harley got indignant at that. "I didn't make up that break-in! Somebody did break into my office. It scared the crap out of me when I saw it! I thought they were still here!"

O'Rourke believed him. He didn't think Fred Harley was smart enough to stage a break in so he could collect on the insurance, although he probably had enough brains to exaggerate the claim.

"Was anything else missing from your office other than money?"

"My desk and cabinets were messed up, but I don't think anything else was missing."

"Why don't we take a look?"

Harley and the three detectives went down to Harley's basement office. The office also smelled of cheap liquor and cigarettes. The room was a mess; O'Rourke couldn't understand how Harley would know there was nothing missing.

"I have a system," Harley said. "I know where everything's supposed to be."

O'Rourke looked out the small rear window of the office. He could see a back yard that led to a locked gate on the street in back of State Street. If someone broke in through the back door, they would only have had to scale a low fence first to get into the yard.

Looking around the office, O'Rourke noticed a wooden rack with keys hanging from it, in back of Harley's desk. "Fleming's apartment number is 2A?"

Harley was eager to please now. "That's right. 2A. First apartment on the second floor."

O'Rourke walked over to the rack. As Harley had said, there were two spare keys for apartment 2A on the hook.

"Told ya," said Harley, smugly. "Two spare keys. I counted all the keys after the robbery to make sure none of them were missing."

O'Rourke took the first gold key off the hook and examined it. The key was gold and had "2A" imprinted on it. Then he took the second key off the hook. The second key looked somewhat similar to the first, but had no number printed on it. Comparing the two keys, O'Rourke noticed the second key wasn't an exact match to the first; it was the same type of key, but the notches and ridges of the key didn't line up. He showed the keys to

Harley, who looked at them for a second before he realized there was no number imprinted on the second key.

"Son of a bitch!" Harley exclaimed. "Where did this come from? This ain't one of our keys!"

Booker looked at the two keys. "Hmm. I'm guessing that whoever broke into the office must have brought several random types of keys with him. After rifling through the drawers to make it look like a robbery..."

"And *maybe* taking some money..." added Valente, looking at Harley.

O'Rourke finished the thought. "The burglar stole one of the spare keys to Fleming's apartment and then replaced it on the hook with a substitute key that he brought with him; one with the same general color, shape and size so no one would easily notice the real key was missing. He then put the other spare key on the hook in front of the substitute key, assuming no one would look closely at every key."

Harley was flustered. "I looked to make sure there was the right amount of keys on each hook. I did! I didn't want somebody to use a stolen key to get into one of the apartments. But I didn't inspect each single key. How was I supposed to know that someone would replace one of the spares? It looks almost like the real one."

Harley's face suddenly lost a little color.

"Oh my god," he said. "I got that poor guy killed!"

ELEVEN

||||||||||||||||||||||||||||||||||||||||

Valente was confused. "If he broke into the building two weeks ago, why didn't the killer just take Fleming's key then, and go up and kill him? He sure went through a lot of trouble coming here twice."

"The killer knew he was taking a big chance by breaking in the building, even if it was through the back door," Booker explained. "Someone could have seen him breaking in and called the police. So he couldn't stay here long. All he needed to do was to take the key and mess the office up a bit to make it look like a burglary. He was probably in and out in a few minutes."

"So he planned this out weeks before the killing," O'Rourke said. "We're talking about someone who is angry enough to mutilate his victims and write obscene messages on the wall, yet has the patience to carefully plan out the murder and then wait a few weeks before carrying it out."

"That also sheds new light on Tucker's murder," Booker replied. "The killer may have planned that out ahead as well. Up until now, we've assumed it was a coincidence that both employees were out the day Mr. Tucker was killed. But maybe this killer had the murder planned well ahead of time and knew both employees would be off that day."

"When we get back, contact Regina Tucker and Bryan Goldstein again to figure out how he might have known that."

Brad Myers returned from outside, where he was helping coordinate with Sergeant Mills. "We have guys knocking on doors in the neighborhood, to see if anyone saw anything last night. Nothing yet."

"We may have better luck tonight when more people are home from work," O'Rourke said.

Before he had a chance to explain, his cellphone rang. It was Grainey.

"What the hell's going on," Grainey asked. "Is this new murder related to Randall Tucker?"

"Yes," O'Rourke answered. He explained the details of the murder and the business about the spare key. "It's got to be the same killer. The same M.O., same paint on the walls, shot twice through the chest. And this time, a finger was cut off."

"Goddamn it." O'Rourke could hear Grainey take a deep breath. "Well, you've got help now. The state police want in on this since Fleming was a state assemblyman. Maybe *they* can solve this thing," Grainey said sharply.

"It can't hurt to have assistance," O'Rourke said, not letting Grainey get a rise out of him. He actually didn't see where the state police could do any more than he and his men had, but there were two men dead now. He wasn't going to feel offended if help was offered. "I guess this eliminates the theory that Coombs and Rivers did it."

"Yeah. I just called Amsterdam and they're still sitting in jail," Grainey said. Embarrassed about his earlier actions, he quickly changed the subject. "I called our Arbor Hill unit too. Tucker's nephew's three friends were on the corner until about eleven last night. And we've had a cop watching Michael Tucker's house. He didn't leave last night."

"Then that also clears them."

"Swell. We've eliminated a total of four suspects in a city of nearly a hundred thousand. Anyway, the meeting with the state police is back here at five thirty. Make sure you're here," Grainey said, before he hung up.

An hour later, O'Rourke, Valente and Myers were still at the apartment. Booker and Oquendo had gone back to the office to start working leads. O'Rourke asked them to get as much information on Fleming as possible. They would coordinate with Sandy Bernstein to have him cross reference people that were associated with Fleming with those associated with Tucker. Maybe there was a connection.

The coroner's office had arrived to remove the body, so O'Rourke and the others decided to head back also. As they almost got to his car, O'Rourke heard Sergeant Mills' calling his name.

Mills was hurrying toward them. A woman of about thirty was with him, carrying a three year old girl in her arms.

"I'm glad I caught you before you left," Mills said, out of breath. "This is Marta Cummings. She lives down the street. She saw a guy come in and out of the building last night. A tall guy."

"We live near the park," Mrs. Cummings explained to O'Rourke as Valente took notes. "I get out of work early and pick my daughter up at day care. Yesterday, it was nice out, so I took Rachel to the playground around 4:30 or so." She pointed to a play area in Washington Park that contained a few swings, a slide, and some seesaws. It was located across the street from the apartment building, although it was more than the length of a football field away.

"There's a bench near the playground. From there, I could keep an eye on Rachel. I could also see across the street from there." O'Rourke could see the bench from where he was standing. From the bench, one would have a clear but distant view of the apartment building.

"I take Rachel to the playground a lot. After a while, just sitting there watching her play gets a little boring for me. So, I like to watch people. People at the playground or walking down State Street. Yesterday, there were a lot of people walking up the street, coming from the state offices to get to their cars."

Rachel was squirming to get down, so Marta Cummings let her down, but held onto her hand.

"A little after five, I saw a man walking from the other direction." She pointed west, away from the state buildings.

"What did he look like?" O'Rourke asked.

"He was tall, at least six feet. He had on glasses. They could have been sunglasses. And he was wearing a hat."

"Did you see him get out of a car?" O'Rourke asked.

"No, sorry. I didn't notice him until he was about a half block up the street from where we're standing now."

"Is there anything else you can describe about him? Old or young? Black or white? Do you remember any facial features or his hair color?"

"From the distance he was from me, I couldn't really tell much. He was walking at a pretty good pace, so he didn't seem old. Like I said, he was wearing a hat. Not a cap, but a big wide hat, so I couldn't see the color of his hair. He was light-skinned; so I'm guessing he was white. I suppose he could have been a lighter skinned African-American though. You know, like Tiger Woods. He had on a dark color backpack, if that helps."

"Do you remember what color and type of clothes he was wearing?"

"I think he had on a short-sleeve shirt and jeans, but I'm not sure. Kind of average type clothes. Not dress clothes. I wish I got a better look at him," she said, apologetically.

"You're doing great. I'm impressed by how well you're able to describe him."

"Well, I mostly remember him because of that big hat. It seemed a little out of place. Maybe he was real allergic to the sun."

"Or maybe he was trying to hide his hair and face as much as possible."

"Then I guess it worked. I couldn't see his face. Plus, the shadows were on that side of the street too."

Rachel was tugging on Mrs. Cummings' arm now, impatient to move on. Myers squatted down next to the three year old and made a face, which got her giggling, and she stopped fussing.

"OK, so you saw the man enter the building…" O'Rourke said to get the woman back on track.

"Yes," said Mrs. Cummings. "He walked up the stairs, opened the door and went in."

"Did he appear hesitant to go in?"

"Oh, no. He went in just like he lived there. Now that you mention it, though, I think he did take a quick look over his shoulder before he went in."

"As if he was seeing if anyone was watching?"

"Well, I didn't think that at the time, but yes. Maybe to see if someone was watching him."

"Actually, *you* were watching him."

"But I was way over there in the playground. Sitting on the bench in the shade. He wouldn't have noticed me."

"OK. What next?"

"Well, I watched several other people go up and down the street. Then, around six o'clock or so, I saw another man go into this building. A distinguished looking man, wearing dress clothes. He had a suit jacket over his arm."

"Assemblyman Fleming."

"Oh, I didn't know who he was. Is that who they just brought out on the stretcher?" Mrs. Cummings probably knew the man was dead, but didn't mention that with her small daughter right there.

"Yes. So you saw him go in?"

"Uh huh. He went right in. He didn't look around like the other man did."

"And did you see or hear anything after that? A loud noise or anything?"

"No. But, I had actually gotten up and pushed Rachel on the swing for a while at that point, so I wasn't paying attention the whole time. But then later, after I had sat down again, I saw the tall man leave the building."

"What time was that?"

"Probably around quarter after six. Less than a half hour after the well-dressed man went in the building."

"Anything unusual as he was leaving? Was he running or in a hurry?"

"He wasn't in any hurry. He did stop at the door before he went down the stairs. I know it sounds weird for the summertime, but it looked like he was putting gloves in his pocket."

"OK. Then where did he go?"

She pointed up the street, to the west. "He walked in that direction, the way he came. I saw him walk to about the end of the block. After that, I didn't see how far up the street he went. Rachel was getting tired, so we headed home."

O'Rourke and Valente asked a few more questions, but there

wasn't much more to learn other than what she had already said. They arranged for her to stop by at the police station after her husband came home so she could give a full statement.

O'Rourke asked Mills to have some cops question people that lived up the street and on the side streets to the right that led away from the park, to see if anyone had seen a tall man walking by. O'Rourke looked at his watch; he figured he, Valente and Myers had time for a quick stop before the meeting with the state police.

The Electric Company was a sizeable nightspot on Washington Avenue in Albany. The exterior windows were tinted so patrons could see out but no one could see in. A small outside sign had a silhouette of two men with drinks in their hand, standing very close and facing one another, and a slogan in cursive lettering that said "Fine Food and Drink for the Alternative Man."

The hours posted on the front door stated the place opened at five. It wasn't quite five yet, but O'Rourke could hear faint music inside so he knocked on the door. A young man with a good deal of mousse in his hair and wearing a name tag that said "Martin" partially opened the door.

"Sorry, gentlemen," he said, "but we're not yet open."

O'Rourke flashed his badge. "We'd like to speak to whoever's in charge."

Martin raised an eyebrow and then opened the door to let them in. "That would be Rolfe. He's the owner," Martin said, pointing to a man in the bar area. The bar was located under a large chandelier at the other end of the restaurant. The bar and restaurant appeared expensively decorated, catering to customers at the high end of the pay scale.

O'Rourke and Valente entered, but Myers hung back. "Why don't I stay outside," Myers said.

O'Rourke could see Myers was uncomfortable with coming inside and saw no reason to force the issue. "OK," he said. "Give Mills a call and see if his men found any more witnesses."

Valente grinned as he and O'Rourke walked toward the bar. "Did you see how red his face got," he snorted.

"Rookies," O'Rourke replied.

The man behind the bar was tall and hefty and wore a ruffled white shirt with a red bow tie. "You must be Rolfe," O'Rourke said as he and Valente showed their badges to him.

"The name's actually Ralph. Ralph Vickers," the man replied. "Only Martin calls me 'Rolfe'. He likes to gay it up around here. What can I do for you?"

"We understand that Bernard Fleming dines here on occasion?"

Ralph looked annoyed. "We try to keep a level of privacy about who comes in here, officers. Our clientele just come in here to dine or have casual conversation at the bar. *Discreet* conversation."

O'Rourke had gotten off on the wrong foot. He recalled that gay establishments in the city had been hounded by the police in the past, and Ralph was understandably touchy about divulging information about his clientele. "Look, I'm sorry. I'm not making myself clear. This is in regard to a homicide investigation. Bernard Fleming is dead." There was no reason to keep it secret. The murder would be on the news very soon anyway, if it wasn't already.

"Holy shit," Ralph said, obviously shocked. "Why didn't you tell me that in the first place? Mr. Fleming stopped by for dinner almost every Friday that the legislature was in session. I kept a table open for him in the back."

"Was he here last night?"

"No, he wasn't."

"Did he usually dine alone or with others?"

"Almost always alone. He usually brought a laptop with him to work on. Some of our regulars would occasionally stop by his table to chat with him, but just for a few minutes. He came in here mostly to have a nice quiet meal and work."

"Did he ever leave with anyone?"

"Not to my knowledge. This isn't some cheap pick up joint, you know. That's not the kind of place I run. I mean, sometimes friendships are made at the bar and men may leave together. But not Mr. Fleming. He would eat his meal and leave by himself."

"Can you give me a list of names of the people who stopped by his table?"

"I'd rather not. As I said, we try to be discreet."

"I understand your position. But you've got to realize that the man's been murdered and it's possible the murderer is someone he knew. It's also likely that the killer has murdered at least one other person and may kill again."

"And," Valente added, "if we aren't able to get some names, we may have to start randomly stopping in here at night, just to get an idea of who hangs out here. We're a little short-handed, so we may have to bring some uniformed policemen with us on occasion."

Ralph pondered that for a moment. He looked toward Martin, who was at the other end of the restaurant, out of earshot. "I'll need a guarantee that you won't leak the names," he said in a low voice. "Some of my customers are out of the closet but a lot of them aren't."

"Unless one of the names you give us results in an arrest for the murder, we'll keep all the names confidential. I have a small team that I can trust working on the case. No one else in the department except them needs to know the names. When we catch the killer, I'll personally make sure the list is thrown out."

Again, he pondered for a minute. "OK. I can live with that." He pulled out a piece of paper from under the bar and wrote down five names. "I don't know the names of everyone that I've seen speaking to Mr. Fleming, but here are the ones I do know. Politicians and local businessmen. I might be able to think of some more later. Just make sure no one knows where you got this."

O'Rourke took the piece of paper and handed Ralph his card. "I know the position you're in. I really appreciate this. Call me if you think of any other names."

Outside the restaurant, they collected Myers who had been standing outside looking at his watch. After they arrived at the station, O'Rourke checked in with the rest of his group, who were already working with their teams, following the same pattern as they did after the first murder. Grainey and the Chief of Police had authorized more overtime - most of the detectives would be working late into the night.

Shortly before the meeting with the State Police, O'Rourke realized he hadn't eaten since breakfast, and headed up to the top floor of the station to the vending machines. He bought a bag of chips, which was probably the most nutritious item in the machine, and headed down the hall toward the stairs.

On the right side of the hallway was a small room with a sign labeled "Prayer Room". Years ago, it was called the chapel, but it had been converted to a prayer room and now contained books of all religious faiths. The last time he had been in there was over a year ago, after his mother had died. He looked at his watch; he had about ten minutes before the meeting.

He entered the room, turned on the lights and sat down in a pew in the back. After a few minutes of silent prayer asking for help catching the person they were looking for, he turned off the lights and left the room. He made a mental note not to wait a year before going back again.

TWELVE

IIIIIIIIIIIIIIIIIIIIIIIIIIIIIIIIIIIIIII

Seven men and one woman were seated around the table in the conference room on the second floor. O'Rourke, Booker, Captain Grainey and Albany Chief of Police Jack Reilly were there from APD. The other three men were with the State Police; Chief Investigator Bill Rusk from the New York office and his assistant Daniel Levitt had caught a plane from LaGuardia immediately after hearing about Fleming's murder and had met up with Dale Mitchell, the head of the State Police office in Albany. O'Rourke didn't know Rusk or Levitt but he had worked with Mitchell on a few occasions; a type A personality, he got a little pushy sometimes, but was pretty sharp. O'Rourke had never seen the woman before. Chief Reilly introduced her as Dr. Elaine Furlani, a psychology professor from the State University at Albany who occasionally assisted the state police.

After all the introductions were completed, Rusk dialed in New York State Police Superintendent Scott Owen in New York City. Until now, O'Rourke had not really considered all the ramifications of the case. The fact that the head of the State Police was on the phone made O'Rourke realize that the murder of a well-known New York State assemblyman was a major deal indeed.

"The reason for this meeting," Superintendent Owen explained, "is to delineate the roles of our departments and use our resources wisely in this case. This will be a very high profile case. Not only was Bernard Fleming a prominent assemblyman in our state, he is nationally known because of his work in the area of gay rights. I don't have to tell you that the media is going to be keeping a close eye on this case and we want to ensure that we are openly cooperating with them. But at the same time, we are not going to give them any information that would compromise our investigation."

O'Rourke shot a brief glance at Grainey, who avoided his gaze.

Rusk, the head of New York City Investigations, spoke up. "I propose that our area take the lead on this investigation. Fleming was a city assemblyman and the most important victim."

"Not to interrupt, but there are two victims here," O'Rourke said. "I wouldn't say one victim is more important than another."

"Well, of course, I was, umm, referring to the one that will get the most media attention," Rusk replied. He gave O'Rourke a glance that implied that he was not happy to have his comments questioned by someone of lesser rank. "I was not saying that was my own opinion of course."

"I'm sure the lieutenant meant no disrespect," Grainey hastily added, glaring at O'Rourke.

"Lieutenant O'Rourke makes a valid point," Owen said. "We have to be careful of our language. We don't want to make comments to the media that can be misconstrued as implying we are placing one victim above the other."

Dale Mitchell spoke up. "Superintendent, I propose that the case be divided geographically. The New York City office can interview individuals in the city that are close to Assemblyman Fleming. Our office can assist the Albany Police Department with any help they require. The Albany police know the city and should continue to take the lead on the investigation up here."

Rusk looked ready to make an objection, but the superintendent spoke first.

"I agree. Now, I'd like to have Lieutenant O'Rourke give us a summary of the investigation so far."

O'Rourke then filled the group in on the latest information, including the missing key and the theory that both murders appeared to have been planned well ahead of time. He mentioned that he had some leads on Fleming's acquaintances in Albany, but didn't go into detail on where he got the names. He concluded with the information that they had received from the witness, Marta Cummings, who had apparently seen the killer.

"I'm impressed, Lieutenant," Owen said, "that you already had determined that the perpetrator was a tall man. Also, that you concluded that he had already been waiting there in the apartment for Assemblyman Fleming to arrive, even before Mrs. Cummings showed up to confirm that information."

"My team had come to that conclusion, yes," replied O'Rourke.

"The lieutenant and his men are representative of the fine men and women that make up the Albany Police Department," Chief Reilly added, in his best campaign speech voice.

"Yes, of course," replied Owen dismissively. "My time is limited, so I'd like to have Dr. Furlani give us some background on these types of murders and possible clues to the suspect we're looking for."

Until then, Elaine Furlani had not spoken. O'Rourke took a good look at her. The doctor's dark hair was pulled back and she wore large glasses, but that didn't hide the fact that she was a very attractive woman.

"Thank you, Superintendent. Before I begin, I must add that what I have prepared has been pulled together very quickly, in just a few short hours. Although we only have two murders to go by, there are certain assumptions we can make, based on the established patterns of serial killers that I have studied as part of my ongoing research. Historically, the majority of serial killers are Caucasian males that work alone. This seems to coincide with the information that was obtained from the witness."

Rusk spoke up again. "There have only been two killings that we know of. Why do you call him a serial killer?"

Dr. Furlani was prepared for the question. "We have a man who has committed two well-planned murders. Robbery was not the motive in either case. He left a message at the sites of both murders and mutilated both victims. This fits the pattern of at least one distinctive category of serial killer, where the killer targets specific victims in advance."

"What else can you tell us about the killer," Superintendent Owen asked her.

Dr. Furlani looked down at a set of photos from each murder. "The terms 'Black Bastard' and "Asshole" are both hateful and profane. It is unlikely that the person is a hired killer or professional hit-man; although those types of killers may on occasion leave a message as a warning, the message would not be similar to this. The killer obviously has a lot of pent-up anger, but it is a controllable rage. That's evident by the very neat lettering in the messages on the walls and also in the precise cutting of the tongue and the finger. This is a person who expresses his anger but acts in a careful and unhurried way. He does not slash at the victims in a frenzied manner. He does not panic and he remains at the scene of the crime until his job is completed. He keeps his cool, so to speak – and that will make him a very difficult man to catch."

O'Rourke was starting to be impressed by the professor, who

had a way of explaining things in a very succinct and clear way. Yet there was also something very detached and distant about her, as if this was just an intellectual exercise for her.

"The reason for using the specific terms he has chosen is not yet clear," the professor continued. "The wording in the first case obviously alludes to the victim's race, but the word used in the second case may or may not allude to the victim's sexual preference."

"He's gay," Rusk said bluntly. "He likes it in the ass. What else can it mean?"

"The word 'asshole' can obviously be used as an insult, as well as a comment on the fact that the victim was gay. The killer could, for example, be making a comment regarding his opinion of the victim's politics."

"It could be both," Booker said, speaking for the first time. "He could be slyly using the word as a double meaning."

Dr. Furlani smiled. "Very good, detective. The killer appears to be very clever. In fact, I would suggest looking into the first victim's family history to see if he was born out of wedlock. A 'bastard' in the strict definition of the term."

"We could be making this more complicated than it is," O'Rourke said. "I know we need to look into all angles, but this killer could just be a guy who personally knew both people and has some sort of sick reason in his mind for killing them both."

"Of course. But investigating that is what all of you will be doing – checking into the victims' background, interviewing acquaintances, going through records, and so on to see if there is a connection between the two victims. You don't need me for that. My job is to provide assistance to you so that we may get an idea of what type of person we are dealing with."

O'Rourke nodded. She was making sense.

"Obviously, it's also possible but unlikely that we could be looking for a killer that is a right-wing extremist," she continued. "Someone who has a political agenda against successful people of color and gays, and perhaps others. We should keep that open as a possibility, but my research has found that serial killers that mutilate their victims like this are rarely motivated by political issues. One more point I'd like to make is that the mutilation pattern is very uncommon. Mutilation itself is not unusual. But the fact that he removed two totally separate parts of the body, a finger and a tongue, is hard to explain. The only thing in common with these two parts of the body is that both can be used for sexual stimulation."

Rusk looked like he was going to lose his lunch. "You don't mean that he's going to use them to…"

"Possible but not likely. Neither corpse was defiled in any other way that would suggest a sexual motive. I think there may be some other reason he removed those two parts of the body. But with just two murders, it's not yet evident."

"You say that like you think they'll be more."

The professor took off her glasses and set them down on the table. "Unfortunately, gentlemen, I would count on it."

For several moments, the room was silent. Finally, Grainey spoke up, with more than a bit of annoyance in his voice.

"You don't know that at all. For all we know, the murderer is just some crazy assassin who was after the assemblyman all along. He probably just wanted to throw us off the trail, so he killed someone else first, using the same M.O. Or maybe he just needed some practice! Let's not get the citizens of Albany all upset with this serial killer nonsense."

Elaine Furlani put her glasses back on and stared at Grainey. "Captain, you are welcome to your hypotheses. However, I was brought to this meeting to give my opinion and suggestions, and I would strongly suggest that the best course of action is to assume the worst, that he will kill again. If this individual never murders anyone else again, that's wonderful. But putting your head in the sand is not going to get us anywhere."

O'Rourke couldn't help smiling as Grainey sputtered for a moment, trying to come up with a response. But Scott Owen spoke before he had the chance. "I've got to brief the governor on this in a few minutes. He's down here in New York, ironically at a tri-state crime prevention conference. So I need to wrap up this meeting and let you all get back to work on this. Bill, your group can work the New York City angle. Talk with Bernard Fleming's friends, associates and the lawyer, Jonathan Grace. Get an idea of who in the city had it out for Fleming."

"Dale," Owen continued, "have your men speak to the senators and assemblymen that Fleming was close to. But let the Albany police handle speaking to Fleming's staff. Also, contact our Office of Counter Terrorism. See if they know of any ultra-right wing groups around here that are active. They have contacts in the FBI that they can talk to as well."

"Chief Reilly, I believe the Albany Police Department should handle the rest of the local investigation; there will be a lot more work following up local leads on Fleming's murder and looking into possible connections with Mr. Tucker's death, I'm sure. Your men are best equipped to do that and Lieutenant O'Rourke seems to be the one to continue leading it, if you don't mind my advice. But use Dale's group as a resource for whatever you need. He can act as coordinator between O'Rourke and Chief Rusk as well. And please keep Dr. Furlani informed as you get more details on Fleming's murder. I hope to God she's wrong about more killings, but let's be ready if there are."

After the meeting ended, Captain Grainey and Chief Reilly escorted the state police contingent out. O'Rourke found himself alone in the room with Elaine Furlani.

"I appear to have upset your captain," she said to him, with a slight smile on her face.

"He wants every case to be wrapped up quickly and simply," he answered. "And if that means coming to the wrong conclusion, that's OK with him."

"He obviously doesn't think our suspect will strike again. I assume you are not in agreement with him, then?"

O'Rourke was reminded of the dream he had a few nights earlier, of the note that indicated the killer wasn't done yet. "After the first murder, I had a…premonition…that this was just the beginning of something. My guess is that there's going to be more."

Dr. Furlani reached out and gave O'Rourke a business card with her address and phone numbers. As she got close to him, he could make out a slight scent of perfume in the air. The kind that comes in a small bottle and costs a lot. "Lieutenant, you and I will need to work together closely on this. With your insight and my expertise, we should make a good team."

"I hope so," he said, giving her his card in return. "There wasn't a long time between these two murders. If your theory that he'll kill again is right, we need to catch this guy quickly."

O'Rourke walked Dr. Furlani to the exit of the building. As he watched her walk away, he was reminded of Ginny. He had promised to take her out to dinner tonight, but she would have to take a rain check. He gave her a quick call and apologized, and filled her in on his day so far.

"I expected that you would call," she said. "The story's been all over the news this evening. Trish Perkins has been on TV non-stop. She's linking it to the other murder you've been working on."

"Well, she's got that correct."

"Look, I know you're busy, so I'll let you get back to work."

"OK. I hope you're not too disappointed. I was really looking forward to our date tonight. It would have helped to make my day a little more bearable. I promise to make it up to you another night, Ginny."

"Yes, you will, Mr. O'Rourke," she laughed. "For tonight, I'll just have to fend for myself. I'll just make myself a light dinner. And then, maybe a nice long, hot, steamy bath..."

"This is not helping..."

Later, O'Rourke got Booker, Valente, Myers, and Oquendo together in his office. Their team members that weren't out in the field were working in the outer room - some looking at files, while others were calling residents of the State Street neighborhood. Oquendo said that no other witnesses had been found yet that had seen the tall man, but there were a lot more calls and visits to be made. O'Rourke and Booker filled the rest of the group in on the meeting with the state police.

"I want each of your teams to note every name they came across in the Randall Tucker investigation," O'Rourke said. "Then, we'll give the names to Sandy's team to cross check with the names we come up with on Fleming."

"You're thinking the killer will be on both lists?" Valente asked.

"I don't know what to think. What I *don't* think is that the killer pulled two names randomly out of a phone book. There's got to be a reason he picked his victims. Why these two particular individuals? Maybe they're connected in some way."

Oquendo looked up from her notepad. "You know, boss, that means you've got to talk to the Tucker family again. If you're looking for a connection between Tucker and a gay politician, you're going to have to ask some real personal questions."

"I know. I'm not looking forward to that. That's why you're going to ask them."

Oquendo started to protest, but O'Rourke held up his hand. "Rose, you've got a good rapport with the family. Case closed."

He turned to Myers. "The state police will be interviewing the other assemblymen and senators, but you can handle Fleming's staff. Take your team and interview everyone that worked in his office. Ask each person if they ever heard of Randall Tucker before he was in the news the other day."

He turned to Valente next. Valente had spoken to Marta Cummings earlier and got her full statement. "She didn't give us any more than we got when we spoke to her on State Street," he said. "She was too far away to get a real good description. I had the sketch artist come up with a picture based on what she said he was wearing, but it could fit almost any tall adult male under sixty."

"Get it on the news tonight. Let the stations know exactly where he was seen and the exact time of day. Maybe someone else saw him."

Valente then pulled out a printout from his computer. "I have a map of the State Street neighborhood. Marta Cummings said that the suspect walked down the street from the west to get to Fleming's apartment building, and later returned up the street when he left. So he was walking away from downtown and the state offices when he left. I figure if he had a car parked somewhere, it was most likely on upper State Street or on one of the streets near there."

"Or he lived in the neighborhood. It's pretty densely populated. But go with the car angle. Coordinate with Mills now and have the neighborhood search team expand further to the west.

There's a firehouse near State Street. Those guys sometimes hang outside on a warm day. Maybe one of them saw something."

O'Rourke asked Booker to remain in his office after the meeting. After the rest of the group left, he handed Booker the slip of paper that Ralph, the bartender from the Electric Company, had given him. He explained to Booker what he had promised Ralph.

"I want you to contact all of these people," he told Booker. "Be very discreet. But don't take no for an answer. We want these guys to tell us anything they know about Fleming's personal life. Anyone that Fleming may have had private relationship with. Fleming spent every Friday night at that restaurant; the killer may have known him from there."

After the meeting, O'Rourke walked down to the Annex to visit the Nerd Squad. Even though it was late, they were at full staff. The three nerds were there, as well as Sandy and Megan. They had all been working hard all day running everything they could on Fleming and all his associates. The men looked hot and tired. Megan just looked hot. "You're here late, Lieutenant," Megan said. "All work and no play. You're becoming a real workaholic."

"You guys are here late, too," he replied.

"I'd love to say it's out of dedication," Sandy joked, "but unlike those in your lofty salary grade, Megan and I are overtime eligible. And we got special approval for overtime for our contract staff too."

"And I thought you guys just did this for fun. So, what do you have for us?"

"Well, we do have something. We ran every name on Randall Tucker's computer, which include his customers and business contacts, against State Legislature databases, which include assemblymen, their staffs and lobbyists. We came up with eight upstate legislators and four legislative staff who have had family or personal portraits done by Tucker."

"That seems like a lot."

"But not that surprising statistically. He was a popular photographer in this area. Anyway, that makes twelve people that may have known both victims. I already sent the names to you and your staff by e-mail. I figured you would probably have to wait until tomorrow to do interviews."

"Anything else?"

"Arnold Polanski, Fleming's aide, sent us a list of individuals from Fleming's e-mail address. People that sent or received correspondence from the assemblyman. There were no matches with the information on Tucker's computer."

O'Rourke rubbed his eyes. He was getting tired. "I also asked my group to get all the names together from everyone they've contacted in the Tucker investigation. We'll get those names to you tomorrow morning and you can run those too."

O'Rourke thought about telling Bernstein about the short list of names he had received from Ralph the bartender, then decided against it. He could give those names to Sandy later, when the rest of Sandy's team wasn't around. If he asked Sandy to run them with no questions asked, Sandy would do it.

Sandy looked at his watch. "We're going to do a little more data analyzing and then we're done and heading home. You look beat. I suggest you do the same."

O'Rourke nodded and headed out the door. Before he left, he took a quick look back. Megan was leaning over Sandy's desk, giving O'Rourke a full view of her long legs that rose up to her tight black skirt with a slit up the side. He wondered if it was too late to call Ginny and ask her if she wanted to stop by his house later tonight.

Later, the tall man surfed through the television channels. Bernard Fleming was the top story on all the local channels, and the story made the national news channels as well. He had mixed feelings about that. It satisfied him that his work was being recognized on such a scale. But he never considered the fact that his missions would become a nationwide story. A little incidental perk. Something to take the sting off of the way that the black bastard and the asshole had messed up his life. His life and one other.

He looked at Channel Seven. Trish Perkins was holding a sketch that someone had drawn. Apparently, some woman had seen him leaving the asshole's apartment. No matter. The picture barely resembled him and could be almost anyone.

This business about the state police being brought in bothered him though. The Albany Police didn't concern him much; he felt that they were mostly a bunch of amateurs. Other than Lieutenant O'Rourke. But the tall man had one big advantage; he knew O'Rourke and O'Rourke didn't realize that. He knew what O'Rourke was capable of. And O'Rourke was not capable of stopping him.

But the state police were involved now. Their resources combined with the local police could present a problem. Given enough time, they might even figure it all out.

The tall man opened his notebook and looked at the names that remained on his list.

Do I stop now? After all this work? End my work before it's completed? No.

I won't do that. It's too important. They must all pay for what they've done.

He would have to expedite his schedule. He would take the next step tomorrow; the longer he waited, the more chance that the police might stumble onto something that would tie him to the incidents.

The tall man picked up a knife that he had placed on a side table. The knife was not quite as long as a butcher knife, but it was very sharp. He hoped he would not have to use the knife tomorrow; it was not as neat as the scalpel. But he might not have enough time to be neat. Eyes can take a long time to remove.

He realized that the knife was too sharp to just stay loose inside of his pack; it could poke a hole right through it. He went into the bathroom and returned with a small hand towel. He carefully wrapped the knife in the towel and placed it in his pack, its blade fully covered up. He smiled at a humorous thought that came to him:

I wouldn't want anyone to get hurt.

THIRTEEN

||||||||||||||||||||||||||||||||||||||||

Dr. Elaine Furlani stood to the right of Steven O'Rourke's bed and unbuttoned the white lab coat she was wearing. Underneath, she was wearing only a black negligee. As she climbed into bed with O'Rourke, he could smell the intoxicating scent of her perfume. He turned and looked to the other side of the bed. Megan Ross was there, peeling off the satin blouse that she had worn to work. O'Rourke could feel the heat from her body as she got in bed and started caressing his chest.

Then he heard a sound at the foot of the bed. Ginny Dixon was lying there, curled up near his feet, wearing one of O'Rourke's dress shirts and nothing else. Oddly, Ginny didn't seem to mind the other two women's presence in the bedroom. The women were hot. Not just a sexy kind of hot though. They seemed to be projecting heat right from their bodies. O'Rourke could feel the intensity. So hot that the bed sheets started smoldering. Suddenly, the smoke from the sheets turned into flames.

The bed was on fire all around O'Rourke but for some reason, he couldn't move. The fire got so hot that it set off an alarm. The men from the firehouse would be here soon, he thought. But they might be too late. Ginny was now lying right next to O'Rourke, the flames circling them both. As he tried to figure out how to get out of the bed, Ginny whispered something in his ear. "Go the right way," she said. "Make sure you go the right way."

O'Rourke was able to sit up now and he looked into the flames. There was a face there in the flames, a man's face that he had seen before. An ugly, evil face. The face was laughing at him. Laughing derisively, as if taunting O'Rourke. But the laughter was being drowned out now, by the fire alarm. The fire alarm sounded just like his alarm clock…

O'Rourke woke with a start, and realized that his alarm clock had been ringing for five minutes. He leaned over and shut it off, and lay back on his pillow for a minute. What a messed up dream, he thought. It was no wonder he was dreaming about heat and fire; he had been so tired the night before, he had gone to bed without opening the windows or switching on the air conditioner. The bedroom was stifling. He got up and opened the bedroom window, thinking about how vivid the dream had been. The flames felt real. Maybe his subconscious was telling him something. He decided to call Valente and Myers before he went to work to see if the firemen they interviewed last night had seen anything.

Valente, who always arrived at work early, answered the phone. "What's up, boss?"

"Just wanted to check and see what the firemen had to say."

"We didn't get too much from them. A couple of them did hang around in front of the firehouse last night, like you figured. We showed them the sketch of our suspect, the one the police artist got from Mrs. Cummings. They don't remember seeing anyone walk by that looked like that."

O'Rourke was disappointed. He had the strange feeling that

maybe his odd, vivid dream had been some kind of a sign.

"So our killer might have gotten into a parked car before reaching the firehouse."

"Yeah. Or he could have just walked by the firehouse without the firemen noticing. They admitted they were mostly focused on the women that walked by."

"That's not surprising," O'Rourke said. He knew a few firemen. "Have you checked on our progress with canvassing the neighborhood?"

"Yup. The uniforms were out late last night checking the area. No one reported seeing anyone that looked like the guy in the sketch. The sketch was on the news last night too. We've received some calls, but nothing of any value."

"All right, thanks. I'll be in within the hour."

O'Rourke frowned. That was disappointing. Aside from Marta Cummings, who had only seen the killer from a long distance away, there were no other witnesses. The killer had walked away from Fleming's apartment in a busy neighborhood in broad daylight and no one could recall seeing him. And several days before, he had done the same at Tucker's shop, which was also located on a busy street. The guy was like a ghost.

After O'Rourke got to the station, Booker stopped by his desk. "I called both Regina Tucker and Bryan Goldstein like you asked. I asked them if they had received any calls prior to the date of the murder asking for their schedule. They each reported that they had received calls at work a few days before asking about whether they would be working in Central Studio on Saturday. In both cases, the caller addressed each of them by their name and said that the employee had helped them buy a camera in the past and would like their help again."

"So the killer did do his homework ahead of time and knew they both would be out that day. But how would he have known their names?"

"Regina said that they wear name tags at work," Booker said. "Their names are in big print. The killer could have walked into the store a few times to figure out who worked there and saw their names."

"If that's true, the killer would have taken the chance that Tucker would have been there."

"True. But I wonder if Tucker, or for that matter Fleming, even knew the killer beforehand."

"I know. I'm starting to wonder that myself."

Booker handed O'Rourke a copy of his notes. "Neither Regina or Bryan were able to tell us anything unusual about the caller's voice, other than that it was male. Regina did say he didn't sound like he was from her neighborhood though. She described him as a "typical sounding white guy". Fortunately, both of them can recall the approximate day and time they received the calls. I'm thinking we could contact the phone company to see if we can see if one phone number called the store on both occasions."

"Good work. Put Valente on that. Maybe we're starting to get somewhere."

O'Rourke got the rest of the team, except for Myers who he had assigned to talk to Bernard Fleming's staff, together in his office. Oquendo had just returned from speaking with Forensics.

"Schade and Wilson pulled another all-nighter," Oquendo said. "They found that the bullets that killed Fleming were from the same gun as the Tucker murder. Even though they still need the state lab to confirm, they're pretty sure from the marks on the bullets that a silencer was used again."

"That makes sense," O'Rourke replied. "The Dumont girl that lives upstairs would have heard the shots otherwise."

"Forensics also confirmed that the spray paint was the same as the paint used on Tucker's wall. Common, ordinary dark blue spray paint."

"Anything else? Fingerprints, footprints, fibers? DNA?"

"No footprints. No fingerprints other than Fleming's. They figure the guy wore gloves again. There was a spot on the floor near the body that had a trace of blue cotton fibers. They're checking the fibers out. Wilson said not to get too excited about it though. In all likelihood, the killer was kneeling next to the body and the fibers are from the knee of his pants, probably jeans. There wouldn't be any DNA on the outside of the pants, so that lead probably won't go anywhere."

"Did they find anything in the other rooms?"

"No. As far as they can determine, the bedroom, bathroom and living room were undisturbed. It looks like the killer never went in any of those rooms."

"That goes along with the idea that he wasn't after anything in the apartment."

"Fleming's wallet had cash and credit cards in it. Schade said that judging from the position of the body, it was unlikely that the wallet could have been removed and put back in Fleming's pocket. Also, Wilson said that there was some cash in the top drawer of Fleming's dresser. The killer would have easily found that if he was looking."

"The killer's obviously not after money. I'm sure the money he took from Tucker's store was just to throw us off."

O'Rourke turned to Valente. "Has there been any more calls regarding the sketch that was on TV last night?"

"Yeah, we've had a couple calls. A man called and said he

saw a tall guy wearing jeans walking up State Street the night before last, but he didn't get a look at his face. Not very helpful, but we're having the man come in anyway."

"Any other calls?"

"Yeah," Valente said, looking at his notepad. "A lady called and said that she saw a man that night that fits the description. She said she invited him into her house and they had sex, and then he left."

O'Rourke raised an eyebrow. "Really?"

"Yup. I got the number she was calling from and called it back. The number was a pay phone at the Albany County Nursing Home. The nurse that answered said the lady that called hasn't left the home in the last three years. She has Alzheimer's."

"And a fertile imagination."

"Yeah. We're going to do more door to door today to ask if anyone saw anything."

"So what do you want me to do?" Oquendo asked O'Rourke.

"You and I are going to pay Mrs. Tucker another visit."

When they arrived, Joyce Tucker let them in. Her eyes were red and sunken. Robert and Angela were sitting on the couch; Angela's eyes matched her mother's.

"Mrs. Tucker," O'Rourke began after they sat down, "you obviously have heard the news about Assemblyman Fleming. It appears that whoever killed him also killed your husband."

"Do you have any leads on the murderer?"

"Not much," said Oquendo. "We did speak to your niece earlier. We think she may have spoken by phone to the perpetrator. We're following that up. We have some questions for you as well, if you don't mind."

"Go ahead."

"We reviewed your husband's records from the store. Mr. Fleming wasn't a customer. Did your husband know him at all?"

"He knew of him. My husband read the papers quite a bit. He was somewhat of a liberal, so he agreed with Mr. Fleming's politics for the most part."

"But he didn't know him personally?"

"No." Mrs. Tucker smiled thinly. "They really wouldn't have traveled in the same circles."

O'Rourke decided to get the question out there sooner than later. "Mrs. Tucker, I'm going to be blunt. It's no secret that Mr. Fleming was gay. Was your husband...inclined that way at all?"

Mrs. Tucker visibly stiffened. She probably knew that the conversation would eventually take that turn, but it still seemed to hit her hard.

"Lieutenant, I know you're just trying to do your job, so I'll try not to get too upset at that question. You can think what you want, but I can tell that my husband never, ever, gave me any cause to think that."

"Mother," Angela said angrily, "I don't think you should talk to these people anymore, if they're going to ask questions like that."

Joyce looked at her, with that serious, practical look on her face that O'Rourke was getting used to. "Angela, the more information they have, the more chance they have of catching the animal that killed your father."

"But mama, for them to ask that about daddy..."

"Your father's not here to be upset about it. Besides, don't you think people out there in the public are already thinking like that? A gay man was killed in the same way your father is killed. People will jump to conclusions that your father was associated with Mr. Fleming in that way."

"That's right," O'Rourke said. "But if we can eliminate this as a possibility, it will help us out. And we can let the press know that it has been ruled out."

"Well, you can eliminate it," Angela said. "My father was not gay, or bi, or whatever. You can ask his friends, our relatives, anyone you want."

"Angela speaks for me too," Joyce Tucker added.

"Actually, our people are already doing just that," O'Rourke replied. "So if Mr. Tucker didn't know the assemblyman, do either of you have any idea why someone would kill both your father and Mr. Fleming?"

"Someone killed a black man and a gay man," Angela snapped. "Doesn't that sound like some sort of bigot to you?"

"It's absolutely possible. And that is something we're all working on. We're getting assistance from the State Police and they're looking at hate groups out there, as well as individuals with a history like that. We're looking into all possibilities."

"Unfortunately, we have another question that we have to ask," said Oquendo. "Mrs. Tucker, you obviously know the word "Bastard" was written on the wall. Was your husband's mother married when he was born?"

"Yes, they had been married for several years," Joyce Tucker answered. O'Rourke could see Angela getting hot again, but she didn't say anything this time.

"I apologize for asking, but was there any chance that his father wasn't his real father?"

Joyce went to a desk at the end of the living room and pulled out a photo album. She brought it over to where O'Rourke and Oquendo were sitting and after a few moments, found a page where there was a photo of Randall Tucker as a teen, standing next to a man.

"This is a photo of Randall and his father," she said. O'Rourke looked closely at the photograph. The man was the spitting image of Randall. "I'm sure you'll both agree my husband was no bastard."

O'Rourke and Oquendo talked with the family some more, asking about any groups or individuals that Tucker had known that may be connected politically or in any other way with Fleming. But there were no leads there.

Later, in the car, O'Rourke asked Oquendo what she thought.

"It doesn't sound like they're hiding anything," she said. "Mrs. Tucker wants this case solved. I don't think she would hide it from us if her husband was gay or went both ways."

"Yeah, I get that feeling too. Whatever connects Fleming to Tucker, it's not that."

They listened to the radio on the way back to the station. The local talk station was all abuzz with the killings. Many of the callers mentioned what Joyce Tucker had said, that the killer was a bigot that hated gays and blacks. It was possible, O'Rourke thought. But that seemed too easy an answer. The guy they were after took great pains to target and kill these two specific individuals. There were surely easier ways to kill people if the killer was just after blacks and gays. Besides, even if bigotry alone was actually the motive, that wouldn't be likely to help them find the killer. This guy wasn't likely to post his ravings on Twitter.

It was lunchtime and there was a small pizza place nearby that had tables outside. It was a sunny day, so O'Rourke and Oquendo stopped there and ordered some slices. O'Rourke wondered as he ate where the killer was and what he was doing right now.

Less than six miles away, there is a large park in the middle of the town of Colonie called the Crossings. The town had decided about a decade ago to create the park in the growing suburban neighborhood between Sand Creek and Shaker Road to maintain a green area where town residents could walk, jog, bike, or otherwise enjoy themselves. As the tall man walked along a paved path in the park, he considered that the people who planned this park had not even remotely considered that it could also be used as a valuable tool for a mission of vengeance.

The tall man rarely took time during working hours to do research on his missions. He didn't want to give anyone at work cause for suspicion. But, today was an exception. With more and more police trying to catch him, he had to move up his schedule.

As he looked around the park, he noticed that aside from the families one would expect to be in the park, there were also other men in working clothes walking through the park on their lunch hour. All the better to fit in with the crowd.

The tall man was in good physical shape and did not need a break from walking. But when he had arrived at his particular destination, he casually walked over to a bench on the side of the path and sat down. From that vantage point, he could see the back yards of several houses located on a small street adjacent to the park. He opened a bottle of water that he had been carrying. As he sipped his water, he focused very carefully at the back of the third house on the right. It was a fairly nondescript white house with aluminum siding and an attached garage. He had viewed this house from the park and from other angles several times before.

Ron Morton, the regional supervisor of McCann Security Systems, resided in that house with his wife Loretta and 17 year old daughter Ashley. Loretta was a state worker in the Department of Tax and Finance in Albany who did volunteer work at Memorial Hospital. Ashley, a high school cheerleader, was preparing for her senior year at Colonie High School. They appeared to be a nice wholesome family. But the tall man knew the evil behind that facade.

Although he had originally planned his mission for next Thursday, he realized that he would now have to act tonight. Mrs. Morton attended yoga classes on Thursday evenings; that was the only night she was routinely away from home. The tall man had already devised a way to get Mr. Morton out of the house. As long as Ashley Morton stayed home tonight, he could proceed with his plan.

He once again studied the house. The windows were all closed. The house, like many others in this area, probably had central air conditioning. The first floor and basement levels had windows facing the park, but the second floor which included Ashley's bedroom did not. The back yard was illuminated at night by a light above the back door which appeared to be on a timer that went on at 8 PM every night. So the back door of the house was not the best option for breaking into the house at night. There was a door to the garage on the side of the house, where it would be dark. The problem was that to get to that door from the park, he would have to run through the back yard.

He estimated that he could sprint from the park, which was pitch dark at night, to the side door of the garage in less than two minutes. In that time, he would be exposed for about ten seconds in the well-lit back yard, but that was a chance he would have to take. The side door itself could probably be broken into fairly easily, in much the same way that he had broken into the back door of Fleming's apartment building. Once inside, he would have to head for Ashley's upstairs bedroom as quickly as he could. He figured that the whole operation could be done in less than twenty minutes from the time he started running from the park; less than that if he decided to use the knife on her instead of the scalpel. The timing was important since there was no way of telling exactly how long Mr. Morton would be away from the house.

After a few more minutes, he was satisfied that his plan would work. He got up and started walking back the way he had come. A jogger ran by and waved to him. The tall man waved back. "Have a nice day," he said.

When O'Rourke got back to the office, the autopsy report was in. Because Fleming was a state legislator, the autopsy was done by the State Police Lab and they had wasted no time in getting it done. The report confirmed that the cutting instrument used on Fleming's finger was the same used on Tucker. The bullet wounds were similar, but closer together this time; the killer was getting to be a better shot. The autopsy report also stated that the victim had not had sex of any kind in the hours prior to the murder. That ruled out the scenario that he had been killed by a man he had recently picked up for sex, a theory that already seemed unlikely. The report also confirmed that Fleming was dead before his finger had been cut off.

O'Rourke realized that it had been some time since Myers had reported in from Fleming's office, so he called his cell phone.

"Hey, chief," Myers answered.

"How's it going down there? You've been at it all day."

"Exhausting. I've interviewed everyone in the office except Fleming's secretary. She's been swamped, dealing with calls from other legislators as well as the press. But I told her to make time for me in about a half hour."

Myers sounded worn out. "You sound beat. Have you taken a break?"

"I had lunch. But the busy day was worthwhile. I've got a ton of interview material."

"Anything valuable so far?"

"Hard to say. Fleming definitely had political enemies. Some people didn't like him. But no one here seems to think that a colleague could have killed him. I did get some names anyway of some of the other senators and assemblymen that he butted heads with the most."

"Good. We can give that to the State Police to check out." O'Rourke looked at his watch. "I can be there in fifteen minutes. I'll interview the secretary with you."

"Sure. See you then."

The secretary, Lisa DeMarco, was an attractive blonde in her mid-thirties. Apparently, even gay men hired pretty secretaries. At her desk outside of Fleming's office, Myers had just started asking De Marco routine questions when O'Rourke arrived. O'Rourke had a few of his own.

"Ms. DeMarco, the State Police in New York City have been asking around to see if anyone connected to your boss there could have killed him. We're handling the personal end of the investigation. You said that you've worked for Mr. Fleming for many years. Do you know much about his personal life?"

"I know some things. He wasn't really shy about talking about it with me."

"Apparently, he's had a relationship with Mr. Grace for some time. But had he ever talked about any other men in his life?"

"Not for a long time. He seemed pretty content with the relationship with Jonathan. I'm pretty sure he wasn't cheating on him or anything like that."

"You said not for a long time?"

The secretary fidgeted in her seat a bit. "Well, yes. Years ago, before he met Jonathan, he seemed to get around a lot."

O'Rourke smiled, trying to put her at ease. "You mean he had a lot of encounters with men?"

"Yeah. I mean a *real* lot. He used to tell me stories. I think he liked to make me blush. I was a lot younger then, more naive. Arnie used to complain to him about all those…um…encounters, as you put it."

"You're referring to Arnold Polanski?"

"Yes. Bernie's advisor. He told Bernie to cut that stuff out. Even though everyone knew Bernie was gay, Arnie was afraid that specific details about his sex life would come out. He felt that most of Bernie's constituents accept Bernie as a gay politician but if they heard stories about how often he had those encounters with men, they wouldn't much care for that. But Bernie never seemed to listen."

"But he stopped after he entered the relationship with Jonathan Grace."

"Actually, he stopped his carousing a year or two before he met Jonathan."

O'Rourke considered that for a moment. Until now, he had assumed that the relationship with Grace had caused Fleming to settle down. "Are you sure about that?"

"Oh, yes. Arnie once told me how pleased and surprised he was that Bernie took his advice. And that was a while before Bernie settled down with Jonathan."

"So, you think Mr. Fleming changed his lifestyle for political reasons, as Mr. Polanski suggested he do?"

She thought for a moment. "No, I don't think so. Bernie was pretty headstrong. He liked to do things his own way. I don't know why he stopped carousing around, but I don't think it was politics."

They interviewed DeMarco some more, but there was nothing else new to be gained from her. Having completed interviews with Fleming's entire staff, Myers and O'Rourke headed back to the station.

When O'Rourke returned, he had voice mails from Bill Rusk's office and from Dale Mitchell. He returned the call from Rusk's office first and spoke to Rusk's assistant, Levitt. Rusk's office had no new leads. Levitt did say they spoke to Jonathan Grace, who had been in New York City the entire day that Fleming was killed. He had solid alibis to prove his whereabouts, so that ruled him out as a suspect.

O'Rourke called Dale Mitchell back next. O'Rourke gave Mitchell the names that Myers had obtained of Fleming's political enemies. Mitchell, through his interviews with state politicians, had the same names already and his team had already spoken to them all. Although Mitchell wouldn't rule anyone out yet until he double checked where they were at the time of the murder, he said none of them looked promising as suspects.

Soon after the call from Mitchell, Derek Booker walked into his office. "I've contacted all the names on the bartender's list," he said to O'Rourke.

"And?"

"Most were cooperative. One of the men took my number and called me back later, where he couldn't be heard. From what I could surmise, these men were just casual acquaintances with Fleming. They couldn't think of anyone they knew that would want Fleming dead."

"You said most were cooperative?"

"One of the men, Stanley Koblenz, is an executive at Albany Banking and Loan. He got upset. He said that he had never been to the Electric Company and didn't know what I was talking about. When I tried to press him, he hung up."

O'Rourke looked at his watch. It was almost 3:00. "I assume Mr. Koblenz has banker's hours. Maybe we can catch him."

Twenty minutes later, O'Rourke and Booker stood a few yards outside of the prestigious Albany Banking and Loan Tower, a downtown Broadway building recently added to Albany's skyline in the past year. Before they left O'Rourke's office, O'Rourke had looked up Albany Banking and Loan on the internet, and one webpage had photographs of all the executives. He had printed out Koblenz's photo and now had it folded up in his hand.

"So, how's Carole," O'Rourke asked Booker while they were standing there. Booker and his wife Carole were expecting their first child in a few weeks. O'Rourke and Booker had been so busy lately that there had been little time for small talk.

"She's doing pretty well. She's getting a little nervous though."

"That's natural."

"I guess. Every woman's probably nervous the first time they have a baby. She's worried about the long labor and all that."

"You can always have her talk to Valente's wife. She's pregnant with their sixth kid. She pops them out like candy from a Pez dispenser."

"Thanks for that mental image. I don't think I'll be eating any Pez anytime soon…Hey, is that our man over there?"

Booker pointed out a tall, thin man walking out of the building. The man appeared to be about fifty and was wearing a dark, expensive looking suit and had a leather briefcase in his hand. O'Rourke looked at the photo in his hand. "That's our man."

They let Koblenz walk past them and then started walking behind him in the same direction. After half a block, O'Rourke called out to him. "Excuse me, Mr. Koblenz?"

Koblenz stopped and turned around. "Yes?"

"I'm Lieutenant O'Rourke for the Albany Police Department and this is Detective Booker. We'd like to ask you a few questions."

Koblenz was startled for a second, but quickly regrouped. "I believe I spoke to the detective on the phone earlier. I'm sorry I couldn't help him."

"We'd just like to ask you a few questions about your relationship with Assemblyman Fleming."

"I already told the detective that he was mistaken," Koblenz said coldly. He glanced past O'Rourke and Booker, looking back toward the building where he worked to see if any co-workers were looking his way. "As far as I know, I've never met Mr. Fleming."

"We have it on good authority that you have."

"Lieutenant, I have nothing more to say," Koblenz said, raising his voice a notch. "I've had a long day and would like to go home now, if you don't mind. If you persist in this, I will consider it harassment and I'll be contacting my attorney."

From the list of names that O'Rourke had received from Ralph Vickers, O'Rourke had no way of knowing if Koblenz was someone who had been seen talking with Fleming on many occasions or just once. He wished now that he had asked Vickers more questions about the men on the list. But Koblenz's attitude set off a red flag that indicated he was hiding something. O'Rourke decided to bluff.

"Sir, we've already been told that you had a very close relationship with the victim. So you're welcome to call your attorney. In fact, you can call him right now and we can make an appointment to discuss this at the police station this evening. Right after we announce to the local media that we have a person of interest in the Fleming case."

The color suddenly drained from Koblenz's face. Then, in a low voice, he responded. "My car is parked a few blocks from here. Perhaps we can discuss this quietly as we walk there."

O'Rourke nodded and they started walking down the busy sidewalk.

"I'd like to keep this very discreet," Koblenz said. "I work at a very conservative business – very much out of touch with the times. I therefore have to keep my personal life very private. If the fact that I was gay got out, it could cost me my job."

"Whatever you say will be kept in the confines of the investigation," O'Rourke said.

"Very well. I've known Mr. Fleming for several years. We still have a few friends and acquaintances in common. I presume that you interviewed one of them and they threw me in."

O'Rourke needed to keep up the bluff. "I can't reveal our sources, just as I won't reveal your name to anyone outside of the investigation. All I can say is that we have very detailed information about your relationship."

"Then you probably know that Bernie and I were an item a long time ago. But that ended more than ten years ago, and we haven't been together since then. Of course, we would still run into each other at times. As I said, we share common friends, and they have private social gatherings on occasion. In addition, I would see him once in a while at a restaurant that we both frequent."

"How would you describe your relationship with him after you two were no longer together?"

"We weren't friends anymore. I'd exchange pleasantries when I saw him and that's about it. But I wouldn't wish to do him harm, if that's what you're getting at."

"I wasn't getting at that. Yet. But since I don't like it when people lie to me or my detectives, I will now. Can you account for your whereabouts on the night Mr. Fleming was murdered?"

"I was at home. I was tired and went to bed early. Unfortunately, I live alone, so I can't prove that."

"What about Saturday afternoon and evening," Booker asked.

"I was home alone then as well. I believe I can prove that I had Chinese food delivered around 8 PM, if that helps."

That wouldn't do for an alibi, thought O'Rourke. Randall Tucker was killed earlier in the evening.

"You say you would have no motive to do Mr. Fleming harm," O'Rourke said. "Do you know anyone that would?"

"I said I wouldn't *wish* to do him harm. I didn't say that I would have no motive to. I imagine that many people in my situation would wish to do him harm."

"And what situation would that be?"

Koblenz studied O'Rourke's face for a minute, and then smiled wryly. "I believe that you've put one over on me, Lieutenant. I assumed that you already knew everything about my relationship with Bernie. But I suppose at this point, there's no sense in hiding anything. In fact, I actually still care enough about Bernie to give you information that might assist you in investigating his death."

"And that information is..?"

"I've been HIV positive for nine years. Because of Bernard Fleming, I might end up with AIDS."

FOURTEEN

IIIIIIIIIIIIIIIIIIIIIIIIIIIIIIIIIIIIII

It was after nine and the temperature was in the low sixties, a cool summer night by Albany standards. The tall man stood in the dark empty parking lot of Sparky's Auto Repair Shop on Sand Creek Road in Colonie. From the exact spot where he stood facing the rear of the shop, he could not be seen from the street; that was one reason he had chosen this place. Behind the tall man was an open wooded area; unless someone was hiding in the trees back there (and he had checked - there was no one there), the tall man would not be seen from the rear either.

The tall man put his hand in the pocket of his lightweight hooded sweatshirt and pulled out a few heavy stones that he had gathered. He stood about five yards from the shop's rear window. The window was large enough for someone to climb through but there was wire mesh visible behind it. Even if an intruder broke the window, he would have difficulty getting into the shop. But the tall man's intent wasn't to enter the shop.

He tossed one of the stones at the window. It made a thud against the window, sounding louder than the tall man expected in the quiet night, but the window didn't break. He waited a couple of minutes, listening intently to see if anyone responded to the noise. Comfortable that no one was coming, he threw a second stone, this time much harder. That worked. The glass window shattered and a loud burglar alarm went off. He had expected that and took off immediately. By the time anyone arrived on the scene, he would be long gone.

Ron Morton was sitting on his couch watching the Mets game. He had the sound turned up high because there was a party going on at the house next door. His neighbors, Marion and Gordon Lemme, had gone on vacation and left their college age son home. The kid had apparently invited all of his friends to a keg party. They had that new alternative music cranked up too loud. He thought about calling the cops on the kid, but then thought about some of the parties he used to go to years ago and decided to cut the kid some slack.

He had just opened a second Coors Light, and David Wright was up at bat with two men on base, when Ron's beeper went off. There was a message on it showing that there was an alarm going off at an auto repair shop on Sand Creek Road. The police had been automatically contacted. Ron's job, as regional boss of McCann Security, was to meet them at the store. He set down his beer and put on his shoes. Before leaving the house, he called upstairs to his daughter Ashley, who was in her bedroom.

"Ashley, I've got to go out for a while. My beeper went off. Your mom should be home in a couple hours."

"Yeah, OK," she called back.

"I've got my cell phone on me if you need to call."

Ashley popped her head out of her room. "I'm almost eighteen. I think I can handle being alone for two hours."

"Fine. Just remember to tell your mom that I got a call."

"Whatever..."

Ashley Morton lay back down on her bed and turned up the volume on her TV remote. There was some reality show on MTV that was set in New Jersey or somewhere stupid like that. She probably should be studying since she was going to summer school to make up the eleventh grade science and social studies classes she flunked during the school year. But screw that. The only reason she flunked was her parents had made her get a part-time job at the Colonie Library, and that interfered with her studying time. How was she supposed to work a part-time job, go to school, attend cheerleading practice, spend time with her boyfriend Mark, and still have time to study? It was so unfair.

She looked out the window at the house next door. The shades were drawn downstairs but she could see the shadows of a lot of people behind them. Rock music was blaring from the house, and now and then, she could hear the people laughing loudly like they were drunk. The college kid next door, Peter Lemme, was having a party. He was a boring geek, but the music sounded cool. She wondered what the party was like. Maybe she should just go over there and ring the doorbell. The guys would of course invite her in because she was so hot. There was probably a lot of liquor over there. But they were all probably just a bunch of boring geeks like Lemme.

The keg party did give her an idea though. She got up off the bed and walked down the stairs. It was rare when her mother and father were both out of the house. It would be a shame to spoil the opportunity. Her mom and dad both drank beer, but she was willing to bet that they didn't know exactly how many bottles were in the fridge. She could easily drink a beer and no one would notice as long as she got rid of the empties.

The tall man arrived at the Crossings. It was a dark cloudy night so he had to make his way carefully through the unlit park.

Finally, he got to the bench that he had been sitting on earlier in the day. He looked out at the Morton house. The neighborhood was usually quiet at this time of night. But tonight, it was not quiet at all. Loud music was coming from the house to the left of the Morton's home, so loud that he could hear it from the park. There were several lights on in that house. But fortunately, shades were pulled down over the windows facing the Morton home.

What now? The activity next door definitely heightened the risk level. Someone could look out the side windows at the wrong moment. *Abandon the mission? No, it's been planned too carefully to scrap it now. Postpone it? That wouldn't work. I can't pull the same ruse to get the father out of the house again. Besides, I need to complete the mission as soon as possible.*

But maybe, the changes in the scenario can be used to my advantage. The loud music may cover me if the girl screams. There would be no way anyone outside the house would hear it with all that noise going on.

He opened his backpack and took out the gun, the scalpel, the knife, and the spray paint. He put the gun in the right pocket of his hooded sweatshirt and the other items in the left so he could access them quickly if he needed to. Then, he removed a ski mask from the backpack and put it on over his head. He slipped the pack on over his back and took a deep breath. He was ready to go.

Moving quickly and silently, he ran from the park until he reached the Morton's low back yard fence. He clambered over it as fast as he could without making undue noise. Dropping to the ground, he stopped for a moment on one knee just outside the lit area, looking to his left and right. Then, he sprinted through the back yard. The back door light was very bright, lighting up most of the yard. He was screwed if anyone happened to look his way. Finally, he reached the shadows at the side of the garage between the Morton's house and the adjacent house. It was still fairly dark there, even with the light behind the shades of the adjacent house filtering through. Wearing the warm ski mask and sweatshirt, he was sweating from the exertion even though the night was cool. He stopped there for a few seconds to catch his breath before it was time to strike.

Ashley sat at the kitchen table, listening to the music from the radio on the counter. The song was an oldie – "No More Tears" by some hippie relic that her dad liked. She had downed half a bottle of Coors Light and was already feeling a little buzz. She pulled her cell phone from her jeans and sent her boyfriend Mark a text. An X-rated one, the kind he liked. He was busy at basketball practice, but he could read it later. The only problem with Mark was that he had this thing about her drinking. Mark had no hang-ups about sex, but heaven forbid she had a sip of beer. "Screw him," she said, and chugged the rest of her beer.

Outside the house, the tall man crept along the side of the garage slowly in the dark, toward the side door. Suddenly, he bumped into something. It was a plastic garbage barrel, one of the big types that the companies that collect the garbage give out to customers. It was nearly empty and almost toppled over, but he caught the handle just before the barrel hit the ground. He waited a second to make sure no one had heard and then continued on. Cursing silently to himself, he moved around the barrel, and got to the garage door. Although there were four small panes of glass on top of the door, he could not see into the garage, which was pitch black. He pulled out his knife and inserted it into the door latch to pry the door open.

Ashley finished her beer and rinsed it out in the sink. The old guy on the radio was singing something about not talking to strangers. Ashley decided she needed to hide the empty beer bottle. She couldn't put it in the kitchen trash for fear of having her parents find it. She remembered that there was a Hefty trash bag in the garage that was almost full with empty bottles. She could put the empty bottle in there to get rid of the evidence. She opened the kitchen door that led into the garage and switched on the garage light.

The tall man had almost broken through the door latch with the knife when an inside light was suddenly turned on. The garage was flooded with light and if anyone happened to look through the side door, they would be staring right at him. Startled, he backed away quickly from the door and crashed right into the plastic garbage barrel. He went sprawling to the ground as the empty barrel fell over with a loud thump.

Ashley thought she heard a noise outside the garage a moment after she turned on the garage light. It was hard to tell though; the music from next door was so loud. She wondered if some of the college kids next door were hanging out in the side yard, between the two houses. Climbing down the three steps that led from the kitchen to the floor of garage, she walked past the second refrigerator the family kept in the garage and over to the side door. She stood on her toes and peered out through the glass windowpanes. She couldn't see anyone out there.

The tall man had quickly gotten to his feet and now stood flattened against the outside wall of the garage, just inches to the right of the door. He could sense someone inside the garage, possibly looking out the window, only a few feet away from him. Ashley Morton. The garbage barrel that he had tripped over was right under the door, but would be under her line of vision. He stayed in that spot for what seemed like an eternity, not moving a muscle for fear that she would hear him. All the while, he was afraid that someone next door would glance out through the window shades and see him there, flat against the wall.

Not seeing anyone outside, Ashley went back through the garage to the trash bag and put the beer bottle inside, shoving it down under some empty soda bottles. She thought about closing up the trash bag now and putting it outside in the recyclable barrel but then decided to have another beer first. She went inside the house, shutting off the garage light and closing the kitchen door behind her.

Finally, the light from the Morton's garage went off. Ashley Morton had gone back inside.

The tall man had to work quickly now. He quietly picked the garbage barrel back up and quietly set it up again next to the house, further away from the door this time so it wouldn't be in his way on the way out after he killed Ashley. He suddenly realized that he had dropped the knife when he fell to the ground. Unable to see in the dark, he got down on his knees and swept the ground with his gloved hands until he found it. He used it to go back to work on the lock until he felt the lock pop. He put the knife back in his pocket, and cautiously opened the door and stepped into the dark garage.

Ashley had grabbed a bag of chips from the pantry in the kitchen and snacked on a few before reopening the fridge. There were only three bottles of Coors left. Her dad would probably not miss the one she had already had, but she might be taking a chance if she drank a second one.

She remembered that there were a few bottles of Corona in the second fridge in the garage, left over from her mom's backyard birthday party last month. Her parents probably didn't know exactly how many were left. She decided to have one of those.

She opened the door again to the garage, flicked on the light and walked down the three steps. Suddenly, she stopped dead in her tracks. A tall man wearing a ski mask was standing less than ten feet in front of her.

The tall man was making his way across the garage in the dark when the garage light suddenly went on again. He froze in his tracks, dumbfounded, as the girl walked down the steps. The moment she saw him, he reacted quickly. He put his hand in the pocket of his sweatshirt to grab his gun. It wasn't there! It must have fallen out when he fell to the ground after colliding with the barrel. Ashley Morton was screaming now. She turned back toward the kitchen. Moving fast now, he ran toward her. As she reached the top step, he leaped at her and grabbed her left ankle just as she reached the door.

Ashley fell face down on the stairs. The man in the ski mask had his hands around her left ankle. Reacting quickly, self-preservation at stake, she turned her body around, so she was face up. She lashed out with her right leg, kicking the man in the face with all her might. Although she was just wearing sneakers, the kick caught him full in the face and he let go of her ankle. The force of her kick almost toppled her over onto him, but she caught herself before she could fall. She got up quickly and flung the door open, got inside the kitchen, and quickly slammed the door shut behind her. She saw the door knob turn just as she locked the door. The knob shook violently, but the lock held.

She realized that she had been yelling, but no one outside would be able to hear with the racket going on next door. She looked around, frantically trying to remember where she had put her cell phone. There was another phone in the living room and she was headed there when she saw her cell phone on the kitchen table. She grabbed it and speed dialed her father's number.

The tall man looked around the garage for something he could use on the door. There was a red fire extinguisher on the wall. He pulled it off the wall and walked up the stairs with it. It was heavy; hopefully it was heavy enough. He bounded up the steps and lifting the extinguisher above his shoulders with both hands, he slammed it into the door. It put a good size dent in the door, but it didn't go all the way through. He tried again, as hard as he could, and a golf ball sized hole opened in the door at about his eye level. He looked through and saw the girl. She was yelling into a cell phone.

Two Colonie patrolmen, Officers Riley and Cole, were talking to Ron Morton outside of Sparky's Auto repair when his phone rang.

Ron saw the call was from Ashley and answered. "So," he said sarcastically, "I thought you said you could handle being alone for two hours. What's up?"

"Daddy, there's someone in the garage," Ashley shouted. She sounded hysterical and out of breath. Ashley hadn't called him daddy since she was a young kid. "He grabbed me and he's trying to get in the house!"

"What?"

"There's a guy in a mask and he's trying to…Oh, god, he just broke a hole in the door and he's looking right in at me."

Ron looked at the cops, who apparently saw the alarm in his face. "Honey, we'll be there in ten minutes."

He told the cops what Ashley had said. One of the cops, Riley, pointed to the back door of the police car and told him to get in and they were on their way.

The tall man quickly calculated his options. He could get through the door with a few more blows. But he could hear that the girl was on the phone with her father. The tall man knew Ron Morton was probably less than a fifteen minute drive away, ten minutes maybe if he was with the police. If the tall man hadn't dropped his gun outside, he might be able to shoot the girl through the door and still have time to escape. But without the gun, there was not enough time to get inside, kill her and get away safely.

"Damn you," he yelled through the door. And then he was gone.

Sean Chen knew that he had been stupid. *Really stupid.* He had been one of the first guests to arrive at Pete Lemme's party and was there when Bill Kirby started making a concoction called Jaeger Bombs. Kirby said that it contained Red Bull so it would allow you to drink all night without getting tired. Sean and the others had alternated Jaeger Bombs with cans of Budweiser. That was dumb. But the three Kamikazes he did later were just *stupid.* About 15 minutes ago, Sean felt sick and ran for Lemme's toilet. Unfortunately, there was a line of three guys outside the bathroom door. One of the guys said that Bill Kirby was in there tossing his cookies, so don't expect to use the bathroom anytime soon. So now, Sean was leaning over Lemme's backyard deck in the dark, puking his guts out.

After throwing up, he slumped over the façade of the deck, hoping he would die soon and be out of his misery. But then, he heard something off to his left. He looked over at the house next door. A man with something over his face was coming out of the side door of the garage. The man dropped quickly to his knees outside the door. Although Sean could barely see the man in the light that came from inside the garage, it appeared as if the guy was frantically searching in the dark for something on the ground. After a moment, he apparently found it and picked it up. The man then got up and ran into the back yard of the house. Fast. As the man ran through the well lit yard, Sean saw what was in the man's hand. It was a gun.

Sean must have made a sound, because the man suddenly turned toward him as he ran away. He had on a ski mask, which Sean thought was weird in this weather. The man stopped, and for a second, Sean was afraid the man was going to shoot him. But the man just started running again. When he got to the fence, he tossed the gun over to the other side, climbed the fence quickly, retrieved the gun, and kept running. Within seconds, the man disappeared into the dark.

Moving unsteadily, Sean started to go back in the house. He figured he should tell the guys what he just seen. But that would have to wait. His stomach lurched again and he ran back to the edge of the deck. As he upchucked, he could taste the Kamikazes coming back up. *Stupid.*

Ron Morton stayed on the phone with his daughter for the entire ride to his house, which took nine and one half minutes on the nose. The police officers gave him instructions during the ride that he relayed to her. The police had her look out the front window. Once she saw that no one was out there, she followed instructions and ran to the Walkers' house across the street. She was still at the Walkers when Morton and the police arrived.

The Colonie patrolmen had called for backup during the ride to Morton's home. Sergeant Vince D'Alessandro arrived along with two other patrolmen about ten minutes after Riley and Cole, and he took charge of the scene. By then, Riley and Cole had established that the intruder was no longer in the house. Ronald Morton had gone across the street and brought his daughter back home. D'Alessandro spoke to the Morton girl and she told him of the attack by the man wearing a mask. He asked the two patrolmen that he rode with to look around outside the house.

D'Alessandro noticed there were several cars in front of the house next door to the Morton's home. Many of the cars had State University stickers on the window. Riley told him that loud music was blaring from that house when they first arrived, but the revelers inside had turned off the music when they saw the police cars. D'Alessandro and Riley walked over to the house, while Cole watched the back of the house to make sure none of the partiers ran off.

D'Alessandro knocked on the door and a young kid around nineteen years old answered. The kid wore glasses and smelled of alcohol. He identified himself as Peter Lemme and told the officers that he was just having a few friends over. D'Alessandro and Riley went into the house and looked around.

D'Alessandro had probably been to a hundred houses breaking up parties like this in his twenty years in the Colonie Police Department, and he could size up a crowd pretty quickly. These kids were bunch of college nerds trying to have a beer blast and not succeeding too well. Half of the crowd already appeared to be sick and the other half nearly passed out. He doubted the attacker had come from this crowd.

While D'Alessandro was speaking with Lemme, one of the other kids came over. The kid's face was as white as chalk and he was unsteady on his feet.

"Excuse me, sir," the kid mumbled, "I need to tell you something."

The kid was obviously drunk, but there was something in the kid's demeanor that indicated he was being very serious.

"What's your name, son?"

"Sean. Sean Chen. I was outside on the back deck ...um... well, getting sick actually, and I saw a man run from the house next door. A tall guy with a mask over his face."

D'Alessandro pointed to the Morton house. "From that house right there?"

"Yes. He started from there. And he turned around and saw me when he got near the fence. He had a gun in his hand."

That seemed odd, D'Alessandro thought. Ashley Morton hadn't mentioned a gun.

"Are you sure it was a gun?"

"It was definitely a gun. He came out of the side door of the house and knelt down near the door looking for it for a minute. He must have left it there. Then, he found it and ran through the back yard. And then he hopped over the fence and ran into the park. "

Leaving Riley to question the other kids, D'Alessandro went outside. He told the other officers about what Chen had said and had them search around the side of the house and the back yard. Then, he called into dispatch and asked them to send some patrol cars to the Crossings to look for the attacker, who was possibly armed.

It had now been a while since the attack, so D'Alessandro

figured the attacker would be long gone from the park. If the man had a car waiting in one of the park's lots, he would have had plenty of time to get to it.

Officer Cole came over to D'Alessandro. He was carrying something in a small clear evidence bag.

"Sergeant, I found this outside, near the side door of the garage. It was on the ground, right next to the house."

D'Alessandro looked closely at the evidence bag. Inside it was a surgeon's scalpel. The sharp end of the scalpel appeared to be covered with dried blood.

"Call dispatch back right away," he told Cole. "Have them tell the cops in the park to be very careful. The suspect should be considered extremely dangerous. Then get me the Albany Police Department. Ask for Lieutenant O'Rourke."

FIFTEEN

||||||||||||||||||||||||||||||||||||||||

As soon as O'Rourke returned to the office after talking to Koblenz, he arranged for a plainclothes detective to watch the man's house. Although O'Rourke didn't have any evidence that would cause Koblenz to be a prime suspect, he was the best lead they had. The detective reported in shortly after six that Koblenz had arrived home, and O'Rourke asked him to keep watch all night.

Myers ran Koblenz' name through all the records they had on Randall Tucker, but there was no connection. O'Rourke then contacted Joyce Tucker. She didn't recognize the name either.

O'Rourke had asked Koblenz for more information about Fleming's history. Koblenz said that once Fleming found out that he was HIV positive, he immediately changed his ways. No more late night dalliances with men he barely knew. A year or so after that, Koblenz had heard that Fleming started living with Jonathan Grace. Koblenz said that he believed there were other men that contracted HIV from Fleming, but he didn't have any idea who they were. It would be difficult to track down the names now, so many years later.

O'Rourke filled in the State Police on the Koblenz interview and then called Elaine Furlani.

"I'm intrigued by the idea that Koblenz or someone else that had an affair with Fleming years ago could be the killer," Dr. Furlani said. "Revenge for contracting HIV could be a powerful motive."

"But Randall Tucker doesn't appear to be a homosexual, so the HIV angle doesn't work with that murder."

"Let me think about that. I'm on my way home now, but I'll call you if I get any ideas."

It was late, and O'Rourke thought about going home himself. He decided to call the kids before they went to bed. When he called Ellen's house, his daughter answered the phone. He told Lauren that it might still be a little while before he could have Tyler and her overnight again. Although she tried to hide it, he could sense the disappointment in her voice. *Sometimes this job really sucks.*

O'Rourke was shutting down his computer when Valente, who was working the late shift, told him that he had a call on his line from Colonie PD. It seemed odd that he would get such a call at this hour. O'Rourke had Valente transfer the call to him.

"This is O'Rourke."

"Lieutenant, this is Sergeant Vince D'Alessandro. We met regarding a case a few years back. I've seen the details in the papers about this double homicide of yours and we may have found something of interest to you."

O'Rourke vaguely recalled the sergeant from the past case. He remembered him as being intelligent and efficient. "Go on."

"We're investigating a B&E and attempted assault that just occurred less than an hour ago. A private home in South Colonie. The perp appeared to be after a teenage girl. He ran off but left something behind that seems to tie in to your case."

"What would that be?"

"A scalpel. It appears to have blood on it."

O'Rourke sat up straight in his chair.

"We'll be right there."

O'Rourke got some more details and took down the directions to the home. He arrived there with Valente as quickly as he could. Sergeant D'Alessandro, a stocky man in his forties with jet-black hair, was speaking with some other officers and came over as soon as they arrived. He showed O'Rourke and Valente the small evidence bag with the scalpel in it and then took them around to the side of the house. The Colonie police had placed a large light there to illuminate the entire area.

"The scalpel was found right there," D'Alessandro said, pointing to a spot on the ground near the side door to the garage. "We've pieced together that the perp must have fallen before he broke into the house. The girl thought she heard a noise just before the break in. He must have dropped both his gun and the scalpel then. He was wearing a hooded sweatshirt, so they could have fallen out of the open pocket. A neighbor said he saw the perp on the way out, looking around on the ground in this area. The perp found his gun and ran toward the park, but he left the scalpel behind."

D'Alessandro handed O'Rourke the evidence. O'Rourke peered closely at the scalpel through the clear bag. The thin brown crust on the end of it definitely looked like dried blood. The scalpel appeared sharp enough to easily cut through human tissue.

Valente visibly shuddered. "Gives me the creeps thinking about what he did with that," he said.

"We don't know for sure that the scalpel is related to the

Albany murders," D'Alessandro said.

"How often do you find a scalpel near a crime scene? I never have," O'Rourke replied. "I'll bet you a steak dinner that it was the one used in the murders."

O'Rourke handed the bag back to D'Alessandro. "Sergeant, I know it's your jurisdiction but if you don't mind, I'd like to send this to the state police to have them test the blood on this as soon as possible. If it matches the blood type of one of the victims, we'll know we have a solid lead."

"No problem. We don't mind cooperating on something like this. I'll just have you sign a form later."

"I appreciate it. Did your men find anyone in the park?"

"No. There's a parking area not too far from where he ran into the park. He probably had a car waiting there and took off before we even got here."

"Probably. Did you say that the girl is still in the house?"

"Yup. We've got the witness from next door there too. You can talk to both of them."

Before he went inside, O'Rourke called Dale Mitchell's home phone number. He was in bed but his wife was still up and woke him.

"I hope this is important," he told O'Rourke with a yawn. "You interrupted my beauty sleep."

"Forget it. It's not working," O'Rourke replied.

"Screw you."

"Look, I need a favor." He briefly explained the events of the evening and asked Mitchell if he could have a test done on the scalpel.

"I'll call the forensic lab at the State Office Campus and they'll be waiting," Mitchell said. "It'll be a little while before we can get DNA results, but they should be able to get the blood type tonight. Why don't you have one of the Colonie cops run it over there now?"

"Thanks. I owe you one."

"Yeah, you do."

O'Rourke, Valente and D'Alessandro walked through the garage to the kitchen of the home. O'Rourke eyed the hole in the door, which had been made by the fire extinguisher that now stood on the garage floor. After confirming that it had been dusted for prints, he lifted the extinguisher up to shoulder level. The girl had told D'Alessandro that the attacker had hit the door with it twice. Based on the height of the hole in the door, he would have had to lift the extinguisher over his shoulders.

"This thing is very heavy and that's a pretty solid door," O'Rourke said. "The guy made that hole in the door with just two blows. He must be very strong."

D'Alessandro nodded. "The girl's lucky," he said.

Inside, the kid that witnessed the attacker, Sean Chen, sat at the kitchen table talking with a Colonie cop. O'Rourke introduced Valente and himself to Chen, and asked him to wait until they spoke to Ashley Morton first. Chen, who was sobering up with a cup of black coffee, was fine with that.

Ashley Morton was in the living room, sitting between her parents. Her mother, Loretta Morton, still had her jacket on. She was holding Ashley's hand. Ashley, a young petite girl, had been crying and had mascara streaked under her eyes, which made her look like a ten year old that had gotten into her mother's makeup. Ron Morton sat on the other side of her, clenching and unclenching his fists. O'Rourke imagined that Morton was picturing what he would do if Ashley's attacker was there in the room.

"Ashley, I'm Lieutenant O'Rourke and this is Detective Valente. Mr. and Mrs. Morton, we'd like to ask Ashley some questions, if you don't mind."

The Morton's got up and shook hands with O'Rourke. "I heard someone say you're from the Albany Police Department," said Mr. Morton. "Why are they involved?"

"We believe that Ashley's assailant may also be a suspect in a crime committed in Albany."

"Ashley's very upset," Mrs. Morton said. "She's already told the story to the other officers. Can't this wait?"

"It's OK, mom," Ashley said with annoyance.

"It's important that we get some information about the attacker as soon as possible," O'Rourke said to Mrs. Morton. "I've already got the basic facts from the other officers. I'll try not to repeat the same questions."

"Fine," Mrs. Morton said, obviously not fine with it.

"Ashley, you said the man was wearing a hooded sweatshirt, dark pants, gloves, and a ski mask. Is there anything else you can tell us about him?"

"I'm not sure. It all happened so quickly."

"You said he was tall. Do you know how tall?"

"Well, I think he was at least as tall as my dad."

"I'm six one," Ron Morton interjected.

"I realize that his face and hands were covered, Ashley, but could you tell if he was white or black?"

"He was definitely white."

"How do you know that?"

"He grabbed me right here," Ashley replied, pointing to her left ankle. "When he reached for my leg, I could see his arm. You know, between his sweatshirt and his glove. I don't think I'm gonna get that friggin' sight out of my head for a while."

"So he had light skin."

"Well, yeah," she replied rudely. "That's what I just said."

This girl has a real attitude. But O'Rourke could ignore it for now. He needed the information. He held his arm out next to Valente's. Valente had an olive complexion, quite a bit darker than O'Rourke's lighter skin.

"Light like Detective Valente's or light like mine?"

"More like yours. His skin wasn't dark at all."

"What about his build? Was he heavy, medium build, or thin?"

"It's hard to tell. His sweatshirt was baggy. Definitely not heavy though. Either average or on the thin side. Like Mark."

"Who's Mark?"

"Mark Dannon. My boyfriend. He's on the high school basketball team."

Interesting. "Is there anything else you can tell us about the attacker?"

"Well, I can tell you that he's strong because he had a pretty good grip on my ankle."

"That was just before you kicked him?"

"Yeah. Right in the face. I hope that sucker's got a black eye!"

Sean Chen was on his third cup of black coffee when O'Rourke and Valente sat down at the kitchen table to talk with him. Chen's eyes were open a bit wider than before, but O'Rourke could still tell he had been partying all night.

"Sergeant D'Alessandro tells me you got a pretty good view of the attacker," O'Rourke said.

"Yeah. But he was all covered up with dark clothes and a mask, so that probably doesn't help much."

"Could you tell how big he was?"

"Tall. I would say over six feet."

"What else you can tell me about him?"

"He can run pretty fast. He was really moving. At least, before he heard me."

"Then he turned toward you?"

"For a second. He had the gun in his hand and at first, I thought he was going to shoot me. But then, he just turned around and started running again, and hopped the fence."

"You're lucky. He probably realized you weren't a threat to him," Valente said.

Chen looked at the two officers as if seeing them for the first time. "A threat? I thought he was just some guy breaking into a house. Hey, how come there's so many of you detectives here, anyway? Who was that guy?"

"A burglar. It's just routine," O'Rourke answered.

"Routine, my ass," Chen said belligerently. "What the hell is going on around here?"

"Just settle down."

"Hey, man, I deserve an explanation. There's a ton of cops around and you guys are acting like you're after the Unabomber!"

O'Rourke needed to get the kid to cooperate. "You're a little young to know who the Unabomber was. I don't think I saw your identification. How old are you, anyway?"

The question surprised Chen. "What? I'll, uh, be twenty next month."

O'Rourke stood up straight in front of Chen. "The legal drinking age is 21 in this state. I'm guessing there are quite a few other underage youths next door that were drinking. It would be a shame for you and all of them to get arrested, if you catch my drift."

"Yes, I do," Chen said, his voice quieter now. "Sir."

"I think we can come to an arrangement. You can answer the

rest of our questions. Then, we can call some cabs and get all your friends home safely. No arrests, no hassle. In return, you keep that Unabomber talk to yourself. If anyone asks, it was just a routine break-in. Right?"

Chen nodded meekly. "Right."

Later, O'Rourke and Valente spoke to the two officers, Riley and Cole, who first arrived at the house with Ron Morton.

"So, what was that all about at the auto repair shop?" O'Rourke asked.

"The back window was broken, which caused the alarm to go off, which then automatically notifies Colonie PD," Cole said.

"And Mr. Morton," Riley added. "He works for McCann Security. His pager goes off at the same time we get notified. We got there just before him."

"What happened then?"

"He had a key to the building. We went inside and made sure no one was in there. There was a small rock on the floor that someone tossed through the back window. Probably some kids."

"Was there anyone around?"

"Just some neighbors. There are a few houses near the store. The alarm was loud enough that some of them heard it. A few people were standing around watching us. We told them it was just a broken window, and they went home."

"Then what?"

"We had some paperwork for Mr. Morton to complete. We were just about done when his daughter called him."

"How long was it from the time you were notified of the alarm going off until the time he got the phone call?"

Riley pulled out a small note pad from his back pocket and did some calculating. "47 minutes."

"And it took you, what, ten minutes to get here from there?"

"About nine. We were hauling ass," he said, grinning.

"So," O'Rourke said, "let's suppose that it was the attacker who broke the store window. He had this all planned out ahead of time to get Mr. Morton out of the house. Let's say he had a car parked in the back lot of the store. He would then have had to drive from there to a parking area in the Crossings, walk through the park in the dark, and go from the park to the house all in about 47 minutes. I guess he would have had just barely about enough time to do that."

"There's a problem with that," Cole said. "One of the neighbors I spoke with at the store said that she went outside as soon as she heard the alarm. She didn't see a car leave at all. If the car came out of the parking lot, she would have seen it."

"That's one reason we initially assumed that it was kids that broke the window," Riley said. "They could have run off through the woods in back of the store. The wooded area comes out on the next street over."

"The attacker could have done that and had a car parked there," O'Rourke said.

"That's assuming it was the attacker that broke the window," Valente said. "Maybe it was just kids that broke the window at the store and it was just a coincidence."

"I don't think so. According to Sergeant D'Alessandro, Mrs. Morton is usually out of the house only one night a week, on Thursdays. I think the attacker intentionally chose tonight to break the window to get Mr. Morton out of the house as well."

"Maybe the attacker had an accomplice break the window."

"If the attacker is the guy we're after, he works alone. At least so far."

D'Alessandro walked up to the group. "I heard what you

were saying. There may be another problem with your time line. There's only one parking area on this side of the Crossings, the South Lot. The only other parking lots are way on the other side of the park. There's no way the attacker could have run to the house in that amount of time from those other lots. He would have either had to park in the South Lot or somewhere on a side street."

"So how is that a problem?"

"I just spoke to one of our patrolmen. He drives into the lots on occasion, to check them out. Kids tend to congregate there in the dark, drinking or smoking pot. He happened to drive through the South Lot just about the same time the house was broken into. There were no cars in the lot."

"So the attacker probably parked on the street, somewhere on this side of the park, and gone in from there."

"Yeah. But that's risky. In Colonie, everybody has a driveway. People notice when cars are parked on the street."

O'Rourke recalled how no one had seen a car parked in or near the store where Tucker was killed. And the sole witness who had seen the attacker leave Fleming's building didn't see the man get into a car there either. Valente must have been thinking the same thing.

"The guy's a phantom," Valente said.

Ron Morton came into to the kitchen to get a glass of water for Ashley, and O'Rourke took the opportunity to speak to him alone. "How well do you know Mark Dannon?"

"A little bit. He's seventeen. Going into his senior year like Ashley. He's been going out with her for a few months," Morton said. "I don't know how long that will last, though. I heard he tends to go from one girl to the next."

"Has she seen him this week?"

"Not since Sunday. He's been busy with basketball practice every night, she told us. But they text back and forth a lot." Morton put down the glass of water. "You think he was the attacker?"

"I'm just trying to follow every lead."

Morton looked at O'Rourke with a thoughtful expression. "You're asking a lot of questions for a case that's out of your jurisdiction. I'm going to ask you a question and I hope you can give me a straight answer."

O'Rourke knew what was coming. "I'll give it to you straight. As long as you promise not to repeat it to anyone. Including your wife."

Morton nodded. "Especially my wife."

He took a deep breath and asked his question. "Does this have anything to do with those murders of the photographer and that assemblyman?"

"I think it's connected. But we're not certain yet. We found an item outside your house that we have reason to believe may have been used in the murders."

Morton looked toward the living room. His wife and daughter were arguing about something. Not paying him any attention.

"But what would my daughter have to do with that," he whispered.

"That's what we're trying to figure out. Did you or your wife or daughter know Mr. Tucker or Bernard Fleming?"

"I certainly didn't. And I'm sure Loretta or Ashley would have mentioned it after we saw it on the news if they knew one of them."

Morton looked at O'Rourke pleadingly. "So what do we do now? Wait for him to attack her again?"

O'Rourke put his hand on Morton's shoulder. "Let me give you a piece of advice. Take your family and stay in a motel for a few nights. Somewhere remote; at least twenty miles from here, where someone wouldn't find you easily. We could station a police car outside your house for a while, but I think it would be safer if your family went somewhere else. I'm sure that we can get one of the police agencies to spring for the tab. And don't tell anyone except the police where you're staying."

Morton nodded. "I'll just tell my wife that the police are afraid the attacker will return. But I won't mention the murders."

O'Rourke looked at the beeper on Morton's belt. "You do security work. Do you own a gun?"

"Yeah. I don't carry it to work, but I have one. If you work for a security company, it's not hard to get a permit."

"Good. I think you'll all be fine. But just to be on the safe side, bring the gun with you."

Valente had been talking with D'Alessandro. None of the cops had found anyone in or around the park that had seen anything unusual. It was late, though, so they would try again in the morning.

As Valente and O'Rourke rode back to the Albany station, O'Rourke filled Valente in on his conversation with Mr. Morton. "If Ashley's attacker is our guy," O'Rourke said, "we know he's fast and strong."

"So he could be an athlete," Valente said.

"Right - which makes it important that we talk to Mark Dannon. Run his name to see if he has any kind of juvenile record. We'll also check him against the names we've accumulated in relation to the two victims."

"You really think this kid could be our man?"

"I don't know. But I'll tell you one thing. I played some hoop in high school. And I know that there's no basketball practice in July."

O'Rourke's cell phone rang. It was Dale Mitchell.

"The lab checked the blood type on the scalpel," Mitchell said. "There were two distinctive blood types found on it. A-Positive and AB-negative. Guess what two people happen to have those blood types?"

"Randall Tucker and Bernard Fleming."

"You got it."

"So Ashley Morton's attacker was definitely the person that killed Randall Tucker and Bernard Fleming. The question is: what do a black store owner, a gay assemblyman, and a suburban high school girl possibly have in common?"

"That sounds like the beginning of a bad joke," Mitchell said.

"Yeah. Now we just have to figure out the punch line."

Back home now, the tall man looked down at his notebook. It annoyed him to see Ashley Morton's name there, still not crossed out. The little slut had ruined his plans. He had expected her to be in her bedroom upstairs. When she opened the door to the garage and switched on the light, it caught him by surprise and he hadn't reacted quickly enough. He should have been able to kill her once he had her by the ankle, but she moved quicker than he had expected and the kick to his face stunned him for just a second. The fortunate thing is he had escaped without incident, other than that neighbor seeing him. But the tall man's face had been covered so there was no way he could be identified. He had briefly thought about eliminating the witness. But that wouldn't be right. The neighbor had done nothing to deserve that. He was an innocent.

The tall man looked at his face in the mirror. The kick had caught him in the cheekbone. There was a small bruise there, but it could be concealed with some make-up. He didn't need anyone at work noticing it.

He thought about the ramifications of the night's events. The police would probably just assume the incident was an attempted attack on the girl by some random deviant. They don't know what the girl has done – the *slut* that she was. How he wished he had been able to complete his mission – to kill her and write that four-letter word, "SLUT" in large letters on her bedroom wall.

The tall man went through his hooded sweatshirt to put his things away. He removed the knife and the can of spray paint. But the scalpel wasn't in the pocket. He checked his other pockets. It wasn't there either. Perhaps he had put it in his backpack.

He combed through his backpack, carefully at first, then urgently. It wasn't there either. *What the hell had happened to the scalpel?*

He mentally retraced his steps. *The gun had fallen out of my pocket before I entered the garage. After I tripped over the trash barrel. Had the scalpel fallen out then also?*

Could the scalpel possibly be traced back to me??

He took a deep breath, then another. *Let me think this through. I didn't clean the scalpel off after using it in the last two missions. There was no need to. The people I used it on were not going to be developing an infection.*

That means there is blood on the scalpel. Tucker and Fleming's blood. The black bastard and the asshole.

If the police find the scalpel, they can determine that it was the same one used on those two. But so what? They can't link the scalpel to me. None of my DNA will be on it. I've never handled it without wearing gloves.

So there was no way they should be able to trace it all back to him. Calmer now, he looked at his notebook once again. He put a circle around Morton's name. He would have to get back to her later. The police will be watching her house now.

The tall man went to his computer desk. In the top left hand drawer, there was a plastic bag containing three more identical scalpels. He took one out, wrapped it in a small hand towel, and put it in his backpack to replace the one he lost. Like a Boy Scout, the tall man was always prepared.

SIXTEEN

||||||||||||||||||||||||||||||||||||||||||

O'Rourke leaned over Ginny Dixon's sleeping form to look at his alarm clock. He was surprised to see it was already eight AM. Ginny had come over an hour earlier and suggested a morning jog. O'Rourke suggested a better alternative. They had decided to go with O'Rourke's suggestion.

O'Rourke was tired, working on about four hours sleep after staying at the station late the previous night. After returning with Valente, he had contacted the detective that was watching Koblenz' house. Koblenz never left his house. O'Rourke told the detective to take off; Koblenz was just another dead end.

O'Rourke had then contacted the Colonie Chief of Police and asked if Colonie PD could keep watch on the Morton house. The chief told O'Rourke that Colonie PD had been contacted by the State Police who had arranged for the family to stay at a motel over 20 miles away out in Schoharie, and gave him the name and address of the place. O'Rourke convinced the chief to keep an unmarked car near the Morton house anyway, in case the attacker decided to return there. Just to be on the safe side, O'Rourke also contacted the sheriff's department in Schoharie County and they agreed to station an unmarked vehicle outside of the motel room for protection. He would have Myers and Oquendo interview the Mortons further at the motel in the morning.

O'Rourke had all the staff that had still been around at that hour check the names of family members and friends that they had obtained from the Mortons against the files that had been accumulated on Tucker and Fleming, which were now getting sizeable. Sandy Bernstein's group would do a more extensive search this morning, but O'Rourke had wanted to get started on it as soon as possible. Their target had committed three attacks in six days' time. Who knew when the next attack would be?

The final thing that O'Rourke had done last night at the office was to pull out Dr. Furlani's card and dial her cell number. He left a voice mail for her with a summary of the attack, asking her to call him in the morning.

Now, O'Rourke climbed out of bed and hit the shower. By the time he has showered, shaved and dressed, Ginny was up, making a pot of coffee.

Over coffee, O'Rourke told her about the dream he had the night before last - the one where Ginny told him to go the right way. He decided to leave the part with the other half-naked women out of the explanation.

"I'm a big believer in dreams," Ginny said. "I'm kind of into that stuff; psychic phenomenon and things like that interest me. I've been into it since college, but I didn't want to say anything to you about it yet. Some people are a little funny about that."

"Well, I've had some strange dreams over the years, but this one – it felt so real. Maybe it means something."

"If I told you to go the right way in the dream, I think it means to follow your conscience or something like that. If you're faced with a moral decision on this case, do what you think is right."

"I'll keep that in mind."

He then filled her in on the previous day's events, not needing to tell her to keep it confidential.

"So why would the same man kill a black photographer and an HIV positive senator, and then attack a teenage girl," Ginny asked him. "What's the connection?"

"That's the million dollar question. I refuse to believe he's picking these people totally at random. If he was, we wouldn't have a prayer in catching him. By the way, he's an assemblyman, not a senator. I thought you were a school teacher," O'Rourke said jokingly.

Ginny stuck her tongue out at O'Rourke. "I don't teach social studies, smartass." She put a cup of coffee on the table in front of him. "And don't be so negative. Random or not, you'll catch him. He'll slip up somehow."

"Maybe," O'Rourke said as he put on his jacket. "But this guy's smart. He plans things down to the smallest detail. He had everything figured just right last night."

"But he still didn't get the girl. He's not infallible."

O'Rourke finished his coffee and kissed her on the cheek. "I like that word. *Infallible.* I guess you are a teacher after all."

On his way to work, O'Rourke drove the Jaguar to Sparky's Auto Shop. Sparky, a short muscular man who reminded O'Rourke of a miniature Charles Bronson, was in the parking lot talking to two men who were there to fix the window. O'Rourke introduced himself and asked if he could look around, and Sparky said sure.

As O'Rourke looked around, he noticed that the parking lot had a nice shiny smooth appearance. But a few feet outside the broken window, there was a stone on the ground that stood out against the smooth surface.

"Did you just get this lot blacktopped?" he asked Sparky.

"Just two days ago. Looks nice, doesn't it?"

"Nice," O'Rourke agreed. "Is this the stone that went through the window?" He thought that Sparky might have tossed it outside.

"What? No. That stone's still inside."

O'Rourke pulled out a pair of plastic gloves from his jacket pocket and put them on. He doubted he would be able to get a fingerprint from the stone, but it couldn't hurt. He picked the stone up with the gloves, and put it in a small evidence bag that he kept in his pocket. He would have someone get the other stone inside as well.

He walked around some more. About fifteen feet from the window, toward the wooded area in the back of the lot, was a small clump of mud on the ground that also looked out of place. O'Rourke knelt down to take a closer look. It looked like it might have come off the bottom of a shoe. He looked at the window from where he was kneeling. He imagined that if he intended to throw a stone hard enough to break the window, this would be about where he might stand. And he would have a few stones with him just in case the first one didn't break the window. He looked beyond the store. If it was dark out, he wouldn't be visible from the street in this exact spot. Plus, from here, he could then turn around and run, and be in the back woods in no time.

As he was mulling it over, a Colonie Police car pulled into the lot. A couple officers came over.

"Judging by that red Jaguar over there, you must be Lieutenant O'Rourke," one of them said.

"My reputation precedes me."

"Sergeant D'Alessandro asked us to check out the parking lot for evidence. It looks like you beat us to it."

"Just by a little bit." He pulled the evidence bag with the stone in it from his pocket and handed it to the cop.

"This was on the ground about a yard outside the window. My guess is our man tossed it at the window from about this spot, but he didn't throw it hard enough. Then, he threw a second one that went through. It's still inside. Sparky may have already handled it. Put some gloves on before you pick it up and have both of the stones checked for prints."

O'Rourke pointed to the dirt on the ground. "And get someone to analyze this. Probably not enough to tell us anything though. I'm guessing that the guy picked up some mud on his shoes from wherever he got these stones."

As O'Rourke walked to his car, the cop called out to him. "Hey, who are you, Sherlock Holmes?" he asked jokingly.

O'Rourke recalled that Ginny had called him a knight a couple of days ago. "You're about five hundred years off," he answered.

From Sparky's, O'Rourke drove the car to the end of a street that bordered the Crossings, not far from the lot where D'Alessandro said the cop had checked out. He used the quickest route possible, but without speeding. There were several traffic lights on the route and it took him about fifteen minutes. That was significantly longer than the police took the night before, but they were moving fast with the siren on, going through the lights.

O'Rourke stopped the car there and tried to figure out the timetable. The attacker couldn't really be sure how long Mr. Morton was going to be away from the house. But an hour would seem to be a reasonable guess as a minimum. So, he would need to get from Sparky's to the Morton house as quickly as possible. He had to drive; even an athlete couldn't run or jog that distance in the time between the alarm going off and the time Ashley called her father. Once at the Morton's house, the attacker needed enough time to kill the girl, use the scalpel on her in some way, probably paint a message on the wall, and then get away. So why take the extra time to go through the Crossings? Why not just park near the Morton home?

Because his car would be more likely to be identified later if he parked near the home. Maybe he even knew there was a party in the neighborhood that night, with potential witnesses. Or maybe the attacker was someone the Mortons or their neighbors might know, so he couldn't leave his car nearby.

So, he parks on a street near the Crossings and enters the park from there. But the Crossings is dark at night. Full of trees. If he parks too far away, it would take forever to get through, even with a flashlight. So, like D'Alessandro said, he parks on a street somewhere around here.

Or maybe he didn't park on the street at all.

O'Rourke called the Colonie Police Chief from his car.

"We're checking with residents of all the homes around the Crossings, to see if they noticed a strange car around," the chief said. "Then, we'll branch out further. So far, nothing. But there's a ton of houses left."

"I had an idea. We've been assuming that the attacker parked his car on the street. But what if he lives around there and just pulled into his own driveway after he got back from Sparky's? He could have then walked into the Crossings from there."

The chief hadn't considered that. "Great point. I'll have my men question people to see if they noticed any neighbors coming home around that time."

O'Rourke then started the car and turned around. He noticed several people on the street or from their windows looking at his Jaguar, a strange car that had been parked at the end of this quiet suburban street where everyone parks in a driveway. If the attacker had parked his car on a street near here last night, someone might have seen it and remembered it, and would contact the police soon. O'Rourke hoped it was that easy. He hoped Ginny was right – maybe the guy's not infallible.

When O'Rourke arrived at the station, he was surprised to see Elaine Furlani waiting there for him. Her expensive, form-fitting suit looked out of place in the drab squad room. Several detectives in the office were eyeing her without trying to be too obvious. He got Furlani and himself a cup of coffee and ushered her into his office.

Furlani reviewed all of the information that he had on the latest attack. "So," she said, "you're certain that the attacker is the same person that killed Fleming and Tucker."

"I'd say the blood on the scalpel confirms it. What do you make of this new attack?"

"I'm surprised. Not that he attacked again; I was pretty certain that would happen. But I'm surprised at the choice of victim and that this attack occurred so soon after the last one. In many serial killings, the subject has a compulsion to kill. An almost sexual compulsion that builds up inside him over time, until he needs to release it. But this is happening too quickly to fit that pattern. This is more calculating. Like he has a specific agenda."

"Like a list or something?"

"Yes. A pre-planned list of victims. He's got some rationale, however twisted it may be in our view, which he uses to pick them. And our only clue to that may be those messages he leaves on the wall. It's too bad we don't have a message this time."

O'Rourke nearly choked on his coffee. "Yeah, too bad that Ashley Morton was able to fight him off so he didn't get the chance to leave one," he said sharply.

Dr. Furlani's face reddened a bit. "I didn't mean it that way. You're of course more personally involved because you met the victim... that is the attempted victim...than I am. It's just that I deal only with the data and what that tells us about our subject. This missing bit of information could have been very valuable."

O'Rourke decided that there was no benefit to pointing out to her how cold hearted that sounded. "OK, so what about this intended victim? Why was the killer after her?"

"Unless your men find some evidence that she knew either of the other victims, there's no way to tell at this point. I'll have to take the data from this attack and analyze it."

"Could this be a revenge thing? Is there something the victims might have somehow done to the killer?"

"It doesn't seem likely that the three individuals did anything in concert with each other. But perhaps, each of them did something individually that offended him."

"So they probably had contact with him before the murders?"

"Not necessarily." Dr. Furlani was toying with her hair, thinking things through. "Fleming was a politician, quoted often in the media. I wonder if our subject follows the news closely. I suppose I'm getting back to the right wing agenda thing again, but maybe he was set off by some remarks they made or something like that. It might be interesting to see if Mr. Tucker ever made any public comments. We could see if he attended any community meetings or was ever quoted in the newspaper. Ashley Morton is in high school. Was she involved with the school newspaper or any social programs in the community? Or possibly a church group that did community outreach? Those might be some avenues to investigate."

O'Rourke wrote that all down. "What about the boyfriend

– Mark Dannon? I think he's lying to Ashley about going to basketball practice."

"He's an unlikely suspect. The man we're after is apparently fast and strong like Dannon, but I don't believe that he's in high school. That doesn't fit the profile. Also, I believe our subject is someone who has difficulty with the opposite sex, especially in a romantic way. I would be surprised if he dates at all."

"But you wouldn't completely rule Dannon out."

"No. My profiles are based on common patterns found in serial killings. But every once in a while, some new pattern comes along. The infamous killer Ted Bundy, for example, did not fit many of the common characteristics of a serial killer at all."

"So, what you're saying is you can't really rule any personality type out as the killer," O'Rourke said, getting frustrated. "If that's the case, then I'm not sure how valuable your…"

Before O'Rourke could finish, there was a knock on his office door. Booker popped his head in.

"We called Mark Dannon's home. He lives in an apartment with his mother. She said she and her son are home now if we want to go talk with them."

O'Rourke got up and handed Dr. Furlani the folder with the information from the attack on Ashley Morton. "Have one of the detectives copy this for you," he said. "We can meet again after Detective Booker and I talk to Dannon."

Dr. Furlani hesitated. "Lieutenant, if you think he's a suspect, I'd like to go with you to interview Mark Dannon."

O'Rourke looked closely at Elaine Furlani. It was unlikely that having her at the interview would really be helpful; she would have access to all the information later. O'Rourke had seen the detectives out in the hallway ogling her and, truth be told, he was having a hard enough time keeping his eyes off of the doctor himself. He considered the type of distraction Furlani might be on a teenage boy who apparently has quite the history with the opposite sex.

"Actually," O'Rourke said, "it's probably more useful to us right now if you look over these records."

Dr. Furlani looked annoyed, but didn't say anything. O'Rourke wanted to get to Dannon's house, so he decided not to worry about it.

On the way out of the station, O'Rourke and Booker ran into Valente, who had several documents in his hands. "I've got those phone company records we asked for," Valente said without much enthusiasm. "We found the phone where the calls that were made to both Bryan Goldstein and Regina Tucker regarding Saturday schedules were placed from. A call was also placed from that phone to the Randall Tucker's store on the day he was killed."

"You don't sound too excited," O'Rourke said. "The phone could belong to the killer."

Valente showed the papers to O'Rourke. "Not quite," he said.

Twenty minutes later, O'Rourke, Booker and Valente were standing outside a Stewarts convenience and ice cream store, located about three miles from Central Studio. They were looking at a pay phone that was on the outside wall of the store, under a sign that said "Phone". Although phones like these were much less common than they used to be, a few still existed in Albany at gas stations and convenience stores.

"Maybe the phone company made a mistake," Valente said.

"Actually," Booker said, "this is the perfect place for the killer to make the calls."

"How so?" O'Rourke asked him.

"Calls from most cell phones can be traced, just like calls from land lines. There are some cell phones from which calls can't be traced, but not everyone is aware of that or which cell phones are safe to use. The killer may have thought he would be safer not using a cell phone."

"But someone could have seen and remembered him using this pay phone."

"Possibly. But how often do you go in and out of stores like these? Probably pretty often. Do you ever pay attention to who's using the phone?"

"Good point."

"And this particular phone is located outside at the back of the store. A very inconspicuous spot. And I don't see any store cameras out here."

"Still," O'Rourke said, "it can't hurt to talk to the guys that work here. Maybe someone remembers something. Tony, why don't you start on that now? Booker and I can go talk to Dannon and pick you up later."

O'Rourke wasn't too hopeful that Valente would be able to get any useful information. Most of the people that worked at Stewarts were part-timers. Chances are the same person wasn't on duty when the killer made the three calls. And even if they were, the phone wasn't visible from the inside of the store. Unless someone was out having a smoke, they wouldn't have seen the caller. While O'Rourke drove the Jag to the Dannon's home, he had Booker call Colonie High School. Fortunately, it was a Friday morning and summer school was in session so he was able to talk to a live person.

"You were right," he said to O'Rourke after the call. "Dannon was lying to Ashley Morton. There's no basketball practice in the summer."

The Dannon's apartment was located in a middle-income complex near the airport, a few miles from the Morton home. The complex had seen better days. Rachel Dannon, a nervous looking woman of about 40 opened the door even before they rang the doorbell.

"Mrs. Dannon," Booker said, "I'm Detective Booker. I spoke to you on the phone earlier. This is Lieutenant O'Rourke."

She invited them in and offered them coffee, which they politely declined. They walked into the living room, where Mark Dannon, a handsome tall, lanky athletic type with a slick haircut, was sitting on the sofa. His pants were low around his waist with his underwear showing, a look that O'Rourke thought looked ridiculous on anyone that lived outside the inner city.

"I was sorry to hear that Ashley was attacked," Mrs. Dannon said. "I hope she's all right."

"Fortunately, she is. The attacker ran away before he could harm her," O'Rourke said. "She couldn't identify the attacker. We're interviewing Ashley's acquaintances for information and we'd like to ask Mark some questions."

"Mr. Booker said you were from the Albany Police. Was she attacked in Albany?"

"No. But it may be connected to a case we're working on."

"I see," Mrs. Dannon said, although she still looked confused. "I'm sure Mark will answer any questions you have."

"Ask away," said Mark. Unlike his mom, Mark seemed relaxed and easy going. Although taller than O'Rourke, Mark was much slimmer. He had big hands and feet, like a puppy that was still growing.

"Mark, do you know of anyone who might want to harm Ashley," O'Rourke asked him.

"You said the attacker was a dude, right? I don't know of any dudes who would want to hurt her."

"Meaning what, exactly?"

"Ashley's a big flirt. Not popular with the girls but very popular with the boys. She's gone through a few boyfriends over the years. The guys like her."

"You don't think any of them would be jealous that she's going out with you now?"

"No. Maybe a few girls might be jealous of Ashley; you know how girls are. But no jealous ex-boyfriends."

"You sound pretty sure of that."

Mark looked uncomfortable and turned to his mother. "Mom, could you get me a soda or something from the kitchen?"

"Wait until we're done talking with the officer," his mother said, not picking up on the hint.

O'Rourke said: "I think I will have that cup of coffee now, Mrs. Dannon, if you don't mind."

Mrs. Dannon finally got the point. "Oh. Oh, yes, of course," she said, going out to the kitchen.

When she was out of earshot, Mark continued. "The thing with Ashley is she doesn't stay with any one guy that long. I've probably gone out with her longer than anyone. I know her ex-boyfriends. They're all into sports, like me. It's not like they were in love with Ashley. I think they all…you know…they went out with her for one thing and they got what they wanted and moved on. There's plenty of other eager girls in school, if you catch my drift."

"Is that what you're planning to do?" O'Rourke asked. "Move on?"

Mark shrugged. "Hey, why not? I'm a young guy. I'm not ready to settle down yet."

Mrs. Dannon approached them slowly with a cup of coffee

and a soda. O'Rourke nodded, indicating it was all right for her to come back now.

"Now this is just a routine question we're asking everyone," O'Rourke lied. "Where were you last night? Between eight and eleven."

"I was home. Here. I was watching the Yankees game the whole time."

"Were you alone?"

"Yup. Just me," he answered.

"I work nights," Mrs. Dannon explained. "I'm a single mother. I waitress at Tony's Place, the restaurant down on Shaker Road."

O'Rourke knew the place, but it was more of a bar than a restaurant. It was a location visited often by the Colonie PD looking to make late night DWI busts.

"What are your hours there?" O'Rourke asked her.

"I go in around three in the afternoon and leave around 1:00 AM."

"Did you work those hours all this week?"

"Except for Sunday. I have Sunday's off." She smiled weakly. "Mark's father and I are divorced. I don't get nearly enough child support, so I have to work a lot of hours to make ends meet."

"Mark, were you home alone every night this week?"

"Pretty much, yeah. I drove out to the mall in the afternoon a couple times this week to hang out with my friends, but I was home every night."

"He texts me every night to let me know he's OK," said his mother.

From his cell phone, O'Rourke thought. That doesn't mean he was home at the time.

"That's interesting," O'Rourke said. "Ashley Morton said you told her you were at basketball practice every night this week."

Rachel Dannon looked like she was going to wet her pants.

"Are you saying my son is lying? Why are you asking all these questions? You don't think Mark had anything to do with the attack, do you? My son would never hurt anyone. He's only eighteen! My god, he doesn't even like to foul the other kids in basketball!" Her lips started to tremble. "Do we need a lawyer?"

"That's up to you," O'Rourke said. "If you want, you can get a lawyer and we can all talk at the police station."

"Don't worry, mom," Mark said calmly. "We don't need a lawyer. I didn't do anything wrong. I'll answer their questions."

He looked right at O'Rourke, not diverting his eyes at all. If he was a liar, he was a good one. "You know what I told you about the other guys moving on after Ashley? Well, it's my time to move on now. I really don't want to go out with her anymore. So I lied about the basketball practice. It was just an excuse not to go out with her."

That seemed to calm Mrs. Dannon somewhat. But O'Rourke decided he better ask his remaining questions before she asked about a lawyer again.

"Mark, you said you drove to the mall. What kind of car do you have?"

"A 2011 Ford Taurus. It's out in front."

O'Rourke could see it out the window. An unremarkable car, he thought. Not too likely to be noticed if parked on a street.

O'Rourke thought about something that Dr. Furlani had said. "I have one more question. Was Ashley involved in any social issues or political causes? Either at school or in the community?"

Mark Dannon let out a laugh. "Are you kidding? Ashley hardly knows who our president is."

"What about you?"

"I really could care less about politics. My concerns are hoop and girls. Not necessarily in that order."

O'Rourke let Booker complete the rest of the interview, which consisted of getting names of Ashley's former boyfriends and other acquaintances that Mark knew of. On the way to his car, O'Rourke knelt down and examined the tires on the Taurus. They were clean. In fact, it looked like the car had been washed recently.

"The car's clean," Booker said. "Were you thinking about that spot of mud on the ground at Sparky's?"

O'Rourke stood up and wiped off his hands. "Yup. It was worth a shot."

"Dannon's a definite suspect," O'Rourke said in the car. "Since we have the resources, I'd like to put a tail on him."

"I don't know," answered Booker. "Dannon seemed pretty calm and collected. It's hard to picture him as a killer. And why would he attack Ashley?"

"He said he 'moved on'. Maybe he's got a screw loose. Maybe he's trying to get rid of her."

"That doesn't explain Tucker or Fleming though."

"I know. But it bothers me that he lied to Ashley about where he was at night all this week. And he has no real alibi for the night of the murders. He just said he was home alone every night. And most of all, he lied to us about where he was last night."

Booker looked at his notes. "He said he was home last night watching the Yankees game on television between eight and eleven."

O'Rourke pulled out a copy of the Albany Times Union from between the car seats. He handed it to Booker. "Check out the sports section. The Yankees were rained out last night."

They picked up Valente at the Stewarts convenience/ice cream store. He was standing out front, eating a chocolate cone. As O'Rourke figured, Valente said none of the employees remembered anyone using the payphone. O'Rourke and Booker filled Valente in on the interview with Dannon.

"I don't think it was Dannon," said Valente, working on stopping the ice cream from dribbling down the side of his cone. "But I was thinking while I was at Stewarts. I've got a theory for you."

"Uh oh." Valente was well known for his wild theories, often way off base. Against his better judgment, O'Rourke said: "OK, let's have it."

"Porn. It's all porn related."

"You'd better explain that. And please keep your ice cream off the upholstery."

"Dannon said that Ashley's a flirt and sexually active. We know she's good looking and has a fairly good rack on her for a seventeen year old. Not that I look at seventeen year old girls, you know, but it's hard to miss. So, let's say she wants to make some money on the side and gets into making porno videos. She finds Randall Tucker, who runs a photography studio, but maybe does some X-rated videos on the side. Then, something goes wrong. Maybe the killer starred in the movies, and Tucker and Ashley didn't give him a fair cut of the profits. So the guy kills Tucker and then makes it look like some kind of crazy did it. Then, he tries to kill the girl."

"That seems pretty far-fetched," O'Rourke replied, trying not to sound too negative. "Tucker didn't have any equipment in the studio to do video. And besides, Ashley Morton's 'rack' isn't all that big."

"So maybe he did the porn videos in his home. We never did check out his house. And Ashley's rack *is* fairly sizeable."

"All right, then, how does Fleming fit in?"

"I haven't figured that out yet," Valente answered. He thought about that for a minute. "Fleming used to be pretty loose with the guys. Maybe when he was young, he starred in gay porn."

O'Rourke rolled his eyes. "Any other theories?"

"Yeah. Suppose Tucker does passport photos. So let's say that there was this international spy agency…"

SEVENTEEN

IIIIIIIIIIIIIIIIIIIIIIIIIIIIIIIIIIIIII

It was three o'clock and O'Rourke sat in his office, thinking about the case. He wasn't convinced that Dannon was the killer. But at this point, they had no other leads. He had called the Tuckers earlier and asked them if they had ever heard of either Ashley Morton or Mark Dannon. Neither Mrs. Tucker nor Angela recognized the names. He also questioned them about whether Randall Tucker had ever written anything political in nature. He even asked if Tucker had ever done any video, just to satisfy Valente. The answer to all of it was no.

O'Rourke then called Bill Rusk, the State Police contact from New York City. Rusk said they had been checking out Fleming's connections, personal and professional, in the city. They had no solid leads yet but would keep checking.

A while later, O'Rourke poked his head in Captain Grainey's office and filled him in on the morning's interview with Dannon.

"I assigned a guy to watch Dannon's home and follow him if he leaves the apartment," O'Rourke said.

"All right. I guess he's our best suspect. And the chief said we can use as many detectives as we want. But don't use too many uniforms. We need to keep our men on patrol in Arbor Hill. It's still a powder keg there with all the niggers fighting with each other."

This is why I never sit down in his office, O'Rourke thought. *If I get too close to the guy, I feel like I need a shower.*

"The news stations are asking about our progress," Grainey said. "What should I tell them about the attack on the Morton kid?"

"Nothing. We would just cause a panic for no reason."

"Damn it, maybe a panic is what we need. People need to be cautious with this bozo out there."

"They need to be cautious, but not terrified. Panic breeds rash actions. We don't want people shooting their neighbors."

"Well, what can we tell the news hounds then?"

"You can tell them that we're still following up every lead. All available officers are working on this. There's no need to panic, but we would advise vigilance as the killer is still out there. Don't let anyone into your homes that you don't know. Lock your doors, and use a dead bolt if you've got one. If citizens see anyone acting suspicious, they should contact the police."

Grainey was writing it all down. "That's good shit, O'Rourke. You may not be able to catch a killer, but you turn a phrase well."

Later, Dale Mitchell called O'Rourke.

"I spoke to Pete Willis in Counter-Terrorism," Mitchell said. "There's a hate group they're keeping tabs on in upstate New York, but they're located out in the western part of the state. He said they're not the brightest bunch. A mixture of bikers, ex-cons and just plain morons. Not smart enough to do the murders in Albany."

"That's the way I felt about the two guys in Amsterdam," O'Rourke said. "And that was before the second murder and the attack on the Morton girl."

"The Morton girl is what throws me," Mitchell replied. "That makes the whole right-wing agenda angle fall apart. If you ask me, I think what you're dealing with is a good, old-fashioned serial killer picking his victims at random."

"Thanks. That's very reassuring."

"Hey, don't say I never help you out. Seriously, though, the State Police have a lot of data on unresolved serial murders. You can have one of your guys come over here and print out whatever he needs."

"I'll have Derek Booker give you a call."

Mitchell is wrong, O'Rourke thought after he hung up. We've got a serial killer on the loose in Albany. But he's not picking his victims at random. There has to be a connection somewhere. They just have to find it before someone else gets killed.

Oquendo and Myers arrived at the station late in the afternoon and their first stop was O'Rourke's office. "We spent hours talking to the Morton family," Oquendo said. "None of the Mortons could think of anyone who would want to harm Ashley. We've got a complete list of the parents' male friends, neighbors, and business associates, as well as a list of all the boys Ashley knows at school. We even asked Ashley about the names of other boys she might have met, like friends of her boyfriends or guys she's met at parties, but no luck with that. She said she's good with remembering faces, but she's not good with names. Bottom line is she's known a lot of boys but she said none of them harbor a grudge."

"That goes along with what Dannon told us," O'Rourke replied. "She seems to get along well with the boys."

"I'll say," Myers said. "She let us borrow her high school

yearbook, and she circled the pictures of her past boyfriends. There are ten of them."

"Let's see the yearbook," O'Rourke said, and Myers handed it over.

O'Rourke flipped through the pages of the yearbook. Ashley had circled in pencil at least ten head shots of boys, mostly photos of students who, like Mark Dannon, would be seniors in the upcoming semester. According to notes under the photos, most were on the high school basketball team. Tall kids.

Out of curiosity, he flipped through the first few pages until he found who the yearbook photographer was. It wasn't Randall Tucker. Another lead dashed.

He handed the yearbook back to Oquendo. "Do me a favor," he said. "Write down the names of the boys in the circled photos. Get that together as soon as you can. Then you and some of the other detectives contact the kids in the photos and see if they can prove where they were last night. If you can't independently confirm the alibis, visit the boyfriends in person. And talk to some female friends of Ashley's as well. Maybe somebody knows something."

A few minutes later, O'Rourke brought the lists down the street to the Nerd Squad. All five members of the team were there, looking very busy.

"You got more names for us, Steven?" Bernstein asked. "We're swamped as it is. You're really keeping us hopping."

"Yeah, but where's it getting us? We're not getting any results," he said.

"We can't get results if there are no connections between the victims," Megan said testily.

O'Rourke handed Sandy the two lists that he had brought

with him, ignoring Megan. "This might help. The long list is all the friends, acquaintances and relatives of the family. It includes Ashley Morton's friends at school. The other list is her ex-boyfriends. If you still have time after you're done with that, Rosie Oquendo has a yearbook belonging to Ashley. You could add all those names to your database too."

"OK," Sandy said. "But this database is getting big. Chances are we're bound to start getting some matches just because there are so many names. The Albany area's not all that big. Once you get this many names, you're bound to get matches, people that have a passing acquaintance with two of the victims, but the matches will just be coincidental."

"Yeah, but all we need is one match that's not a coincidence."

O'Rourke looked at his watch. It was almost six. "Are you going to be able to run all these names against criminal records today? Tomorrow's Saturday. You guys aren't usually here on the weekend."

Sandy picked up the lists. "Get with the times, Steven," he said to O'Rourke. "We don't have to be here to access the database. We can all work on it from home. I intend to be up most of the night working on this."

O'Rourke noticed Sandy did look very tired. Megan too, for that matter. They both probably had been working late every night at home on this stuff all week. O'Rourke felt bad about his remark about not getting results. He was about to apologize when his cell phone rang. It was Valente. "Boss, you might want to get back over here quick," Valente said.

"What's up?"

"Mark Dannon's on the move."

The Communications Room was in the basement of the Division One station, two floors below O'Rourke's office. The dispatching supervisor on duty, a large woman with a round face, was sitting at a large console talking into a head set to a detective out in the field, Pete Richards. Booker and Valente were seated in front of her, and O'Rourke sat down next to them.

Valente filled O'Rourke in. Richards had been watching the Dannon apartment from his car parked a discreet distance away. A little while ago, a few hours after Mark Dannon's mother left for work, Dannon left the apartment and got into his car. Richards was following him. Dannon had driven from the Colonie apartment complex over to Central Avenue and was now driving down Central toward Albany. The dispatcher was keeping in contact with Richards through the car's phone and they could hear Richards' voice on the speaker as he followed Dannon. "So much for the kid who stays home every night," Valente said.

Booker put his laptop at the end of the desk that the woman was seated at and turned it so Valente and O'Rourke could see. "I patched into the GPS of the car that Detective Richards is driving," the woman said. "You can watch on the computer."

O'Rourke could see a map with a flashing red dot moving east down Central Avenue. The cars were actually only a few miles west of Central Studio. Right where this whole thing started, thought O'Rourke.

"Dannon's not going real fast," Richards was saying over the phone. "But I have to stay back so he doesn't spot me. Traffic's kind of light right now."

"That makes sense," Booker said. "All the state workers clear out of Albany by about four on a Friday afternoon in the summer. Most of the traffic now is on the highway."

"He just turned onto Fuller," Richards continued. Fuller Road was a main route that went past the west side of the State

University Campus, connecting Central to Western Avenue. "I'll let a couple cars get between us."

The three detectives were transfixed by the red dot on the laptop as it moved down the map of Fuller Road. If O'Rourke's dad was still alive, he would have marveled at how far technology had come to allow police to watch someone's movements like this.

The dot reached the end of Fuller and turned left, the display now showing the car heading east on Western Avenue. The cars were now in the city limits of Albany, actually heading in the direction of Division One. "He turned just as the light changed," Richards said. "I didn't want to get stuck at the light since it's a real long one, so I had to speed through the red light. I hope he didn't notice."

O'Rourke wondered where Dannon was heading. He thought about the timing of the three attacks so far. They all had occurred within the last six days, the most recent just yesterday. If Dannon was the attacker, there could be another attack this evening.

"He's not in any hurry," Richards was saying. "He's staying in the slow lane. I think he might be planning to take a right somewhere up ahead."

"That's a quiet residential area. If Dannon gets onto those smaller streets, he'll eventually spot Richards trailing him," O'Rourke said to the others, getting out of his chair. "C'mon, let's get a second car."

O'Rourke, Booker and Valente hurried outside and got an unmarked Camry from the parking lot. A few minutes later, they were on Western Avenue, heading west toward Dannon's car, which would be headed toward them from the opposite direction. O'Rourke decided to have Valente, who Dannon had never seen, do the driving, while the other two sat hunched down in the back. The Camry's car phone had been patched into Richard's car. Richards was still following Dannon's Taurus east on Western. Fortunately, there were a lot of long traffic lights on Western and that had slowed Dannon down.

"He's making a right turn up ahead onto South Manning," Dannon said. "I don't want to follow him onto that street. It's only one lane each way, and he might notice that I've been behind him ever since Colonie."

"Just let him turn and keep going straight," O'Rourke told him. "We're almost to Manning. We'll tail him from here."

O'Rourke saw Richard's car pass by them in the opposite lane just before they got to Manning. Valente took the left onto Manning, a residential tree-lined street. A few seconds later, they could see Dannon's Ford Taurus two blocks ahead.

As they followed, Dannon's car continued on South Manning, past New Scotland Avenue and St. Peter's Hospital. At the end of Manning, Dannon took a right onto Whitehall Road, with Valente staying about a block behind.

"He's probably not going too much further on Whitehall," Valente said. "It wouldn't make sense. If he continues this way, it'll just take him back to New Scotland again."

"Unless he spotted a tail," Booker replied. "He could just be returning home."

"No, I don't think so," O'Rourke said. "He's slowing down."

Dannon put on his turn signal and turned left onto a small side street. O'Rourke knew the street; it was only two blocks long because it ended near where the New York State Thruway passed through the edge of the city. Valente pulled over to the side of Whitehall Road and waited to see how far Dannon went down the side street before he followed. Dannon drove almost to the end before he pulled over to the right side of the street.

Valente waited a minute, then turned onto the small side street.

When they got a half block from the Taurus, O'Rourke noticed a commercial van parked on the side of the street. "We don't want him to notice us," O'Rourke said. "Pull in back of the van."

O'Rourke was sitting in the back seat of the car on the passenger side, so he couldn't see the driver's side of the Taurus past the van in front of them. "What's he doing?" he asked Valente after they sat for a couple of minutes.

"He's just sitting there. Wait, he's getting out of the car now. He's walking around the front of the car toward a white house on the right. You'll see him on your side in a second."

O'Rourke pointed to the glove compartment of the Camry. "There should be a pair of binoculars in there."

Valente pulled out a pair of binoculars and handed them to O'Rourke. O'Rourke watched out of his passenger side window as Dannon came into view a half block away, walking down the driveway toward the white house. O'Rourke trained the binoculars on the windows of the house itself. He wanted to see if anyone was at home. He moved from one window to the next. It was a little difficult to see though the late afternoon glare, but when he got to the last upstairs window that faced him, he thought he saw movement inside.

He looked back at Dannon. Dannon had walked right past the small walkway on his left that led to the front of the house and kept going. He was walking around to the rear of the house.

"I've got a bad feeling about this," Valente said.

"Easy," Booker said. "For all we know, he could be visiting his grandparents or something."

O'Rourke looked through the binoculars at the upstairs window again. There was definitely someone inside, closer to the window now. It was a woman. A young blonde from what

O'Rourke could see. Definitely not Dannon's grandmother.

Dannon got to the rear door of the house. Valente had shifted over to the front passenger seat to get a better look, while Booker was looking over O'Rourke's shoulder.

O'Rourke focused the glasses on Dannon. Dannon looked around to his right and then his left, as if he making sure he wasn't being watched. He tried the doorknob but apparently the door was locked. Dannon then pulled something from his pocket. O'Rourke couldn't quite make it out from his distance away but it was larger than a key. A glint of late afternoon sunlight shone off a shiny metal surface.

"That looks like a knife," Valente said.

O'Rourke pushed open the car door. "Let's go!"

O'Rourke was the first one out of the car and sprinted toward the back door of the white house a half block away. Booker and Valente hadn't reacted as quickly and were a few seconds behind him. Mark Dannon was focused on the door and didn't see O'Rourke coming at first. When O'Rourke was within ten yards of him, Dannon took a quick look his way and then started running away. O'Rourke, though winded, managed to yell out "Stop!"

Dannon didn't stop. The seventeen year old athlete was fast. O'Rourke, breathing hard, knew that if he didn't close in soon, Dannon would easily outrun him and the others. He stepped it up a notch and got within a yard of Dannon. Dannon was starting to reach full stride. It was now or never.

O'Rourke hurled himself through the air like a cornerback making a tackle and managed to grab onto Dannon's legs. They both hit the ground hard. Things were moving fast now. O'Rourke saw Dannon turn toward him. He had something shiny in his right hand. Reflexively, O'Rourke grabbed Dannon's wrist and banged it against the ground hard. The object fell out of his hand. Dannon then shoved O'Rourke hard with his other arm. O'Rourke fell over onto his back. Dannon got back up but O'Rourke, still on the ground, barely managed to grab hold of his pant leg. Dannon started running and his low-riding jeans slipped down before he was able to escape O'Rourke's grip. Booker was coming now, moving fast. Booker hit Dannon from behind and they both went down, Dannon's pants now down around his ankles. Valente had just caught up to all of them when the back door of the white house flew open and the blonde woman burst through the door and yelled, "What the hell are you doing to my boyfriend?"

EIGHTEEN

||||||||||||||||||||||||||||||||||||||

O'Rourke, still on the ground, realized things would probably look very strange to someone just coming on the scene. Dannon was face down on the ground in the back yard with his pants around his ankles, with Booker sprawled on top of him. Valente was a few yards behind them both, breathing heavily.

No one spoke for several seconds until Valente finally blurted out: "Your boyfriend? What the hell?"

The woman, a buxom bleach blonde around thirty, was wearing a short robe. It looked like she had thrown it on hastily; she was trying to hold it closed but the straps of her bra were visible underneath.

O'Rourke, confused, got to his feet and pulled out his badge. "Ma'am, we're police officers. We're you expecting Mark Dannon tonight?"

The woman pulled her robe tighter. "Well… yes," she said, flustered. "Is that a crime or something?"

O'Rourke picked up the shiny object on the ground. What had looked from a distance like a knife was actually a thin, six-inch long shiny metal key chain. It had the words Led Zeppelin emblazoned on it, and a couple of keys attached. "That's mine," Mark

Dannon said, pulling up his pants after Booker released his hold on him. "I know it's sort of retro, but it belonged to my dad."

A crowd of neighbors was now gathering near the back yard, as the scuffle had made a good deal of noise. "I think we should go inside," O'Rourke said.

A few minutes later, they all stood in the woman's kitchen. She identified herself as Darla Sorkins. "Has Mark been at your house earlier this week?" he asked the woman.

"Yes," she said, in an annoyed voice. "He's been here a few times."

"Last night?"

"If you must know, yes. He was here last night."

"What hours was he here?"

"From about six to after midnight."

O'Rourke exchanged glances with Valente and Booker. If that was true, Mark could not have been Ashley Morton's attacker the previous night.

"Are you sure he was here for that entire time?"

The woman was now getting angry. "Yes, I am. You know, I don't think I have to answer these questions," she said. "I can have anyone I please over at my house for as long as I want! I opened my door to see the three of you attacking Mark. That's sounds like some kind of police harassment to me."

"We had reason to believe he was trying to break into your back door and cause you harm," O'Rourke answered. "He was back there for several minutes."

"That's because I never used Darla's key before," Mark explained. "She just gave it to me last night. I was having trouble getting the door unlocked."

"If you weren't trying to break in, then why did you run from me?"

"Darla told me she had a jealous ex-husband," Mark said defensively. "I see some big guy running toward me in her back yard, I don't stop to ask questions."

"Why were you using the back door anyway?"

"Darla has nosy neighbors. She asked me not to use the front door anymore. The doorbell's loud and they peek out their windows when I come to the door. She said just come in the back door from now on. I didn't knock because I figured she'd get more turned on if I came in unannounced. One time, she pretended I was some hot intruder and…."

"Shut up," Darla snapped. "You don't have to tell them any details. This is a private situation and none of their business!"

Irate now, she opened the back door and glared at the three men. "You have no right to be in here. You all need to leave right now!" she shouted.

O'Rourke didn't move. "Ma'am," he said, "are you aware that Mark Dannon is only seventeen years old?"

Darla stopped dead in her tracks, looking like she had been slapped in the face. She stood stunned for several seconds, and then lunged at Dannon. "You miserable rotten liar," she screamed. "You said you were nineteen!"

Valente and Booker, who were standing between Darla and Mark Dannon, grabbed her and held her back. "I met him at the mall a couple weeks ago," she sputtered, still trying to get to Dannon. "He gave me a total line of bullshit! He told me he was in college, studying to be a doctor!"

O'Rourke pulled a chair out from the kitchen table, took Darla firmly by the arm from the others, and sat her down gently. "I think you better start from the beginning."

Darla Sorkins explained that she had been shopping in Crossgates Mall a few weeks earlier and had run into Mark

Dannon at the food court. Darla had been recently divorced and lonely. She and Mark started talking and he told her that he was in his second year at college, taking pre-med courses. They ate lunch together and hit it off, even she was twenty-nine and he was (she thought) only nineteen. After a couple dates, she invited him over to her place. He told her that he had college roommates, so they couldn't go over to his place. He had been there almost every other night the past week. From what O'Rourke could gather, he was at her house at the time that Bernard Fleming was killed, as well as during the hours that Ashley Morton was attacked.

"And," she continued, "the third time I invited him here, he seduced me."

"Seduced *you?*" Dannon exclaimed. "You were all over me like a hyena in heat!"

"You lying shit..," Darla said angrily, getting up again.

Valente put a hand on her shoulder. "Easy now…"

O'Rourke saw no point in staying any longer. "As entertaining as all this is," he said, "we're going to take off now. Ms. Sorkins, I don't want you to ever have any more contact with Mark. Although I realize that you were misled, sex between an adult woman and a seventeen year old male is still a crime in this state. If we ever hear that you had further contact with him, you'll be arrested."

O'Rourke steered Dannon toward the back door, but Sorkins pointed to the front of the house. "You might as well use the front door," she said with a sigh. "The whole neighborhood's probably outside by now. They'll see you either way."

Darla was right. There were at least thirty people on the sidewalk in front of the house. The onlookers watched as O'Rourke, Valente and Booker walked Dannon out the door and to his car. Valente turned to the crowd and said, "Go home, folks. Show's over."

"You go right home," O'Rourke said sternly to Dannon through the car window as the teen started the car. "I don't want to ever see you around here again."

"Do me a favor," Dannon said before he drove away. "Don't tell my mom…"

Valente took the wheel again on the way back to the station, this time with Booker sitting in front. O'Rourke, in the back, looked down at his pants and saw that he had a hole in the knee from when he tackled Dannon. "Damn it," he said. "All that for nothing and now I've got a rip in my slacks."

"I wouldn't say it was for nothing," Booker replied, rubbing a sore elbow. "At least we ruled out Dannon as a suspect. And, we got our exercise for the day."

Valente laughed. "That was one hell of a tackle the boss made," he said, looking over his shoulder at O'Rourke. "Actually, you each took that guy down hard. You should have seen the look on that lady's face when she saw the kid's pants off and Booker on top of him."

"Very funny," Booker said. "I noticed you were pretty far behind. What's up with that?"

"I would've been able to run quicker, but I just had a big dinner."

O'Rourke leaned forward, glancing looked down at Valente's belly hanging over the seat belt. "It looks like you've had several big dinners."

When they returned to the station, O'Rourke checked his messages. He had hoped that someone, either Sandy or Dr. Furlani or maybe the State Police would have found a lead for him, but that wasn't the case. After a couple more hours, O'Rourke decided to call it a day. He had been at it since early in the morning and was exhausted, and there was nothing to be gained by staying any longer.

When he got home, O'Rourke grabbed a beer from the fridge and called Ginny, and they talked for a while. O'Rourke apologized again about missing their dinner date the other night.

"I'll tell you what," Ginny said. "When you get all done with this case, we can go to a park and have a summer picnic. Just you and me."

"That sounds nice," he said. "We'll do that. I promise."

After talking with Ginny, he called his kids at Ellen's house. Tyler and Lauren had been fighting about something and he found himself trying to calm Tyler down. As he talked to him, he looked out his back window. He had been so busy at work that he had been neglecting his lawn, and the grass was way too high.

Lauren got on the phone after Tyler and gave O'Rourke an earful, telling her side of the argument with Tyler. Despite his daughter's annoyed tone, O'Rourke was glad to focus on something other than the case.

Several miles away however, the tall man was focusing intently on the case. He knew that Ashley Morton had been moved to a motel in Schoharie County. But the sheriff's department had a car outside the motel twenty-four hours a day. So Ashley Morton would have to wait. He was frustrated but he would have to move onto someone else. There was no need to keep taking the targets in order, he decided; he could work on his most recent target next. He looked down at his list of names, at the one at the very bottom – the one he had just added. *Steven O'Rourke.*

NINETEEN

||||||||||||||||||||||||||||||||||||||||||

Shortly before he woke, O'Rourke had another weird dream. In his dream, he felt that Lauren and Tyler were in danger so he went to Ellen's house to get them. Oddly enough, it wasn't Ellen that answered the door but Darla Sorkins, the woman that Mark Dannon had been having his nighttime liaisons with. She told O'Rourke that she didn't know where the kids were; she said she couldn't watch them anymore because they were underage. Then she said something else odd; she couldn't remember their names but she was good with faces. She then asked if O'Rourke had some pictures of them.

O'Rourke looked down and found he had glossy professional photos in his hands of each of his children. He knew he needed to show them to someone. When he looked back up, Darla Sorkins was gone; instead, Dr. Furlani was standing there now. She took the pictures from him. "I'll have to analyze these," she said coldly stepping back into the house. "It's too bad we don't have a message with them."

Before she closed the door, Dr. Furlani added in a whisper: "They're not the ones in danger. Make sure you go the right way."

He woke up from the dream to find Ginny next to him in bed

looking at him with concern. "You were talking in your sleep," she said. "You sounded upset."

O'Rourke climbed out of bed quickly. "There's something I have to do."

It was very early and not yet light outside, but it was Oquendo's early day, so he figured she might be awake already. "Hello," she answered dully when he called her at home. "Who's this?"

"Rosie, it's me."

"Whaz wrong," she said, half asleep. "Is somebody hurt," she asked like most cops do when getting a call in the middle of the night.

"No, sorry, I shouldn't have called this early. I need to know how long it will take to print out all the customer photographs that Randall Tucker had on his computer. Good copies of all the photos. Wedding photos, family portraits, everything..."

"Wait a minute, let me think....There's thousands of photos and we only have two color printers. I assume we'll have to label them as they print out so you know whose face belongs to who. It'll probably take all day even if we use the whole team."

"No good. We need to move on this. Could you have that done by 2 PM?"

"Maybe, if I have the whole office work on it. Why?"

"I still think there's a common thread in these three attacks. Ashley Morton said she was good with faces but not with names. We need to visit her and see if she recognizes anyone in those photos. And we need to do it quickly. I think this guy's going to strike again soon."

By 2:45, O'Rourke and Oquendo arrived at the small motel in the town of Schoharie. A black car was parked about twenty feet in front of the door to the Morton's room. Oquendo had made O'Rourke stop for coffee on the way to Schoharie, and she brought a cup of coffee and a doughnut over to the young guy sitting in the car while O'Rourke waited. "That's Deputy Rodriguez of the Schoharie Sheriff's Department," she said to O'Rourke with a big smile when she rejoined him. "He's got the day shift."

"Good looking guy. Did you let him know that you're married with three kids?" O'Rourke teased.

"You know, you're a real dick sometimes…"

Inside the motel room, Mrs. Morton looked worried. She shot a nervous glance at her husband. "I think you should tell him," she said to him.

"I, um, told Loretta and Ashley about the connection between the attack on Ashley and the murders you're investigating," Ron Morton said to O'Rourke. "I don't like keeping secrets from them."

"Actually, I was going to tell them anyway," O'Rourke said. "We'd like to get some information from Ashley that might help us with the murder investigation."

"I'm scared," Mrs. Morton said with tears in her eyes. Ron Morton, who was sitting on the couch between Ashley and her, put his arm around his wife's shoulders.

Ashley rolled her eyes. "Here we go again with the histrionics," she said.

"You're safe here, Mrs. Morton," O'Rourke said. "Unless you've told anyone where you are, the only ones that know you're here are the police officers working on the case. We issued strict orders to them not to disclose this location to anyone outside the police department."

"My parents haven't told anyone," Ashley said. "They're scared stupid."

The way Ashley treated her family irked O'Rourke. "Well, you seem to be holding up just fine," he said dryly.

"I'm not worried," Ashley answered. "It's all so random. First some photographer in Albany, then some gay senator, then an attack on me. There's like no pattern. The guy's picking out people out of the blue and attacking them. So why would he go through the trouble to attack me again?"

"We don't think it's random. That's why we brought these." Oquendo opened one of the large manila envelopes that they brought with them and slid out a large pile of photographs onto a small table. O'Rourke said: "This may take a while."

For hours, Ashley looked over the photographs, which included wedding pictures, family portraits, modeling photos, and other assorted photographs. O'Rourke was considering calling somewhere for a pizza when Ashley finally saw something. She pointed to a group of three photos. "I know this girl," she said.

O'Rourke looked at the photos. They were modeling photos of a young girl in three different poses. The labels on the back of these three read "Cheryl Nottingham, age 18, $300 paid," with an Albany residence listed for her. The photos, which were dated about ten weeks ago, looked to be of high quality to O'Rourke's untrained eye. The girl, a thin brunette who looked more like fifteen than eighteen, was wearing trendy clothing. Probably what one would normally wear in a modeling shoot, O'Rourke assumed. Although well dressed and wearing makeup, the girl appeared gaunt and pale. Cheryl Nottingham was not pretty, but Randall Tucker had done a good job of making her look reasonably attractive.

"Where do you know her from?" O'Rourke asked.

"I met her at a party a few months ago," Ashley answered. "I had a real problem with her."

"Why?"

"Mark brought me to a birthday party for some guy he knows. I went to get a beer…I mean soda…and when I came back, I saw this girl flirting with him. I told her to get lost and she just walked away. But I remember her since I'm surprised Mark was even letting her flirt with him. I mean she wasn't even good looking."

"So that's it? No fight or anything?"

"No. She just slinked away like she was going to cry or something."

"What else can you tell us about her?"

"Not much. I didn't even know her name. Somebody said another girl, her cousin I think, brought her to the party. I think they left a little while after that. I guess that's all I know."

"Okay. Well, at least this gives us something. Please continue looking at the photos. Maybe you'll recognize someone else also."

O'Rourke pulled Oquendo aside. "Get some information on this Nottingham girl," O'Rourke said to her. "Your team made calls to all of Tucker's customers after the first murder. Find out what she told them. Now that we have a connection with Ashley, we'll talk to her in person next."

Oquendo took out her cell and went outside the door to call in.

Ashley looked at more photos for almost twenty minutes when Oquendo came back inside. She had an odd look on her face. "We won't be taking to Cheryl Nottingham," Oquendo said to O'Rourke.

"Why not?"

"She's been dead for two months."

O'Rourke was stunned. "I thought we contacted all of Tucker's customers. How did we miss this?"

"Sorry boss. That big ape Joe Wendell worked on this one. I just tore him a new one over the phone. He said he called the phone number in Tucker's records and reached the Nottingham family. When he asked to speak to Cheryl, her father answered. He said she had passed away two months ago from an accidental drug overdose. Wendell figured he wouldn't be able to get any information from her so he just made a note in the file and went on to the next customer. He never even thought to tell me about it."

"Can we confirm that's what she died of? Could this be another murder?"

"I'm already ahead of you. I called the coroner's office. I told them it was associated with the Bernard Fleming case and they put me right through to the coroner himself. He said there was no foul play involved. The girl died of a prescription drug overdose. No marks or abrasion of any kind on the body, and no signs that the drugs were forced down her throat. But the coroner did say that even though the official report says 'accidental', sometimes in these cases it's not so accidental. They'll put accidental on the report if they're not certain, for the family's sake. But this girl had been on anti-depressants for a long time. He said with the number of pills found in her system, it wouldn't shock him if this was an intentional suicide."

O'Rourke looked at the family, who had been following all this intently. "Ashley, please continue looking at these photos. We have to leave now but call me immediately if you recognize anyone else."

When they got outside, Oquendo asked O'Rourke: "What now?"

"Now we talk to the Nottinghams."

TWENTY

||||||||||||||||||||||||||||||||||||||

O'Rourke recognized the street that the Nottinghams lived on. It was located in an upper middle class area of Albany, not far from the Albany Municipal Golf Course. Oquendo didn't speak until they were out of Schoharie, when she said quietly: "Boss, I'm sorry. I should have checked over Wendell's work. We might have caught this sooner. If I had, maybe Fleming would still be..."

"No," O'Rourke said. "Don't think that way. Even if we had known that this Nottingham girl had passed away, I don't know if it would have meant anything to us then. It's only now that we have a connection with Ashley Morton that it might mean something."

"But what? All we know is that Randall Tucker took some photos of a girl that had an issue with Ashley Morton and who recently passed away. It doesn't explain why someone would kill Tucker. And what does that have to do with Fleming?"

"I don't know yet. But it's all we have to go on right now. See what information you can get on her from DMV and other records."

Oquendo pulled data and made some calls from her smart phone and by the time they got to Albany, she had some useful data. "Nottingham graduated from high school in June but just barely. Grades were low and she missed a lot of days. No criminal record at all. She had a driver's license but no car registered to her; no traffic infractions reported. No work history reported. That's it – not much out of the ordinary."

"Except she's dead at age eighteen. That's got to mean something," O'Rourke said as they pulled up in front of the Nottingham's house.

The Nottinghams lived on a quiet street. Most of the houses on the street had fine-trimmed front lawns. The Nottingham home, though, stood out from the rest on the street. Garbage bags were piled on top of overfilled plastic trash containers; no one had brought the trash to the curb for a while. The grass hadn't been cut for a few weeks and weeds sprouted in several spots. There were two cars in the driveway, but no lights on inside the house except a light coming from the basement.

O'Rourke and Oquendo walked to the door. It looked like it was going to rain and it was starting to get dark outside even though there was still a few hours of daylight left. O'Rourke rang the bell but there was no answer. He rang it again and then knocked on the door until he heard someone stirring inside.

A thin woman that appeared to be about sixty opened the door. She was dressed in a loose housecoat and bare feet, and had dark circles under her eyes.

"What do you want?" she asked in a flat voice.

O'Rourke held up his badge. "Police. We'd like to ask you some questions," he said.

The woman didn't express any surprise, or any other emotion for that matter. "Come in," she said softly. O'Rourke guessed that she was heavily medicated.

The door opened to the living room; it was dark and it took a second for O'Rourke to adjust to it. He noticed the blinds and curtains were all closed. There was a blanket and pillow on the living room couch and a pair of woman's slippers next to it; apparently, the woman had just been sleeping. For her not to hear the doorbell on the first two rings indicated she must have been in a very deep sleep.

They stood, expecting her to offer them a seat. O'Rourke was about to say something when they heard someone else coming up a set of stairs from the basement.

"Who was at the door?" a man's voice called out.

A second later, a tall thin man that looked to be in his forties entered the room. He was wearing a sweatshirt and jeans and had on a pair of work gloves. He looked at them warily. "My wife shouldn't have let you people in the house," he said, annoyed. "Whatever you're selling, we're not buying."

O'Rourke again held up the badge. "I'm Lieutenant O'Rourke, Albany Police Department," he said. "Are you Mr. Nottingham?"

"I'm John Nottingham," the man said.

"We need to ask you some questions. It's related to a case we're investigating."

He looked at his wife. "Theresa, can you get me a cup of coffee? And some for these folks too, if they want."

"Actually, that would be good," O'Rourke said.

As Theresa Nottingham went to the kitchen, O'Rourke realized that his first impression had been wrong. The woman wasn't close to sixty at all; in fact, she was probably only in her forties. Although thin, she had an athletic build, like someone who jogged or swam often. It was her demeanor and slow movement, as well as the lack of makeup and the deep circles under her eyes that initially made her appear much older.

"I apologize for my wife," the man said. "She hasn't been herself lately. I'd rather we not talk in front of her. Now, what is it you want?'

"We'd like to talk to you about your daughter."

"My daughter is dead," the man replied. He said it wearily, without anger or sadness.

"We know that," Oquendo said. "But we believe she may be connected in some way with a current investigation we're working on."

"I can't imagine my daughter being mixed up with any criminal activity. She had some…issues, but nothing like that."

"Actually," O'Rourke said, "we're concerned that someone she may have known, a male acquaintance, may be involved with some current criminal activity. It's very important that we find the person."

John Nottingham paused for a few moments. O'Rourke looked at him carefully. O'Rourke would not be surprised if he was a runner or swimmer either. The man was the tall and lean type. The type that could probably sprint quickly through a back yard after attacking Ashley Morton.

"Lieutenant, I'd like to help you, but I'm sure you're mistaken," Nottingham said. "Cheryl had some mental health problems. She was prone to depression and had very low self-esteem. She never had a boyfriend. Or any close friends, for that matter. She really wasn't involved with many activities at all, much less criminal activities."

"The person we're looking for may not have been a close friend or boyfriend. It could have been someone that she knew from school or somewhere else."

Nottingham's eyes narrowed. "Just why do you think my daughter would have known the person you're looking for?"

O'Rourke decided not to beat around the bush. "Because she had some photos taken by a Randall Tucker, who was murdered a week ago. And she had contact with a girl named Ashley Morton, who we believe was subsequently attacked by the same person."

Nottingham looked stunned. "Perhaps…perhaps we should all sit down."

Theresa Nottingham returned with a tray with three cups of coffee, set it down on a table, and then went back to the kitchen without saying a word.

"My wife has been devastated since Cheryl died," Nottingham explained. "She and I have both been out of work since it happened. Theresa has been taking some very strong anti-anxiety medication. I thought she was about to be able to discontinue the meds, but then last week her mother passed on."

O'Rourke nodded sympathetically.

John Nottingham pointed to a picture on the wall. "There's a picture of Cheryl and Theresa, taken shortly before Cheryl died. Look how different Theresa looked."

The framed picture on the wall was a photograph of Mrs. Nottingham with one arm around Cheryl and the other around an older woman, probably her mother. Mrs. Nottingham indeed appeared to have aged several years since the picture was taken. There was something else about the picture that struck a note with O'Rourke, but he couldn't quite put his finger on it.

"Cheryl had modeling photos of herself taken," O'Rourke said to Nottingham. "But you said she had low self-esteem."

"My wife did some modeling when she was young. She felt that if Cheryl had modeling photos taken, it would boost her self-image. The problem was that Cheryl was not…how do I say it… well, she wasn't what most people would consider an attractive girl. Anyway, Theresa kept trying to convince Cheryl to have some photos of herself done. Cheryl finally reluctantly agreed to go along with it. Theresa gave her the money for the photos."

"How did they pick out the photographer?"

"Cheryl did it herself. She just looked through the Yellow Pages. Totally at random."

"Did you know the photos were taken by Randall Tucker?"

"Not until you just told me. I read about Mr. Tucker's death recently, but never connected that to Cheryl. Theresa and I actually never saw the photos. I actually suspected that Cheryl was so embarrassed that she never actually followed through with having them taken. I didn't want to ask her about it, since she was so fragile at the time, so I just dropped it."

It sounded odd to O'Rourke that the family would just drop the subject after giving Cheryl three hundred dollars. He wondered if Nottingham was telling the whole truth.

"Mr. Nottingham," O'Rourke continued, "did you or anyone in your family know Bernard Fleming at all?"

"The assemblyman that was murdered? Just what we read in the papers."

"What about a high school girl from Colonie named Ashley Morton?"

Nottingham shook his head. "The name doesn't ring a bell. I don't think Cheryl knew anyone from Colonie."

"You said that Cheryl didn't have many close acquaintances."

"Almost none. There were a couple of girls she was acquainted with when she was in middle school, but they moved away or went on to different high schools. She didn't hang around with anyone in high school. We had her try after school activities to meet other kids, but she would just drop out of the activities. Cheryl does have a cousin, Lori, who lives in the area. Once in a while, Lori would take her places, but Cheryl never seemed very interested."

"Did Lori ever take her to parties?"

"Yes. Once or twice. They went to a birthday party shortly before Cheryl died."

The party where she met Ashley Morton, O'Rourke assumed.

"Okay. We'll need to get a list of your family's friends and relatives, just to cover all the bases."

"Of course," Nottingham said. "But I can't believe any of them would be involved in something like this. Besides, Cheryl wasn't really close to anyone other than my wife and me."

O'Rourke tried to think outside the box. "What about teachers she was close to?"

"I don't recall her ever mentioning any in particular," he replied.

"Did she have a therapist?"

"A female therapist, years ago, but it wasn't working so we dropped it. We were hoping her latest medication would help."

"She had a driver's license. So she must have gone out sometimes."

"We encouraged her to get the license because she thought that might encourage her to get out more. But she rarely used it. I believe that the last time she drove my car anywhere was when she went to have those photos done."

"She recently graduated. Was she looking for a job?"

"No. And we didn't push the issue. We didn't want to create any more anxiety for her."

"Are there any men or boys you can think of that Cheryl knew?"

"Lieutenant, I can't think of anyone. When Cheryl wasn't at school, she was almost always home. She spent a lot of time alone in her room, watching television or on the computer. It was a vicious cycle. Her depression made her hard for others to warm up to. Then, I believe her loneliness made her more depressed."

O'Rourke let it all sink in. Cheryl Nottingham was a depressed girl who died from an overdose, either intentionally or by accident. She had no real friends and rarely went out anywhere. She must have had some interest in the opposite sex though, since Ashley said she was flirting with Mark Dannon. But if Cheryl had no other known male friends or acquaintances, this lead could be at a dead end.

But there was something Nottingham had said...

"You say she spent a lot of time on her computer?"

"Yes. Like most kids her age."

"I assume you have Internet access?"

"Of course."

"Can we see her computer?"

Theresa Nottingham was nowhere in sight as they went to Cheryl's room. Mr. Nottingham explained that his wife was probably sleeping again. They walked quietly to Cheryl's room, which was on the first floor down the hall from the living room.

"I've tried to get into her computer myself several times in the last few weeks," Nottingham said. "Nothing will come up without a password. And we don't know what it is. I can't access her information from my computer; she had a separate account."

"Why did you try to get into her computer after she died?"

"Lieutenant, the official cause of my daughter's death is listed as 'accidental overdose'. My wife believes that. I don't."

"You think she intentionally overdosed?"

"Yes. She suffered from depression, but I thought she was getting a little better lately. The new medication - I thought it was helping..."

He paused for a moment to regain his composure.

"Anyway, she used to keep a diary, not that long ago. After she died, I looked all over her room for that, but I guess she probably outgrew it and got rid of it. So I figured that maybe she put her thoughts on the computer. I was thinking…if I could just get an idea of what her mindset was just before she died…Well, I guess I thought if I could do that, then maybe it would help me understand."

According to Mr. Nottingham, Cheryl's bedroom had been left mostly intact since she died. The room was well lit with sunshine coming in from a window facing the front of the house, and at first glance seemed pleasant enough. But upon looking closer, O'Rourke noticed that the bedroom contained no decorations on the walls and very few personal items. A black sweater was still draped over the back of the desk chair, one of the few signs that this had been a young girl's room.

John Nottingham looked like it would hurt him to enter the room. From the doorway, he pointed to a laptop computer on the desk. "The computer's over there."

O'Rourke turned the laptop on. It took a few minutes for the screen to come up. When it finally did, a password was requested.

O'Rourke tried all the obvious passwords, such as combinations of the names and dates of birth of the family. No luck.

Oquendo, who was good with computers, tried a few things herself. After a few minutes, she said: "We're not going to be able to get into this without help."

"We can contact the Internet provider and see if we can get access to her e-mail account," O'Rourke said. "But, that may take a while and it won't help us if she kept information in documents on the hard drive. We need to get into the computer now."

"The Nerd Squad's gone for the weekend," Oquendo said.

"Sandy said he would be working at home though. I've got his cell number."

O'Rourke punched up Sandy's cellphone number on his phone. Sandy answered after a few rings.

"Hello?"

"Sandy, it's O'Rourke. We've got a possible lead on the killer. There's a deceased girl that may have been connected to him and there's a laptop computer in her house. But it's password protected. We need your help."

"You mean now?"

"Of course now. I'll give you the address. It's right here in Albany. How soon can you get here?"

"Well, see, that's a problem. I'm not in Albany. I took off for the weekend. I'm in a motel room in Lake Placid right now."

Lake Placid, a popular vacation spot in upstate New York where the Winter Olympics took place in 1980, was located in the Adirondack Mountains, about two and a half hours north of Albany.

"I thought you were working on the case over the weekend," O'Rourke said.

"I am," Sandy said. "Can't a guy go on a working vacation? I'm actually sitting here right now, playing with all the data you gave me. I haven't found anything useful yet though."

"Well, we need someone to get into this damn computer. This dead girl is our best lead so far. Do you have Megan's cell number?" O'Rourke was now sorry he deleted it after he and Megan Ross broke up.

"Uh…well…that's a problem too. Megan's away for the weekend also."

"How far is she away from here?"

"She's pretty far away also."

"Damn it," O'Rourke said. "What about the rest of the Nerd Squad?"

"They're fairly proficient, but this is too important to trust them with. There are ways to get into computers that are password protected. I've got some special software for that. But you have to be very careful with it. If you mess up, there's a chance you'll accidentally delete important data."

O'Rourke could ask for help from the State Police. But their computer experts were located in New York City. They wouldn't be able to get to Albany any quicker than Sandy would.

"This is too important to wait, Sandy. Sorry to disturb your working vacation but I'm going to have to ask you to get down here as soon as you can. Either that or call Megan wherever she is and ask her to get here."

Sandy didn't answer right away. It sounded like he had his hand over the phone. There were muffled voices talking in the background. Someone was there with him.

Then another voice came on the phone. A female voice that O'Rourke recognized.

"O'Rourke, it's Megan. We'll be down there as soon as we can."

TWENTY-ONE

IIIIIIIIIIIIIIIIIIIIIIIIIIIIIIIIIIIIIIII

It took O'Rourke a few moments for it to sink it. His first thought was that Sandy had patched Megan in from somewhere else. But then he realized that Megan was right there with Sandy. On a weekend vacation in Lake Placid. In his motel room.

"What the hell…," he blurted out into the phone.

"O'Rourke," Megan said, "you obviously want us down there as soon as possible, so I'm not going to waste time on phony excuses. Sandy and I have been…dating for some time now. We went away for the weekend. But we really have been spending a lot of time on the data you gave us."

O'Rourke was perplexed. Sandy was a skinny guy, shorter than Megan, and at least twenty years her senior. He would never understand women.

"So, all those insanely hot looks you've been giving me…," he said.

O'Rourke looked up from the phone and noticed Oquendo staring at him. He turned his back to her. "So what was that all about?" he whispered into the phone.

"Just a little misdirection," Megan replied. "Sandy and I didn't want anyone to know we're together. The Department frowns on that sort of thing in the same unit; they would probably transfer me if they knew. By the way, I'd appreciate it if you would keep this quiet."

"I will," he answered, annoyed. "Although I don't know why I should." But there really was no point in doing otherwise.

"I'm actually surprised you didn't catch on,'" she said teasingly. "Some detective you are."

"Well how was I supposed to know you and your boss would be in Lake Placid working on setting a new Olympic record in his bedroom?"

"You're so funny. Look, we've got to pack. We'll be down there as soon as we can. I'll put Sandy back on."

Sandy got back on the line. "The computer," he said. "Is it a wireless connection or is it connected with an Ethernet cable?'

"It's attached with a cable," O'Rourke said. "We can disconnect it and—"

"No, don't do that," Sandy said, sounding worried. "I don't want you amateurs monkeying around with anything. Just leave it there. Megan and I will head down there right now, and we'll disconnect it ourselves. Then, we'll get it to the Annex and bring my whole team in to analyze what's on it."

O'Rourke was concerned about leaving the computer in the house where John Nottingham could get to it. But he realized there was a solution to that.

"Okay," he said to Sandy. "But get down here as soon as you can."

O'Rourke walked over to Nottingham, who was still standing just outside the bedroom. "Do you have a key to lock up Cheryl's room? We want to keep the computer safe."

"Yes, I think it's in the kitchen. Hold on, I'll get it."

While he went downstairs, Oquendo said: "Is Sandy coming?"

"Yeah, but he won't be here for two and a half hours."

"What was all that other stuff about?"

"Nothing," O'Rourke said awkwardly. "Personal business."

John Nottingham came back with the key. "You don't have to lock her door," he said. "I'll be in the house."

That's the problem, O'Rourke thought. He locked the door and double checked to make sure the room was secure.

"Is this the only key to her room?"

"Yes," Nottingham replied.

"Good," O'Rourke said and put the key in his pocket.

They went back to the living room. Theresa Nottingham was still in her bedroom, probably in a deep sleep. O'Rourke and Oquendo sat down with John Nottingham for another half hour, getting the names of family friends and relatives and any other people that Cheryl had contact with. When that was completed, O'Rourke and Oquendo went to leave.

"Mr. Nottingham, I'm sorry for your loss," O'Rourke said on the way out. "I have a daughter of my own, so I can imagine how you feel. But, I'm required to ask you if you can account for your own whereabouts over the past several evenings."

"Lieutenant, I don't have much of a social life anymore. I wouldn't feel right going out somewhere and having a good time so soon after my daughter's death. So I've been in my basement every evening, refinishing our family room. If you don't believe me, I'll take you down there for a look. My wife has been home every night with me, although she sleeps most of the time."

After a pause, Nottingham said: "I guess that's not much of an alibi, is it?"

"It is what it is," O'Rourke said.

Inside the car, Oquendo said: "Do you really think John Nottingham's our guy?"

"We can't rule him out," O'Rourke answered.

"Maybe he's some kind of psycho overprotective father," Oquendo theorized. "He could have found out about Cheryl's altercation with Ashley Morton. And maybe he had some beef with Tucker taking the photos. But that doesn't explain the murder of Bernard Fleming."

"Nottingham doesn't seem like a psycho," O'Rourke said. "Just a father dealing with a lot of grief. If he's our guy, he's able to hide it well."

"Are you sure the computer is safe with him in the house?"

"It's safe. If Nottingham tries to break in her room to get at it, then we know he's our man. But I'm thinking if he's not the killer, he and his wife could be in danger. There's someone else out there who has attacked two people associated with Cheryl Nottingham."

O'Rourke called into the station. Myers and Booker had left for the day, but Valente was still there. O'Rourke filled him in and asked him to assign a detective to park in front of the Nottingham home for the night. O'Rourke waited until the detective's car got there before heading to the station.

On the way back to the station, O'Rourke could sense that Oquendo wanted to ask about his phone call to Sandy Bernstein. But thankfully, she didn't bring it up.

At one point on the drive back, there was a slow moving car in front of the Jaguar and O'Rourke passed it, going over the double yellow line. A couple of young men were in the car and the driver raised his middle finger in a vulgar gesture as he passed them. Oquendo responded with the same salute right back to them out of the open passenger window. "Asshole," she said.

O'Rourke chuckled at Oquendo's actions for a few seconds, but then suddenly pulled over. The other car sped by them, its horn honking, but O'Rourke paid no attention.

O'Rourke stared straight ahead for minutes, working something out in his head. Finally, Oquendo said: "What?"

"That guy just gave us the finger," O'Rourke said, still lost in thought. "And then you did the same."

"Sorry, boss. I didn't mean nothing by it."

"No, it's just that I haven't seen too many people do that when they drive. Not around here."

"That's because you upstaters are soft when it comes to driving," Oquendo replied with a grin. "You oughta drive down in New York City more often, where the traffic is terrible. I lived down there until I was twenty. They do it all the time down there."

"Bernard Fleming was from New York City," O'Rourke said. "And he had a car up here that he drove on occasion."

"Yeah, but what's that got to do with…Holy shit! His finger!'

"Right! Fleming's left middle finger was cut off by the killer. The finger on the left hand which a driver would use to stick out the window if he was annoyed with another driver. In fact, I could picture the other driver responding to that by calling the guy an 'asshole', just like you did. The same word that was written on Fleming's wall."

Oquendo let that sink in. "It's kind of a reach, but definitely possible. So you think that this killer is just murdering and mutilating people who cut him off in traffic or did something else impolite to him?"

"Maybe. Or maybe people that did something impolite to Cheryl Nottingham."

O'Rourke was still pondering his theory about the finger as they arrived at the station. If that did explain why Fleming's finger was removed, then Tucker must have had his tongue cut out because he said something to someone. But what and to whom? And how did the words "Black Bastard" fit into that?

Once inside, O'Rourke asked Valente and Oquendo to have everyone on their teams go through the list of family friends and relatives they got from Mr. Nottingham and compare the names to people associated with Tucker, Fleming, and Morton. Valente would call Mark Dannon and Cheryl's cousin Lori, while Rose Oquendo would check with the Tuckers and Arnold Polanski.

O'Rourke then called the state police and updated Dale Mitchell on the events of the day. "The Nottingham girl might be the key to these attacks," Mitchell said. "But let's face it, Albany's not as big as New York City. I've only lived up here for ten years, but whenever I'm introduced to someone else that lives in Albany, it seems like we always have someone in common around here that we both know. This could just be a coincidence that she's connected to both Tucker and Morton."

"Maybe. But I don't like coincidences. Plus it's the best lead we have right now."

"Yeah. But we need to keep a lid on this. If the killer is associated with this girl and finds out we're looking at her computer, the Nottinghams could be in danger."

"We're keeping a car outside the house around the clock. But I'm concerned about Captain Grainey leaking this to the TV stations."

"Let me handle that," Mitchell said. "I'll have Superintendent Owen personally call your chief. This has to stay out of the news."

Valente had some information. "I called Mark Dannon," he said. "He had a different take on the incident at the party. He said this girl looked really shy and was all alone so he started talking to her while Ashley was getting a beer. He said the girl wasn't really flirting with him; she just seemed happy that someone was talking to her. Then Ashley came back and scared the girl off. He never even knew her name. The bottom line though is that he doesn't know any guy connected with Cheryl Nottingham."

"What about the guy who hosted the party? The birthday boy?"

"Dannon gave me his name and number, but he's not our guy. Dannon said the guy's about five foot eight."

"Call the guy and see if he can give you the names of the other guys that were at the party. I feel like we're grasping at straws here, but we've got to follow any lead we have."

"Okay," Valente said, jotting that down.

"Were you able to get hold of Cheryl's cousin?"

"Yeah. Lori Nottingham didn't see the incident, but said that Cheryl came over to her, really upset, and had Lori take her home. Lori said that she would be surprised if her cousin was involved with any guys. She said Cheryl wasn't gay or anything; she definitely liked guys, but was just too shy to go out with them."

"Well, unless I'm totally off base on this, some guy obviously took an interest in Cheryl. Hopefully, there's something on that computer that will tell us who."

Detective Jim Farrell was getting bored as he sat in his car in front of the Nottingham home. He enjoyed working on cases and interviewing suspects, but he hated sitting in the car doing nothing. He was assigned to guard the house until 2 AM, when someone else would take his place. Fortunately, he had time to stop at the bakery on Quail Street on the way over and had a plentiful supply of coffee and muffins.

It was dark out now and raining steadily, but he had a clear view of the house because the streetlights were on. He had been there for an hour and a half; it was his understanding that Sandy Bernstein and the hot woman that worked with him would be showing up at the Nottingham house within an hour to look at the computer. They would probably have to wake up the mother when they got here since the first floor of the house was dark. The only lights on in the house were from the basement, where the father was working. Every once in a while, Farrell could hear the sound of a power tool coming from down there.

Farrell opened the bag of muffins and looked inside. There was one blueberry muffin and one chocolate one left. Probably the biggest decision he would have to make this evening.

He finally decided on the blueberry. As he looked back out the car's front window, he was startled to see a man walking toward him from down the block. He was certain he hadn't heard a car come down the street.

Lieutenant O'Rourke had left instructions with Farrell to call for back-up if he saw anyone, and Farrell wasn't one to disregard orders, especially when serial killers were involved. He picked up the radio and called in. "Dispatch, this is Detective Farrell, outside the Nottingham house. There's an unidentified man walking toward the house. Request back-up assistance."

"Roger that," came the response. "Will send back-up immediately."

Farrell reached into his jacket and unsnapped his gun holster. But then he realized it was a false alarm. The man was waving toward the car and Farrell recognized him. Farrell picked up the radio again.

"Dispatch, cancel that request for back-up. Repeat, no back-up assistance required. I can identify the man. He's one of ours."

"Roger that."

The man walked over to the driver's side of the car and Farrell rolled the window down. "I'm surprised to see you here," Farrell asked. "Has there been a change in plans?"

"Yes. I guess you could say that," the tall man said, just before he fired two shots into Farrell's forehead.

TWENTY-TWO

|||||||||||||||||||||||||||||||||||||

O'Rourke was feeling exhausted. He had slept only a handful of hours combined over the last few nights and had been at it today for over twelve hours. He bought a large coffee from the vending machine upstairs before heading back to his office.

Oquendo was there when he returned with a copy of the coroner's report on Cheryl Nottingham that had been faxed to her. She also had called the Tuckers and Arnold Polanski. None of them had ever heard of Cheryl Nottingham.

"One more thing," Oquendo told him. "I asked Polanski if Bernard Fleming was an aggressive driver. You know – to test out your theory about the finger."

"What did he say?"

"He said yes. One of the most aggressive and rudest drivers he ever met."

O'Rourke decided to call Dr. Furlani to fill her in on the day's activities.

"Very interesting," she said after he filled her in. "It's possible that the killer had a close protective relationship with this Nottingham girl; perhaps there's even a sexual component at work here. That's common with serial murderers."

O'Rourke looked at the coroner's report again. "I don't think so. The autopsy showed Cheryl was a virgin. And a 'sexual component' doesn't fit with what her cousin said about her being too timid to have a boyfriend."

"Hmm. Yes, you may be right about that. Let's see what else I have..."

She paused for a few moments. O'Rourke guessed she was looking through textbooks on serial killers. He started to feel angry again about the fact that this was all just some intellectual exercise to her.

"Another thing is that the girl's father also can't be ruled out as a suspect," Furlani said. "Guilt can be a powerful motivator. He may have felt that he didn't do enough to prevent her death. He could be lashing out at..."

O'Rourke interrupted her. "Hold on," he said. "I've got another call."

Megan Ross was on the other line, all out of breath. "O'Rourke, get over to the Nottingham house now! There's a cop down!"

"What?"

"Sandy's calling it in to 911 right now. Jim Farrell's dead. We just pulled up to the house and we found him in his car. He's... oh God, the house...I'm looking at the house now and the bedroom window's broken. The computer...I bet it's gone...I better check..."

"No! Get back inside your car and wait for the patrolmen to respond. The killer might still be around. I'll be there soon."

"Goddamn it," O'Rourke said fifteen minutes later.

He was standing outside Jim Farrell's car in the rain looking through the open driver's side window at Farrell's dead body lying on the front seat. Although it was getting late, the area was bright from police lights that had been set up. There were two entry wounds in the man's forehead. O'Rourke could see a mass of blood and brain tissue stuck to the inside of the passenger side window. Next to Farrell's body, an uneaten blueberry muffin sat on the passenger seat with one small drop of blood on top.

"I've known Farrell for years," O'Rourke said to Valente and Oquendo, who were standing behind him. "He started on the force a year or two after me. I should have assigned more cops to guard the house..." he said, his voice trailing off.

Valente put a hand on O'Rourke's shoulder. "No one could have guessed that this would happen. Nobody outside the Department knew about the Nottingham lead. Who would have known a cop was involved?"

O'Rourke had already heard the 911 call. Farrell's last words sent chills down O'Rourke's spine: "He's one of ours."

O'Rourke's mind was jumping ahead now, trying to figure out his next steps. Every cop that was on duty tonight at Division One was either working on the Cheryl Nottingham lead or had heard about it. It was likely that some cops in other divisions knew about Nottingham as well; news gets around fast in the police department. The word may have even gotten out outside the department, but that was irrelevant; Farrell had plainly said the man coming toward him, the man that must have killed him, was one of them.

Every male officer on the police force, detective or uniformed cop, was a suspect. They could probably rule out shorter police officers as suspects; but by nature, most cops are fairly tall so that didn't help much. There had been less than an hour between the time of Farrell's last call into Dispatch and when Sandy and Megan found his body, so they could find out which cops that were on duty during that time had been outside the station. The harder part was verifying where those that weren't on duty tonight were at the time of the shooting.

But that would have to wait right now. The three of them walked toward the Nottingham house, past a dozen Albany cops and detectives. The flashing lights from all the police vehicles lit the neighborhood up like Christmas. The front door to the Nottingham house was open slightly and O'Rourke could see two detectives talking to Cheryl's parents inside. Megan Ross and Sandy Bernstein sat on the front porch of the house, staying dry under an overhang. They looked like they had been through a war.

"So let's go through it again," O'Rourke said to them sympathetically. "What happened when you got here?"

"We pulled up behind Farrell's car," Sandy said. "We knew you assigned someone to watch the house so we figured we would check in with him first. I knew something wasn't right when I saw the open car window since it was raining pretty hard at the time. We couldn't see anyone in the car until we got right up to the window. He was just lying there on the seat…"

"You didn't move him at all?"

"There was no need to," Megan said. "He was obviously dead – he had two frigging holes in his head."

"And there was no one else outside anywhere?"

"No one. So then Sandy called 911 and I called you. Then we got in our car like you told us too. We kept an eye out from there – we didn't see anyone until the first cops arrived."

"Did the Nottinghams leave the house?"

"No. And all the lights in the house were off in the house except for in the basement."

"Okay. You guys just sit tight for now and try to relax. You can probably go home soon."

While Oquendo stayed with Megan and Sandy, O'Rourke and Valente walked outside the house toward Cheryl's Nottingham's bedroom window. The rain had stopped now but there was still a chill in the air. When they got to the window, they saw that most of the glass in the window had been broken and was on the floor inside the bedroom. With the police lights shining on the house, O'Rourke could see inside enough to determine that the computer which had been sitting on the desk earlier in the day was now gone.

"That's what he was after," Valente said. "He killed Farrell first and then stole the computer."

"There's no doubt now that Nottingham's connected to the killer," O'Rourke replied. "And the killer must have felt there was a chance something on the computer could lead to him."

"But the M.O. is all different. There's no spray-paint message this time. And so far, it doesn't look like the killer mutilated Farrell in any way."

"I think that's because this wasn't a part of the killer's original plans. Farrell's not related to the other killings; he only killed Farrell because he had to, to get to the computer."

"Farrell shouldn't have let his guard down," Valente said. "He opened his car window to talk to the guy."

"I also noticed his gun holster was unsnapped but the gun was still inside the holster. Judging by what was on the calls to Dispatch, he initially couldn't identify the man, so he must have unsnapped the holster then, maybe even drew his weapon. But then he recognized the man and like you said, he let down his guard."

"So the shooter had to have been a cop, right? There's nothing else Farrell could have meant when he said the guy was one of ours."

"Yeah. I wish to hell it could mean something else, but I don't think so. The guy we've been after ever since Randall Tucker's murder is a cop."

O'Rourke saw another car pull up on the street. The car was a small, powder-blue coupe – definitely not police issue. A woman got out of the car, holding an umbrella. It took O'Rourke a moment to realize that it was Dr. Elaine Furlani.

"What's she doing here?" Valente asked.

"I was on the phone with her when Megan called me," O'Rourke said as they walked over to her car. "I told Furlani that I had to go to the Nottingham house. She must have decided to come here to look at the scene first hand."

O'Rourke saw Dr. Furlani show a cop her identification and he let her through a barricade that they had set up. She was walking over to Farrell's car when O'Rourke called out to her.

"Dr. Furlani, wait! The crime scene's a little, uh, intense."

"I'm fine, Lieutenant," she replied coolly. O'Rourke and Valente were too late. She was already at the car. "I just wanted to see our suspect's latest work."

"Sorry, no message for you to decipher this time," O'Rourke said pointedly.

"It doesn't um, look like the earlier crime scenes," she said, as she leaned in and peered through the car window to get a better look. She sounded differently now, less cool and controlled.

"No, but we're sure it's the same killer. He was after the girl's computer."

"I see," her voice wavering. "I assume that he therefore had to…uh…kill this man to get to the house, and…oh, what's that over there on the passenger window?"

"Blood and skull fragments," Valente said. "He was shot in the forehead at close range and it splattered all the way over to the opposite window."

Dr. Furlani suddenly put her hand over her mouth and bolted away, nearly knocking Valente over.

"Women…," Valente said. He was about to add something else until the look on O'Rourke's face made him think better of it.

O'Rourke waited a few minutes, then went over to Dr. Furlani. She looked pale and dizzy as she leaned against a tree for support. Her earlier aura of cold professionalism was totally gone.

"Take a few deep breaths," O'Rourke said gently. "It helps."

She nodded and took his advice. After a few breaths, she looked a bit better.

"I've studied hundreds of crime scene photos at the university," she said quietly. "But I've never actually gone to a crime scene. To actually see it all up close…"

She wiped her brow with the back of her hand. "I'm sorry, I seem to be perspiring quite heavily," she said.

O'Rourke pulled out a handkerchief that he kept in his jacket pocket for collecting evidence, and handed it to her. She wiped her face off thoroughly with it and went to hand the damp cloth back to him. O'Rourke held his hand up to her. "You can keep it," he said with a smile.

Furlani laughed nervously. "Thank you."

She took off her glasses and wiped them with a dry corner of the handkerchief. Without her glasses, she had a vulnerable look about her. "I'm so embarrassed," she said apologetically. "You must think I'm a real amateur."

"No. I just think you're human."

A half hour later, Chief of Police Reilly showed up. By then, news vans were on the scene as well. O'Rourke spied Trish Perkins from Channel Seven down the block, interviewing neighbors

"This case is getting out of hand," the chief said. "I still can't believe one of our men may be involved in this. I'll have to make a statement to the press soon. I'm not happy about all this."

"I'm angry as hell myself," O'Rourke said. "I feel responsible for Farrell."

"You can't second guess yourself," the chief replied. Then he added: "The press will do enough of that for you."

O'Rourke spoke with the chief for a while, filling him in on the latest information.

"The killer was taking quite a risk," the chief said. "Up until now, he's been planning these attacks ahead of time. Slipping quietly into places. But now, he kills Farrell right out on the street and then breaks a window and climbs right into a house. The only reason the neighbors didn't hear it all was because it was raining so hard outside. But if someone had come walking by…""

"He's getting desperate," O'Rourke replied. "He must have wanted to steal the computer pretty badly to take the risks."

"What about the Nottinghams," the chief asked. "Didn't they hear anything?"

"They said no," O'Rourke replied. "John Nottingham was downstairs, working in the basement. He was using a power saw; if he had that on when the window was broken, he wouldn't have heard a thing. And the mother takes heavy medication; I'm not surprised that she didn't hear anything."

As they spoke, O'Rourke spotted Captain Grainey pulling up and coming out of his car. He looked upset.

"Why the hell am I always the last to know about everything?" he shouted as he stormed toward O'Rourke and Chief Reilly. "I never even heard the name Nottingham until a half hour ago!"

"That's my fault," the chief said, covering for O'Rourke. "I hadn't had a chance to call you yet."

"O'Rourke should have told me," Grainey fumed, glaring at O'Rourke. "I'm his boss!"

"We were concerned that the Nottinghams themselves could be a target," O'Rourke said angrily. "We had to keep access to the information about the girl within the department. If it got out, lives could be in danger."

"What a great job you did with that," Grainey replied, pointing to Farrell's car.

O'Rourke was close to a boil now. "Well, maybe I'd keep you in the loop if you didn't blab everything to Trish Perkins. I can only imagine what you might be getting in return!"

Grainey, almost speechless, moved threateningly toward O'Rourke. "You…you can't…who do you think you're talking to…"

O'Rourke took an angry step toward Grainey, but Valente, who had heard the commotion and had come running over, grabbed O'Rourke's arms to hold him back.

Chief Reilly, his face red, got between Grainey and O'Rourke. "That's enough of this," he shouted. "There are news cameras watching us! I've got a mind to take you both off this case!"

"It's too late for that," a voice said from behind them. It was Dale Mitchell, who was trailed by two men in suits and several State Troopers.

"I just got the order from State Police Superintendent Owen," Mitchell said. "Since there's a likelihood that an Albany police officer is involved, we're taking over the entire investigation."

"What?" Chief Reilly asked, not quite comprehending.

"The Albany Police Department is off the case. By order of the governor of New York State. You can all go home."

TWENTY-THREE

||||||||||||||||||||||||||||||||||||||

The tall man sat at his desk late in the night looking through Cheryl Nottingham's laptop computer. His initial plan had been to make Steven O'Rourke his next target, but when the tall man heard that O'Rourke found out about Cheryl Nottingham, his plans had to change. There was no way the tall man could let anyone see what was on that computer. He regretted the business about Jim Farrell, but Farrell was an acceptable casualty.

The tall man originally had just planned to destroy the computer and discard the pieces separately. But he knew he could get into the computer and curiosity got the better of him.

As expected, the tall man found the e-mails between Cheryl and himself on the computer; the same correspondence that he looked at over and over again on his own computer almost daily. He also noticed that Cheryl had created lots of documents on her computer; accounts of very personal information and thoughts about herself. But as he searched though those, he was upset about what he didn't find. He searched for hours, but was unable to find any mention of himself at all in those documents. That couldn't be possible. After all they had been through together...

Then he realized that Cheryl was just being smart. She didn't want anyone to know about their relationship, so she must have started deleting everything about him from the computer. She never had the chance to delete the e-mails though. The woman he loved so passionately had tragically passed away before she could get to that. Thinking about that brought up that rage in him again – anger at the black bastard, the asshole, the slut, and all the others.

After he calmed himself down, he searched through the documents some more and found something else. There was mention of a diary that Cheryl used to keep. Of course! That's where Cheryl would keep her innermost thoughts. That's where she would have written about him.

He kept at it until he found another mention of the diary. Cheryl had left a note about where the diary is now. But the location she mentioned presented a major problem. The diary was at the woman's house. The woman he had killed first. Before he had decided to leave messages and take mementos during the missions.

The diary is secure where it is now, he thought. He would eventually need to retrieve it since it could identify him. But no one else knew about it; he could get it later. It was getting late now and although it was a Sunday, he was scheduled to work in a few hours. He shut the laptop down and went to bed.

After Dale Mitchell made his stunning announcement, O'Rourke, Oquendo, Valente and Chief Reilly returned to the station with Mitchell and the two plainclothes state police officers that had accompanied him. (The chief had wisely sent Grainey home.) The uniformed state policemen stayed at the scene of the crime, planning to bring their own forensics unit in.

Under order of the governor, all data on the case from Division One computers had to be made accessible to the State Police. O'Rourke's staff, as the team leaders, had most of the key information on their own computers; the remaining bits of information that the other detectives had on their computers could be retrieved later in the morning. O'Rourke kept passwords for Myers' and Booker's computers, and had to give it to the two state policemen. O'Rourke, Valente, and Oquendo watched as the men systematically downloaded information from O'Rourke's computer, then those of each of his team. O'Rourke felt disheartened as he watched the men complete the process on the last computer.

The final step was the hard files. O'Rourke, doing it the old-fashioned way, tended to keep a lot of information in hand-written files rather than on computer. The two men had brought large boxes with them, and began taking O'Rourke's file folders related to the case and packing them in the boxes.

O'Rourke couldn't stand being in his office while they did that. As he walked out, Chief Reilly put a hand on his shoulder. "You look exhausted," he said to O'Rourke. "What time did you get to work this morning?"

"Before eight," O'Rourke answered. So much had happened today that it was hard to believe it was just this morning that they interviewed Ashley Morton.

"It's late. How much sleep have you had in the last three days?"

"I've had enough," O'Rourke lied.

"Look, you've been doing a good job on this case, no matter what Grainey said. But the State boys have the case now. You need some rest. An exhausted cop is no good to us."

O'Rourke started to protest but Jack Reilly cut him off.

"Steven, I want you to go home. Now. Keep your cell phone

on in case Mitchell needs you for something. But otherwise, relax. Get some sleep. I don't want to see you here tomorrow. That's an order."

Later, O'Rourke sat in front of the television in his house, beer in one hand, remote in the other, still angry at being taken off the case. On the television, the story was not only the headlines on the local channels but on CNN and Fox News also. He switched on the Channel Seven news. They were about to show something from Trish Perkins about the murder case that seemed to be a re-airing of an earlier report. He turned the volume up.

"Bill," Trish said in an earnest voice, "this case has taken quite a turn tonight. We can confirm now that an Albany police officer has been killed. His name is being withheld right now until the next of kin can be notified. But we can say now that his death appears to be related to the murders of Randall Tucker and Bernard Fleming. In addition, it appears there was a recent attack on a teenage girl in Colonie that also appears to be related."

Most of the rest of what Trish Perkins had to report was about the State Police taking over the investigation. O'Rourke's name popped up twice, as the detective formerly in charge of the case. He decided he needed another beer.

When he got back to his seat, the report was still on. "Trish," Bill Reynolds asked, "it appears the Albany police officer was surprised and shot without having a chance to even try to defend himself. Is that correct?"

"Yes, Bill. It looks like the officer was shot at close range before he even had a chance to pull his gun."

"Can you give us your take on all this?"

"Well, Bill," Trish opined, "the person who has been committing these crimes, the one we refer to now as 'the Tall Man', is obviously deranged, but also very clever. He's been able to stay one step ahead of the Albany Police Department for a week now, and even the State Police have no clue where or when he'll strike next."

After Bill asked her to expound on that further, Perkins added in her best imitation of Nancy Grace: "This man attacks at night and doesn't give his victims a chance. He preys on those that least expect an attack, and then robs these people of their dignity by disfiguring them. He's sick and he's a spineless coward to boot, in my book."

Wow, thought O'Rourke. Trish wasn't holding anything back. She knew this was a big story and was making the most of it. O'Rourke shut off the tube and went to bed. One last thought occurred to him as he was falling asleep. He hoped for Trish's sake that the killer wasn't watching her report.

When he woke up, O'Rourke was surprised that the alarm clock read 7:46 AM. Normally, he was up by six. He was still in a bad mood, yet he realized that he had slept soundly for the first time in a week. He couldn't recall any nightmares or dire warnings from the night before. The only thing he could remember dreaming about was mowing the lawn, a task that he realized was long overdue.

After getting dressed and going out to get the morning paper, he dialed Ginny Dixon's number. Ginny picked up on the first ring.

"Well, hello stranger," she answered.

"Have you finished your morning run?"

"Just finished. How are you doing?" There was concern in her voice. She must have seen the morning news. In addition to the full coverage on the local news, the headlines in the Times Union read "Murder Suspect an Albany Cop?"

"As well as can be expected. Do you have some time to come over and talk?"

"By talk, do you mean talk? Or something else?"

"Actually just talk," he said, then added: "But maybe we can get to the something else after that..."

After some talk and something else, they sat at a table on O'Rourke's back deck under the morning sun, coffee mugs in hand.

"I'm still pissed off about being booted off the case," he said. "We put all that time into it and then they just pull it out from under us like that."

"It definitely doesn't seem fair," Ginny said.

"I just hope those state guys know what they're doing. The last thing that Mitchell said was that they're going to see what they can find on the social networking websites. Although, to be honest, that's probably a dead end. From what we know of Cheryl, I can't see her having a ton of friends on Facebook."

"What about e-mail? Can they check with whatever company handles Cheryl's internet access to get her records," Ginny asked. "Are they even allowed to do that?"

"We already looked into that. Her particular internet provider only stores e-mail records for 30 days. They don't have enough total storage space for more than that. And Cheryl's been dead for two months."

"Do you think that's why the killer wanted the computer? Because they had corresponded with each other?"

"Maybe. Or maybe she wrote something on her computer that might identify him."

They were interrupted by the ring of O'Rourke's cellphone. He thought it might be Dale Mitchell calling so he picked up right away. It wasn't Mitchell.

"O'Rourke here."

"Lieutenant? This is Ralph Vickers. From the Electric Company."

O'Rourke recalled that he had given the bartender his number in case he thought of any more patrons that might have spoken to Bernard Fleming.

"What's up?"

"I saw the morning paper," Vickers said. "It said that the killer might be a cop."

"That's one possibility."

"Well, here's the thing. There's something I didn't tell you the other day when you were at the bar."

O'Rourke put down his coffee and sat up straight.

"What would that be?"

"When you came into the bar, there was another cop with you."

"Tony Valente?" O'Rourke had no idea where this was leading.

"No, no. There was another one outside, that didn't come in. Young guy, tall and slim. Good looking. I saw him from the window after you left."

He was referring to Brad Myers. O'Rourke recalled that Myers was hesitant to go into the gay establishment. Valente had even ribbed Myers about it a bit.

"What about him?"

"I didn't want to say anything before. No need to out the guy. But when I read the paper this morning, I figured I had to tell you. That guy was a regular at the restaurant."

"You must be mistaken," O'Rourke said. O'Rourke didn't want to believe it. He knew what being suspected of being gay could mean to a cop's career.

"No. I got a good look at him. Martin saw him too. He recognized him right away."

"Maybe he was doing some undercover work at the bar…"

"I saw him putting lip locks on other guys more than once," Ralph said. "If the guy isn't gay, he sure does a good job of hiding it."

"Damn it," O'Rourke said. Myers' presence in the same place that Fleming hung out certainly raised suspicion, considering the killer might be a cop.

"Did you ever see him talking to Bernard Fleming?" O'Rourke asked Vickers.

"Not that I recall. I asked Martin also, and he doesn't remember either. They both came in a lot, but we can't remember seeing them hanging around together. But the place gets pretty busy sometimes, so there's a lot we don't see."

"Thanks," said O'Rourke. He couldn't think of anything else to ask right now. "I know you don't like to give out information on your customers, so I do appreciate it."

"Sure thing," Vickers said. "Just trying to help."

"What was that all about?" Ginny asked. "It sounded serious."

O'Rourke knew he could trust Ginny not to say anything, so he told her of the conversation with Vickers.

"There was a comment that I remember Brad making in that bar in Amsterdam," O'Rourke said to her. "He said that he didn't hang out in that type of bar in college. That makes sense now."

"You don't think he had anything to do with the murders, do you?"

"I don't know. All we really know is that Brad spent a lot of time in the same place that Bernard Fleming did. It could be just a coincidence."

"It doesn't fit with your theory about a traffic incident being the reason Fleming was killed."

"That's just a theory I came up with. There's no way to be sure about that."

Ginny thought about it some more. "Maybe Brad just avoided

going into the Electric Company with you just because he thought Ralph Vickers might say something to out him. It might have nothing to do with the killings. And what connection would Brad have with the other victims?"

"None that we know of right now," O'Rourke said. "The thing is Brad's a good kid. I personally don't care if he's gay or straight or likes to shag sheep in his spare time. Gay marriage may be legal now in this state, but the Albany Police Department's still very conservative. If other cops found out he was gay, it could mean the end of his career as a cop. I don't mean that in any official way. You can't be canned for being gay. But the way the guy would get treated; trust me, he wouldn't last long on the force."

"This is the kid whose father was a cop, right?"

"Father and grandfather."

They both sipped their coffee in silence. Then Ginny finally said: "So what are you going to do? Are you going to contact the State Police?"

"I'm going to have to think about it."

Ginny went inside to get them more coffee. O'Rourke found a piece of paper and started writing down the approximate times of the three attacks. He tried to remember where Brad was at all those times. He couldn't recall offhand if Brad was on duty at any of those times. The only way to know for sure would be to check the timesheets in his office.

The smart thing to do would be to call Dale Mitchell right now and tell him about the call. But once he did that, there was no keeping a lid on Brad Myers' secret.

Ginny came out and handed him another mug of coffee. "Your grass needs mowing…" she said, looking out at the lawn.

"I know. I actually had a dream about mowing the lawn last night," he said, smiling. "I guess I'll have time to get to my personal stuff now."

"Speaking of personal stuff, Molly's coming home tomorrow," she said. "My mom thinks she's over her fear of her dad coming to the house and trying to take her away. I miss her being home."

"That's good. I'm glad Ellen was willing to take my kids all week," O'Rourke said. "The kids are great but I wouldn't have been much good around them lately."

"I keep thinking about what you said about Mrs. Nottingham," Ginny said sadly. "To lose a child like that…I don't think I could bear it."

"Yeah, the woman's a wreck. Her husband said she lost her mother recently as well. There was a recent picture on the wall of Theresa Nottingham, but she's changed so much since the picture was taken. You wouldn't recognize her from the…"

O'Rourke stopped abruptly in mid-sentence.

"You've got that look in your eyes again," Ginny said. "I know that look. You're on to something, aren't you?"

"I think so," O'Rourke said. "I knew there was something about that picture. But I was too tired and couldn't put my finger on it yesterday."

He pulled out his cellphone and dialed Oquendo's number at work. Luckily, she was at her desk.

"Rosie," he asked her, "do you have your report of our interview yesterday with the Nottinghams?"

"Boss, we're supposed to stay out of this case now."

"I know, but I just need you to look something up. But don't tell Mitchell."

"You're going to get us both in trouble…"

"Please, it's important," he said urgently.

"Okay, okay," she said. "I turned over my typed report to the State Police, but I still have the original handwritten notes I took at the house." There was a rustle of papers and Oquendo came back on the phone.

"What do you need?"

"Theresa Nottingham," O'Rourke said. "What was her maiden name?"

"I think it was Jackson or something like that. Hold on...It was Johnson."

"Remember that accidental death case that we were looking at the morning that they found Bernard Fleming's body? The old woman on Second Avenue? Wasn't her name Johnson too?"

"Hey, her name was Johnson! Gertrude Johnson! I never even made the connection. I mean, there's a million Johnsons around. It's like Perez."

"Shhh. Not so loud. Let's keep this between you and me."

"Okaaay..," she said quietly. She clearly didn't understand the reason for the secrecy, but she was going along with it.

"Now," O'Rourke said, "I want you to look up the names on the Lexis system. Check to see if Gertrude Johnson and Theresa Johnson are related. As a matter of fact, see if Theresa went by the name Terry at all."

It took Oquendo a few minutes to retrieve the information from LexisNexis, a system the department utilized to get public records such as credit information, birth records and motor vehicle data.

"Holy cow, boss, you're right," she said in a hushed voice. "Theresa Nottingham is Gertrude Johnson's daughter. And she occasionally used the name Terry Johnson on some documents years ago. What's this all about?"

"That picture that Mr. Nottingham showed us. I just realized where I had seen Mrs. Nottingham's mother before. She was the dead lady at the bottom of the stairs on Second Avenue. I didn't recognize her at first."

"No wonder! The lady was dead for a couple of days and her face was really messed up from the fall. She didn't look much like the picture."

"I still should have caught it. The sports trophies I saw at Gertrude Johnson's house had two names on them: Todd Johnson and Terry Johnson. I didn't look closely at the trophies at the time and assumed the two were brothers. But Terry was a girl – short for Theresa."

"So what does this all mean? Cheryl commits suicide and then two months later her grandmother dies in an accidental fall. How does that help with the case?"

"Because I'm thinking that maybe the fall was no accident."

"Holy crap!"

"Shhh. Listen, Rosie, I need you to keep this to yourself. Remember what Mitchell said – we're all suspects. Well, not you, but any cops that are tall and male. Which means most of us."

"Okay. But we have to tell Mitchell. This could be a real lead."

"I'll handle it myself," he said. Rosie was silent on the other end. "Rosie, I can't tell you why, but you've got to let me do this myself. At least for now. I'll call you back later."

"You're also keeping this information from the State Police," Ginny said after he hung up. "This is not a good idea…"

"I can't very well call them and tell them part of what I know and leave out the part about Brad," he said. "I think I can get to the bottom of all this soon. Maybe I can figure it all out today before I have to go back to work. I won't have to bring up Brad's name if I can show that the killer is someone else."

Ginny was about to ask him how, but he was already calling Sandy Bernstein on his cell.

"I need a favor," he said as soon as Sandy answered. "I need you to get some information for me quick. On the Nottinghams."

Sandy paused, then said: "I thought we were all off that case. All of us. Including you."

"That's why it's called a favor."

"That guy Mitchell was pretty adamant that he wanted the Albany police off the case."

"Don't worry about him. He makes things sound more serious that they are."

"Yeah, right. Those State Police, they're a barrel of laughs."

"Sandy, I really need this."

"I don't know, Steven…"

"I hesitate to bring this up," O'Rourke said without hesitating, "but you have a little secret that I'm keeping. Something about you and a Miss Megan Ross…"

"You fight dirty," Sandy replied with a sigh. "All right, what do you need?"

"I need you guys to run the name Gertrude Johnson. There's a recent file on her in the Accidental Death folder on the main drive."

"The lady that fell down the stairs down in the South End?"

"Yeah. She's related to the Nottinghams. Check out everyone she's connected to. All her relatives, in-laws, friends, acquaintances. No matter how distant. Make a list. Then check that against the names you've compiled on Tucker, Fleming and the others. Call me on my cell as soon as you can if you find any connection."

"I still say you should call Mitchell. Don't do this on your own…"

"Everybody seems to be telling me that. Good thing I'm not a good listener."

O'Rourke dialed up Nottingham's number next. Ginny, despite her misgivings about O'Rourke deciding not to call the State Police, was watching him, fascinated by it all. O'Rourke put his phone on speaker so she could follow the conversation.

Nottingham didn't pick up and let the call go to his machine. "Mr. Nottingham," O'Rourke said, "if you're there, pick up. I need to ask you something. It's very urgent -"

"Lieutenant O'Rourke?" Nottingham said, picking up. "What is it?"

"I need to ask you about your mother-in law. Gertrude Johnson."

"Hold on," he said quietly. "Let me go to the other room." He came back on a moment later. "I don't want my wife to hear," he explained. "What did you want to know?"

"Did Cheryl have problems with her grandmother?" he asked. No time to sugar coat things.

"As a matter of fact, yes," he answered. "Cheryl used to adore her. When Cheryl was at a low point a couple of weeks before she died, we suggested she stay with her grandmother for a while. Gertrude was getting pretty frail and couldn't do a lot of things around the house. So we asked Cheryl to stay there for a while to help out. We thought it would benefit both of them. It didn't work out though. Gertrude was getting cranky because she was losing her independence and Cheryl – well she was being Cheryl, getting into dark moods. There was a big blow-up and she had to come back home after only a few days. That was the beginning of her last downward spiral."

"Is there anyone else in Gertrude's family that lives in this area? Any men?"

"My brother in law Todd, her son, lives in Virginia. Other than that, no other living relatives. Why do you ask? Do you think what happened to Theresa's mother wasn't an accident?"

"What about friends?" O'Rourke asked, ignoring the question. "Did Gertrude have male friends that you know of? Acquaintances? Anything like that?"

"Not really. Well, I shouldn't say that. She was friendly with the mailman."

O'Rourke remembered the mailman, the one that looked like a chubby leprechaun. He could be ruled out.

"How about home aides? Helpers? Anyone that cared for her?"

"No, as I said, she was very independent. It took all we could do to convince her to allow Cheryl to stay there."

O'Rourke was out of ideas. He stared straight ahead, trying to think of something and then it hit him.

"What about her lawn? Who took care of that?"

"I did. She was way too frail to do it herself. She would let us know when it needed mowing. Now that you mention it, she hadn't mentioned it in a month. The lawn must look awful."

"No, as a matter of fact, I was there a few days ago and it looked recently mown. I'll call you back."

He looked up after he was off the phone. Ginny was wide-eyed.

"Wow," she said. "Remember that dream you had? It was about mowing the lawn…"

"Maybe it doesn't mean anything," O'Rourke said, uncomfortable with the idea that his dreams had a bearing on the future. "But it's worth checking out."

O'Rourke went inside and got his gun and holster out of the locked drawer in his bedroom, with Ginny following. He put them on and put on a jacket over it.

"Now, wait a minute," Ginny said emphatically. "You're not going over to Mrs. Johnson's house, are you?"

"Why not? The house is just a site of an accidental death that my unit happened to investigate. As far as anyone else knows, it has no connection with the case the State Police are working on. I have every right to take another look at the house."

"I know *this* is not a good idea."

"The worst that can happen is that I get into some hot water for not letting Dale Mitchell know about it."

"Actually, I can think of a lot worse things that can happen. A person may have been murdered there…"

"That's what I'm counting on. If her death was a murder, it happened before Tucker was killed. And it doesn't fit the pattern of the others. It could be it was the first of the string of murders, before the killer got so good at it. Maybe he slipped up and left a clue."

O'Rourke hurried out to the Jag. He looked back and Ginny was still standing in his doorway, chewing on a fingernail. She was worried about him. And he was worried that it bothered him that *she* was worried. This relationship was getting serious a lot quicker than he had expected.

"Listen," he said to her out the car window, "I'm not going to get hurt. I'll call you in two hours and let you know I'm all right."

She smiled, trying to act upbeat. "I'll hold you to that. Don't forget, you promised me a picnic."

"Deal," he said, and took off down the street.

TWENTY-FOUR

||||||||||||||||||||||||||||||||||||||||

Gertrude Johnson's house on Second Avenue was only about fifteen minutes from O'Rourke's house. He spent the drive trying to convince himself that not calling the State Police was the right thing to do because he was trying to protect Brad Myers. But deep down inside, he was still hurt by being taken off the case and wanted to solve it himself.

He left the Jaguar across the street and walked across Second Avenue to the house. The yellow police tape was still in an X shape over the front door; the Albany Police Department had been so busy this week, no one had taken it down.

Two kids about eight or nine, one white and one black, were sitting on the front steps of a house two doors up the street, playing some kind of a card game that had superheroes on the cards. As O'Rourke walked toward the Johnson house, they came over to him.

"Hey, mister," one of the kids said jabbing a finger at him, "you can't go in there. The cops have it all taped up. A lady fell down the stairs and killed herself in there."

"I *am* a cop," O'Rourke said. "Did either of you know the lady?"

"No," said the second kid. "I live right over there but I hardly ever seen her. She never went outside."

"I think she was a witch," the first kid said.

"You're so stupid, Jimmy," said the other one.

"No, you are, Aaron!"

"Okay, settle down," O'Rourke said impatiently. "Did you ever see anyone come to her door? Or mow her lawn? A tall man?"

"No," Aaron replied. "You can't see her yard over her high fence. Plus, we really don't play outside all that much. We're only out here now because my mom said we need to get some air."

"That means we were getting on her nerves," Jimmy explained.

"Yeah, I can see how that could happen," O'Rourke said. He pulled two five dollar bills out of his wallet. "I'll tell you what, maybe you guys can help my investigation out. Go back to your game, but keep an eye on my car. Make sure no criminals try to steal it."

"Okay," the kids said excitedly. They took the money and ran back to their steps.

The outer door of the Johnson house wasn't locked. O'Rourke pulled the police tape aside and walked into the small vestibule. The door to the upstairs apartment to his right was locked, the broken window now covered with a thin piece of plywood. With his pocketknife, he was able to pull out a few nails and remove the wood. He carefully climbed through the doorway around the jagged glass where the officers had broken through, just like he had done a few days before. The only difference now was that there was no dead body lying on the other side.

After climbing up the stairs, he stopped at the trophy case on the landing. He opened the opaque glass door of the trophy case and took a close look at the trophies that he had only briefly glanced at a few days ago. The trophies that had "Terry Johnson" written on the base, which were for bowling and soccer, were indeed trophies for a girl, which was evident by the vague female shape of the gold figurines on top. Something he missed the first time when he only gave them a quick glance.

He was about to move on when he noticed that one of the large trophies on the top shelf was not lined up properly with the others. He put on his gloves and carefully turned it over. The bottom of the trophy had a crack in it, as if it had hit something hard. Like Mrs. Johnson's head. The coroner's office naturally assumed that the fractured skull was caused by the fall. But now, O'Rourke knew better.

O'Rourke knew he was on the right track now. The killer had murdered Gertrude Johnson for a reason, something associated with Cheryl Nottingham. Cheryl had a recent falling out with her grandmother, according to the father. Could that have been the motive for the murder?

This killing didn't fit in with the murder of Tucker and Fleming though. No message on the wall and no parts cut off the victim as far as he knew. But this would have been the first killing, unless there were more he didn't know about yet. Perhaps the killer changed his M.O. after the first murder. Maybe he wasn't satisfied with just killing his victims.

O'Rourke put the trophy down and walked down the hallway of the house. There was something else he needed to check out.

There were two bedrooms on the second floor. The one on his left with the handicapped rails inside must be Mrs. Johnson's. But it was the other one that he wanted to check out. When Cheryl stayed here for a few days, that's where she would have slept. O'Rourke didn't know exactly what he was looking for but it couldn't hurt to look inside.

He opened the bedroom door and switched on the lights. Luckily, the power hadn't been shut off yet. It was stifling hot in the room so he opened a window on the far side of the room before looking around.

There were a few framed pictures on the dresser, as well as on a night stand. One picture was a photo of the three Nottinghams and Mrs. Johnson. Cheryl was the only one not smiling.

He opened the dresser drawers and looked through them. Many were full of the grandmother's things, but one drawer had some clothes and a bracelet in it that looked like they must have belonged to Cheryl. Upside down, under the clothes, was a framed picture with the glass broken out of it as if someone angrily threw it in there. O'Rourke recognized the photograph. It was a copy of one of the photos he had seen of Cheryl - one that Randall Tucker had taken.

The nightstand had just two drawers and both were empty. The bed was an old-fashioned type that had two small sliding wood doors on the headboard. O'Rourke opened up the first door. It was empty. He leaned over across the bed and slid open the second door on the bed's headboard. There were a few old books inside that looked like they could be forty years old. Moving the books aside, he found something hidden behind them. A small pink and black book with a metal clasp.

A diary.

John Nottingham had said that his daughter used to keep a diary but that he couldn't find it after she died. Could that be because Cheryl had left it here after her spat with her grandmother and had never had the opportunity to go back for it?

O'Rourke, gloves still on his hands, picked up the diary. Feeling a little creepy about looking through a dead teenage girl's personal diary, he opened it anyway and started reading.

A few blocks away, the tall man walked along Delaware Avenue toward the corner of Delaware and Second. He had signed out at eleven AM, telling his co-workers that he didn't feel well. He risked throwing suspicion on himself by leaving early but it was a risk he had to take. Besides, he was feeling a bit ill. He had just learned that O'Rourke had realized that Gertrude Johnson was connected to the other missions.

He couldn't put it off any longer – he needed to get the diary today. This might actually work out well for him, he thought. *O'Rourke knows about Johnson but he hasn't told the State Police. For some reason, he's going it alone. He could even be heading to the house himself.*

If so, the tall man would be ready for him. His backpack contained a pair of gloves, a ski mask, a knife, a scalpel, the gun with silencer attached, and a small container of kerosene that he had put in it this morning. He had everything he needed to be able to cross Steven O'Rourke's name off his list.

O'Rourke noticed that only the first two thirds of the diary had writing in it. Cheryl never had a chance to fill it up. The first thing that struck O'Rourke was that the quality of the handwriting changed dramatically as time went by. The early sections were written when Cheryl was younger. The handwriting, although that of a younger child, was fairly neat, improving gradually as time went on. But the writing on the last fifty pages or so began to progressively get more and more sloppy and distorted. That's when she started going downhill, O'Rourke realized.

An entry in the diary not far from the end was the first to catch his eye. It read: *I went back to the photography store today. I told Mr. Tucker that I demanded my money back. The photos came out awful!! At first he was calm about it. He said he couldn't refund the full price. He tried to tell me the photographs look fine. But I didn't look pretty at all in them! Then he handed me a mirror and asked me to compare the photos to my reflection. I'm sorry, those photos are what you look like, he said. He was so damned condescending!*

I was furious! I said to him who do you think you are! I started swearing at him and he asked me to leave the store! THAT BLACK BASTARD!!

The last two capitalized words of the paragraph stunned O'Rourke. Those were the exact two words written on the wall inside Central Studio. Had the killer also read the diary?

It was obvious that Randall Tucker had been murdered because of this disagreement with Cheryl Nottingham. Cheryl was upset about the perceived insult, and it resulted in someone killing the poor guy and cutting his tongue out because of what he said. But who? He needed to read more. Not far below, he found another entry:

I know I'm not the greatest driver in the world, but why do people have to act this way! I was driving down the street in the left lane on my way home from Central Studio. I was going slow but I needed to stay in the fast lane because I had to make a left turn up ahead. This old guy in the car in back of me was so inpatient! He kept flashing his lights at me, like I was going too slow for him. Why didn't he just go around me? But I got even with him. I slowed down even more and kept tapping my brakes. I think that really pissed him off. He finally passed me in the right lane. But then he did something that really upset me. He gave me the finger! Stuck his arm out the window and gave me the finger!

I saw his license plate too. BERNARD F. Yeah, he's a real "F" all right! And he's some kind of big shot too. The sticker on his license plate had NY ASSEMBLY on it.

It's people like that that depress me. They think they can get away with anything they want. The whole world sucks, even the people in charge. Especially the people in charge. It makes me want to...no, I won't write those words down...

O'Rourke couldn't help but feel a bit impressed with himself that he had made the right guess about a traffic incident being involved. O'Rourke then looked through all the surrounding pages in the diary, but couldn't find any reference to the word ASSHOLE. So apparently, the killer didn't get the wording for his vulgar message on Fleming's wall from Cheryl's diary. If he didn't get it from the diary, did Cheryl tell him in person of her experience?

He found something else a few pages further:

I need to stay positive. That's what mom said. She said I need to stop dwelling on the negative. Make more friends, she said. Well, I'll try. Maybe this new guy. He seems really interested in me – in my feelings and what I have to say. Maybe he can help me get out of this darkness I'm feeling. Maybe...

Was it the killer that Cheryl was referring to? But her father said she had no men in her life. Was this someone she was keeping from her family?

O'Rourke was getting absorbed in the diary. He needed to tell someone about this. He would just read a little more first...

The tall man walked briskly down Second Avenue. Although it was warm out, he had the hood of his sweatshirt up over his head. People might think it odd, but it was better than exposing his face. As he neared the Johnson house, he thought back to the last time he was there. Killing Gertrude Johnson was his first mission. It was something that he needed to do for his soul mate. For Cheryl.

Before she died, Cheryl had told him all about the evil old lady – how she had tormented Cheryl. How she, along with the others, had given Cheryl such aggravation. The aggravation which ultimately forced poor Cheryl to take her own life. He had decided, therefore, that the old woman's life must end too. She had ruined Cheryl's life, and therefore his as well. It wasn't fair that she should go on living while Cheryl was gone.

Using his police ID, the tall man easily convinced the gullible old woman to let him into her home. Three weeks ago, he pretended to be part a charitable police association that helped the elderly with mowing their lawns and jobs like that in order to gain her confidence. Although seething with rage on the inside, he came across as a friendly young man just doing his part for society. But he found that he didn't have the nerve to kill her right away though. He actually mowed the old woman's lawn for her, just as he told her he would.

He came back twice after that, mowing the lawn both times. He was confused – she didn't seem to match Cheryl's description of her. The old woman seemed nice, but it must be a disguise. Cheryl said how the woman used her. Always asking her to do things for her, as if she were her slave or something. Asking her to wash the dishes or mop the floor. Pretending that she was too frail to do it herself.

The third time, it was a very hot day. When he came inside, sweating from the exertion of mowing the lawn, the old woman had a cold drink and a piece of cake for him. After eating, he followed her to the front stairs. He actually almost left the house again without doing anything. But she started talking about her family, how her son-in-law usually did the mowing. She showed him the trophies that her son and daughter had won years ago.

But then she mentioned her poor granddaughter, who had passed on recently. She started saying some disparaging things about her; how the poor dear had problems, needed help. As she spoke, she didn't notice him putting the work gloves back on that he had earlier used for mowing. When she took a step down the stairs to lead him out, he acted quickly. Grabbing one of the trophies, he struck her squarely in the back of the head with it. She caught her heel in the carpet before she tumbled down the stairs, hitting the bottom with a loud thud. He didn't plan it to look like an accident, but after she fell, he realized that it would look that way.

He remembered how his heart was pounding after that, as if he were going to have a heart attack right then and there. And he recalled looking down at the body and then going through the house to make sure there was no evidence left behind. The last thing he had done was to take a key to the back door from the hook on the wall, where he had seen her put it after he mowed the lawn. He wanted to keep the key in case he later realized that he had left some evidence behind. But now he realized there was a better way to get rid of any evidence. A good fire would take care of the old wooden house.

He pulled the key from his pocket as he got within a block of the house. His plan was to get in the house through the back door, retrieve the diary, and get out. Do it quickly. Nothing complicated. Unless O'Rourke was there.

O'Rourke found the part he was looking for near the end of the diary:

Grandma really pissed me off today. I'm really getting upset. Doesn't help that I left my pills at home. I'm not her goddamn slave! I've got to get out of here! I can't take it anymore! She's killing me!!!

That was the last entry in the diary. But what about Ashley Morton?

He flipped back and found an entry:

My cousin asked me to go to a party with her! I can't believe it! Lori's so cool. Why would she invite ME? I wonder if my mom called her and asked her to? It doesn't matter. I'm going to go! I'll hang out with the cool kids!

Then a few pages later:

That party was a disaster! It started all right. Then Lori went to get something to eat and I was alone with some boy. His name was Mark. He was really nice. He asked me how I knew Lori and where I had gone to school. I told him. He said he went to Colonie High.

We were getting along real well. I think he really liked me! Then this blonde tramp comes along! She gave me this look like who the hell was I. She said I shouldn't be talking with her boyfriend and told me to get lost. By the time Lori came back, I was crying. I asked her to take me home. I told her what happened on the way home. She said she thinks the slut's name was Ashley. Ashley Morton.

I still can't get over the way that bitch Ashley Morton looked at me. Like I was some disgusting bug or something!

O'Rourke wondered what the killer would have done if he had gotten to her. The diary described how Ashley looked at Cheryl Nottingham. Would the killer have cut her eyes out? Written "BLONDE TRAMP" or something like that on the wall in neat letters?

It was all falling into place now. Hopefully, there was something in the diary that identified who this guy was that Cheryl met. He flipped the pages to the end of the diary. If it was anywhere, it would be there.

TWENTY-FIVE

|||||||||||||||||||||||||||||||||||||||||||

The tall man was approaching the woman's house now. There were two young boys playing some game on the steps of a house two doors down. He kept his head down, the hood of his sweatshirt shielding his face from them. They didn't seem to pay him any attention.

He stopped dead in his tracks when he saw the red Jaguar parked across the street. O'Rourke was definitely inside.

Could others be with him?

No. The information that the tall man had learned this morning was that O'Rourke was on his own. He didn't know what O'Rourke's exact plan was, but he knew that he was alone.

When he got to Gertrude Johnson's home, he walked down the alley between her house and the one next to it. He reached the back door and opened the door with the key.

Inside, he took his backpack off and set it down. He pulled a ski mask from it and put it on over his face, covering all but his eyes and mouth. He then put on a pair of gloves. Finally, he took out his .38 and attached the silencer.

He was ready for O'Rourke now.

Inside the house, O'Rourke located the section he was searching for:

I found this new friend online. He seems to really care about me. About my issues. I told him all about those people that have been ruining my life, like that Norton girl and Mr. Tucker at the photo studio. He said he's sorry that everyone has treated me so bad. He said he could sympathize. I think maybe he has some issues too. He said he'll keep in touch. He said at first that he was seventeen but later admitted that he was in his twenties. I told him my name but he didn't want to tell me his yet. But he told me I could call him Biker Boy. Cool! Guys with motorcycles are sexy!

Biker Boy? O'Rourke recalled that Brad Myers had a motorcycle.

O'Rourke had assumed... had hoped... that it was just a coincidence that Myers was in the Electric Company at the same time as Bernard Fleming. But now he wondered.

Could Myers have been on the internet and have somehow come across Cheryl Nottingham? Myers was apparently gay; but could he have established some sort of rapport with her – something beyond a sexual attraction?

It could add up. The killer always seemed to be a step ahead of them. But Brad had been a key part of the investigation. How could he have kept so cool all this time?

O'Rourke went back to the diary.

The tall man reached the top of the stairs and quietly opened the door to the kitchen. There was a light on in one of the rooms ahead. It was the spare bedroom. The one that Cheryl had slept in. He walked deliberately toward the room, the gun in front of him. He had to be ready for anything.

O'Rourke found another passage later in the diary:

Biker Boy wrote today that he's in love with me! Isn't that weird? I'm not in love with him or anything. I mean he's nice and asks about my feelings when we e-mail each other but I hardly even know him! I asked him what he looks like - he said that he's tall and in good shape. But wouldn't everyone say that? Then I asked him if he's in college or does he work. He wrote something strange. He said he's actually at work right now. He said he works for the police department! But he said don't worry – no one knows that he's online with me.

Is that true? Or did I just dream all that? I can't tell. Grandma is driving me nuts. I can't remember anything. Life sucks.

O'Rourke was about to turn the page when he heard a sound behind him. He turned and his heart skipped a beat when he saw a tall masked man there in the doorway, silently pointing a gun at him.

For a few seconds, neither man moved. O'Rourke quickly looked the man over to see if there was anything that might identify him. He was tall; taller than O'Rourke. About Myers' height. He had a ski mask on, but O'Rourke could make out that he was light-skinned from the open areas around the eyes. The man had blue eyes. Did Myers have blue eyes? He couldn't remember.

The man wore a hooded sweatshirt, dark pants and shoes, and had on a pair of gloves. O'Rourke could see a small patch of pale yellow showing from the man's shirt collar that was showing under the neck of the sweatshirt. It was a yellow dress shirt, the kind that detectives often wore.

Where O'Rourke was standing, the bed was on his left and the dresser was to his right, with the bedroom wall behind him. The window near the foot of the bed was still open, but it was too small for a man to easily fit through. The only way out then was the bedroom door past the tall man. He tried to calculate the distance between the man and himself. Six, maybe seven feet.

O'Rourke needed to do something, try to distract the man. "There's no reason to keep that mask on anymore," he said. "We know who you are. I figured it out. I called into the office a while ago. There all on their way here right now. Oquendo, Booker and the rest. They'll be here any minute."

O'Rourke had hoped for some reaction, but the man hadn't even blinked. His cold eyes, as well as the gun with the silencer in his right hand, were still focused right on O'Rourke. The desperate gamble hadn't worked. O'Rourke was quickly running out of time.

He could almost see the man's finger tightening on the trigger. O'Rourke had one last card to play.

"Is this what you're looking for?" he asked the man, holding out the diary.

The man reacted this time. His eyes were on the diary now.

"This is what you came here for, isn't it? There's a lot about you in here. Very interesting."

The man held his left hand out and pointed at the diary. He motioned for O'Rourke to toss it to him. It didn't take a genius to figure out the man's next move once O'Rourke did that. O'Rourke recalled how accurate the man was with his gun.

O'Rourke slowly moved the diary toward the man. Then with a quick move, he tossed the diary through the open window to his left.

"No!" the man shouted, turning to watch the diary sail out the window.

O'Rourke immediately took two quick strides and lunged at the man. He managed to grab the man's right arm so he couldn't fire the gun. O'Rourke smashed into him with his right shoulder, pushing him back. The man hit the wall hard but didn't let go of the gun.

The tall man was strong. O'Rourke had the man pinned against the wall, but he was struggling hard, trying to get free. O'Rourke's own gun was in his holster, under his jacket. If the man would just let up for a second, he might have time to reach for it.

He was about to make the move when the man managed to get his right knee up, striking O'Rourke sharply in the midsection. O'Rourke staggered for an instant and the man brought the butt of the gun down hard on the back of O'Rourke's head. The force of the blow sent the gun flying out of the tall man's hand. The gun clattered to the floor and slid under the bed as O'Rourke sunk to his knees.

The tall man didn't know what to do. The diary was outside, in the alley next to the house. O'Rourke was down on his knees, dazed but still conscious. The tall man's gun had fallen under the bed and he was all out of breath. The man had a scalpel and knife in his backpack but it would take precious moments to get them out. O'Rourke was starting to get up already and he surely had a gun on him.

In a state of panic now, the tall man turned around and fled. He dashed toward the front of the house, pulling his ski mask off as ran.

O'Rourke had gotten to his feet and saw the man running away. He started after him but never get out of the bedroom. After two steps, there was a throbbing pain in the back of his head where the gun had hit him. The tall man hadn't been able to get his full weight behind the blow, but it had hit O'Rourke hard enough. Everything went black and he hit the floor hard...

The tall man was halfway down the front stairs before he realized that O'Rourke was no longer chasing him. Was he calling for back up? Or was he hurt?

The tall man decided to take a chance. He pulled off his backpack and pulled out the small container of kerosene. He quickly poured the gas haphazardly up and down the stairs, not caring which way it went. Descending the stairs, he pulled a book of tall kitchen matches from his pocket. When he reached the door, he lit a match and tossed it behind him onto the flammable liquid. The stairway erupted in flames. Even with that small amount of kerosene, the old wooden home should burn quickly.

He went outside and pulled the hood of his sweatshirt back up. He walked quickly into the alley between the house and the one next door. The diary was there, on the ground. He put it in his sweatshirt pocket and walked back to the front of the house, turning up the Second Avenue hill. The kids were still playing on the steps of the nearby house and didn't seem to be paying any attention to him. He chanced a look back at the Johnson house. If you looked carefully, you could see a small plume of smoke starting to come out of the front of the house.

The tall man walked faster now. He took a deep breath and tried to concentrate as he walked up the hill. He didn't know if O'Rourke was telling the truth about calling into the team, but he had to assume the worst. The end might be near for him now regardless if O'Rourke survived the fire.

As he walked up the street, he pulled out his cell phone. Fumbling with the phone, he punched in a number that he had put on his speed dial earlier in the day. By the time he got to the top of Second Avenue, he had all the information that he needed for one last mission.

O'Rourke was somehow back in the meeting room at work. It was very hot and smoky in there. He was at the podium addressing a group of people, all sitting in chairs in the front row. Randall Tucker, Bernard Fleming, Jim Farrell, and Gertrude Johnson. Each of them was covered in blood from head to toe.

They were all saying something to him. He couldn't make it out at first, but they kept repeating it. Finally, he understood.

"Help us," they kept repeating. Then they added something else: "Make sure you go the right way."

A ringing noise woke O'Rourke up. For a few seconds, he couldn't remember where he was. He was laying down and it was very warm. He smelled smoke. Maybe he was still dreaming…

Then he realized it was his cell phone that was ringing. Still groggy, he got to his knees and answered it.

"H'lo," he said, still groggy.

"Steven…is that you? Are you all right?" It was Ginny.

"What?" The back of his head hurt like hell.

"You were supposed to call me in two hours, remember? You promised."

It was coming back to him now. He was still in the spare bedroom in Gertrude Johnson's house. His assailant had smashed him in the head with the gun. He glanced at his watch. He had been out for fifteen minutes. He probably had a concussion.

But that was the least of his worries right now. There was heavy smoke out in the hallway, starting to come inside the bedroom. The house was on fire.

"Ginny, I gotta go. Call 911! Give them the address of the Johnson house. Tell them it's on fire, and that I'm inside."

He shoved his phone into his pocket and went to the bedroom door. The hallway was hot and filled with smoke. He was reminded of his other dream, from a few nights ago.

It was impossible to see much in either direction. He didn't know which way to go. There seemed to be slightly less smoke to his right. But if he went left, that would take him to the front of the house, the closest exit. He took a step to his left and then stopped.

What was it that everyone kept saying to him in his dreams? "Make sure you go the right way."

He had taken that to mean to do what he knew was right. But was there another, more literal meaning to the message?

Still unsteady, he turned and headed to his right, toward the back door. With one hand on the wall, he made his way down the hallway through the dense smoke. After taking a few steps, he heard a loud crash behind him. He turned around and it took a second for him to see what had happened though the haze. The ceiling had caved in, right where he would have been if he had headed to his left.

Coughing heavily now, he reached the kitchen. There was light up ahead filtering through the window of the kitchen door that led to the back stairs and porch. He made it to the door and pushed it open. The stairway ahead was fairly clear. He slammed the door shut behind him and made his way down the back stairs.

The door at the bottom of the stairs led out to the yard with the well-mowed lawn. Once outside, he fell to his knees and took a few deep breaths. Fresh air never felt so good.

He didn't stop there long. He got up and ran through the alley toward the street. On the way, he noticed that the diary wasn't in the alley anywhere. The tall man must have taken it.

Once out of the alley, he called Oquendo.

"Where are you?" she asked. "There's a 911 call on the Johnson house. It's on fire."

"No kidding," he said. "I just barely got out of there."

"What? Are you-"

"I'm OK. Is Myers in the office?"

"He was until a while ago. He's out to lunch now."

"Do you know how long ago he left?"

"Yeah. I've been keeping a close eye on the whole unit. You really got me suspicious when you said don't tell anyone anything. He left for lunch a half hour ago."

O'Rourke tried to calculate if that time worked. But he was too groggy to figure it out.

"His shirt," he said. "Do you remember what color shirt he had on?"

"Yeah. It was blue."

"Are you sure?"

"Wait a minute. He's coming back right now. Definitely a blue shirt."

"OK. I have to go. Have the team get down to Gertrude Johnson's house as soon as they can."

O'Rourke tried to focus despite his still throbbing head. Was it still possible that Myers was the one who had attacked him? Even if he had gotten to the house quickly, could Myers have returned to the office so soon and changed his clothes?

He was at the front of the house now and he could hear a fire engine's siren in the distance. The whole top floor of the house was engulfed in flames. A crowd was gathering near the house.

O'Rourke noticed the two young boys, Aaron and Jimmy, at the front of crowd and approached them.

"Did you guys see anyone come out of this house before me?"

he asked them.

"Yeah," Aaron said. "Some big guy in a hoodie. Was he a cop too?"

"No…well, yes. Probably. What did he look like?"

A woman standing next to Aaron that was probably his mother was staring at O'Rourke but he didn't have time to explain.

"It was hard to tell. He had his hood over his face. We thought that was weird since it's warm outside."

"I saw him too," Jimmy shouted out. "He was a funny looking white dude."

"You couldn't see that," Aaron said. "He had his hood on."

"Yes, I could," Jimmy argued. "I could see a little bit of his face when he came out the door. Before he pulled his hood up."

"No way. You couldn't –"

"Which way did he go?" O'Rourke interrupted.

Both boys pointed up the hill toward the top of Second Avenue.

"He walked that way," Aaron said.

"I watched him walk all the way to the top," Jimmy said proudly. "Then he turned left onto Delaware Avenue."

"No, he turned right," Aaron said. "Right is the hand you write with, remember?"

"Oh yeah. I mean right."

O'Rourke told Aaron's mom who he was and asked her to tell the firemen when they arrived that he got out okay and that there was no one else in the house. Then he jogged up the street, not running his fastest since his lungs still bothered him from the smoke.

The corner was only two blocks away. When O'Rourke got to the intersection, he noticed two old men sitting on a stoop of a house a few doors to his right.

"Have you guys been sitting here long?" he asked them.

"You smell like smoke," one of them said to O'Rourke.

"Yeah, and you look like hell," said the other. "Are you all right, son?"

"I'm fine," O'Rourke said. "Did either of you two see a tall guy come by here, a little while ago? Wearing a sweatshirt?"

"Yeah," one of the men said. "Maybe a half hour ago. I think he was one of those gangbangers. You know, those black kids that sell drugs and always wear their hoods up. Like that kid that got shot in Florida last year."

"No," the other man said. "He wasn't black. I saw his hands. He was a white guy. Sometimes they wear hoodies too, pretending to be cool."

"Did you see which way he went?"

"Yeah. He got on his bike and took off."

"A motorcycle?"

"No. A bicycle. He had it chained to the post in front of the store at the corner. He took off really fast down the street on it."

A bicycle?

It had never occurred to O'Rourke that the killer could be riding a bicycle. Cheryl wrote in her diary that the guy called himself "Biker Boy" and like Cheryl, O'Rourke had assumed that meant a motorcycle. But a bicycle made sense. They had been trying to figure out all along how this guy could get to and from the crime scenes so quickly without anyone noticing him. There were no car tire tracks in the alley in back of Tucker's store. But a bicycle wouldn't be likely to leave any noticeable tracks. And Fleming's neighborhood was a particularly tough place to park a car, but someone could leave a bike chained nearby and walk to the building easily enough. Someone with a bike could get in and out of those areas quickly and quietly. And no one really pays much attention to someone on a bicycle.

O'Rourke thought about the attack on Ashley Morton. The attacker could conceivably have gotten from Sparky's Auto Repair to the Crossings and stashed a bike in the park within the timeframe they had calculated if he took the shortest route through Colonie. But they would have to be moving at high speed. The attacker would probably have to be a really good rider to go that fast.

Like a racer...

He called Sandy Bernstein but got his voice mail so he tried Megan Ross' work number.

"Megan, it's O'Rourke."

"Hello, handsome. We're almost done with the list of contacts for Gertrude Johnson."

"Never mind that. Sandy said a few days ago that one of the Nerd Squad won a bike race in Saratoga recently. Which guy was that?"

"That would be Harold. Harold Lyons."

"Is that the tall skinny one? The redhead that looks like Napoleon Dynamite?"

"Are you insulting our contract staff again?"

"I'm in a hurry, Megan," O'Rourke said gruffly. He was in no mood for games. "Is he or isn't he?"

"Yes," she said curtly. "Harold Lyons is the tall one with the red hair."

"Is he in today?"

"He was. We called all the contract staff yesterday and asked them to work overtime today. That was before we found out the computer was gone and APD was off the case. Once they all re-arranged their schedules, we couldn't tell them not to come in. But Lyons left around 11. He said he wasn't feeling well."

"Did he know I was asking about Gertrude Johnson?"

"Yeah. We all did. Sandy had us pulling up data for you all morning on her."

"He was one of the guys you used for the perv patrol, wasn't he?" The perv patrol was what they called the staff that went online pretending to be minors in order to try to track down pedophiles.

"Yes. All the contract staff do perv patrol duty when they aren't busy with other things."

It made sense. Lyons could have first made contact with Cheryl Nottingham when he was online at work. That would explain the comment in Cheryl's diary that Biker Boy at first said he was seventeen before he admitted that he was older. Lyons was probably on perv patrol duty pretending to be a lonely teenager when Cheryl responded to him.

"Do you know if he rode his bike to work today?"

"He rides it every day. He doesn't own a car."

"What's his home address?"

"Hold on."

She came back on the line a minute later and gave him the address, which he wrote down on a slip of paper. Lyons lived on the second floor of an apartment building on Ontario Street, only about two miles away. Lyons could easily be there already.

O'Rourke could see a lot of things that pointed to Lyons, but they were all circumstantial. Was he just adding it all together because he wanted Lyons to be the killer? There was one way to be pretty sure.

"One more question," O'Rourke said. "Do you remember what color shirt Lyons was wearing today?"

"Of course. I always check out the clothes men are wearing. It was yellow."

O'Rourke called Dale Mitchell next.

"I know who the serial killer is," he said to Dale Mitchell as soon as he picked up the phone. "We need a warrant quick."

"APD is off the case, Steve," Mitchell said patiently. "You're not supposed to be officially involved in this anymore. If you've got a hunch, let's set up a meeting in my office. "

"We don't have time for a damn meeting. The son of a bitch clocked me on the head with his gun less than an hour ago."

"Holy shit! Okay, okay, give me what you've got."

O'Rourke explained his last few hours to Mitchell, making sure he told him that he decided to go the Johnson house only because something bothered him about her "accidental" death and that he connected it with the serial killer case after he got there. If Mitchell saw through that, he didn't say so.

"There's a judge I have a good relationship with," Mitchell said. "I should be able to get a warrant, but it might take an hour or so. I'll have some of my men get to Lyons' house right now, in case he's there and tries to take off."

O'Rourke saw Valente pulling up to the curb in his car, a big beat up Buick. Myers, Oquendo and Valente were all with him.

"Okay, Mitchell, we'll meet them there."

O'Rourke thanked the two old men, who had been listening to O'Rourke's calls with quite a bit of interest, and walked toward Valente's car.

"We were looking for you down at the burning house," Valente said. "A couple of kids said you went up this way."

"We're heading to Ontario Street," O'Rourke replied, getting in the car and handing Valente the slip of paper with the address on it. "We need to get there quickly and wait for a warrant. Harold Lyons lives there, on the second floor. Lyons is the tall redhead that works in the Nerd Squad - he's the killer. I'll clue you all in when we get there."

Valente and the rest of the group looked puzzled, but held their questions. They could tell from O'Rourke's voice that time was of the essence.

"Drop me off at my car first," he said to Valente. "It's across from the burning house."

"Are you sure? You don't look like you should be driving."

"I want to make sure we have at least two of our cars there in case the killer tries to take off on his bike. The more cars we have, the easier it will be to box him in."

Valente pulled his car up to the Jaguar. Across the street, a crowd had gathered while firemen were hosing down the Johnson house, which was now charred black and in ruins. Aaron and Jimmy waved to O'Rourke as he got out of Valente's car. "Nobody tried to steal your car," Jimmy yelled out to him.

Oquendo got out of Valente's car also and got into the Jag with O'Rourke. Once they were inside, O'Rourke pulled out from in back of a fire engine and followed Valente up the street.

On the way, O'Rourke got out his phone to call Ginny back but Oquendo grabbed his arm first.

"Hold on. I think you have some explaining to do," she said.

TWENTY-SIX

||||||||||||||||||||||||||||||||||||||||||

"Harold Lyons is the killer," O'Rourke explained to Oquendo as they drove down Delaware Avenue. "I just figured it out while the four of you were on your way here. I'll tell you the whole story when we get to the house so I don't have to repeat it."

"That's not what I mean," Oquendo answered angrily. "I want you to explain why you couldn't let me or the rest of us know what was going on. You had me paranoid this morning, thinking the killer was one of our team."

O'Rourke looked at Oquendo, who was so angry she was almost in tears. He had known her a long time and knew she could keep a secret.

"I'm going to tell you something just between you and me," he said. Then, he repeated the conversation he had earlier in the day with Ralph, the bartender at the Electric Company.

When he was through, he said: "I couldn't believe that Brad was the killer, so I didn't want to tell anyone about this. At least not until I had a chance to look through the Johnson house to see if there was anything that led to someone other than Brad. In the end, I guess it worked out."

"That doesn't justify going it alone," Oquendo said indignantly.

"You could have gotten yourself killed, you idiot."

He didn't have a good response to that; she was right. "I'm sorry."

"Okay," Oquendo said. She knew apologies didn't come easily to O'Rourke.

After a few minutes, she said: "I guess I should be shocked that Brad is gay. But now that I think about it, that does explain a lot. That's why he never talked about his personal life."

"Despite your prodding."

"So I'm a little nosy."

"Brad has been keeping it a secret, and I can understand why. No police force is very liberal-minded in that way."

"No one's gonna hear it from me," Oquendo answered.

As they got close to Ontario Street, O'Rourke finally called Ginny.

"Are you all right?" she asked frantically. "I've been calling you, but it just goes into voice mail."

"I'm fine," he said. "I've been on the phone a lot." He explained to her what had happened at the house, playing down the blow to the head. He figured that he had at least a mild concussion. But if he told her that, she would insist that he go to the hospital immediately.

"Jesus," she said. "You're lucky that you got out of that house all right. You're having one hell of a day."

"That's putting it mildly. I've got to go. We're on Ontario Street."

"You better be careful," she said to him. "You still owe me that picnic."

Valente pulled his car behind an unmarked black sedan and O'Rourke parked behind him. They were about half a block from Lyons' apartment, far enough away where they could see the front door of the building without being noticed. The neighborhood was near the downtown State University campus, and a lot of summer semester students were strolling around in the afternoon sun.

O'Rourke walked over to the black car and one of the two State Police investigators inside rolled down his window.

"Lieutenant O'Rourke," the investigator asked and O'Rourke nodded. "I'm Mark Bennett and this is Hector Hernandez. Dale Mitchell should be here in a little while with the warrant."

O'Rourke could see the second floor windows from where he was standing. "It looks like the shades are drawn. No lights on. Has anyone been in or out of the building?"

"Not since we got here. And we have another team on the next block over watching the back of the house in case he takes his bike out that way."

"Good. I'll wait in the car until Mitchell comes."

O'Rourke walked back to Valente's car and got in; Oquendo was there too.

While they waited for Mitchell to arrive, O'Rourke filled his team in on how what transpired at the Johnson house, glossing over why he went there in the first place. "I didn't get a chance to look through the entire diary, but I didn't see Lyons' name in it. Just 'Biker Boy'. But I think we have enough to connect Lyons with the murders. There's the bicycle connection and the yellow shirt. And he left work early this morning, not long after I asked Sandy to have his team get more data on Gertrude Johnson."

"I know Jim Farrell liked to use the Nerd Squad as a resource," Booker said. "He would have known Lyons. No wonder he was caught off guard."

Less than an hour later, Dale Mitchell pulled up. He had Elaine Furlani in the car with him.

"I have the warrant," Mitchell said, holding it up. "Dr. Furlani was in my office when you called me, so I asked her to tag along."

Dr. Furlani noticed a couple of the men looking at her with concern. "Don't worry," she said. "I'm staying here in the car until the coast is clear."

"So how do you want to handle this," Mitchell asked O'Rourke. "You figured it out, so I'll let you make the call."

"If he is inside, we'll have to move fast. Let's take two cars, pull up quickly right in front of the door, and get inside quickly. Have your other guys come in from the back."

"Okay. You lead the way."

O'Rourke got back in Valente's car with the others, and Mitchell got in Bennett's car. O'Rourke watched out the back window and waited until there was no traffic behind them. When the road was clear, O'Rourke shouted: "Go!"

Valente gunned the big Buick down the street, with Mitchell's group following. Both cars pulled up to the house with a screeching halt and everybody got out. O'Rourke led the way quickly up the outside stairs. The front door of the building was unlocked. O'Rourke turned the knob and pushed it open with his foot, his gun drawn. The doorway led into an empty hallway, with a set of stairs going up on the left. A bike lock and chain was sitting on the floor next to the railing, unconnected to anything.

"He didn't even bother to take his bike lock with him," Valente said to O'Rourke.

"That's not a good sign."

O'Rourke ran up the stairs, two at a time, with the others following. At the top of the steps, they stopped in front of the door to the second floor apartment.

Mitchell stood to the right of the door while O'Rourke stood to the left of it. Both men had their guns held out in front of them. "Kick it," Mitchell shouted.

O'Rourke raised his foot and gave the door a swift hard kick, yelling "Police!" The door flew open and the whole group piled in behind O'Rourke. O'Rourke and his team went to the left and Mitchell's to the right, cautiously searching the apartment room by room.

After a few minutes, they established that no one was in the apartment. Mitchell called in to his men on the next block and they informed him that no one went out the back way. The tall man was nowhere to be found.

While the teams combed through the apartment, O'Rourke and Mitchell called their respective headquarters to have an APB put out on Harold Lyons. "Better notify neighboring towns too," O'Rourke said to Mitchell. "He can move pretty fast on his bike. He could be out of the city already."

Myers called out from a bedroom on the left. "Look in here, lieutenant."

O'Rourke went into the bedroom. A dresser drawer was open, clothes spilling out of it, as if Lyons grabbed some clothes hastily before he left. On the bed was a hooded sweatshirt, a pair of slacks and a wrinkled yellow dress shirt.

"So he definitely came back here after he confronted me," O'Rourke said. "He must have been in and out before Mitchell's men got here. But why come back here at all?"

"He changed his clothes," Myers replied. "But it doesn't make sense that he would come back here just for that. He obviously wasn't worried that the clothes would tie him to the attack on you or he would have gotten rid of them."

"That's not all he left behind," Oquendo said, kneeling down near a closet. "Look what I found."

Oquendo had a backpack in her hands, the type that bicyclists commonly wear on their backs. Inside was a scalpel, a pistol, a silencer, two cans of spray paint, an empty container that smelled like gasoline, and a variety of bicycle tools. "If there was any doubt he's our guy, there isn't anymore," O'Rourke said.

"That's strange," Oquendo said. "He took his bike. Why not just take the backpack with him?"

Booker walked into the room. "We found two computers in the living room. One of them looks like Cheryl Nottingham's laptop."

"Call Sandy and Megan and get them over here," O'Rourke said.

They searched the bedroom some more, finding a ski mask under the bed and more scalpels in a dresser drawer.

Dale Mitchell came into the room. "I heard you found some good stuff in here."

"Enough to prove Lyons is the killer," O'Rourke answered. He handed the backpack to Mitchell. "There's a second gun in here. It looks just like the one he pulled on me. I'm hoping he doesn't have any more weapons on him."

"Me too," Mitchell said. "Maybe we can catch him without a fight."

"I doubt it," said a voice from the hall. Dr. Furlani was standing there. "Based on his patterns, I don't believe he's going to give himself up easily. And I notice there's another thing we're not finding here."

"What's that," Mitchell asked.

"His souvenirs. There's no finger or tongue in the apartment. I was expecting that he might have kept them as a trophy of some sort."

"Eeww," Oquendo said. "I'm glad we didn't find them."

"Maybe he just tossed them in a dumpster somewhere," Mitchell said.

"Regardless, Lyons is still out there somewhere," O'Rourke

said to Dr. Furlani. "The thing we need to know right now is if he's done killing."

"No," Dr. Furlani said. "I don't believe that he's done at all."

Harold Lyons rode his bike up the steep hill, his tall body pedaling the racing bike in one of the lowest gears. He was hardly breaking a sweat. He was used to steep inclines from riding his bike in regional races and he had one of the best bikes money can buy.

The bicycle was one of the few things that Harold owned that he had actually purchased in a store. Harold did almost all of his shopping over the internet. If Harold was the type that gave advice to friends, which he wasn't since he had no friends, he would have told them to do all of their shopping that way. It was amazing what one could find on the net, and if you did it right, the items were virtually untraceable.

After some digging, he had found someone in Texas who was willing to sell him two pistols and silencers, no questions asked. The same for the other items that he had used for his missions – the gun, scalpels, knife, and spray paint. Even the item he now had in the long, narrow carrying case on his back, the item he returned to his apartment to retrieve.

In addition to being skilled at finding hard to buy things online, Harold also was an accomplished hacker, which had come in handy for gathering the information that he needed on his targets. Two years ago, just before he left the Midwest, he used his hacking abilities to erase all traces of his past, including his involuntary commitment and the nasty business with his mother. It was easy for him to create phony work history records and after he moved to Albany, it wasn't hard for him to use his computer abilities to land a job working for a local company. The firm provided skilled computer contract staff to various public and private entities. He was surprised when the company told him there was a job available at the Albany Police Department. That unexpected bonus had worked out well, for that allowed him to find Cheryl. That was back when he was happy.

But now, Lyons was not happy at all. He had to assume the police were onto him. After arriving at his apartment, he took what he needed and got out fast, not caring that he left his backpack, his clothes, and other evidence behind. He had changed into lightweight biking clothes and a helmet, taking only the long carrying case that was stretched across the back of his shoulders. He would have liked to have taken the handgun and some of the other things. But he needed to move fast up the hills, traveling as lightly as possible, and he knew from experience that even a few extra pounds on his back made a difference on a steep climb.

He didn't need all those things anymore anyway. The carrying case on his back contained the only weapons he would need now.

While O'Rourke's men and the state police continued to look through the apartment, several more detectives and officers arrived. Mitchell had agreed to officially allow the Albany police to assist now that the killer had been identified. Sandy and Megan were there, trying to get access to the two computers while other cops were out canvassing the neighborhood, asking if anyone saw a tall man riding a bike. At the very least, they hoped to get an idea of which direction he was heading.

"So you don't think Lyons is running away," O'Rourke asked Dr. Furlani as his group stood in Lyon's living room.

"No. But I do think he's desperate. He probably believes it's close to the end for him. But I don't believe he'll bow out quietly."

"He's already gone after some of the people that Cheryl felt were ruining her life. But I'm sure there are a lot of others left. More lives could be in danger."

"That's possible. Anyone that offended or upset Cheryl is a target."

"So is that what this is all about? He's just going after people that wronged this girl?"

"Basically. I've heard of this sort of thing before. He's fixated on her. To him, she was his whole life. But then after she died, it all fell apart for him. He couldn't go on with his life without her. So he fixated on something else – getting revenge on those he felt caused the pain that led to her suicide."

Dr. Furlani wiped her glasses with a soft cloth. Without her glasses on, O'Rourke was reminded how fragile she looked the night before.

"The diary said they first found each other on the Internet," she said to him. "Did the diary indicate where or when they met in person? Maybe that would give us a clue to where he's going."

"I didn't get that far," O'Rourke said. "I would have read more but the guy interrupted me with that gun of his."

Mitchell pointed to Oquendo and Myers. "Can you guys call Cheryl's father and get a list of who else might have caused problems in Cheryl's life? They'll need protection."

"Don't forget Ashley Morton," Booker said. "He could be making another attempt at Ashley Morton's life. He may know where she is."

"We've got that covered," Mitchell replied. "We moved Ashley and her family again. But we have some men watching the motel where they had been staying just in case Lyons shows up there."

"He could also be changing his fixation now," Dr. Furlani said. "He could be seeking revenge now on those who tried to stop him from carrying out his plans, rather than just those who wronged

Cheryl. Perhaps that's why he targeted Lieutenant O'Rourke."

O'Rourke suddenly realized that it would not be hard for Lyons to get personal information on him. The man had obviously been using his computer expertise to get very detailed information on his victims.

He walked into the next room and called up his ex-wife.

"Where are you?" he asked before she could even answer.

"I'm at McDonald's with the kids. Why? What's wrong?"

O'Rourke was relieved that they weren't at home. He was sure that if Lyons wanted to, he would have been able to find Ellen's address.

"Do me a favor. Take the kids and go to a friend's house. Just don't go home or to your parents' house. Go somewhere that you usually wouldn't go."

"Steven, you're scaring me," she said in a whisper. "What's going on?"

"It's probably nothing. But I just want to be careful. Just do it, okay?"

"All right. The kids are almost done eating. We'll go to Denise Kerr's house. She's the mother of one of Lauren's friends at school."

Myers and Valente were motioning to him, so he finished up. "Good. I'll call you later."

Valente had something in his hand. A spiral notebook.

"There's an access panel for the shower pipes inside the bathroom. We opened it up and found this inside."

O'Rourke opened the notebook. Inside the cover was a small manila envelope. There were six photos in the envelope, all of Cheryl Nottingham. They weren't photos like the ones Randall Tucker had taken though. These were more like surveillance photos, shots taken from a distance with a zoom lens, some at odd angles. One was a photo of Cheryl leaving her house, another of her getting on a city bus, a third photo of her walking down a city street. The others were all similar. Stalker stuff.

He looked through the notebook. Only the first page had any writing on it. It was a long list of names, one on each line, written in black ink. Gertrude Johnson's name was listed first, followed by Randall Tucker, Bernard Fleming, and Ashley Morton, and then some other names. The first three names had a red line drawn through it.

O'Rourke didn't recognize any names listed after Ashley Morton except the last name on the list, which was written in pencil. *Steven O'Rourke.*

"I guess I'm lucky there's not a red line through my name," O'Rourke said.

He pointed to the line below his name. It contained simply the number '7' with a circle around it, also written in pencil.

"What the hell does that mean?"

"We can't figure out that out," Myers said. "There are way more than seven names."

O'Rourke showed the notebook to Mitchell and Furlani. Mitchell pointed to O'Rourke's name. "You made his list, you lucky son of a bitch."

"What about the number on the bottom?"

"Perhaps it's a symbol for another person that he's after," Dr. Furlani suggested. "Your name and this symbol are in pencil, unlike the other names. They were added later, apparently after the investigation started."

"Could the symbol stand for one of us here?"

"I don't think so. I'm sure Lyons saw you as the face of the investigation. After all, the news stations play that clip from you on television so much. You know, the one where you're calling him a…well, I believe the term you used was 'sick bastard'."

"So maybe my name isn't on the list just because he thought I was ruining his plans. Maybe he wants me dead because of what I said."

"I've got it," Myers exclaimed. "I know what the number means. The seven with a circle around it is the logo for Channel Seven!"

"I don't get it," Valente said. "He's going to attack a television station?"

"No, not the entire station," O'Rourke said worriedly. "He's targeted the person on Channel Seven that called him a spineless coward. He's after Trish Perkins."

TWENTY-SEVEN

IIIIIIIIIIIIIIIIIIIIIIIIIIIIIIIIIIIIIII

Booker, Oquendo, Valente and Myers each took some of the names on the list to try to get addresses for them while O'Rourke found Channel Seven's number. He dialed it, putting his cell phone on speaker so Dale Mitchell and Dr. Furlani could hear. He asked for Trish Perkins and the receptionist put him on hold on for a moment. As the three of them waited anxiously, a soft 70's song played pleasantly on the other end of the phone.

A man's voice came on the phone. "This is the station manager. Can I help you?"

"This is Lieutenant O'Rourke from the Albany Police Department. I need to speak with Trish Perkins right away."

"She's not in the office right now. She's out on assignment at Thatcher Park."

"Can you give me a number where I can call her directly? It's an emergency. She may be in danger."

"What do you mean?"

"It's possible someone may be after her. Can you give me her number?"

"Yeah, sure. Hold on a second."

The man came back on the line a moment later and gave

O'Rourke the number of Perkins' cell phone.

"This must be serious," the man said. "This is the second call I've had from you guys today asking where she was."

"What?"

"We got a call earlier this afternoon. Someone from your department. An Officer Harold Lyons."

"Did you tell him she was up in Thatcher Park?"

"Well, yeah. He said he was a police officer."

"Damn. Where exactly is Perkins in the park?"

"I'm not sure. She hasn't called in for a while. I asked her to do a general feature on the different areas in the park. Trish could be anywhere up there."

Thatcher Park, a forested area high up in the nearby Helderbergs, was only about fifteen miles outside Albany. "Lyons is an experienced bike racer used to climbing hills," O'Rourke said to Mitchell after he hung up. "He could be up there already."

O'Rourke dialed Perkins' number. The phone went right to her voice mail. "Ms. Perkins, this is Lieutenant O'Rourke. We have reason to believe that your life is in danger. When you get this message, please drop everything and get to safety immediately. Get in your car and go to the Thatcher Park police building, located right off the main road. This is no joke. The man after you is the one your station calls the 'tall man'."

"She's not answering," he said to the others after he hung up.

"I just called the State Park Police," Mitchell said. "They're sending some of their men out to search the park for her and her cameraman. And for Harold Lyons."

"The Park Police aren't really experienced with this sort of thing," O'Rourke said. "They spend most of their time confiscating beer from teenagers and giving out directions to visitors.

They're going to need some back up."

"We're not accomplishing much standing here," Mitchell said, putting on his jacket. "Let's go."

Thatcher Park was a two thousand acre forest located on a 1300 foot high plateau called the Helderberg Escarpment, about a twenty minute drive from Albany. People drove there to picnic and sightsee in the summer, where the higher elevation made it a good ten degrees cooler than Albany on hot days. The park included a scenic overlook, Lookout Point, which offered gorgeous views of Albany and the surrounding area hundreds of feet below. Further down the road in the park was the Indian Ladder Trail, an impressive two-mile long hiking path along the side of the cliff, about fifty feet down from the top, that was accessed by walking down steep metal stairways leading down from the park on both ends of the trail.

Harold Lyons biked up to the park often, since it was a good workout to strengthen his leg muscles. He was very familiar with the layout. There was no charge to enter the park, although there was a fee to park a car in the lots located near the picnic areas. When they weren't patrolling the park, Park Police officers were usually either situated near the pay booths in the parking areas or in the main Park Police building alongside the road.

Lyons had arrived in the park about twenty minutes ago. The television station manager had said that the Perkins woman was somewhere in the park, along with her cameraman. Lyons had watched a good amount of Trish Perkins' coverage of the case on television and had twice noticed a white Channel Seven van in the background when she was doing her live reports. So he was now cycling through the park, glancing into the park's various parking areas looking for the van.

At the second parking area past Lookout Point, Lyons saw the van. It was parked on the far side of the lot and it looked empty. He got off his bike, pretending to stretch his legs, and took a look around. Dozens of picnickers were out enjoying the sun. About a hundred feet from Lyons, a park policeman was standing near the parking booth, talking to a cute twenty year old girl manning it. Neither of them took any notice of Lyons.

He scanned the picnic area and didn't see any sign of Perkins. The van was parked not far from a sign pointing to the entrance to the Indian Ladder Trail so he had to assume that's where the two of them had gone. The scenic view from the trail would be a logical spot to film a feature for the news.

Lyons had an idea. He got back on his bike, turned around, and started back the way he came. He was out of sight for less than two minutes before the policeman got an urgent call on his walkie-talkie, notifying all officers to be on the lookout for a tall man riding a bike.

Jeremy Conrad, the husky Channel Seven cameraman, stood with his back against the side of the cliff wall, filming Trish Perkins. Perkins was standing on the Indian Ladder Trail with her back to the valley below, talking into the camera about the beautiful view behind her.

Jeremy was shooting this feature segment about the trail for the fourth time and was getting increasingly frustrated. Although there were not too many hikers on the trail right now due to the hot sun, a few had come by. Most of the hikers were polite enough to wait while they were filming before walking past them. But about thirty yards to his left, there were two openings cut naturally into the face of the cliff right along the path, known as "the caves". Although each cave was less than ten feet long, kids loved to run in and out of them. A couple of young children had done that while Jeremy was shooting the first take, making all kind of noise, and they had to stop that shoot.

The next two times they tried the shoot, Trish had become tongue-tied and flubbed her lines. When he complained, Trish, who Jeremy figured was well on her way to being a functional alcoholic, told him that she still had a hangover from the four Cosmopolitans that she had drank the night before at the Recovery Room Sports Grille. So Jeremy was now on take number four.

Jeremy had experience with difficult working conditions. A year ago, he served in Afghanistan. After an explosion that cost him part of his hearing, he left the Army and hooked up with Channel Seven. A good job, except when Trish Perkins came to work after a binge the night before. One more goof up and he was really going to lay into her.

While Trish was talking into the camera, it never occurred to her that someone might be trying to reach her on her cell phone. Normally when she was being filmed, she kept her cell phone on vibrate in the pocket of her skirt where it wouldn't interrupt the shoot. But today, since she was doing a shoot along the rugged trail, she had traded her skirt and high heels in for a pair of designer jeans and very expensive hiking shoes.

Her jeans were purposely as tight as can be to accentuate her flattering figure - so tight that she couldn't fit her cell phone in her pocket. She had put her phone in her purse, which now was on the ground behind Jeremy as they continued filming. Neither of them could hear the faint buzzing from the phone inside her purse as she continued with her descriptive monologue.

"- you can all see," Trish was saying into the camera, "the beautiful pamanera below..."

"Stop," Jeremy said disgustedly, turning off the camera. "C'mon, Trish, not again! The word is 'panorama'. Let's try it one more time…"

O'Rourke sat in the passenger side of Valente's Buick, with Oquendo in the back. Booker and Myers were riding with Furlani and Mitchell in the car right behind them. The Buick was doing eighty out Route 85 toward Thatcher Park. Oquendo was on her phone with the Park Police, while O'Rourke had just finished calling the Albany County Sheriff's Department.

"The Sheriff's Office sent some deputies up to the park to assist the Park Police," O'Rourke told the others. "They'll be arriving soon."

"The Park Police just spotted the news van in one of the parking lots," Oquendo said when she got off the phone. "They're searching for Perkins in that area. It's possible that she may be on the Indian Ladder Trail. Some men are heading down there now from each side of the path, but it's a long trail. If she's there, it could take a while to get to her."

Just before talking to the sheriffs, O'Rourke had tried for the fifth time in fifteen minutes to contact Perkins, to no avail. He had also called the station, but they didn't have a current cell phone number for Jeremy Conrad, the cameraman. O'Rourke was starting to get worried that Lyons had already gotten to them both.

The turnoff to the road that Thatcher Park was on was still a few miles ahead. "Faster," he told Valente.

Harold Lyons realized that it would make no sense to try to follow Perkins on the trail. It was a winding trail along the side of the cliff, so he would probably have to get very close to her to kill her if he went onto the trail. And after he killed her, he still would have to make his way back up the trail's long stairway to escape.

He had a better idea. He biked back toward the entrance to the park, passing Lookout Point on his left. Several people were there looking out at the scenery, near the long low wall that ran along the edge of the cliff. Lyons rode past that area as the road curved sharply to the left. Soon the woods appeared again on his left side. He was almost at the beginning of the park now, on the way back toward Albany. He stopped his bike and made sure that no cars were coming in either direction. Then, he quickly pulled his bike right up to the edge of the woods, got off, and slid the bike under a large evergreen tree until it was out of sight.

He walked into the woods, the carrying case still on his back. The woods were thick and it was slow going without a path to follow. Normally, it would not be safe to walk through this area with bike shorts on; deer ticks that carried Lyme Disease were common in this area. But that was the least of his concerns right now.

He ignored the thick branches on the trees and bushes that scraped his face as he plodded through the dense woods. After several minutes, he finally reached the clearing on the other side of the woods. In front of him was a small dirt trail that ran along the top of the cliff. There was a barrier there to prevent someone from falling off. Off somewhere to his right was an old parking area that was no longer open, a victim of state budget cuts; that meant this trail was never used anymore. He walked to the barrier, which was just an old ranch style wooden fence railing; two old long parallel horizontal planks of wood were all that stood between him and the steep drop below.

One hand on the barrier, Lyons looked out from the top of

the cliff. The Indian Ladder Trail was about a half mile to his left. As he anticipated, he could see it quite clearly from here since the escarpment curved around in a horseshoe shape. In the distance, he could see people walking along the trail, which was about fifty feet lower in elevation from where he was now.

After setting his carrying case down on the ground, he unzipped one flap and pulled out a small pouch containing a large sharp knife. He clipped the pouch to his shorts. *Just in case,* he thought. He opened the long zipper that ran the long way along the case and pulled out the hunting rifle that he had purchased over the internet a few months ago. He had considered trying to buy a semi-automatic assault weapon, but had decided against it. New York was currently one of the toughest states in the country on gun control. Someone online said that the state could monitor online purchases of those types of guns. He didn't know whether to believe that or not, but there was no sense in taking a chance by purchasing an assault weapon.

The problem with the hunting rifle he bought was that Lyons had never actually fired one. Although he wasn't actually a police officer, the fact that he worked under contract with APD allowed him to use the police shooting range. He had gone there several times with his handgun and had gotten quite good with it, but he had never used the rifle. He had never really thought that he would need it. He preferred the up close approach.

But he had no choice now. Time was too short. He had to show the world how Patricia Ann Perkins had wronged him. That he was not a coward.

As he loaded the rifle, his hands were shaking. He took a deep breath and tried to calm himself. *Just get through this one last mission.*

Fumbling with it, he finally got the bullets loaded in the rifle.

The gun could fire five shots before he had to reload. More than enough.

He knelt on one knee and pointed the rifle toward the Indian Ladder Trail, leaning it on the higher of the two wooden rungs of the railing. Hikers were clearly visible through the powerful scope of the gun. At the far end of the trail, he could see two park policemen moving quickly down the stairs. Were they somehow onto him?

He moved the scope to the closer side of the trail. There were two policemen starting down the stairs on that side too. Obviously, he needed to work quickly. He panned the scope from left to right. Suddenly, he saw her. Trish Perkins was talking to a large man, almost right in the middle of the trail. No one else was around them.

He aimed the rifle carefully. It was now or never…

Trish Perkins had finished the segment and put down the microphone. "Finally," said Jeremy. "It's a wrap."

"It's about time," Trish answered. She was getting thirsty.

"Hand me my purse, will you? I've got a bottle of water in there," she said as she walked toward the cliff wall where Jeremy was standing.

Jeremy picked the purse up from the ground and handed it to her. She opened it and saw her cell phone flashing. She was surprised to see five new messages on it, all from the same person; a person she now kept on her list of contacts. Steven O'Rourke.

She dialed the number and it was picked up immediately. "What's going on, Lieutenant?" she asked. "Changed your mind about talking to me?"

"Listen to me," he shouted urgently. "You're in danger. Where are you?"

"I'm on the Indian Ladder Trail. In Thatcher Park. We're doing a -"

She stopped when she felt something hit her face. A bee sting? No, more like several sudden small stings. A second later, she heard a loud bang echoing through the cliffs.

Jeremy Conrad, who had seen his share of sniper fire in combat, saw the small fragments of rock explode from the side of the cliff near Trish Perkins' face and recognized what he was seeing almost before he heard the gunshot. He reached out and grabbed Perkins' wrist and threw her down onto the dirt path. "Stay down," he shouted, just before he got shot in the back and crumpled to the ground.

O'Rourke heard the shot outside his window a second before he heard it over the phone. Someone close to them was firing at Trish Perkins, who was farther away. "It sounded like it came from just up ahead," Oquendo shouted from the back seat. "On the right!"

Valente's car had just entered Thatcher Park. An abandoned parking lot was several yards ahead on the right. A wooden gate with a sign on it that said "Closed" blocked the entrance to the lot.

"Hang on," Valente shouted as he gunned the accelerator. He turned the Buick to the right and the big car crashed through the gate, the sign flying over their heads. As the car sped through the lot to the far end, O'Rourke heard a second shot from up ahead and then a third.

The car reached the end of the lot and Valente drove it onto the grass, as far as he could go before they reached the trees. Trish Perkins was yelling something into the phone and O'Rourke tossed the phone to Oquendo. "Tell her to find cover," he shouted and was out the door before the car came to a complete stop.

There was a path a few yards ahead and O'Rourke ran toward it. He could hear Valente behind him, calling Mitchell, who had fallen behind them on the drive up the mountain. O'Rourke reached the beginning of a wooden railing on his right and realized that he was running along the top of the cliff. Another shot rang out and it sounded like it was several hundred yards in front of him. He ran faster along the path, his gun out now. Lyons had to be somewhere up ahead.

Lyons missed with the first shot, striking the rock wall near Perkins. He tried again and missed completely. By then, a large man had grabbed Perkins and pushed her down near the cliff wall. The man was between him and Perkins, blocking the shot. Frustrated, Lyons shot the man in the back.

The man fell to the ground and Perkins scampered behind the big man's body. This made her a smaller target, but her head and one shoulder were still visible to Lyons. Lyons took dead aim and fired quickly again. The shot hit the large man's prone body, spraying blood into the air. He took a fifth shot. Success! It hit Perkins in the shoulder. He was getting used to the gun now. One more shot should do it. He had used five shots and had to reload now but that would only take a few seconds. He saw her get up and start running. But it didn't matter. There was nowhere for her to hide. She was in the middle of the trail, a mile from either end and in full view. She would be an easy target now.

Trish Perkins took it all in as if she were watching a newscast of it happening to someone else. She didn't know what Jeremy was doing as he grabbed her wrist and pulled her down. Before she could ask him what was going on, he fell to the ground in front of her. Something splattered onto her shirt and she realized it was Jeremy's blood.

Trish still had her cell phone in her hand. A woman was on the cell phone now instead of O'Rourke. "Find cover," the woman was yelling.

Somehow, Trish had the presence of mind to dive in back of Jeremy's body, curling up into a fetal position behind him. Whoever was shooting at them was on the top of the cliff, way off to their right. She squeezed as much of her small body behind Jeremy's large body as possible, but it wasn't enough. Her head and shoulders were still exposed.

Somewhere in the distance, she could hear hikers screaming. Another shot rang out and it hit Jeremy, who was probably already dead. She tried to hunch down even further. The next shot hit her in the shoulder and she screamed out in pain.

The shots suddenly stopped. She couldn't stay here in back of Jeremy anymore. With her head and shoulders exposed, she was a sitting duck.

But where could she go? If she ran along the trail in either direction, she would be out in the open.

Then she remembered the small caves. They were about thirty yards away. She got up and started running as fast as she could.

O'Rourke was running fast along the dirt and gravel path that ran along the top of the escarpment, the flimsy wooden railing to his right the only thing between him and the woods hundreds of yards below. The sound of the shots had stopped. Was Trish Perkins dead?

Valente and Oquendo, neither of whom were fast runners, had fallen way behind him. Up ahead of him, the path veered sharped to the left. A blind curve. If Harold Lyons was waiting there for him, he was done for.

It took Lyons a little while to reload because his hands were shaky, but he got it done, wasting just a few seconds. He re-aimed the gun, ready to finish the job.

But Perkins was gone.

Where the hell had she gone? There was no one on the trail for a hundred yards in either direction. She hadn't had time to run farther than that. Did she fall off the cliff?

He was in a panic now. The park police would be here soon, following the sound of the gunshots. What should he do?

Then he heard sounds behind him. Someone was coming.

O'Rourke got to the curve in the path and threw caution to the wind. There was too much at stake. His gun in front of him, he rounded the turn.

No one was there.

But there was something on the path in front of him, on the ground. A hunting rifle. Why would Lyons just leave his rifle on the ground…?

Suddenly, a figure came charging out of the woods at him. O'Rourke swung his gun around but not quick enough. Lyons' plunged his knife into O'Rourke's right arm and O'Rourke's gun fell to the ground.

Lyons pulled the knife back again and this time aimed it toward O'Rourke's face. O'Rourke grabbed Lyons' wrists with both of his hands, despite the searing pain in his arm. He was barely able to hold Lyons off; the tall man was stronger than he looked.

While O'Rourke struggled to keep Lyons' knife away from his face, he felt himself sliding backward on the loose gravel of the path. He pushed against Lyons as hard as he could, his arm throbbing. But Lyons had the advantage and was moving O'Rourke back toward the cliff. With his bright orange hair and his face contorted in rage, Lyons looked like a tall, deranged clown. O'Rourke couldn't hold his ground and he felt his back hit up against something hard. It was the wooden railing. The only barrier between him and the steep drop hundreds of yards below.

It was all happening too fast. He could hear the voices of Valente and Oquendo calling out to him in the distance. But they were too far away. Suddenly, he heard a splintering sound directly behind him. The railing was about to give way.

"I'LL KILL YOU," Lyons yelled, his face inches from O'Rourke's. "For what all of you did to her!"

Lyons was out of control, single minded in his anger. O'Rourke's hands were still clamped around Lyons' wrists, but O'Rourke was tiring. The knife was now only inches from O'Rourke's face. He needed to do something drastic.

"Cheryl didn't love you," he shouted at Lyons. "You never even met her, did you, you sick son of a bitch?"

Lyons' expression changed, resembling someone who had just had cold water thrown in his face. He hesitated for just an instant.

That was all the time O'Rourke needed. With all his might, he yanked Lyons' arms to the right, swinging the tall man's body against the wooden railing as hard as he could.

The wooden barrier give way. Lyons crashed through it and went sailing backwards off the cliff, his arms flailing in the air. O'Rourke could still hear the tall man screaming out the word "Cheryl" until he hit the trees five hundred yards below.

O'Rourke suddenly felt light-headed and sank to his knees, only a few feet from the cliff's edge. He noticed there was a lot of blood on the ground and realized with a shock that it was his. Someone was coming. He could hear Valente say: "Easy boss, we've got you," just before he passed out.

TWENTY-EIGHT

IIIIIIIIIIIIIIIIIIIIIIIIIIIIIIIIIIIIIIIII

O'Rourke couldn't quite open his eyes, but he had a sensation of moving fast. He could hear a siren close by. Someone was holding his hand and saying something to him. It was Oquendo. He mumbled something to her and passed out again.

The next thing he was aware of was being in a white room with a bright light over him. A woman with a white surgical mask on said to him, "You're going to be all right." She put something over his face and he fell back to sleep.

Now O'Rourke was back in the conference room at work. The bloody corpses of Randall Tucker, Bernard Fleming, Jim Farrell, and Gertrude Johnson were all still sitting in their chairs in the front row again, watching him.

There was a large green chalkboard next to O'Rourke, the kind he remembered from school. There with several names on it, one name listed under another. Michael Tucker's name was on top, then Earl Coombs, followed by several other suspects. O'Rourke picked up an eraser and slowly erased each name one by one. Soon, there were only two more names left, at the bottom of the board. He erased Brad Myers' name from the board. Harold Lyons' name was the only one left. He picked up a piece of chalk and drew a line through Lyons' name. A great sense of relief washed over him as he did that, as if a heavy burden was lifted from him.

He looked back at the four persons in the front row. They were no longer bloody; in fact, they were all dressed in clean white clothes now. They were all smiling. Slowly, they all started fading away before his eyes. The last to leave, Gertrude Johnson, said something to him before she disappeared. It sounded like "Thank you."

When O'Rourke woke up again, he was in bed in a hospital room. His right arm was heavily bandaged and he was still pretty groggy. A nurse that was in the room noticed he was awake and said she would get the doctor.

Dr. Patel was a friendly, heavy-set man in his forties.

"That was quite a gash you had there," he said. "You lost quite a lot of blood. It's a good thing you were brought here as quickly as you were. The good thing is there doesn't appear to be any permanent tissue damage. You're going to need physical therapy but your arm is going to be fine."

"So I'll be able to shoot a bull's-eye from fifty yards out?"

"I suppose so."

"Good. I was never able to do that before."

The doctor smiled at his stupid joke and then pointed at O'Rourke's head. "You have a concussion. You should have gone to the hospital right after you hurt your head."

"I was a little busy at the time."

The doctor did some poking and prodding for a while. When he was done, he said: "There are many people out there waiting to see you. We asked the reporters to go home, but there are several others. Do you feel up to visitors? Just a few at a time."

"Sure. I'm more awake now. And my arm doesn't hurt that much."

"You're full of pain killers," the doctor said. "It will hurt like hell later."

The kids came in first with Ellen. Tyler gave him a hug so hard that Ellen had to tell him to be careful of O'Rourke's arm. Lauren, gave him a smaller, more grown up hug.

"Promise you'll stop being a cop, daddy," she said. "It's too scary. For Tyler, I mean."

O'Rourke looked at her. Although she was thirteen and usually looked fifteen, she looked much younger right now.

"Sweetheart, there are some promises I can't make. Being a cop is what I do. I'll tell you what though. I'll be more careful from now on. I'll try not to go running around blind corners any more. Or if I do, I'll wait for the rest of my team to catch up. Okay?"

Lauren had tears in her eyes, so she just nodded.

Ellen and the kids stayed for a while, and O'Rourke was in no hurry to see them go. But finally Ellen said: "We should go now. There's other people that want to see Daddy."

Oquendo, Booker, Valente and Myers came in next, accompanied by Chief Reilly. "Captain Grainey offered to stay behind and hold down the fort," Reilly said. "I didn't think you'd miss him."

"So how are you feeling, boss?" Valente asked. He still had blood on his shirt from helping O'Rourke out of the woods.

"Not too bad. I probably won't be running after any more crazies right away though."

"You look a lot better than you did in the ambulance," Rosie Oquendo said.

O'Rourke recalled Oquendo holding onto his hand during the ride as he drifted in and out of consciousness. "I thought that was you getting fresh with me in there," he said.

"In your dreams, old man."

They all laughed and then Reilly said, "You know, you're a celebrity now. Reporters from all the local channels and some of the New York City stations were here earlier, until they were told to leave."

"They're calling you the man who saved Albany," Myers said.

"Dale Mitchell might be pissed off about that. It was his case at the end."

"I'll handle him," Chief Reilly said. "By the way, when you're feeling better, you'll have to do some interviews. After what Lyons did, the Albany Police Department can use some good press."

"Wonderful," O'Rourke said wearily.

"It's not so bad. I heard Trish Perkins is already booked on Good Morning America. I can see the story now. The brave newswoman who narrowly escaped death..."

"I was going to ask about her. So she's all right?"

"She was shot in the shoulder. She made it into one of those caves on the trail, where she hid until the park police came to get her."

"Unfortunately, her cameraman wasn't so lucky," Valente said. "He took one in the back. He didn't make it."

"I'm sorry to hear that. What about Harold Lyons? I'm sure he didn't survive that fall."

"They're still looking for his body," the chief said. "It's really dense in those woods and hard to get through. It's dark out now, but they'll try again tomorrow. But we did find out something interesting about him."

"What's that?"

"We were able to get his fingerprints off the rifle and ran them. It turns out his real name was Lawrence Howard. Several years ago, he spent some time in a mental hospital in Iowa. While on a weekend release, he killed his mother and ran off. No one ever knew where he went, until now. And get this – after he killed his mother, he cut her heart out."

They all talked about the tall man for a while longer, until a nurse came in and asked them to leave because O'Rourke needed his rest.

After they left, the nurse poked her head in the door. "I think you can handle one more visitor. She's been waiting a long time."

O'Rourke nodded. A minute later, Ginny Dixon came in the room. O'Rourke smiled broadly. Although he had been with Ginny for less than a week, he realized that he felt closer to her than any woman since Ellen.

"It's about time," Ginny said. "I never met such chatty cops."

"If I knew you were out there, I would have shooed them away. You're a lot better looking than they are."

She put her hand on his. "I was worried sick about you," she whispered. "You take too many chances."

"I'm sorry," he said quietly. "That's why they say never get involved with a cop."

"Too late now."

He told her what had happened in the Johnson house during the fire – about how he narrowly escaped being buried under the falling ceiling.

"I'm sure you remember that dream I told you about," he said. "You told me in the dream, the one where my room was on fire, to go right way. When I was in the middle of the real fire, I decided to take your advice literally. I was going to head left toward the nearest exit, but instead I decided to take a right. That choice saved my life."

Only half-joking, he added: "Maybe you sent me a psychic message."

"It wasn't me," she answered quietly. "It was you. These dreams you have - I think you have a gift. I can see it in the way you put things together in your head, making connections that others don't see right away."

O'Rourke just nodded. He was too tired to think about all that.

He had noticed that Ginny had brought a wicker basket into the room when she came in, which she had left on a chair in the room. "What's that over there?" he asked.

"You'll see," Ginny said.

She brought the basket over near the bed and opened it. Smiling, she took a big plaid blanket out of it and carefully un-folded it onto the floor right next to O'Rourke's bed. Then she pulled out a bottle of Perrier water, two empty glasses, and two wrapped sandwiches one by one from the basket, laying them all down neatly on the blanket.

"Did you forget?" she asked, sitting down on the blanket. "You promised me a picnic."

THREE MONTHS LATER

|||||||||||||||||||||||||||||||||||||||

Jake Harley tossed his empty sack through the back window of the dark vacant building and climbed through the window after it. His out of shape Uncle Fred was already inside, trying to catch his breath after climbing through the window before Jake. Fred's day job was working as an underpaid building manager of an apartment building on State Street; by night, he and Jake illegally stripped copper wire from vacant buildings, at least on those occasions when Fred was sober.

"Are you sure this is a good idea, Uncle Fred?" Jake asked. "The police station is right down the block."

"No problem," Fred Harley wheezed. "The cops can only see the front of this building from there. We're just gonna get what we can from this back section."

"I don't know. Maybe we should do it some other time…"

"No way," Fred said, pulling out a small flashlight from his own sack and switching it on. They started to climb a set of stairs. They always started at the top and worked their way down; Jake had forgotten why. "If we wait, somebody else will get to it. They pay good money these days for copper wire."

They got to the second floor and continued up to the third

and final level.

"What was this place anyway?"

"The cops used it for offices and storage and stuff," Fred explained. "But they closed it down a couple weeks ago, once they finished renovating the police station. In fact, this was the place where that guy we heard about on the news worked. You know, the one they called 'the tall man'."

Jake shivered. It wasn't a particularly cold autumn night, but hearing that gave him the creeps.

They got to the top floor. It looked like they were in luck. This floor apparently hadn't been used for anything but storage for years. The area was full of dust and several taped up boxes. More importantly, several of the ceiling tiles were gone. It would be easy to get up into the ceiling and pull out the wiring.

Jake started pulling some tools out of his sack. He watched while Fred started opening some of the boxes.

"Hey, there's some good shit in here that we can sell," Fred said. He pulled two dusty walkie-talkies out of a large cardboard box. "Look what the cops left behind! I guess they forgot to look up here before they cleared out."

"That's the city for you," Jake answered. He pointed to a smaller white box in the far corner of the room. It looked newer than the others. "Don't forget to check out that box way over there," he said.

While Fred looked around, Jake took a few of the boxes closest to him and stacked them one on top of another, so he could get up to the ceiling. The quicker they could get done and out of here, the better.

Suddenly, he heard Fred cry out. Jake turned around and saw Fred running past him toward the exit, faster than Jake had ever seen the old man move.

"Uncle Fred, what's wrong?" Jake called to him, but Fred was already halfway down the stairs.

"The old drunk's going nuts," Jake muttered to himself. Fred had left his sack and flashlight on the floor on the far end of the room, and Jake went over to get it. It wasn't a good idea to leave that stuff behind.

Fred's sack was on the floor next to the white box that Jake had pointed out to Fred. Jake retrieved the flashlight and sack, and started toward the exit. But then his curiosity got the better of him. He turned around and knelt down on the floor in front of the white box, which Uncle Fred had already opened. Later on, he would swear that a chill ran down his back just before he looked inside.

Inside the box were three mason jars, two small ones and a bigger one, filled with some kind of murky liquid. There were things floating in the liquid, but he couldn't make them out in the dark. He shined the flashlight onto the jars.

The first small jar contained an object that looked to Jake like a plastic replica of a tongue. The second small one had something that looked like a human finger inside. His first thought was that someone had put Halloween stuff in the jars.

Inside the largest jar was something vaguely shaped like a heart. He was suddenly acutely aware of a very strong odor which reminded him of when he had to cut up frogs in ninth grade science class. These were no Halloween decorations.

Jake let out a scream, letting the jar fall back into the box. Then he made a mad dash toward the stairs himself, leaving behind the abandoned souvenirs of the tall man.